Hidden Messiah

Old Prophecies and Modern Times

Marinella F. Monk, MD

HIDDEN MESSIAH

Copyright by Marinella F. Monk, MD

Published by KDP

Printed in the United States of America - 2019

ISBN 9781086240993

Thank you for buying an authorized edition of this book and for complying with the copyright laws by not reproducing, scanning, or distributing this document and any part of it in any form without prior permission.

Hidden Messiah being a work of fiction, any names, characters, events or places are either the product of the author's imagination or are included in the story in a factitious manner. Any resemblance to actual living or passed persons, businesses, establishments, events or locations, is entirely coincidental.

Photographs courtesy of Joshua Earle for the front cover and Benjamin Davis for the back cover.

Cover deign by Chris Franzen.

"I saw the Angel in the marble and I carved until I set him free"

Michelangelo Buonarroti

Other books written by Marinella Monk:

YOU ARE NOT ALONE

GENTLE THERAPY

HEAVEN REDISCOVERED

Looking into our humanity, we witness history fulfilling prophecies and science discovering the divine of the universe, leading us to accept that which is to come, it shall.

Marinella Monk, MD

This book could not have been written without the contribution and presence of dear friends and family members. I am filled with gratitude for their words and gestures of kindness that inspired me to pursue my dreams and keep writing.

To my beautiful and talented daughter, Béatrice, who gives me great joy, and who always brings happiness and pride into my life.

To my ravishing, spirited, and immensely talented sister, Gabriella, I give my heartfelt thanks for always being there for me, encouraging and supporting me with her unrestrained passion.

I am grateful life gifted me with two more sons, Richard and Philippe, who, upon coming into my life, knew how to bring more love into my heart to share.

And to Robert, my husband, my love, and my friend, I am forever grateful for being the breath that lifts my wings above my limits, for the wisdom that helps to expand my understanding in the face of adversity, and for the vision he inspired in me like a beacon shining in the middle of life's storms.

INDEX:

Chapter 1 - Hidden Messiah　　p. 1

Chapter 2 - An Unusual Couple　　p. 25

Chapter 3 - Lamentations　　p. 49

Chapter 4 - Tribulations　　p. 81

Chapter 5 - Transformation　　p. 91

Chapter 6 - Transfiguration　　p. 111

Chapter 7 - Transcendence　　p. 157

Chapter 8 - Refugees　　p. 181

Chapter 9 - Armageddon　　p. 189

Chapter 10 - Exodus　　p. 205

Chapter 11 - Apocalypse　　p. 269

Chapter 12 - The New Jerusalem　　p. 287

Epilogue　　p. 299

CHAPTER 1 - HIDDEN MESSIAH

TREBOR

Trebor woke up drenched in sweat. He was screaming and he heard screams around him, but no sounds were coming out of his throat and no one was around in this elegant hotel suite.

"The same damn dream" he thought, trying to calm his breathing and grabbing the glass of water from the night stand. Then, he sat on the edge of the bed, his eyes looking faraway, searching deep into the vision of his dream.

After a while, Trebor became angry; he was determined to get rid of this nightmare, this 'nocturnal terror' he was afflicted with since he could remember. The same dream was resurging and haunting his nights, then lingering for a longtime. He was now in his early thirties, and the bad dreams were back only once or twice a year, but they were so vivid and their effect lasting so long the following days, that they made him wanting to find out their meaning. He was certain that if he knew the reason of it, he could find the way to control the problem, to solve it and make it go away forever. In the same way he knew how to take care of the problems of his financial empire.

Walking toward the balcony of the Plaza Hotel in Los Angeles, Trebor leaned against the railing, admiring the beautiful color of the sky and the sea, announcing the approaching evening. He was still wrapped in the feelings that deeply stirred his being; because the dream was mostly that, a deep and inexplicable emotion. Feelings of terror, his souls calling for help, for sustenance, to remain alive, and somewhere not far, in the dark, he felt someone else. He did not see anything, but he felt very strongly this other presence, and although it was a loving presence, all was shrouded in terror. He could hear screams, then a soft crying, then, nothing.

"All this makes no sense once or ever", he said to himself, almost aloud. He recited again, all the good reasons to consider himself a very lucky person, for he had everything one could expect in life. He was young, handsome, successful, and immensely rich. He had loving parents and many friends. In his work, he was respected and admired, and he could go out with any beautiful girl he desired. Then why, where is all this unsettlement coming from? He did not recall any traumatic event in his life, and he had always been protected by his powerful parents.

After a while and a little calmer, Trebor entered his room, then into the shower of his bathroom. He needed to shake off all these feelings before meeting some important investors expected for dinner.

Coming out of the shower, Trebor started shaving in the front of the marble double sink. The reflection seen in the mirror was of an extremely attractive young man, a lean body with perfect proportions. Although he had oriental features, he was tall; his slanted eyes were of an intense, deepest blue, and his dark hair tempted to form some waves. Trebor was of an exotic appearance, his unusual looks however, did not queried many questions. Since he was of a different race as of the white people with whom he was most of the time in contact, he was perceived as some racial combination that westerners had a hard time to recognize. Trebor considered himself as different, not a 'freak' anymore as he did sometimes when he was a child, but somewhere he admitted that he must be different as his parents liked to tell him, "he was special".

TREBOR'S PARENTS

Lynn and Irvin Young belonged to a Chinese family well-established in Hong Kong for as long as the British were present, after the First Opium War of 1838-1842 and until now, even following the handover of the British colony to China in 1997. The ancestors of this Cantonese family had seized the opportunity to get out of misery during a time when foreigners, like the Englishmen establishing outposts far east, were considered heathens and were avoided by the local population. The Yong family migrated to Hong Kong as servants, following a newly arrived couple coming from England and assigned to the British Governor's office. The Yong household breeding easily, formed an ample resource for various employments readily needed for the creation of the new colony. The move from the mainland China to the rocky island appeared to be a strike of luck for the Chinese understanding the dynamics of new changes, or just looking for an opportunity to support their families.

The Yong descendants were hard working and very smart individuals; they quickly learned the ropes of trades and penetrated the web of business and politics, the finesse of negotiations whether on the market place or during refined multinational dinners. They had the instinct of sensing the underground play, when opposite cultures observed each other and kept a cool face as high stakes were in the game. Men and women of the Yong lineage absorbed rapidly the polished manners of the upper-class colonial representatives of each side, and soon started their own enterprises. Keeping tight relations with the British Governor office and some succeeding to occupy important administrative positions, many realized the importance of creating a variety of services providing the young colony with the much-needed supplies. Steadily, they branched out in all directions, from diplomatic to high finances, cargo shipping industry trading from Victoria Harbor, to construction companies building the skyline of the new city, elegant hotels, and attractive commercial centers.

It helped that the Yong women were beautiful and became skilled at navigating within the highest social circles, shrewd business women or influential mistresses to powerful dignitaries. One or two generation into their Hong Kong arrival, some men were sent to London to achieve a greater understanding of the western culture and obtain a formal education in the banking and stock market trading.

Lynn and Irvin Young, stemmed from the direct lineage of the Yong and Ying family descendants and their ramifications, and as many of the Chinese living in Hong Kong territory, adopted the use of English names with a little twist of their Chinese given names. This way, Li Ying, meaning elegant and brave, used the English counterpart of Lynn Young marrying Wang Yong, meaning brave, who became officially Irvin Young. For the arrival of their child Trebor, in 1990, with the approach of the handover of the island of Hong Kong to China expected in 1997, they chose for Lynn to give birth of her child in the United States, anticipating any potential changes of the regime and looking to protect the future of their child.

Toward the end of the millennium, there were quite a few luxurious private clinics on the west coast of the US offering to Asian families arrangements to receive medical care, or bring into life their children. It became a way for some fortunate Chinese, Japanese, and even Russians with influential connections, to obtain a visitor visa for three months and spend a relaxing time preparing for their child to arrive. These families, for whatever personal reasons, thought that it was clever to take advantage of the best medical care available in the western world and, by the same occasion, obtain for their child privileges offered by the American citizenship.

Lynn Young, arriving in her mid-thirties without being able to produce any offspring, but desperately desiring a child, had the means to come to Los Angeles, as soon as she was sure she will have, at last, a child. She arrived on a private Gulfstream IV of the latest model and checked in in an exclusive and very luxurious clinic tucked in the shady hills of Belair, where she was immediately met by her obstetrician-gynecologist.

Once the baby's birth certificate was registered by the civil officer at the court house, things went without worries for little Trebor's future. Back in Hong Kong, he was raised by his very loving parents, and even after the handover, when he was almost seven years old, Trebor was still enjoying a relatively posh life style. He received a mixture of traditional Chinese and Western education, benefiting from his American nationality secured at his birth.

Trebor completed his college education at the University of California-Berkeley in San Francisco and followed with the Graduate School of Business at Stanford, in the San Francisco Bay area. He specialized, as expected, in international finances and business, attentively groomed by his father for the banking and holdings of the family business. When Trebor was found able to juggle with ease complicated business matters within the private companies of his close family, he was initiated on the fine international negotiations between East and West.

After the handover in 1997, the situation became considerably more delicate since the Chinese communist regime scrutinized the transnational trades of the newly added province of Hong Kong. However, the knowledge of intricate dealings and ramifications of the Young Family financial holdings far beyond into the western nations, allowed Trebor to have a high level of negotiating advantage, once becoming an adult.

Following its annexation to China, Hong Kong fought to maintain its privilege and continued to function under the principle of "one country, two systems", trying very hard to remain separated from the Chinese political and economic domination. Because of the enormous amount of exportations and being the largest world re-exportation center, taking advantage of its geographical location, Hong Kong was already benefiting from an infrastructure combining one of the busiest container ports and offering the busiest airport in the international cargo transport in the world.

On the other hand, for over one hundred years of British domination, the Chinese population of Hong Kong formed extensive ties with the most competitive financial centers of the world, along with places like London, New York City, Tokyo, Boston, Toronto, San Francisco, and Singapore. The Hong Kong Stock Exchange placed the former colony amongst the top global international Financial Centers, while investment companies are found in great concentration in the high-rise business center, maintaining strong relations with the World Trade Organization, APEC (Asia Pacific Economic Cooperation) and many others.

The Chinese government having initially serious ideological and logistic considerations, inheriting a capitalistic and highly cosmopolitan way of living of the Island of Hong Kong, quickly understood the advantage of this annexation. Thus, the communist China became inclined to "tolerate" some of the capitalist legal system regarding the independent customs and emigration, but also in relation to fields of finances, trade, shipping, tourism and sports, along with communications with the western world.

It soon became clear, although never openly admitted by the official Chinese position, that there was suddenly an unexpected window of opportunity for China to take advantage of an underground infiltration into the western establishment. Through the dense and deeply rooted financial and industrial network already existent, refined over the years by the new territory and recently falling into their lap, the Chinese superpower aspirations could take advantage of two opposite worlds.

If the economical explosion experienced between 1961 and 1997 allowed the gross domestic product to increase 180 times, during a period of time when China experienced an acute economic decline, in contrast, Hong Kong, thanks to its competitive simple taxation, enjoyed the highest income per capita in the world. Hong Kong remained one of the most visited cities, in spite of its cost of living notoriously elevated. Along with the British Common Law independent from the mainland Chinese civil law system, Hong Kong succeeded to maintain the Hong Kong dollar as its currency.

Social systems such as education, health, and transportation, remained very advanced within the far eastern populations, while the Hong Kong population is known for its longest life expectancy in the world. Hong Kong recognized some degree a religious freedom, however, close to three quarters of its inhabitants do not have any religious affiliation any longer, in a place encompassing the fourth highest population density in the world.

During the second decade of 2000, Trebor Young benefited from the relative openness of business climate in Hong Kong, aided by his American citizenship as he started the management of International Holdings, keeping him mostly in North America and Europe. Something that Trebor was not aware of, though, was the fact that a highly secret bureau of the Chinese international security was following his every move.

There was no specific reason or need of his services for the moment, but his impressive knowledge in trading, investments, and projects of the other superpowers, and the ease with which he navigated in the westerner circles, were all enough reasons to consider that one day Trebor could become an enormous unsuspected asset for the interests of the Republic of the People of China. Although Trebor lived an exemplary life, mostly working or traveling, all was noted, recorded, anything that could become a reason for him to be compromised and have to accept an eventual collaboration with the communist Chinese secret police, was scrutinized.

Above all, Trebor did not know that his father had an old debt to pay one day for a favor given to him many years in the past.

MAI

Mai Lee stopped for a moment to look out the window and admire a little arrow of rays piercing through the cloudy skies. She could almost feel the cold dampness enveloping her once going out, and she could not retain a shiver. But here it was cozy, and she felt fortunate for her situation at this elegant hotel, by the North Korean standards, where she had a job as a house keeper. Continuing to make the bed and tidy up the room following the same routine she now repeated for a while, Mai continued her daydreaming. For she secretly knew that she was able to keep her sanity, to survive, finding refuge in her dreams. She often repeated, as a string of prayers, the reasons she so was grateful for.

Around 1978 or 79, her parents stricken by extreme poverty and with two little girls in tow, living on the desolate hills of North Korean border with South Korea, the Lees' were offered a job to work at a small compound build by the military ministry for exchanges and negotiations with the South and their allies. She could remember when she was seven or eight years old, going hungry and growing in a gloom of sadness and deprivation. Her parents, sweet and patient, were nevertheless crushed people under the oppression and complete control of the communist totalitarian regime, with no expectations of a better life, and losing hope. Their vision of the world was restricted to the few news arriving to their isolated village or diffused by the local propaganda of the Communist Party.

With this new and unexpected opening for a steady job, although representing a very limited resource of nourishment, Mai's parents regained some promise for surviving and finding the means to raise their children, maybe even offer them an occasion to ensure their own existence in the future. Sunjin, the father, was provided with an uniform, and held a variety of add appointments as a night guardian, along with some maintenance jobs for plumbing, heating, and painting. He was courageous and hardworking, and he assumed very quickly a number of other small chores likes luggage handling, locksmith work, electrical wiring and even learning how to drive one of the hotel's old Lada for the guests' transport. Becoming almost indispensable,

Sunjin saw himself placed at the head of the maintenance personnel, after an important visit of some dignitaries coming for an inspection of the south border installations. During that winter in 1985, Sunjin worked day and night to repair the shabby heating system before the commission arrived. However, even after his promotion, Sunjin remained modest and knew how to make himself almost invisible. This kept him and his family unhurt from the instability and many purges of the communist system, known to throw people into labor camps just to maintain terror and intimidation.

Mai's mother, Jia, was employed as a genitor, cleaning and mopping the corridors, the cantina-restaurant, and the limited public toilets of the hotel. After a renovation, the work at the hotel became more pleasant, and Jia learned how to keep a room cleaned and place furnishing in a more refined way, the way the members of the Party acquired a liking. However, Sunjin and Jia Lee preferred to remain unnoticeable. As expected from the general population of the north Korean regime, they kept their eyes down and never fully smiled, moving like shadows away from the hotel guests.

Over the years, the Lee family made some improvements to their modest dwelling built low on the hills and practically invisible from the hotel where they worked. And they intended to keep it that way, avoiding anything that could create any kind of suspicion in this intensely distrustful climate and possibly endanger their safety. They attended the daily mandatory assemblies at the hotel with all the other employees reunited at the crack of dawn before starting their work day, or for Sunjin at the end of his night, when they were to listen to the party's messages. As it was the everyday communist indoctrination method of the entire country, if the Lees' did not have a television and had no desire even for a radio, they had, however, the mandatory speaker installation in their house constantly barking routine party slogans. The speakers could never be turned off and broadcasted news every early morning, waking up the entire nation at the same hour, and continuing at regular intervals during the day with the same insipid refrains, as part of the brain-washing process of the North Korean inhabitants.

Struggling to stay alive during the times when the country's population was starving and people were dying either in the labor camps or just from lack of nourishment, groups of homeless orphaned children roamed the streets and scoured through the trash, taking away from one the ability or desire to own a domestic animal. The Lee family members considered themselves lucky having a stable source of food and clothing, and some heating to fight the constant cold. The father planted a few rows of yams and potatoes, and with little rice from the monthly ration, Jia skillfully invented a variety of dishes. Adding different flavors and spices, Jia made thick soups providing them the nourishment needed for most of their long working days.

Sunjin even managed to have a water faucet in the main room, functioning as living room/kitchen, where the girls had also their little cots at the back side of the room. Behind a hanging old drape, was set a basin on a small stand, where they poured a little bit of warm water to wash at the end of the day. The parents had the luxury of a small room at the back of the house, and the whole place if modestly decorated, was always impeccably clean.

The girls, Sun-Hi and her little sister, Mai, attended the village school, wearing the uniforms and the red Young Communist Party's scarf, and followed the usual daily chanting of the adoring allegiance to the Party and its leaders. When Sun-Hi was fifteen, she started going to the hotel more regularly to help as a young party volunteer, a great opportunity for her to learn on the job the complex dynamics of the hotel industry. She was eager to help at any task, and could be seen in the kitchen washing dishes, shining shoes in a back-storage room, and bringing down the dirty laundry. Mai followed her soon after, although she was under thirteen, but free labor was always needed and appreciated at the hotel, especially when coming from members the employees' own families.

Mai remembered very clearly her first 'job', when she was only a little child. The Red Star Hotel received many military groups coming for border inspections or meetings with the leaders of troops in charge of defending the frontier with the South. The hotel needed help with the potato peeling, and other small tasks. It was in the middle of the winter and Mai loved to be in the restaurant's kitchen where it was warm and smelled so good. And there were produce she had never seen before, Brussel sprouts, endives, asparagus, and some otherwise never found during the winter, like carrots, tomatoes, string beans... And meat, oh that smelled so good, it almost made her head turn. But not for too long, because Eunji, the 'first chef' would push in front of her a full bowl of the most delicious thick preparation of her own. Oh, life at the hotel was all that one could dream of, and Mai decided that she would do her best to work there when she would be a grown up, and where she "will keep her job forever". Later on, she learned about other delicacies she had never heard before, such as coffee, Cherry, and so many different wines! Why one would want to drink anything else than chai? Nevertheless, the smell of the coffee was surely intriguing! And then, the lady guests were taking their coffee and tea with those deliciously looking and smelling cookies and slices of cake!!

With time, Mai, along with her entire family, was attached to the Red Star Hotel one way or the other. After school and finishing her homework making herself small by the stove in the kitchen, she offered her help for whatever chores were needed. She loved it there, the warmth, the food she was given regularly after serving dinner to the guests. Then, Mai waited for her mother and her sister to finish their assignments, sitting on a little chair behind the door close to the stove, where sometime she would end up dosing off. The Lees' never knew a real dinner before starting their posts at the hotel, and, like most of the people around, they didn't have but a bowl of hot water thickened with lentils or rice, to which were added some herbs for the flavor. It happened many times in the past to have only chai, and were happy if they could sweeten it with a little sugar when the ration was distributed every three to four months. Lee's children never had eggs or milk before, and the period of plenty they discovered in the service of the privileged class was received like a celestial gift, and was helping the little girls to grow healthy and strong.

No employee of the hotel was allowed to bring home food or any other item from the hotel, with the exception of one or two brioches half eaten or left untouched by the hotel guests. Mai could not believe that they would have been discarded anyway and the chef was stashing them in their pockets instead. That was making a 'yummy' addition to their thin bowl of soup at breakfast.

Summer time, Mai offered all her free time as a helper of the hotel, and no one was complaining. Her teachers even facilitated her assignments of the summer patriotic duties for the functions requested at the hotel, as a "major national participation". Thus, Mai was happy to consecrate all her summer vacation to her new occupation. When she and her sister were very young, they did have a short stay in a young communist vacation camp and enjoyed some limited 'scout times'. However, since all superfluous expenses had been diverted to the military branches, those children vacations have been revoked a long time before.

Many children in the villages were bored during the off-school periods, their homes being very small, with one little stove for cooking outside, no indoor plumbing and not much to see or to do. Once the sweeping of their only room done, children were uninterested in reading the same used school books, for no other reading was allowed nor available in the country that defended the infiltration of the 'imperialistic influence' to penetrate the country and the young minds.

In the late part of 1980s, the Korean government made some attempts to display a more open policy toward the outside world, even inviting a few tourist delegations from the free world, with visits during which the south side of the country noticed most of the 'détente'. Very limited groups of visitors, a few journalists strictly accompanied and having a pre-approved itinerary, stopped by the Red Start Hotel in their way to the capital. Military representatives from Americano-South Korean alliance were periodically seen meeting with their northern counterpart for constant need of reassurance from both sides of 'non-threatening collaboration'. The location was convenient for the military teams and meetings were easy to arrange for members from across the border.

Although the general population stood at a respectable distance from any foreigner, having no direct contact, not even exchanging a few words, always avoiding to stare, the locals observed discreetly the way the foreigners acted. The villagers and in particular the employees of the hotel, people working at the gas station and border agents, they all noticed the way the visitors held themselves straight, heads lifted and looking up, speaking confidently, and surprisingly, laughing often. They moved with ease, even drove cars, and showed kindness and respect to others. That created some confusion or surprise, the residents usually being treated and spoken harshly. But for the employees, the most difficult situation was refusing presents or tips, for they were absolutely forbidden to accept anything from a stranger, when they had to firmly push away any gift, at the consternation of the guests.

The two sisters, Sun-hi and Mai, were appreciated for their joyful disposition and for their pleasant looks, which helped to give a little improvement to the hotel personnel image, in times when the lodging industry was expected to become more polished.

When Sun-Hi turned 18, she was an attractive young girl, with an open expression and delicate features. She felt at home in the hotel, and everyone appreciated the way she interacted with the guests and the hotel personnel. Loh Gim, a young officer assuming some of the team meetings with the border regulations and exchanges with the south side, became a regular guest of the hotel, and, like many other visitors, he noticed the young girl. Loh enjoyed some of the advantages of the specialty stores and other perks the highly ranked party members benefited from, thanks to his complete allegiance to the Party.

Sun-Hi working regularly at the reception desk, became soon the hostess for the group meetings and receptions. This position implied for her to learn and be fluent in English, task that she assumed most seriously. She was in no time followed by her little sister, Mai, who occasionally helped her with the receptions, and Sun-Hi hoped to prepare her little sister for a similar job in the future. This new opportunity appeared to be also an opening for the two sisters to discover a world they had never imagined, a world they did not suspect could even exist.

All the restrictions put in place by the communist regime had to leave occasionally some room to the personnel dealing with foreigners. This allowed Sun-Hi, and then to Mai, to read simple booklets of customs, etiquette, expressions, and preferences of some of the western guests. Some magazines were also carefully selected and made available with the strict directions to be used as source of information, and demonizing the imperialist life style.

The more the two sisters learned about the existence of the 'free world', a term that could not even be whispered openly, the more their hearts and imagination became filled with thrilling expectations. Bursting with hope for something different, something they could not clearly define, their young minds aspired to knowing more about the real world, where people could laugh and play, have nice homes and decent clothes. A world where young people could meet and have fun, dance and watch any programs they wanted on television, read any book they heard about, could travel, and even possess a car and go on vacation.

Above all, Sun-Hi and Mai dreamed about a happy life, where freedom and joy were possible, where they did not have to contain every smile, be under constant criticism, act submissive, and obey blindly the Party directions. And mostly, a world where they would not have to live in fear, in terror that at any time one can be found 'guilty' of some kind of subversion against the regime and be thrown into a labor camp and disappear.

SUN-HI

The four members of the Lee family have been conditioned their entire life to keep their feelings deep inside, and tried their best to juggle between acting professionally and at ease with foreigners, as though the Korean life was not that much different from theirs. Nevertheless, there was a tight rope to walk on, and they continued to show their total devotion to the Party and persisted to reject the capitalist attitude.

Loh Gim approaching his 30th birthday, felt pressured by his parents to take a wife and establish his social status, now that he consolidated a good military career. Loh lived with his parents in an apartment block, a typical communist dwelling of the party members, while his three sisters were already married and out form the rundown old family home in the country, remaining only Loh, the youngest of the children and the 'spoiled' one by his sisters and his mother. When Loh became an officer in the army, he was entitled to a new home and took his parents with him to live in his new place. The apartment allocated had a sink and a private toilet with two rooms and a separate entrance, but the kitchen and shower facilities were common for all the apartments of the same floor, and located at the end of each level of the building. This might seem rudimentary to a westerner, especially for a privileged member of the party, but it was definitely un improvement from living in a shack up in the mountains and having to draw the water from a well or carry it from down the river, especially during the cold and long winters.

Loh was not very used to see a woman occupying a public function and was intrigued by the Lee young girls appearing so much at ease and interacting so professionally with well-mannered people. He was very impressed and almost intimidated by the refined way Sun-Hi conducted herself; she was so elegant and pretty, and most of all, so respected and sought after by everyone, the hotel members and the guests, all the same. However, Loh considered himself an important member of the Communist Party, an officer of the Army for that matter, and started openly courting Sun-Hi. Loh made all the efforts to be on his best behavior, and shortly after showing his interest on Sun-Hi, went to her father, Sunjin Lee, and told him that he wanted to marry his eldest daughter. Loh, was a little surprised when the father suggested to make his demand to his daughter, but he complied however. Sun-Hi, sincerely flattered and looking forward to having a husband and starting her own family, accepted.

Thus, a couple of months later Sun-Hi and Loh became engaged and within a year, married. The Red Star Hotel held a little reception shortly after they signed the simple civil formalities, offering some appetizers, the traditional wedding cake and some Champagne. That was a first for the newlywed couple as for many from the attendance. The head manager of the hotel, Chung, jokingly declared that he would let Sun-Hi get married only with the promise that she will be coming back to work at the hotel. Sun-Hi and Loh had their lavish wedding, thanks to the good heart of Chung and his appreciation for Sun. Chung also offered the newly married couple a beautiful room with the adjacent bathroom to spend their first night together. Sun-Hi felt like a princess, when, before wearing her bridal gown, indulged herself taking a long bath and lavished in the fragrant shampoos and lotions, then, aided by her mother and her sister, prepared for her big day.

"Oh, life looks so wonderful", she thought!

DISILLUSIONS

Since her sister's marriage, Mai increased her time working at the hotel. Soon she would end her high school education and for her the choice was clear, she would continue to work and advance her career at the Red Star Hotel. Mai was full of expectations and exulted with joy for her work. She continued to attend to a variety of activities organized by the management, with increased responsibilities as the hotel was more in demand for hosting meetings and important visitors' stay. By the age of sixteen, she was a beauty, gracious and discreet, her manners were perfect and held with a natural elegance. Mai was constantly, but silently, inquiring about everything regarding the prompt assistance to the smallest needs of the attendees. From the material needed for the conferences, projectors and microphones, to the minutes details as the disposition of the water carafes and glasses, papers pads and pencils, or the proximity of telephones. She was equally attentive and learned about the perfect running of the dinners and receptions, while she became quite proficient in English language and gained some knowledge in Mandarin and Russian.

Later, when she completed her school and was finally free to dedicate her entire time to the hotel obligations, Mai received a little allowance for her clothing. She made a few visits to a store in the town of P'yonggang near to the hotel, a special store reserved to the Party dignitaries. One of the hotel managers took her there using a special card issued for these stores, and she discovered in awe the huge perks certain members of her country could have access to. Although Mai did not make any overt remarks about this surprising discovery, she could not help, however, taking mental notes. For the first time in her life, Mai felt the unrest sensing that there were some unspoken layers of social covenants in a country that had always been presented to her as a regime based on complete equality.

She had learned her entire life, that her country was 'the workers' country' where everyone was equal with similar distribution of their efforts, and now she witnessed that some benefited from deals just like she has been told were the privileged people in the capitalist countries. Her trust was shuttered and she was saddened to observe now clearly that there were enormous social and political inequities. And above all, Mai discovered that her own country lived in a tacit understanding, where no one would question, not even mention, the existence of privileged life enjoyed by some, hidden under a veil of hypocrisy. "At least, she thought, "the westerners are not trying to hide it!"

If Mai was a blooming young woman remaining polite and pleasant with everyone, she was keeping herself very private, knowing that she was, like everyone else, watched and reports were handed regularly to the next in the Party's hierarchy. The dictatorial and oppressive system functioned like a clock, everyone watching and everyone being watched. It was the best way to control the masses, there was no need for hired spies, people were policed from within.

Mai did not trust anybody, except for an unspoken agreement with her parents, she matured in the face of necessity and cultivated a more formal demeanor, using her new position as events coordinator. She was dressed in a very professional manner, using the suits bought at the Party members' store, which helped to give a little more credibility to her child-like face.

As she took the habit without even realizing it, Mai was lost on her thoughts looking out the window, this time from her small office, considering her jobs over the years. She remembered herself as a house keeper, after been advanced from peeling vegetables and cleaning pots and bowls. Then, after her sister married, she was frequently asked to take her sister's place for the reception and coordination of conferences, and this was handy, since Mai had already been trained on the job by Sun-Hi.

More recently, Mai, now 17 and freed from her school education, could fully assume the event coordinator position, and Sun-Hi begun asking even more often to have her work hours given to her sister. No one was really questioning Sun-Hi, since the oriental women, and particularly Korean ones, were expected to take care of their husbands and family in the first place, and they rarely continued to work after being married. However, Mai, deep in her thoughts and getting ready to leave for home, reviewed in her mind the events slowly scrolling by: one morning Sun-Hi tried to hide some blue marks on her arms pulling down on her sleeves, then calls came in frequently announcing she would not come to work that day. Mai tried to find out what happened, worried sick about her sister and realizing that she was not as cheerful and as happy as she always appeared to be in the past.

Sun-Hi, as a married woman, was expected to take care of her in-laws as well, and living in a tight space, soon she realized that her mother-in-law was an exigent and mean person, demanding that she attends to all her needs. Sun-Hi hoped for some support from her husband, after all she was an educated woman and they were practically in their honey moon. But Loh Gim soon showed his insensitive nature, expecting his wife to obey without questioning, and treated her more like a servant than a wife. Too soon, the sweet and gentle Sun-Hi became disillusioned and sad, although she made all efforts to keep it for herself.

That was until last night, when the Lee family was woken up in the middle of the night by Sun-Hi, who, out of breath and covered in blood, managed to run through the night back to her parents' home for protection. They finally learned the truth, Loh was drinking every time he had a chance, and this habit let surface his brutal nature, beating his wife. This beast started striking his wife as a show to his parents that he was in charge and he knew how to control a woman, to the sadistic satisfaction of his mother. Their low level of education and primitive minds considered that "a woman was to get regular beatings to keep her straight". So, Sun-Hi was humiliated and hurt as a matter of principle. But after one of these beatings, she could not take it anymore, suspecting also that her husband, who enjoyed hitting her in the face, wanted to render her unable to present herself to work in that condition. And quitting her job, Sun-Hi would become completely at the mercy of her husband and his family.

In the following morning, Sunjin took his daughter to the hotel manager. He was a simple man without any political power and no means to fight his son-in-law, who was a member of the Party and an officer in the army. With his wife and Mai by his side, Sunjin explained to Chung, the same manager that married Loh and Sun-Hi, the terrible way Loh Gim was treating his wife. Chung, a kind man, at first at loss considering the situation, and with no authority outside the hotel, decided however to call Loh's superiors. Chung informed Loh's colonel about the way he behaved and he insisted that these actions dishonor the military conduct.

Loh was called and reprimanded, and although furious, had to make a formal promise to his colonel that he "will treat his wife nicely". However, Sun-Hi was terrified to go back and obtained to stay a little longer at her parents' house and heal before being able to show up at work.

Eventually, Sun-Hi had to go back to her husband, after Loh kept coming to the hotel and to Lee's house, and tempted to make sincere amends promising to treat her well, as during the time he was courting her.

PUPPY

Mai, still looking out the window and remembering this sad turn of events, felt a cold shiver running down her back, wondering for how long this would last, not trusting her brother-in-law in the least. She was also preoccupied with another worrisome incident, her dog she called "Puppy". Mai found him over two years ago, a little abandoned puppy, on a cold rainy day coming back home from work. Hurrying under the slashing curtain of rain drops in the early dark of the autumn, she heard a light squeal coming from a ditch. Glancing to the side of the road, she stopped to see what was there and discovered a little baby dog, eyes barely opened, obviously discarded by the mother's owner. The baby dog was so little, trembling and cute, and as soon as Mai took him in her arms and felt her warmth, he tempted to suckle one of her fingers. Mai thought that the puppy dog was the most adorable, but so defenseless, and without any hesitancy she took him under her coat and brought him home.

At home, she gently cleaned the baby, made him a little preparation with some yams crushed in puree and some goat milk given by a neighbor, after she helped with her meager savings to take her son to the doctor. That night, after the puppy filled his belly and fell asleep next to the bowl of food, Mai took him to her bed. Since then, Puppy, a name that Mai had learned from her English education texts were given to the baby dogs, slept with her every night. From that day, or more precisely, that night on, Puppy became the tender and much-loved companion for Mai and another member of the Lee family.

However, there started the problems; in a country doomed to starvation, where dogs are eaten and considered a delicacy, Puppy risked any day to disappear and become someone's unexpected source of meat for several days. Mai, almost fifteen at that time, spent most of her time between her school and her job at the hotel and was rarely at home. She worried constantly that Puppy, who was loving and playful, would leave the surroundings of their home and be stolen. They managed having the father, Sunjin, who worked mostly at night, watch him day time after work, but he needed his sleep during the mornings. Nevertheless, the mother or the girls kept Puppy close by every time someone was home.

Mai could not help not to worry, since in the past and getting older, Puppy decided that he would please his mistress welcoming her home, and was getting further and further out on the road to meet her. Mai became terrified of losing Puppy, as it was clear that they were hiding the dog to keep him alive. She was happy every time she found Puppy home, well and jumping with joy, leaking her face and enticing her to play with him. Mai found the meaning of true and unconditional love in Puppy, and she considered Puppy the only friend she ever had besides her family.

JO

Joseph Godson arrived at the Red Star Hotel an early-morning at the beginning of the cold season. He was attending, as part of a South Korean-American team, routine revisions of the border control between North and South Korea and her allies. It was the first time that he was visiting any part of the North Korean territory, but he possessed an extensive amount of information from his detailed briefings in his preparation for this type of exchanges. Joseph, twenty-five years old, going by Jo with the people who knew him, was taking in the whole situation and location of the meeting place, in this October of 1987. He was a marine, trained in special forces and considered exceptionally gifted by his espionage and counter-espionage training masters. He was a diamond black belt in martial arts, and spoke fluently Korean and Cantonese. However, this time, Jo was there to oversee the interactions of the two team members, as an observer from the outside, paying attention to details of the way the two camps behaved, their reactions, and in particular to notice anything out of the ordinary. He was as attentive to the north team comportment as much as of the south team and its American colleagues, looking for possible leaks of information passed voluntarily or involuntarily.

Jo was a natural on making himself at home anywhere and in any circumstance, carrying a nonchalant demeanor and addressing people with a disarming smile. In reality, he was a lover of the nature and of all people in general, and resisted vehemently when approached to be recruited by the CIA. However, Jo was already very attracted by the special force training, liking the challenge of pushing to extreme the physical and mental abilities in dangerous situations. He was a fighting machine with lighting reflexes, and owned a mental capacity retaining details, memorizing visual and written information as no one else could. In addition, Jo had the faculty of solving problems that ranked him to an IQ off the charts. He was finally persuaded to become a CIA officer when told how much he could do for his country and for the world stability. After all, Jo was a dreamer at heart, in a quasi-robotic body.

The meeting with the North Korean delegation was not scheduled until 10 am, and the members of his team, three other Americans and five South Koreans, went to their rooms at their arrival, planning to meet around nine in the hotel's restaurant for an unhurried breakfast. Jo, used to a Spartan regimen, decided to go out and jog his 5 miles, fault of any other exercise space available at the hotel. At seven he already had changed into unnoticeable sweat pants and jacket, went out through the back door of the hotel and chose to leap into the natural paths beyond, toward the hills. In reality, this was giving him an opportunity to free his mind and observe this part of the 'enemy' landscape. He prepared an explanation in case he would be intercepted by someone from the territorial surveillance, he would 'play dumb' and simply say that he was running and lost his directions.

Jo warmed up taking in the fresh air and the desolate land, with dark tree trunks and branches, the leaves long gone laying a soft layer fallen on the ground, helping to mute his strides. As he was going up on a gentler slope, he increased his speed, bringing up his cardio work. After a while, close to the top of the hill, he arrived at a sort of assembly of homes, a king of scattered hamlet, with simple dwellings hiding behind shrubs, while others took protection against the back of the hills. All seemed so quiet, very few roosters calling or goats bleating. Making a tour of the hamlet, he started his descent taking the direction of the hotel. He arrived at a little wood bridge across a small dich where the rapid waters of a brook made the only happy sounds in this grey morning.

On the middle of the bridge, he heard, rather sensed a movement behind him, and in a quick reflex he turned around to face whatever tried to 'attack' him. And attacked he was, by an adorable Golden Retriever running after him, and, as if he were happy to see him, almost jumped into his arms. Before Jo could 'defend' himself, his face was licked through and through. Surprised, Jo looked around to find out where the dog was coming from, all the while padding his head. And plop, the dog dropped on his back, ready for a belly rub. Jo had no choice but to oblige, when he saw a young silhouette approaching, running down the narrow path. Because of the tall bushes along the road, Jo was not able to clearly see the person coming until she arrived at the foot of the bridge. And the image was of a lovely girl, cheeks warmed by the run, hair flowing in the wind and her delicate face bearing an expression of intense apprehension.

Although Jo was smiling, amused by the friendly reception of this innocent creature, so unexpected in an enemy territory, the young girl was still frightened and started apologizing profusely, as she went to the dog and wrapped him in her arms. She was holding him rather in a protective gesture than to correct him from running off. And this was the moment when Jo had the opportunity to test his fluency in basic North Korean, as he was reassuring her that no harm was done.

Mai was a little rattled by the presence of this tall stranger, but she did not seem to have any trouble communicating with him. For now, she wouldn't want to understand where was he coming from, only to take Puppy home and lecture him for escaping again and making her worry to death. Still, while she didn't see much of the stranger's head, which was covered deep to his eyebrows by a black woolen cap, she was stricken by the intense color and expression of his blue eyes. She was certain that she had never seen this man before.

LIFE IN NORTH KOREA

During the late 1980s, North Korea remained the prototype of a totalitarian communist country, while some of the Eastern European nations under the Iron

Curtain were opening under a fresh liberating breath from the Russian oppression. After President Ronald Reagan made his speech in Berlin in 1987, addressing the Soviet Secretary, Mikhail Gorbachev, the world watched as a wave of freedom swept through the entire Eastern Europe, after many failed attempts in the past to obtain independence. Starting with the falling of the Berlin Wall in November 1989, which happened after 27 years of separating the East from the West Berlin, by the end of 1989, other countries unleashed their hatred for the communist regime in violent acts of revolt.

In summer 1990, virtually all former eastern communist countries were replaced by democratic governments. East Germany was on the way of reuniting entirely with its western sister, while Poland, Hungary, Czechoslovakia, Bulgaria, Romania, elected freely their government. Throughout Soviet Union, the collapse of the colossus was under way, fragmented like a shattered piece of glass as it was losing the annexed nations during the dark years of Stalin era. On the Asian countries, however, China managed to crush the students' movement in Tiananmen Square in 1989 and save its domination, while reinforcing its ties with North Korea.

By 1990, North Korea was under complete control of the Kim family, who established the supremacy of the Chairman of the Communist Party as 'the Father' figure of the nation, imposing an adoration of the masses reaching the level of madness.

Kim Il Sung, the first in line to create the communist nation of Korea, born in 1912 and very active during the World War II supporting the Bolshevik military, placed his connections on a strong position to obtain the control of the newly formed communist satellite. Thus, at the end of WWII, he came back from the Soviet Union to Korea. He already had two sons, and Kim Jong Il is believed to be born in one of the military camps in URSS sometime in 1941, was then only a child.

Kim Jong Il, the second in line of the Kim dynasty, son of Kim Il Sung, the "supreme leader" or "father of the nation", grew up under the complete domination of his father, although himself treated and venerated as a god. He was a mixture of conflicting personalities, spanning from love of power and cruel and vicious habits of maintaining the family privileges. He had a spoiled nature and was surprisingly attracted by the 'western imperialistic' culture. Kim Jong, learning from his father the barbarian and merciless technics, maintained complete authority using torture and starvation of the population, and imprisoned hundreds of thousands of his people in labor camps at the most insignificant sign of complaint.

He assumed the position as the head of the State Security, while he spent his time impersonating Elvis, his obsession, and directing movies in a Hollywood style. For he was secretly known of having very decadent tastes, considering himself an artist and holding a true passion for the western movies and actresses, in particular for the 'Western Movies'. In a country where all was devoted to the military power and the military service was mandatory for any young male for a duration of 10 years, Kim Jong Il indulged in Hennessy cognac, fine cigars, and expensive food, during times when the country was going through the worst famine.

Until July 1994, when his father died at age 82 from a heart attack, Kim Jong Il was mostly involved in the behind-the-scenes intrigues and manipulation, particularly after he took charge of the secret service, safeguarding his position as the sole successor to power. At his father's death, Kim Jong Il was 52 years old, and very well versed in the matters of complete control and terror instituted by his father for some 50 years of his totalitarian domination of North Korean territory. In order to eliminate any potential competition to the succession of Kim Il Sung, it is said that Kim Jong Il did not hesitate to extreme cruelty and there are strong rumors that he had his younger brother drown and his step brother shot.

Kim Jong Il, after establishing the image of his father as the absolute leader of the nation, practically as a god on Earth, extended this concept to his own cult of personality. During this time, he continued, though, his obsession of the movie making to the point of kidnaping an Asian actress from Hong Kong and forcing her to star in his films.

Full of contradictions, pulled between his desire to serve the long-lasting domination of his father over the political direction of North Korea, and his unsatisfied desire to affirm his own position, Kim Jong Il continued an ambiguous and conflicting life. In the early 1990s Kim Jong Il was giving a semblance of détente with the outside world, while continuing his merciless work as the head of the security services, and eliminating many of his opponents.

His son, Kim Jong Un, the third in line for the Kim family succession, born in 1980, was even sent to complete his education in Switzerland, and continued to be groomed to walk on the family steps in order to pursue the same practices insuring the family tradition and supremacy.

This pale image of détente lasted the last decade of the 20th century and until 2011, at Kim Jong Il's death at the age of 69. By that time, Kim Jong Un was well prepared to take over the family legacy and to continue the disastrous governance of the North Korean state, while his distorted and vicious mind reached new heights in the desire to maintain his power at all cost.

Kim Jong Un concocted a devious plan to obtain some means of feeding his famished nation by threatening the Western countries, and in particular the United States, flaunting a constant nuclear menace. To his satisfaction and against all powerless protests of the capitalist countries, with the backstage support of superpowers such Putin's Russia and the Communist China, all seemed to be working for Kim. His unrestrained ego relentlessly pushed his party members and top scientists to fabricate and test one after another nuclear missiles, while using all means available to this end with total disregard of depleting his country's economy.

This paradox and through this evil manipulation made Kin Jong Un hold the whole world at his merci and provided him with substantial aids against his vaunting nuclear threats. This insane ruse had only one scope, maintain his power. Because Kim Jung Un was well aware that without the nuclear menace, his position, his own life, were in danger in the outside world, and even inside his homeland.

PYONGYANG

In this early year of 1987, in the northern side of the Korean peninsula the atmosphere of détente was somewhat reached un underground feeling. At least, this was the impression the Kim family intended to project around the world: the supreme leader, Kim Il Sung, still alive and at the summit of his authority, along with his son, Kim Jong Il, in his late forties, and his grandson, Kim Jong Un, 7 years old, who seemed to become one day an iron-handed ruler as well.

The Democratic People's Republic of Korea (DPRK), continued its propaganda of filtered and well-orchestrated images of the country towards the outside world. There were mostly impressive marches of thousands of people chanting and praising the party leaders, who proudly watched parading military equipment meant to impress the imperialist world. Those endless demonstrations of the 'success of the revolution' staged on immense boulevards, were practically the same shown over and over again. Very few from the free world would know that, beyond these large public places, life in Pyongyang was significantly more modest, with rows of apartment blocks in communist style built in the Stalin era of 1960s, long past their need of renovation.

Some 2.5 million Koreans were living, or better said, were squeezed in a place suffering from a chronic housing problem, and trying to obtain one of these apartments, mostly same size and quality, quickly built for the post-war necessities. They were uniformly utilitarian high-rise blocks, twenty and up to forty story high. While the young people living in the upper levels had to start their descent early in the morning in order to make it on time to work or to school, the elderly felt 'trapped' in their small apartments and many never went out since the time they moved in. And because the electrical supply was exceedingly defective, the very few elevators still functioning were unreliable and therefore, rarely used.

During the long and cold winters, the erratic power supply created a serious heating problem, and the people resumed to wearing their day-time cloths on as well as during night time. Some kerosene lamps used for heating or candles for lighting were hazardous and expensive, and many could not afford them.

The 'alternating supply system' spread in Pyongyang, could have been the subject of a comic movie if one would not consider the sad impact in people's everyday life: monitoring the electrical distribution from one side of the street to the other, children and some adults would 'rush' from one place to the one of friends across their block to finish homework or, for the most fortunate ones, watch television.

FIRST TIME AWAY FROM HOME

It was during these times when Mai had the first occasion to visit the capital, as it was the first time she had to leave the close perimeter of her village and her work at the hotel. Mai was summoned to attend one of the Party's annual anniversary celebrations, during the time she attended an intense training in the hospitality hotel business. Found that she had a future for this type of employment, for she had a real talent when dealing with delicate interactions between the Korean hotel employees and the inevitable meeting with the world across the south border, her supervisors and the comrades from the capital thought of outmost importance to give detailed briefings to all exposed to foreigners.

The classes were schedules for four weeks in the capital, lodging in the community dormitories annexed to the central buildings allocated to the Ministry of the Interior and the Institute for National Reunification's White Paper on Human Rights.

Before leaving for the capital, Mai found out that she had to fill and register a form at the local police office, after showing her documents requesting her attendance to the party education classes. Only then she could obtain a written authorization to leave the place of her living, providing the reason and the duration of it. This was the first time she had heard about these formalities, mandating all citizen to inform the authorities about all movements outside their domiciliation, and obtain an approval prior to their departure.

Finally, when the day of her leaving came, Mai left from her hotel in a van looking very much like an old military vehicle, already occupied by four other young people going to the same classes. Mai was quiet and observant during her five-hour ride. She was apprehensive of what she would find in Pyongyang and tried to retain as much as she could from the novelties discovered during her trip.

The comrades in the van, three other girls and an arrogant young man, had diverse functions in hotels along the border; two of the girls were shy and expressed their anxiety having to learn how to react when taking care of South Korean customers. The third one, was nice enough and had already several years of experience working on a job similar to Mai's. Reassuring the other two girls, Tania, adopting a Russian name for the convenience of her work, gave them some tips concerning their work as receptionists.

With Mai, Tania became more open and, appearing at ease, even made some jokes about how to manage conferences with clients from the free world. Mai was somewhat impressed by Tania, who had an open, almost joyful personality. Mai had learned during her entire life to be reserved and restrain her reactions, instinctively not trusting anyone. Not long after being removed from her familiar places, Mai felt instinctively the desire to 'stick' to Tania's presence, and was glad to learn that they were attending the same hotel management courses.

Mai also learned that these classes contained several hundred of attendees, as the state had limited funds, the sessions being organized far and few in between. However, since it was imperative for the Party to keep the employees under strict discipline, the control of their interactions with the western world was overriding at times the meager economical resources available. The classes were taught by very devoted Party members, who volunteered for these courses. They were making sure that the number of each class was limited to 10 or 12 members chosen for specific job needs, and that the students were entirely indoctrinated with the communist views of the people they were to encounter.

The young man traveling with them in the van and holding a distant demeanor, was well dressed instead of the usual gray or kaki plain cloth available around. He had even a warm looking pullover under his heavy coat, and boots in good condition. His head was covered with a fur hat having extended ear covers, in a Russian style, which was habitual to this country, but this seemed to be of a better quality as well. Soni, started smoking and soon filled the small back cabin with fumes, making Mai feel uncomfortable as she remembered that the people at the hotel were taught not to do this without asking permission first.

Soni, however, after keeping for himself for a while, pitched a few commentaries intended to impress, and took a patronizing tone towards the girls. Overall, he was giving them the impression that he was not intimidated by his superiors, he was laughing at 'bending the rules' and going out drinking with other young men and accepting gifts from the hotel customers. He made sure to let the others know that he was to attend the classes reserved for the head manager of the hotel and that, once back to his work, he would be in charge and he "will make everyone tremble."

The trip, which normally should not have taken more than two hours, view the poor conditions of the roads, mostly dirt tracks when traversing rural areas, made the ride last five hours. Mai was noticing everything she saw, all so new to her. Passing through villages, she watched the desolate lands, barren this time of the year with humble dwellings in pitiable conditions. People seem to stay away from open areas, particularly when a rare vehicle was passing by. No machinery was seen in the collective farming, no cows, just a few chickens and an ox cart were all that Mai could spot through the narrow side windows.

Finally arrived into the capital city, they traversed a few large avenues with impressive Party buildings. Mai had never seen anything that big and tall, and she felt a surge of pride and anticipation stirring her heart with hopes for new and many good experiences coming into her life. The van finally stopped near the entrance of a building, and everyone was shown a side door leading to the dormitories allocated for the duration of the classes. Boys and girls were directed in opposite sides of a long corridor in the basement of the building, after being told that the classes were held on the higher floors of the same building.

They quickly found out that their dorm rooms hosted twenty girls and there was a common washroom and a private area for the toilettes. Mai, used to rudimentary living conditions she lived in her life, was however, repulsed by the sight of it: a few holes in the cemented area, and the nauseating smell made her stomach turn.

Back to the dormitory, she found a bank bed in a corner of the room and sat her few belongings by the bed and in the small wooden box functioning as nightstand. After that, all the students had to present themselves at the main floor and have their registration completed and be assigned to the classroom to which they were expected to attend in the morning. Once the formalities over, they were directed to the cantina where they would be taking their meals for the duration of their stay.

But until then, everyone was expected to gather into a large meeting room, where fault of siting space for everyone, most of them had to stand and listen to the instructions given. This is where the students were informed that going outside of the building on their own and wandering into town was not allowed. There was the promise, however, of a visit of their "glorious capital city" along with a participation to a marching day in the People's Square.

The regular session of indoctrination completed, everyone was finally led to the cantina and Mai could reach for a glass of water. Then, she joined the others, and grabbing a rudimentary wicker tray, followed in a single file the other members of the conference. When she had a glance at the food, she saw two matrons slapping some dubious paste of unappealing color into their small plates. She was happy to see that she would have a bowl of brown rice next to the un-nameable concoction. Mai was right, even though she was starving, after taking a bite of the food, she knew she could not get down any of it. Tasting the rice, she decided that it was 'eatable', although she detected an after-taste of spoiled grains. Trying to take her eyes off the food while eating, she looked around and noticed that most the other comrades were insensitive to the quality of the food. She also noticed that on a small table next to the counter serving the food was a large cauldron where people would stop and ladle some soup to fill a bowl. Feeling too hungry, Mai summoned her courage and went to get a bowl of soup for herself. Once sitting down again, she was glad of her decision, the soup was warm and making the rice tastier, something to fill up her stomach.

Mai was accustomed to simple nourishments, growing up with small samplings of basic but natural foods. She thought that even with meager means one could manage to prepare something more appealing than what she had seen so far.

GEEA

The Youth Preparation Classes for Hospitality, a long title like all the names communist society favors, were well into their second week. Mai longed for her little village close to P'yonggang, wishing for a solitary walk in the nature, for she did not have any privacy since her arrival to the capital. Her classes were boring and she felt she did not learn or achieve anything since there were no topics with specific situations presented to them; the long hours consisted of basically the same indoctrination with flat slogans, repeated to the point that Mai continued to hear them in her sleep. The daunting underlying message was to intimidate anyone that would ever forget they were the 'People of the Democratic Republic of Korea', and never drop the guards when dealing with foreigners or 'succumb' to their 'decadent' manners.

The highlights of those four weeks were, however, the parade they attended in the People's Square. Never had Mai seen anything that glorious and gigantic; under a thundering noise and a ground rumbling under the hundreds of boots keeping a stork like cadence, rows and rows of military squadrons were presenting in front of highly impressive and solemn bleachers where Kim Jong Il and the Party leaders smiled down at them. Then gigantic assault chars presented on mounted platforms rockets and other GAG, ground-air-ground weaponry, that surely 'made the whole world tremble'. Mai was completely taken by the feeling of pride for her country, in the middle of a crowd possessed by the general hysteria of the images exhibited in front of them. These images engrained for over forty years, the only exciting moments people were to look at, became their beliefs as they were the only events and news presented to them, keeping most of the population in complete isolation with the outside world, and having nothing else to compare with what it was displayed to them.

Mai interaction with the other students in her class was limited, as everyone was carefully observed, while congregations amongst the students, even of the same class, were 'not encouraged'. Tania was cheerful as always, but stroke a friendship with an older girl from another south-border town. They were sitting together at the cantina sometimes, and Mai was always impressed by their jolly demeanor. Soon after she started her classes, Mai was assigned to a small desk further back by the window, but close to the single wooden stove, sitting arrangements for which she was glad to remain unchanged until the end of their stay. Although accustomed to the long winters, the cold seemed to her a little more tolerable in the south part of the country where she lived, than the bitter cold she felt here.

During one of the breaks, Mai was standing closer to the stove and reading some of the notes she had taken, trying to retain some useful ideas for her work once arrived home. She was not very interested in these plain sentences, and her gaze had drifted towards the flames, lost in a strong yearning for her home and family. Her thoughts were interrupted by a cheery voice who was addressing her with an amusing look:

"Do you really need to study all this?"

"Oh no, I think that I could repeat everything by heart by now", Mai answered.

"You shouldn't worry, at the end of our course, you will be able to pass the test in your sleep!"

"That's reassuring! Mai replied, "But, are we going to pass any language classes?"

"Although Russian, Chinese, and even English are needed in our profession, there are not included in the official curriculum. It is understood that we have to learn them 'in private' and rely on the quality of the instructions available locally."

Their conversation came to an end as it was time to restart another class. Mai noticed that the young and pretty girl she just spoke with, came to sit behind her, and doing so, she whispered to Mai, "I am Geea, by the way."

To which Mai discretely turned to mutter her name.

As these uninspiring days went by and everyone fought to stay focused during the classes, Geea had even a harder time to concentrate on the subject. The two young girls started spending practically all their break time quietly chatting close to their desks. Mai noticed that, if Geea was a little chubby and short in stature, she had a pleasant smile and her clothes and shoes were of a good quality. Her manners were polite like in the South, and, although Mai could discern a little shyness behind her assurance, Geea presented herself as someone assuming charge in most situations.

To her surprise, Mai received an invitation to spend the night at Geea's home; when the school ended, Mai would be introduced to her new friend's parents and they would have dinner together. Geea was all excited and explained that the occasion was to attend to a special musical, where her mother was the main singer and a popular star of the socialistic productions of the People's Opera. Mai learned also that Geea's father was one of the well-respected generals of the country. When Mai, although very attracted by this highly unusual invitation, panicked realizing that she did not have anything proper to wear, her very few belongings being simple work pants and tops, worn out form constant usage, she received a quick reassurance:

"Not to worry, I have exactly what you need and we will have a great time; besides, you mustn't refuse my parents who can't wait to meet you".

"They want to meet me? Are you sure you told them that I am a very simple peasant from the South?"

"Yes, they know that, and they also know that you are smart and gentle, and the prettiest think anyone had seen since my mother was 17, like us."

"Now you really make me feel intimidated, I can't come!"

"My parents are very nice and they spoil me very much; I am sure they will do the same with you," was Geea's prompt replay.

Thus, it was decided, and some unexpected adventure came into Mai's life. When their courses came to term, Mai followed Geea as she stopped by the building entrance of their education classes, where an always-present desk with an annoyed looking employee checked every person coming in or going out. Shortly after Mai obtained her pass to leave the building, the two girls went out, climbing down the stairs with a light footing and big smiles on their faces.

CHAPTER 2 - AN UNUSUAL COUPLE

CHAPTER 1 - MAI AND JO

When Joseph Godson learned about Mai being arrested and thrown in jail, he was devastated. He also learned that, along with her, her family had been arrested as well, all of them condemned for treason and sent to a labor camp for many years. He was at that time in San Diego, California, for a special review and training, and asked permission to take a leave of absence. Because he wanted to go to the Far East and investigate on his own, Jo was told that, in these particular circumstances and for his own security, it was more appropriate if the matter was dealt with by the secret services. As soon as his leave was obtained, Jo flew to Seoul, South Korea, where he tried to obtain more information from his colleagues who worked recently across the border. But once arrived there, it was very little he could learn.

The last time that Jo saw Mai was in mid-August 1990, when he came for a routine stay at Koryo Hotel, in Pyongyang, in one of the periods when Mai was working there as well. It was a situation that would hardly permit them to have any interaction, when they rarely and secretly exchanged a few stolen moments and kisses. When Mai accompanied some members of Jo's delegation on a bus tour, Jo came along just to be with her, even though he had already seen the few places shown to the western visitors. But they did not have the opportunity of a private encounter against all the longing they craved for each other.

Jo had promised Mai that he was working to find a way for them to be together. But against all their wishes and for their own protection, they had to continue to hide their marriage. Mai insisted that, for the time being, even if she could manage to leave the country as the wife of an American, her family would suffer terrible consequences.

Following the visit in the North Korean capital, Jo had to stop at the Red Star Hotel in P'yonggang for three days before regaining Seoul, regrouping with some other members of his team. It was also when Mai found out that she had a little and rare break from work and she could go home for a few days. Seizing the unexpected opportunity, Jo asked the chauffer of the van bringing the two other delegates to the Red Star, if Mai can come along, as it happened on another occasion in the past. The two lovers had a hard time hiding their joy of being together during the few hours of the ride. With all their reserve, they might have shown a little too much tenderness toward each other when Jo reached for Mai's hand, expression of affection barely tolerated in public in this part of the world.

Once arrived at the Red Star Hotel, Jo managed to use all his abilities acquired during his training and make himself invisible, while visiting in secret Mai, who was at home resting. The two of them shared these rare moments with the most intense joy two young people in love can do. Inquiring why Mai was thinner than usual and felt tired lately, Jo pressed his questions and she finally announced to him that she was pregnant, and if it didn't show yet, she was well into her sixth month of maternity. Jo's first reaction was an explosion of joy, but he was called to reality by Mai's

25

worried look, when she admitted that her troubles kept her awaken at night, constantly considering the situation and her limited options. Jo, regaining more sense of reality, became frantic, pacing the room in deep concern. They talked for a long time and Mai spoke of her utter determination to take care of their baby against the preconceived judgmental criticism she expected to face soon.

Mai added that she already confessed to her parents about her pregnancy, and when they cried under the shock, she could not bear their sorrow and told them that her baby was a legitim one, and that Jo was the father. Surprisingly, they became very supportive and, knowing that once Mai's pregnancy becomes visible, she will be fired and treated as a shameful person. Mai's parents anticipating hard times ahead, promised her that they would help raise the baby. However, it was understood that the name of the father and Mai's marriage to a foreigner were to remain an absolute secret, in order to preserve their lives.

It appeared that under continue scrutiny, as people in North Korea lived constantly, the chauffer, one of the regular informers to the local Party cell assigned to Red Star Hotel, started suspecting that a possible 'courtship' was going on between Joseph Godson and Mai Lee. Even though some of the pretty employees were often covertly encouraged to 'sympathize' with westerners, they were, however, held to report the information obtained during 'private discussion' and even received orders for particular subjects on which to question them.

When Jo visited Mai at home, a Party security service officer was spying on Mai's home and caught a glimpse of Jo leaving her house a couple of times, lifting any doubt of their affair.

After the three days that Jo spent at The Red Star Hotel after which he left for South Korea, then for the US, Mai went about her usual activities, unaware she was under tight observation. Returning to work after her vacation, a week went by without Mai bringing up any information regarding her involvement with Joseph Godson to the comrade in charge with the hotel surveillance. At last, this called her to his office and asked if she thinks that Jo Godson showed her any special interest. When she denied, he pressed more rudely about her having an affair with him, and when she denied again, he snapped into a rage, calling her a liar and a traitor.

Shortly after that, Mai was handed to the Security Services of the Republic of Korea, brutally pushed into a black van, and disappeared into the underground levels of a communist jail.

Shortly after, her parents were arrested and followed the obscure path of the communist legal system. The employees of the hotel were one by one interrogated by the Security agents, who, after the initial shock of Mai's arrest, all loving sincerely their 'little girl', they secretly felt sorry for her. However, the officers of the Secret Police, against all their efforts of intimidation, could not obtain much information from any of the hotel employees.

BRUTAL REALITY

It took a little time until things went back to normal at the hotel, and another month or so until Jo, now far away in San Diego, California, learned from the team members left in Seoul, about Mai' arrest and Lee family's imprisonment. And he felt not only enraged, powerless, and crushed about Mai's condition, but he considered himself responsible of what happened to her. He was afflicted with guilt, thinking that his selfish feelings made her take all the risks, that he endangered her all this time, and now she was risking her life and the life of their future child. He could not find any sleep, images of Mai being mistreated by the bullies of a brutal regime only fueling his rage.

To the wedding vows promising to love, cherish, and protect his wife, Jo added the vows of making the impossible to save her and his child, even though at the present time he was at loss of what he could do.

Jo also realized that he needed to lay low for a while and he could not go to North Korea yet, as much as he would have wanted to. He was jeopardizing not only his life, but the work done by other fellow Americans for their country, and that only contributed to heighten his distress. There were now new members of the team allowed only sparingly to work above the south border, and they were assigned to different locations, and obtaining information became even more difficult. Somehow, an idea came to Jo's mind and he discretely sent someone to make a contact with Geea, Mai's friend, hoping she would know more.

Geea appeared to be of a great help; she discretely informed Jo's friend that Mai had been summarily judged and condemned to 25 years of labor camp and her parents, to 20 years. She avoided to mention that they were not expected to survive more than one or two winters in the camps' conditions. Filled with sadness, she uttered however, that Sun-Hi, Mai's sister, was promptly brought directly to the Police Security quarters by her husband as a testimony that he dissociated himself completely from his wife's doings. When Sun-Hi protested against being part of a conspiracy against her country, Loh Gim, her husband, grabbed a pistol from one of the officers standing by in observation, and shot himself his wife to death in front of the security agents.

Geea cried desperately telling all this to Jo's friend. She also revealed that she was aware of Mai's pregnancy, and that she was the one who took Mai to a friend gynecologist for a first visit. Then Geea said that she was also present when the doctor informed Mai that she was carrying twins.

While Jo continued to stay in South Korea and remained in alert for any new details concerning Lee family's condition, slowly the incoming news averted more devastating than the other. He learned about Sun-Hi, Mai's sister tragic death, then about her mother's. Jia, who after contracting pneumonia in the harsh labor camp's conditions, perished only a few months into her sentence.

Toward the end of November 1990, Joe felt that his heart shredded to pieces and his mind was lost, when bits of information were whispered by some villagers working on the grounds of the Red Star Hotel, to the regular employee friends of Mai's. Lingering sadness could not be completely shrouded and sorrowful whispers had been heard by friends of the South Korean members staying at the hotel. Eavesdropping gathered even more devastating news: Mai and the two babies she delivered were left to die soon after the delivery took place.

With all the discreet efforts made by Jo's friends and colleagues attending the conference sessions at The Red Star Hotel to find more details of what happened to Mai and her family, they remained practically disheartened by the brutality of North Korean practices, virtually a prison-like state. The reception and conference assistant staff were replaced with personnel keeping a cold face at all times, not engaging anything else beyond the strict information or instructions given to the visitors of the hotel. Chung, the hotel manager, would give the impression to someone who knew him before that he had aged by 10 years. Although his face expressed sadness, he remained kind with his older employee team. One detail came to their ears, though, and they reported to Jo, for whatever meaning this might be to him.

When one of the American team had seen Chung going on the hotel premises accompanied by a pretty Golden Retriever and asked about the dog, he volunteered to tell that the dog was 'adopted' by the hotel management. One day, Eunji, the old chef, found him at the door of the kitchen in a morning before down, when she was coming to work. "He must have followed somebody's sent and come to the hotel", she thought. The dog was weak and starving, and the chef must have known him, so she let him inside, where he spends now his time behind the kitchen stove. Eunji told the manager about the dog and asked permission to keep him as the 'hotel guardian', and he agreed, as long as the dog would not create any trouble.

Chung mentioned that the dog, although friendly and sweet, seemed lost and sad, and that he leaves every day for a few hours to stay by a small dwelling up in the hills, waiting for his masters to come home. A neighbor, who knows him since he was a puppy, brings some water outside for him, and sometimes sits with him for a while, petting him. They don't have to say much, just look at the abandoned little home in silence. If they feel the same sadness, the dog is looking for his masters to come back, while she knows that they never will.

After lingering for a little longer in the Korean peninsula, time going by without bringing anymore news, Jo finally returned to San Francisco, the place of his residence, and asked for some personal time off. Colleagues and superiors respected his sorrow. However, in mid-December 1990, Jo was given an opportunity to offer his powerful skills and competency to a bigger cause and extract himself from this mourning state: The Gulf War, the First Iraqi War, was declared Aug 2d 1990, and Operation Desert Shield was in full swing. At that point, Jo threw himself into the American Forces, combating another tyrant, Saddam Hussein, not keeping himself from taking all the dangerous missions. He was acting as if he did not care if he would die the following minute.

Fortunately, the war ended in February 28, 1991, after the second part of the war aligning the coalition forces with Saudi Arabia and Kuwait into Operation Desert Storm, from January 17, 1991, until the end of the war, when the Iraqi invading army retrieved from Kuwait. This being considered as a victory for American intervention, president George H. W. Bush ordered the end of the military action in Iraq.

Freed from participating to imminent military interventions, Joseph Godson continued to be an active part of the American-South Korean alliance and preferred to remain in the region, holding great expectations to learn more about the events that, a few months before, devastated his entire life. With the time Jo spent in the Iraqi war, the episodes lived in Korean peninsula seemed so far away! Jo had a hard time to believe that it was just a little more than two years since he had met Mai. He played in his mind the enchanting progression of their love, then their secret marriage during one of the few unexpected opportunities for Mai to cross the border separating the two sister countries.

MEMORIES

Joseph Godson clearly remembered the summer of 1988, when Mai was assigned more frequently to work in Pyongyang, soon to be attached to the international delegations staying at Koryo Hotel. Every time Jo came to the North Korean capital, he stayed also at the same hotel and often Mai was in charge with the coordination of conferences and city visits of their group. Their first separate encounter, hers from the hotel, his from his work team, happened and it was facilitated by Mai's friend, Geea. Without much forethought, as the two friends took the habit to spend time together, Geea invited Mai to a traditional theater/dinner presentation, one of the most popular leisure times in the city.

It had happened that Mai, during a casual exchange with Jo at the end of a conference day, dropped in the conversation the name of the theater where she was looking forward to spending the evening with Geea. It was also during one of the few times of 'détente' toward the western countries when the Korean president struggled to made believe that the foreigners could circulate more freely and attend some of the cultural events of their city he was so proud of.

Jo's interest and curiosity fired up, he inquired about that particular evening and arrangements were made for him and two of his closest coworkers to be accompanied to the theater. 'Casually' running into Mai and Geea, the trio insisted to have them, along with their 'guide', sitting at their table. Mai was resplendent in a simple red silk dress, straying from the rigid work suit, and wearing her long hair falling from a ponytail in two strands spiraling down. She even allowed herself a little make up on her already rosy cheeks and had applied some red on her beautifully designed lips.

As the evening advanced, everyone became more comfortable and relaxed with a conversation alternating from Korean to English. The two girls appeared to be very good guides themselves explaining to the 'heathen' guests the story of the play and the traditional characters found in most of them. Slowly, the uptight official guide started paying less attention, reassured by the innocent conversation and particularly impressed when he learned that Geea's father was a general of the army. Without much difficulty, Jo managed to serve their guide a generous amount of liquor, and this soon became a 'giddy' observer.

During this delightful evening, Jo had the opportunity to engage in a private conversation with Mai, and the two young people learned more about each other's life. As they become rapt in their animated exchange, there was a conceding attraction growing between the two of them. If Jo answered to her questions about his childhood, parents, and hobbies, Mai was more discreet about her own less impressive life, and concentrated on giving him details about the dishes served or the subject of the play. Jo seemed to drink her image with his eyes, and cared less about the subject of the conversation. During that evening, Joseph Godson was falling head over heels, or rather heart over mind for Mai, without even realizing the emerging emotions flourishing within him. For a few rare moments, he relaxed and without trying to resist, he allowed these exquisite feelings to invade him.

At the end of the evening, as everyone was making their farewell, Geea, with the most natural smile, invited the other attendees for a dinner at her parents' house. As Jo's friends declined, for they were expected by their families to have a home dinner, the guide stepped forward telling Geea that he will be glad to accompany Jo to her house. Geea gave him her most seductive smile, saying:

"Oh, not to worry, my father will send an official car to take Mr. Godson and Miss Lee to our home."

It looked as they found a breach in the communist security vice, and Mai and Jo could meet privately a few more times, thanks to their good friend Geea. Most of the times, Geea's parents were out busy with their own professional and social obligations, and Geea found excuses to discreetly retrieve to another part of the apartment, aiding the two lovers talk and learn more about each other. In no time, a very special and profound relation developed and intensified between the two young couple in love.

This special summer of 1988, Mai and Jo had seen each other either in Pyongyang or at the Red Star Hotel, sometimes enjoying a few private moments, other times for only a few whispered tender words exchanged furtively. By the end of the summer of 1988, Jo feelings were clear and he was certain of his deep love for Mai, to the point that he concluded that only a marriage was the way to continue their relations in the future. He was aware of the difficulties and dangers of such an association between a person subject of a totalitarian regime and a member of a politically enemy country. However, Jo was convinced that his love and determination were strong enough to overcome the obstacles and that the two of them would find a way to finally be together in a free world.

Thus, Jo approached his chaplain at the American Mission in Seoul and obtained his agreement to officiate a religious alliance in the event that he could manage to bring Mai to South Korea. It seemed after all, that a little more distention was felt between the two Korean sister countries. And hope took roots as a result of the Summer

Olympic Games of 1988 held in Soul, South Korea, and against all the troubles created by the norther counterpart boycotting the event.

SOUTH KOREA

If summer of 1988 made possible the bourgeoning of a romance between Mai and Jo Godson, earlier that year Mai lived another important and unusual episode on her life. The month of April remaining frigid in the Korean peninsula, this lessened the incentive of summits or conferences scheduled that time of the year in the North Korean capital. Miraculously, with the slowdown of the activities at the Red Star Hotel, Mai was considered well trained and ready for learning more from the western hospitality customs in order to introduce similar quality in the main hotels in the South Korean side. Thus, Mai learned that she was sent, at first two weeks, then to stay a few weeks at a time, in Seoul. She was briefed at great length about her duties and expectations of total allegiance to the Party.

Mai was completely taken aback by everything she witnessed during her first impression of the South Korea. Although only a few dozen miles separated her country side from the southern sister land, she felt that she stepped into a different planet, a wonderland of an existence she could never imagine as she discovered with every glance she was taking around.

Until her trips to Seoul, Mai's visits and sojourns in Pyongyang impressed her quite enough for her to believe that the North Korean capital represented the summit of what one could expect from an advanced metropolitan life, including the technology and the display of a prosperous economy.

When her small group of comrades going for training packed down in a small van on the way to Seoul, Mai found out that she was the only girl in the group of five men, who were assigned to a different program and stayed at a distant hotel from hers. She restrained her joy when at the next and final stop at Kaesong, before crossing the border, the girl that came on board was Tania, the young and cheerful Tania who attended the same first training Mai had in Pyongyang the year before. Since Mai sat on the isolated two seat bench close to the driver, the men gathered together to the back benches, Tania swiftly climbed in the van and sat next to Mai.

The van did not stop at the JSA, Joint Security Area, usually presented to the few western tourists as the main area of contact between the two Koreas, but at a heavily guarded check point near to Panmunjom, on the North Korean side of the DMZ, the Demilitarized Zone. After the group stopped at the border gate and had their documents checked by some stern looking solders who handled their official permits with the outmost suspicious consideration, the small group of comrades was allowed to cross the separation made by the border North Korea had traced with the entire world.

The eerie short drive through the no man's land, the DMZ, a powerfully militarized sliver of land running some 250 kilometers between the two countries, led them to its equivalent south border post near Minsan, where they were received by the counterpart orderlies on duty. There, they could notice already a change in the attitude of the officials; although remaining professional, they did not try to be intimidating. Holding themselves somewhat straighter and their uniforms appearing cleaner, after making the sign to go pass to the van, they continued to talk among themselves and laugh at their story they seemingly interrupted for a few moments.

Once passed the south frontier and entering the southern territory, an unexpected change in the mood of the group took place. The team members seemed more relaxed and adjusted to the landscape seen through the windows, with tiny changes in their reactions slowly progressing to less restrained exclamations of surprise. During the 50 km, some 30 miles until Seoul, their final destination, the surprises only continued to increase with images of roads, buildings and fields well maintained, leaving behind the military scenery.

Seemingly, none of the members of the group had seen before billboards with appealing posters for products that most of the time no one could guess their utilization. Approaching the southern capital, the traffic increased as well, displaying a flow of beautiful private cars in impeccable condition. Then, along with the presence of more traffic lights, the bemused visitors could see rows of skyscrapers with their shiny glass walls and stores parading the most attractive items, where people were coming out carrying marvelous shopping bags.

But the most astonishing impression everyone experienced, sharing it with the others or keeping it for themselves, was people's behavior. They moved with confidence, at times engaged in passionate conversations, holding hands, laughing and interacting without retention. They were dressed in a manner that all seemed coming out from a fashion magazine, with clothes of a large variety of colors and designs, accompanied by delightful accessories. Their boots had beautiful shapes and the scarves and hats were so attractive, they must have been a pleasure to wear.

At that point, no one was talking anymore lost in this overwhelming novelty, but what the comrades in the van thought mostly, was that these people on the street were their brothers, sharing the same origins and cultures, and yet, they had such a different way of living. They would have liked their ride to last for a long time, so much of a contrast was to be absorbed in a short lapse of time, when they eventually arrived to their destination.

SEOUL

North Korea does not have a formal embassy nor a consulate in the South Korea, and a possible overlook of the communist party had flawed the hosting arrangements for its 'visiting' citizens in Seoul. It might have been that a more normal integration in the regular life of the south would allow their spies to learn how to act naturally in a western environment, while the very few trainees being assigned close to the place of their meetings, would look less suspicious. This was suitable to the northern government's finances, since the southern institutions offered complimentary lodging arrangements, cutting also the transportation expenses, and along with it, limiting the opportunity for the delegations to circulate across a 'decadent' city and freely interact with the locals.

The van took the direction of one of the districts, or 'Gu', south from the Han River, the Gangnam-gu, an older district of Seoul already changing to become one of the hippest areas of Seoul. Rich in history, it was a fast-growing neighborhood with shopping centers, a business center and trendy fashion stores, along with a new generation of night clubs. The World Trade Center completed in anticipation of the summer Olympic Games of 1988, and the Coex Convention & Exhibition Center were close by. With time, Gangnam-gu became this "Mayfair" of Seoul, one of the most exclusive neighborhoods, with lavish apartment buildings and high-rise professional towers, but where more affordable shopping streets had survived as well.

On a small alley, the van pulled close to a service entrance giving access to the older Gang Nam Hotel, which had its main entrance on Bongeunsa-ro. There, the driver told Mai and Tania that this was their destination and a comrade from Pyongyang hospitality department was waiting for them inside. Tania had a little more information before hand and she already knew that they were staying at the same hotel where their training was taking place.

Later on, the five other members of the group were dropped off at a small hotel close to the Gangnam Official Tourism Center by the Gangnam subway station, where they were to attend a variety of activities scheduled during the Olympics. The joke of the fate was that none of the various disciplines of the games agreed upon with South Korea and scheduled in North Korea had ever taken place. The two countries never met a final conclusion of the choices available, and North Korea decided to boycott the games and even sabotage them. It was much later determined that the South Korean commercial flight 858 from Bagdad to Seoul disappeared crushing with its 115 passengers in the Andaman Sea, it was in reality a scheme plotted by the North to give the impression that the South Korean airlines were not safe and discourage the participants to the Olympiads to come. Kim Hyon Hui and her partner in crime, Sung Il, had disguised a bomb in a radio and got off the plane at the stop made in Abu Dhabi before continuing to Seoul. They had eventually been arrested and each of them swallowed a cyanide capsule, but while Sung Il died, Hui survived and later on admitted to the plot.

Meeting Jiye, their 'chaperon' in charge for the duration of their stay in Seoul, Mai and Tania were also introduced to the aid manager of the hotel. Jiye was a short, heavy-set woman with a shining moon-like face, some makeup barely covering her acne, who assumed from the beginning her role as supervisor of their small delegation. She had already been on the same position for several weeks with other trainees, and she seemed at ease around the hotel. However, Jiye had no choice but to follow from close distance the directions given by the hotel manager who intended to remain in control with the proceedings of the newly arrived.

To their surprise, Mai and Tania, now feeling almost as longtime friends brought together by circumstances, learned they had been allocated their own room for the duration of their training! Indeed, the rooms weren't very large, but the comfort, decor and the attached small, but complete bath with a shower and indoor toilet and sink, seemed to them as an unexpected luxury. They had hot and cold water at all times, and the baths were supplied with divinely smelling soaps, shampoos and body lotions, tissue boxes, all offered for them to use, not a customary indulgence while training or working in their own country. It took a little time to admire all the amenities, although the two friends had been working in hotels offering some necessities to the visitors staying there, but nothing could be compared with the ones they just found in their own rooms. The young age of the two friends made their hearts sing with happy expectations, and indeed, they were to enjoy other pleasant surprises. It was almost as though the management of the Gang Nam Hotel took a real interest in showing the people from the north how other Koreans could live, and tried to make up for their deprivation every time there was a chance.

And occasions to make their stay worth presented often: they reduced the 'chaperon's' control and allowed the hotel personnel directing the training at all times, as a condition of offering to forfeit the expenses incurred. By the same way, the direction of the hotel insisted that a good knowledge of the city is a prerequisite before properly directing and interacting with the hotel clients, thus arrangements were made for guided tours with small groups of the people in training. In consequence, every member of the northern Korean staff enjoyed a degree of freedom and exposure to the western life beyond their remote expectations, if not quite to the liking of the Party supervisors.

Therefore, the schedule prepared for Mai and Tania had included visits of the historic districts in town. However, the other members of the northern delegation joined these visits, along with one or two other persons with an unclear designation, which made Mai and her friend remain on their guards and avoid showing too much enthusiasm at the amazing spectacle.

The stay in Seoul became for Mai by far the most extraordinary and unexpected experience in her life. The town visits brought her across contrasting sites from the old history center built under the Joseon dynasty, with many palaces, like Changdeok Palace, or the Hwaseong Fortress, and the Jongmyo Shrine. They had been shown the Royal Tombs, the business and financial hubs with a large concentration of headquarters of international companies, banks, along with the commercial areas, like the one on Jongno street. And everywhere Mai turned, there was this dizzying display of advanced technology and electronics, gigantic neon signs of all colors running the whole length and width of commercial buildings, hotels, restaurants, and malls.

Mai had a glimpse at the many parks or stadiums, where she learned that people loved to spend time, choosing their favorite spots, take a stroll in the nature, have picnics or watch the sunset. If she was almost stricken with panic when stopping at the Coex Mall, a few streets away from her hotel, when guided through the immense indoor center to a mechanical escalator, however, Mai was pleased to discover that there remained also quite a few traditional shops and markets.

During future visits, Mai learned about the 'cheap eats' like the gimbap, seaweed rice and veggie-filled rolls, or other delicious gimbap flavors. She enjoyed the charm of the Tapgol Park Ikseon-dong located in the heart of the downtown, There, along with the old Seoul cinemas, could also be found some of the traditional old houses converted into trendy small restaurants and bars, where at night, the soft lights of the hanoks made the small streets glow.

Mai admired some other impressive and well-maintained buildings and later on she was surprised to learn that they were Methodist, Protestant or Lutheran churches, and that the Roman Catholic Church represented a strong influence in Korean society. Thus, the contrasting life style Mai found so close to home, where people of her own traditions could enjoy freely, continued to amaze her at each turn.

From the beginning of their training at Gang Nam Hotel, the two young girls have benefitted from the special and kind attention of the hotel personnel, who were acting almost as trying to compensate them for the limitations they must have known in their Democratic People's Republic of Korea. It was in particular Sea-na, the assistant manager, who took to heart to give the best education on westerner life style to her two pupils, albeit for a short time in their life.

Sea-na was a beautiful, stylish young lady of 28 years old, who had the chance to travel and follow international hospitality classes in London and Chicago. Her open vision of the political realities of the world, although the business protocol would forbite her to discuss it at the work place, enabled her character to feel free and at ease around customers coming from all corners of the world. As the meaning of her name, free and beautiful as the bird's fly, Sea-na flowed graciously but efficiently through the hotel receptions areas, while Mai and Tania usually followed in her footsteps, learning and admiring.

Since the multi international interaction was one of the most important areas to guide the new students, the chaperon accompanying the North Korean team did not have the necessary qualifications and had to step aside and observe from the distance. However, the two young trainees were expected to write a daily report of their happenings.

Besides the regular outings scheduled as part of their orientation, Mai and Tania were gratified with a few isolated getaways Sea-na took them as a 'girl-time' during a few spare breaks. One was to question if it was the girls' genuine enchantment to discover this new 'wonderland', or Sea-na's delight observing their reaction and appreciation of things that she and others would take for granted. From that point on, Sea-na promised to herself to do all that was in her possibilities to help the 'sisters from the North". She gave the girls a more detailed description than she was expected about the way people from South Korea lived, explained how the society and in particular their government functioned, and how the young generation enjoyed spending their free time.

Mai and her teammate did not receive any financial compensation for their work during their training, thus they had no money on their own, no wons, the monetary currency used in the south. However, Sea-na managed to bring them to popular shopping and eateries, and discreetly covered the fees, dismissing them with a smile, as 'customary' for the people in the South. The two visitors having a deeper understanding of the life of in Seoul, realized that the people here embraced their existence with hope and passion, they admired their freedom of expressing their feelings, and above all, they became aware of something new, these brothers and sisters from the South were happy!

At the end of their two weeks of training, weeks that flew by like a dream, Sea-na stopped at some of the street stands and asked the girls to choose a few items they would like, as presents from her. Sea-na was very touched to see that the girls made some very modest choices and all for their relatives and none for themselves.

When their last morning in Seoul came, along with goodbyes, Sea-na made them promise that they would soon come back. But once Mai and Tania joined the other members of their trip climbing into their used van for the short trip back home, they had been promptly reminded of the reality of their life, and made them think quickly that what they just experienced, was only a dream. Their waking up was even harsher with the contrasting conditions they went back to, and along with it, they had to taper their enthusiasm and quickly adopt a subdued attitude.

After a while, Mai had another trip to Seoul, this time announced at the last moment and departing directly from her hotel in Pyongyang, probably in order not to allow her to have any 'undesired contact' prior to leaving the country. She also learned that this time she would go to a different hotel. Mai's eagerness to see Sea-na again was dampened rapidly before even she crossed the border, as she was strongly reminded that she would be under close supervision and she was due to make every day detailed reports to her superiors.

Although Mai went to her second assignment in Seoul without the precious presence of her friend, Tania, and was staying at another hotel, everyone showed kindness and gave Mai encouragement to absorb many of the western ways of the hotel industry. She even had the opportunity to talk on the phone with Sea-na and met her twice, when she could go for short breaks in town and enjoy a small local snack. From that point on, Mai could add to her acquaintances another friend to a short list of people she could trust.

CHAPTER 6 - SEA-NA

The summer of 1988 went by without Mai, nor other member of her team, be able to return to Seoul; the North could not come to an agreement and share some of the games with South Korea and Kim Il Sung's gigantic ego made him mope and boycott the Summer Olympic events. His son, Kim Jong Il, was 46 and regretting a more public interaction with the western world during the summer games, consoled himself with more discreet trips to Hong Kong. The third member of the Kim dynasty, Kim Jong Un, was only eight and little aware of the international intrigues for the time being.

However, Mai's summer and fall of 1988 were filled with activities at her home place, working at the hotel long days and organizing the conference sessions. Since her sister, Sun-Hi, married the year before, her husband tolerated less and less her absence from home. Gradually, Mai took practically over her sister's assigned job and her time was shared between the Star Hotel and Koryo Hotel in Pyongyang, as the delegations from the south visited less often during the busy events occurring in Seoul. Best of all, it was during that summer when Mai appointments in Pyongyang were brightened by the unexpected times shared with Geea and Joseph Godson, while a tender relationship was growing between Jo ad Mai during these special moments spent together.

By the end of the year and with the arrival of the cold weather, the visits to South Korea became so sporadic and remained postponed for the following year, that Mai had to restrain her hopes and secret desires for a return to the southern capital. Her enduring nature helped to contain her impatience as Mai displayed at all times a professional and calm presence, although her thoughts were often questioning the reasons of the dramatic dissimilarities she witnessed between the sister countries; they were the same people and yet, their political believes, life style, and behavior could not be more contrasting. The time slipping toward the end of 1988, Mai realized that it became harder for her to control her eager expectation for a trip to Seoul, and to refrain from overtly approving of the westerner customs.

It took almost another year for the young 'interns' to go to the previously formal assignments to Seoul, and Mai had the immense pleasure to see herself back to Gang Nam Hotel in September 1989, although for only a short week. Seeing her friend Sea-na was again the highlight of her time there, when at the end of that week, Mai was rewarded with the news Sea-na whispered during their farewells, telling Mai that she was scheduled to come back and stay a little longer in December and then in January 1990.

When Mai returned to Seoul training at Gang Nam hotel in December 1989, she was already well-versed on assuming the regular hotel hospitality business and able to handle a variety of duties. It was no surprise when Sea-na informed her that for a few days she would be assigned to hosting a conference intended to maintaining the relations between the two sides of the Korean peninsula and some of the allies present in the region. Thus, a handful of North Koreans coming from the more distant regions of North Korea were to meet some Chinese comrades from the other side of the border, while the south members were accompanied as usual by their American partners.

Although seeing the configuration of the attendees made Mai a little tensed, Sea-na acted nonchalantly, reassuring her there was nothing for her to fear. Indeed, shortly after the morning proceedings were on the way, Mai noticed that the communist members soon conducted themselves like children, happy to take a break. Although they were conditioned to be under constant surveillance, away from the bitter winter cold of their dwellings and enjoying for a few days these lavish living quarters and cuisine, they were making the most of this rare and unusual treat. And for once, Mai noticed that their authoritarian behavior was replaced by caution, though intimidated by such unfamiliar life style. They even gave in at times and joined the others for a good laughter; the Western 'bon enfant' attitude in a way was fascinating them with their relaxed and friendly behavior. It was one of those special encounters that one can witness one more time people getting along just fine, in reality longing to befriend each other.

It was a good thing for Mai to appreciate that she was not under the constant scrutiny of her countrymen, for another, bigger surprise was in for her: Joseph Godson was among the Americans participating to this regular follow up of the discussions between the two camps! A few hours into the deliberations, frequent breaks allowed the twenty some delegates to enjoy free exchanges and sample the well supplied all-day buffet. Earlier, Mai run into Jo during the proceedings of the conference, and after she responded with polite words to his warm salutations, Mai could even engage in a little isolated conversation, when the other members of the conference did not need her help.

As the day unfolded with the usual guidelines, repeated policies and recommendations, the northerners were increasingly aware that the South side of the peninsula was on the holiday mood. With a large Christian fraction of the population, and most of the American military presence being accompanied by their families, Christmas celebration was in the air. The hotel, along with the entire town loaded with alluring articles, was magnificently decorated, creating the spirit and the elation of the Christmas season. This was obviously inexistent in the communist regime, and the festive atmosphere exercised an unexpected enthrallment on the comrades, hardly concealing their own delight. They had even a harder time not to let their hearts ache for their families, when comparing the display of so much prosperity, in contrast with the misery present in their country only at a brief distance away.

Mai and Jo had met for over a year, and during the previous summer they even had the chance to see each other a few times privately at Geea's house. They both felt a powerful attraction and fell in love. Their feelings were perhaps more intense because of the secrecy they had to shroud in their connection, the desperation of knowing that their love was 'forbitten' by the Party. The opposite worlds Jo and Mai belonged to, considered such a passion as treason and it was setting them on a dangerous path in all regards.

No matter how impossible their fondness appeared to any logical person, somewhere in their hearts they kept the hope that, in some unforeseen way, they could be together one day when they would freely express their feelings for each other. And unexpectedly, fate played them favors with an ally, Sea-na, who discovered in her own heart a romantic inkling, and was happy to play Cupid, adding more excitement to this holiday ambiance.

It did not take long to Sea-na's sharp instincts and sense of observation to notice that Mai and Jo had a special connection. A tender chord in Sea-na's heart was telling her that she was right, these two people, from such different backgrounds were in fact fitting perfectly together. Sea-na was aware of the delicate situation they were in, but for once, she wanted to push further her fondness she already felt for her protégée.

"They are in a free world here, after all", she thought, and a plan started to form in her mind. And easy said - easy done, the opportunities were many in this time of the year, especially as she controlled most of her interns' schedule and intended to keep a strong hold on it.

It almost amused her to watch the North Korean party dogs, and play tricks on them, with the deep and secret satisfaction, knowing that they could do nothing against her. Thus, Sea-na, affecting additional professional obligations out the work place, gave Mai a little tour in town to show her the Christmas lights along with some small shops in the old town. And when she suggested a break at a coffee shop, Jo happened to be there as well. Delighted by this 'unexpected' encounter, they had hot chocolate and patisserie together. Then, Jo invited them to see the lighting of the Christmas tree in Jongno, by the Bosingak pavilion.

That evening, Sea-na accompanying Mai to the lighting ceremony, suggested to continue the evening and go to the skating rink. But shortly after arriving there, Sea-na excused herself, having to leave for a few personal errands.

Although living in a country with many months of icy winters, Mai had never skated before. Shy by nature, she refused at first Jo's invitation, but at Jo's insistence, and seeing other young people having such a good time, she agreed to give it a try. Jo guided her attentively, and soon Mai moved along, thrilled by this new experience, while Joe was the most enchanted, not able to take his eyes away from his betrothed. From there, with rosy cheeks, they entered a tea house and had a traditional dinner together. Then Jo accompanied Mai back to her hotel, leaving her at a safe distance from Gang Nam Hotel. However, they did not say their 'good night' without Jo obtaining the promise to see Mai the day after, following the meetings at the hotel. During the short ride in the taxi cab, the first for Mai, Jo held her hand all the way, and before Mai exited the cab, they exchanged a passionate kiss.

A magical time followed for the two young people in love; Jo took Mai out practically every evening, visiting Tapgol Park and wandering on streets where the hanoks held small bars and restaurants. Mai felt like living a dream, discovering how the young couples of the sister country spent time, enjoying life with ardor, laughing, listening to the little bands and dancing, expressing their joy freely and completely. As Mai was overwhelmed by this discovery, she also realized how much she enjoyed all of it, and how much the youth of her homeland was deprived of. She did not, however, want to question the validity of the Party's teachings. She completely blocked out any criticism, even though she could not help comparing, having the guilty feeling that, if she finds anything wrong with the establishment of her country, it would be considered a betrayal.

One time, when Mai happened to stroll with Jo in the Yeouido Park district, she saw two of the North Koreans delegates. The young couple ducked away, but they felt relieved when they noticed that, although both married, the comrades were accompanied by two girls, loudly singing, swaying, and stumbling in the middle of the plaza. Allowing her heart to slow down, Mai laughed with Jo all the way to the Dongdaemun market. There, Jo insisted to buy her a beautiful silk outfit as Christmas present. Mai did not know much about Christmas traditions, and at the end accepted his gift, while Jo added also two nice scarves for Mai's mother and sister.

Sea-na continued all this time to tenderly watch over the two lovers and discreetly helped them to get together after work, finding all kind of ingenious reason to send Mai to places where Jo was to meet her.

FORBIDDEN MARRIAGE

The magic continued in Mai's heart when she went back to her home at the end of December 1989. There was a contrasting change of décor looking at the dark alleys of the near-by towns, Kaesong and P'yonggang, with no attractive window displays, even less Christmas decorations. She was submerged again by the gray sadness of people's expressions, by the poverty and by everyone's lack of enthusiasm. However, Mai was eager to see her parents and her sister, and bring them her presents, as her siblings could not help but share with her the new joyful energy. Mai was full of aspirations, dreaming of her return to Seoul in a few weeks when she would be with Jo again, and where they would not have to constantly hide their special bond. Mai held in her young heart only hopes, looking toward to the next happy step and wishing somehow for more to follow.

During the days approaching her return to Seoul anticipated for January, 1990, Mai became anxious at the thought that the plans could change at the last minute, aware of periods of increased tension the government showed toward the western world. Knowing that all could be cancelled at any moment, Mai almost jumped with joy when she boarded again the puny black van. Then, it was not too soon to her liking when the car went through the check points of the DMZ. At last, Mai could look forward to the two weeks she would be spending at Gang Nam Hotel, her heart filled with expectations and gratitude toward Sea-na, who made all possible for her to come back again.

Thus, Mai entered the hotel with a light heart, at ease with the demands of her job thanks to her excellent training, and started right the way to greet the arriving guests. Sea-na stopped by briefly after lunch and informed her, that, since she travelled and worked for a good part of the day, Mai should take off the remaining of the afternoon to rest. Then, before going on to her duties, Sea-na suggested that she would love if Mai could come by her office at 17:00 hours for a cup of tea.

After eagerly finding her room, now familiar to her, Mai arranged her few belongings with great pleasure. Then, she took a hot and relaxing shower, and finally wrapped on the plushy robe offered by the hotel, she cocooned herself in the soft bed and swiftly fell asleep. Although she slept two good hours, a blissful dreamless rest never happening in the middle of an afternoon during a work day, she had the impression that it had past only five minutes when the wakeup call rang in her room. Mai almost jumped and needed a few moments to recollect and recognize her surroundings, then she smiled and relaxed again.

Since her little social call was actually private, Mai thought that it was appropriate for her to wear the special yellow silk outfit Jo offered her recently for Christmas. She arranged her hair lifting up two large bands on each side of her head making a playful twist, and letting the rear part flow on her back. Mai considered that it was in order for this occasion to apply a light shadow of pink on her cheeks and a little bit of red on her lips, and she quickly made the finishing touches. Approaching the managers' area and passing the large reception lounge, Mai felt almost on vacation, like a guest receiving a special treatment from one of the best-appointed supervisors.

On the hallway leading to Sea-na's office, Mai run into a couple of reception girls she already knew, who showered her with exclamations of admiration. Indeed, Mai looked so beautiful, like a gracious character from old Japanese prints. Still returning the compliment to the two young ladies, Mai knocked at the door and, after hearing Sea-na's voice inviting her in, she stepped inside. Mai could not refrain her surprise when taking in the whole scene, a cozy and elegantly furnished office leaving enough room for three comfortable bergeres and a round table. There was set an inviting assortment of typical British tea small sandwiches, sconces, and petits-fours laid on a tiered plateau, along with a fine porcelain tea service. But the surprise was coming from seeing Sea-na engaged in a friendly conversation with Jo!

What came automatically to Mai's mind was that she interrupted a private conversation and she would be reprimanded for having done something wrong, so much was she conditioned by her communist upbringing. Her worries vanished when the two of them promptly stood up and came to give her a warm hug, then Sea-na invited Mai to seat down for tea. Mai's tension eased up as the two others calmly engaged her into their peaceful conversation.

Lifting up into the soft light of the side table lamp, Jo admired the tea cup: "this is exquisite, the porcelain is transparent in the light. And what a delicate design this is!"

"Believe it or not, this is a Limoges tea service, answered Sea-na. Many years ago, some French missionaries took one of the emperor's china copy to France, and the bishops of Limoges liked it so much, he asked one of the masters the famous porcelain if he could make a French version of it."

Then Sea-na volunteered for more information when she read the interest on their faces. "As you might know, Korea has a large population of Christians, the Catholic fraction being the larger one. When our Prime Minister visited France after WWII, he was gifted with a complete Limoges table and tea service versions of the imperial design. Bringing it home, it was found so exquisite that more copies were ordered, and with time, they became largely fashionable. Now, a variety of patterns are ordered by luxury hotels, official caterers, and private privileged citizens."

During her 'exposé', Sea-na continued her perfectly skilled hostess function, pouring tea, offering delicacies from the trays, and inquiring if there would be cream or sugar added. Mai was fascinated by this refined and yet so tranquil greeting 'ballet', observing every detail and marveling privately. This occupied Mai's thoughts, who did not realize how entranced Jo was next to her, only to come to reality when, after having had one or two cups of tea sipped and savored, Sea-na getting up and excusing herself, declared she must attend to another function.

Mai hastily stood up, only to be gently rebuked by Sea-na, who insisted for them to carry on without her. "I am sure you two have a lot of things you want to talk about. Please feel at home and enjoy the desserts and the place as long as you would like".

After Sea-na left without giving them time to contradict her, Mai was suddenly invaded by very mixed feelings; she loved so much the sweetness of this place, the presence of her friends, but she was also uncomfortable with suddenly so much intimacy with a foreigner, an American above all, and in the place where she was working. Mai was sorting through her mind to find an appropriate behavior for these unusual circumstances, when she heard Jo complimenting her about how lovely she looked. Then he imperceptibly changed to a lower and softer voice, telling her:

"Sea-na is a good friend of yours, and now I consider her as a friend of mine as well. I am the one who asked her to arrange this date. I wanted, I needed to express to you my feelings and my intentions"...

"Is this a…date? With you? You mean a real date?" Mai started stammering, taken aback by the turn of the events.

"Yes, and Sea-na is aware of our situation and she promised me she would do everything she can to help, if this is fine with you."

As Mai was at a loss of words, a little moment went by, during which Jo, who usually was very much in charge with his actions, trying to control his emotions finally added:

"I confided in Sea-na my feelings for you…I was the one who asked her to help me, to help us…"

Mai read Jo's expression and she was not displeased with the feelings she was seeing, and, fault of words, she started blushing. The two of them were riveted in each other's gaze, an intense emotion seizing them both.

At that moment, Jo suddenly stood up from his chair, approached Mai and dropped his left knee on the floor. In a little awkward gesture, he raised toward her a little box he opened with shaking hands. Then, he summoned all his strength to declare:

"Mai, I love you since I first laid my eyes on you. My love for you is true, this world is not big enough to contain it. It is why, the separation made by any border or regime could not be a barrier to my desire to be united to you for as long as I will live. And, in order to be together there is no other proper way to be united but under the sacred union of marriage." And looking at Mai's astonishment, he added, "Will you marry me?"

Mai's head was turning and along with the sway she felt, a tornado was going through her entire being. She was seized by an immense joy and almost believed that the love she felt all along for Jo could be shared as a real couple. Then, a wave of fear washed over her, "But how are we going to live, we belong to different countries, I will never be allowed to marry an Am.., a foreigner."

"We will find a way, in the meantime we can get married here. With Sea-na's help, we will get married tomorrow and we will seal our love in the holy matrimony. Yes? Please say Yes!"

"Oh, yes, my love!" and the two young people in love fell into each other's arms, sealing their commitment with passionate kisses. Only moments later, Jo remembered: "Wait a moment, you did not see the ring!" and taking it out from the cradle of the little box, he showed it to Mai. Then, he added with a sweet shyness, "It is not a big one, I did not want you to get in trouble if it is too visible. We will have a larger one for you when the time is right."

It was a beautiful sapphire in the shape of a lotus flower, delicate and discreet. While Mai was ecstatic at the beauty of it, Jo was happy that it fitted perfectly, against all worries he expressed to the jeweler when he bought it, thinking that it would be way too small.

The now engaged couple was floating in a time zone not belonging to this world, lost in the magic of the moment. When later on Sea-na cautiously made her way back into the room, she was all smile of understanding that they declared openly their love. Getting herself ahead of the events, she could no longer contain her excitement:

"We need to start the preparations right the way, there is not much time and you two will want to spend all the time you have here, together. It will go by fast, and it will seem to you flying even faster". Looking at Mai, who already started considering all of the obstacles and dangers of such union, Sea-na added: "I know, it looks impossible, but Jo and I came up with a plan that should take all into account. We will manage to cover up your time working at the hotel and distract the attention of possible informers during the wedding."

Then, Sea-na realized that it was the moment to congratulate them, and hugging Mai, whispered to her: "Do not worry, I will do everything I can for your happiness. I will finally have the opportunity to dupe the enemy, and I will take so much pleasure to see at least one couple happy".

After many hugs and congratulations, tears of happiness flowing on the pretty faces of the girls, at Sea-na's request, Jo opened a bottle of Champagne she had made appear by enchantment, and all laughed at the funny expression Mai was making testing for the first time the bubbly ambrosia.

The animated trio continued later into the dinner hours their enflamed discussion, their heads spinning either from the champagne or from their planning fever. When they finally had to part and Mai regained her room, she was filled with gratitude realizing that strangers could show overtly so much kindness and friendship, and that love can transport her into dreams of endless possibilities.

They could not marry the day after; that was the day when Mai, accompanied by Sea-na who invoked the visit to suppliers for the hotel, made some necessary shopping stops, then, they met Jo at the chapel of the catholic church.

A while before, Jo approached his chaplain of the American Mission in Seoul and obtained his agreement to officiate a religious alliance if he could manage to bring Mai to South Korea, and now the chaplain was there to greet them. It was not enough time by any stretch of good intentions of the catholic church to convert and officially baptize Mai, who had been raised without a formal religious affiliation. However, Jefferson Davis, the chaplain who confessed Jo in many occasions, especially before him leaving for dangerous missions, went along and confessed them, then gave the communion to the two of them. After a few very unsuccessful trials in the past to dissuade Jo from such an alliance, he accepted warmly to unite the two young people in marriage the following day.

Thus, it was settled, one more day and Jo and Mai would have a discreet ceremony in the same chapel and after her regular working hours, in order to avoid any suspicion. With the advancing afternoon hours, the anticipation covered by secrecy created an invisible bond between Sea-na, two of the trustworthy reception girls, and Mai. The hotel trio decided to be Mai's maids of honor and pledged to spare no efforts making this event not only possible, but a complete success.

The following day, Kim and Lani were sent early to the chapel for the wedding preparations; in the dressing room reserved for the bride, they arranged the flowers, prepared the dress Sea-na bought for Mai the day before, along with the vail, shoes, hair dressing, and all the other details making bride's day so special. The bridal bouquet was ready, a beautifully arrangement made of lily of the valley, white gardenias and light pink rose buds, brought in by Jo. While giggling and having a great time, they were anticipating all the surprises Mai was to discover, these items all new to Mai, nevertheless expected to bring incommensurable joy into her young heart.

Then Lani and Kim went to a larger room next to the chapel where an intimate reception was to follow the ceremony, all remaining isolated from the public places and as unnoticeable as possible. They made sure that the table was well decorated with garlands of flowers, then disposed on a little table attractive boxes with presents. After that followed a quick check of the catered food for the buffet, before turning to admire the lovely display of the bride's cake.

Finally, Kim glancing her watch, rushed Lani with a friendly nudge back into the chapel, where the two bride maids found the groom, the chaplain, and Jo's best man, Jimmy Rodney, his partner during the South Korean missions. The two girls observed the others and had a hard time suppressing a titter, noticing how handsome the two young men were and how nervous the groom appeared.

Soon after 17:00 hours, Sea-na drove Mai to a back door a few steps from the chapel. In no time Mai was dolled up by the three other young women who were taking great pleasure helping Mai. Here came the dress, then the vail, the shoes, after which they arranged her hair, and insisted on a little color on her cheeks and lips. All this was accompanied by enthusiastic exclamations of how beautiful Mai was, who abandoned herself to her bride maids' hands, completely overwhelmed by the extend of attention and unanticipated surprises.

When all was ready, a choir boy at the small organ of the chapel playing the Bridal's March, announced Mai's entrance. The bride, looking divinely beautiful, slowly met her charming prince and the secret ceremony unfolded like a dream for all of them. The magic was so palpable, making the dangerous circumstances even more surreal.

The ring exchange was anticipated by Jo, who gave Mai his Academy class ring to slip in his finger, after her lotus ring was placed on her left band finger. The love and tenderness were present in everyone's heart, and the chaplain Jefferson Davis made a short, but very touching sermon. It was mostly a wishful statement for the couple to be protected by God's power, finding ways and granting them the joy of sharing a happy life together.

No one saw the time passing as they gathered in the reception room, receiving and giving hugs and repeating wishes of happiness and prosperity. Then Sea-na proposed that the couple opened their presents, and if they were only a few, Jo and Mai were laughing and crying at the same time, with emotions running so high at the generosity of their newly found friends. Then, Mai's bride's maids insisted she had something to eat and have a sip of Champagne. Then, followed the wedding cake and Jo holding his bride tightly, managed to cut together the first piece of cake and gallantly offered it to her. In a way, he was happy Mai did not know of the westerner custom where the bride smudges the groom's face, and luckily, he escaped this silly joke.

Everyone was having a beautiful time, even more as they were aware of the fragility of the married couple's future, having all along the impression of being in another dimension, where space and time were suspended for these very special human beings. For now, it seemed that Mai and Jo did not mind having to continue the senseless game of concealing their love and their union, as long as they were united in front of God.

Too soon came the time when Mai had to change again into everyday clothing, leave with Sea-na her wedding dress who promised to keep it for..."other happy circumstances". It was convened that Jo preserved their gifts, while Mai would wear her wedding ring on her little finger, avoiding a possible indiscretion that could endanger her.

Jo had reserved a room at Gang Nam Hotel, so the married couple would spend the wedding night at the place where Mai had also her room, not missing from her work place. Sea-na played again the good fairy and had switched Jo's room for the honeymoon suite, decorating it lavishly and bringing in the rests of the bridal cake and Champagne. However, she was happy to keep the bouquet she caught when Mai was asked to toss it.

Mai rode in Sea-na's car with the two other girls who were dropped on the way to their homes. Jo had changed into regular cloths but carried a duffel bag with him, having had reserved his room for the entire duration Mai was in town. He took a taxicab and checked in the hotel as a regular traveler. He was getting angry by the moment at the circus they all had to play, feeling more than ever how unfair the political restrictions of the communist regime prevented people trapped in these countries from the sacred freedom of marrying and living a happy life with whoever they would chose. He repeated the words of commitment that he would use all his capacities and power to change the circumstances and give a chance to a life he desired for Mai and himself. As he had declared during their wedding ceremony when making his vows of love and protection, Jo renewed in his mind and in his heart his promise to make Mai happy and to adore her as long as he would live.

Once more, Mai used the delivery door and made a casual stop at the reception desk checking that no one had noticed her absence. She answered a few messages from a younger team member, and in no time, she was in her room and happy to be reassured that she was released from early duty the next day. Then Sea-na casually walked her toward the room Jo was waiting for his bride, after watching that the way was deserted. As much as Sea-na started hating the absurdity of the situation making a couple hide their marriage even in their wedding night, Mai did not care, she was to meet her beloved husband and find the happiness they desired all along. Even if she would die after this night, she thought, it was worth all of it, she would feel blessed having shared a few moments with the man she loved more that her own life.

HONEYMOON

Mai and Jo spent together almost two weeks in Seoul, and, even if they had to meet in secret every night, this was the most idyllic time they ever lived celebrating their love. For they knew that upon Mai's return to DPRK, the two lovers were not to be together for a time that would appear to them a cruel eternity.

Mai had no more assignments to return to South Korean Capital, against all the skillful interventions Sea-na tempted, the North Korean regime was tightening the pressure and control upon its citizens, considering the 'détente' period over. Mai had to assent, resuming her regular duties at the Red Star Hotel and Koryo Hotel when staying in the North Korea's capital. She was making constant efforts to conceal any unusual events that happened recently and assumed her regular and boring life, traying hard to remain invisible to her reporting supervisors. Her mind traveled from the rigor of her usual daily activities to the memory of her recent times of bliss, memory which kept her dreaming and hoping, although she had a hard time to believe that these happy moments had really happened.

Then again, in the middle of a frigid winter day in February 1990, Jo's team came to the Red Star Hotel when Mai was also back working there. However, the newlywed couple, while longing for each other, had to overcome and act on a carefully innocuous manner, which made the few days Jo had to spend for that conference, the most difficult. They were tortured by the desire to be together and having to disguise any possible link between them, constantly surrounded by a whole system that would only condemn them. Struggling with feelings constantly tearing her heart apart, Mai dealt with splitting emotions of having to hide her marriage to her parents, and the confusing guilt that she might be betraying her own country, opposed by her profound conviction that she did not do anything wrong loving and marrying Jo.

As she did many times before, Mai continued to coordinate the flowless functioning of the conference, conference to which Jo participated. Their interactions were intentionally minimum, and hour after hour, day after day, the time went by without offering the smallest opportunity to the couple in love to get close or have any private conversation. They knew to what terribly difficult situation they engaged their lives, but the absurdity of the interdictions they were facing grew harder in them by the minute.

Jo came to South Korea, then participated to the regular exchanges between the two sister countries as part of the American supporting ally to South Korea. He has been trained as a 'spy' and continued to observe the ground situation in each side of the DMZ, providing valuable information to the local military base, but he was not one of the CIA forces infiltrating into the north. If Jo was fulfilling his duties with analytical considerations, all personal judgement detached from his work, he was now enraged by the outrageous reality since his marriage to Mai. The disrespect of basic human rights of choosing with who and how to conduct their private lives made him boil inside. And for once, he was having difficulty disguising his own feelings about the North Korean regime.

The circumstances keeping them apart, reinforced even more in Jo's heart the solemn engagement to the woman becoming his life partner. Besides the desire to share with her the joys of the marital life, dedication and responsibility were now his incessant concern, constantly surveying her surroundings, resolute to defend her from any harm. And as long as his stay at the Red Star Hotel allowed him personally to be on the watch, he became continually worried for the times when he was faraway.

The last evening before the members of the southern delegation departure, the two teams carrying on a quite long-term relationships, even the hosts acting a little friendlier after the party organized by the southern team in the past, decided to have an improvised after-meeting gathering.

Promptly, a buffet was dressed up and drinks were offered at the request of the main Party leader of the northern delegation. Mai felt obligated to stay around until the end of the impromptu party, since her translation skills could be needed. However, as the tone loosened up and the voices became louder, the communication soon resumed to friendly taps on the back and booming laughter of the northern members, staggering and slurring simple greetings mixed with Party slogans, meant to give the correct impression to the guests.

This gave Mai the opportunity to retrieve to her little office next to the reception lobby with the excuse of finishing her reports. Once done with her daily narrative, she risked a quick look into the conference room where the party was held. She felt reassured that no one had noticed her absence and discreetly left for her home, after an exhausting working day. On her way home, climbing the cold snowy trail in the early darkness of a winter night, she remembered that she did not see Jo at the party. As if someone was reading her thoughts, Mai felt two arms embracing her, and there he was, Jo appearing like a ghost from the darkness, gently dragging her out of the open path.

They held each other lost in their passionate kisses, when Jo finally whispered into her ear:

"Everyone was drunk and I could slip out, away from my watchers. Please, come to my room, I can't stand being far from you, and tomorrow I leave, God knows for how long." Then, he added: "You could leave my room early in the morning and be there for the conference, and no one will notice. Please,…"

After a moment of reflection, Mai conceded, and let Jo know that she must first go to her house and pick up some clothes to change in the morning. Inside, she tip-toed around, not wanting to wake up the household, but she undid her little bed, so her parents would not suspect her absence. Mai was also reassured to see that Puppy, her little dog, not seeing her all evening, went to bed with her parents for the night.

Then Jo, waiting for her outside, guided her through his hidden road safely into the hotel. The two lovers, sliding like shadows through brushes and wooden lands, reached the back of the hotel, when Jo went ahead inside using his key to open the back door.

After checking the hallway leading to his room, Jo made a sign to Mai to come along. Jo was glad that he always chose his rooms close to a back exit, one of the safety strategies he learned in the military training. While rounding their way to the back of the hotel, the young couple risked a quick peek at the hotel's main entrance. Although a cold wind sending flurries of snow was announcing a storm approaching, they heard animated voices leaving the hotel in a happy mood, while the last hotel employees gathered at the front entrance bid them a safe return home.

A gust of cold air almost pushed Mai through the door as she followed Jo in, and shortly after, Mai and Jo were together, in the privacy of his room. At last, they could be close and share their love without retention. They spent the night lost in the passionate feelings they had for each other, remembering the nights of their honeymoon in Seoul. However, as a blizzard started raging outside, a sentiment of desperation kept them holding tight into each other, nothing to separate them, for the two of them realized the dramatic reality their marriage was facing. Lost in their love, Mai and Jo travelled into another world, where all was beauty and love, and where all was possible. That night, as Mai was to learn later, it was the night when she became pregnant.

CHAPTER THREE - LAMENTATIONS

CAMP OF BIRTH AND DEATH

Mai was dying. Life was draining out of her body and she did not have the strength to fight anymore. Close by, on an improvised litter, her newly born twins were dying too. Or they were left to die. Since her arrest and imprisonment in the labor camp, she endured beatings and harsh treatment doing laundry work from dawn to dusk, but because her pregnancy was advanced, she escaped the routine raping of all the other women were to suffer. Although seven months gravid with twins, at the time of her arrest she did not show it much, maybe a little weight added to her slender frame would make one think that she was finally eating better.

She was allowed to go to term, fault of any interest of her condition from the camp administration, for she was expected to die soon anyway from the camp conditions or complications of carrying a baby. Somehow, Mai survived these almost two months left until her delivery, and now she was bleeding to death, her body left unattended, emptying slowly from the fluid of life.

Mai did not care leaving this place, this life, but she felt that her soul would forever perish along with her body, as she could no longer stand hearing the cries of her failing babies. For she knew she brought to life two babies, as she was secretly told by the gynecologist lady, friend of Geea, she visited after she became sure she was pregnant. She also heard the two prisoner women talking, when they came to this simple but isolated shack helping her give birth. And they did what they could, not much being offered, only their pity and some remote knowledge as mid-wives from delivering babies in their village. Mai first heard, "here is a pretty little girl, all healthy, shame be to all this". Then, later, when feeling another wave of pain ripping through her entire body, they said, "what a beautiful little boy, ready to suckle". And then, they left without any further concern.

And now she was living the long agonizing last hours of her and of her babies' life. She knew that all the babies were left to die, their mothers not allowed to hold or to nourrice them, and, as supreme punishment, only to hear them cry until their last breath. That was the way things worked in the labor camps in North Korea, in 1990s.

Mai's crime has been of loving another human being. She dared to fall in love, completely, with an imperialist, an enemy of the people.

As her physical strength was leaving her, her mind was gaining more power, and, as the entire energy she could gather expanded, it filled the small space, reaching her newborns. Her soul was engulfing her babies as a real presence, telling them she was there, their mother, giving them love to last for their entire lives. Transcending from this life, she was pouring hers into her babies'. This was the last gesture only the extraordinary love of a mother could do.

CHAPTER 2 - AGONY

As she labored to bring her babies into this world, pain tearing apart her insides, shading tears and blood, Mai became more aware that she would not survive this birth. She was so tiny and her babies so grown, she needed special care in order to make it through. Somewhat relieved to realize that her two babies made it just fine, after long hours of excruciating pain without any medical help, her body gave up and she entered into an acute postpartum defibrination syndrome, her coagulation factors unable to overcome the massive bleeding. The loss of fluids needed to hydrate her could no longer maintain a proper blood pressure. Mai was hemorrhaging profusely, and she was slipping into organ failure. The little liquid flow left in her body sipped into her tears.

Recent images came to her mind as she went in and out of a coma. There were happy images at first, when the cries of the babies were bringing her back to reality.

She remembered seeing Jo for the first time coming down the little road before going to work and frantically looking for Puppy. How relived she felt when she saw him by the little bridge, but Puppy was not alone and she automatically tensed. As she came closer, it appeared that the dog was not in danger, he was making new friends! During the run to the dog, Mai could see that she did not know that man. When arriving face to face with him, she realized that he was definitely not from the area, but a Caucasian showing up from nowhere. Her reflexes went automatically into a shielding gear and reserve in his presence, knowing that all visitors could be under a surveillance never too far behind. She even wondered how he managed to 'slip' through the hotel security, for he must be one of the hotel guests for that week conference.

Never had she seen a more seductive man; getting up from his crouched play with Puppy, he towered her with his tall and strongly built stature, unfolding upright with feline movements. His head was covered with a black woolen cap going down to his brows, hiding most of his head, but his striking blue eyes were the most unusual thing Mai had ever seen. And when he smiled, then broke into a friendly laughter, Mai was seized by a shiver of unknown feelings. After the very first exchange of a few words, Mai discovered manners of a kindness she never witnessed before. She grew up and worked in occasions in contact with some dignitaries, but they all kept a frown expression, never looking in the face, and talking on a burly manner, especially to women.

When Jo, as he introduced himself, turned his face toward her with a spontaneous smile and sparkles dancing in his eyes, it was like an opening into a world where people can communicate in a way totally unbeknownst to her. In the past, she did notice the warm and friendly manners of the westerners attending meetings, and at times she questioned the foundation of the constant reminders received during their mandatory reunions. The westerners were presented as calculated and evil imperialists, using devious means to attract and turn his comrades into spies and enemies of the communist regime. In consequence, Mai learned how to preserve a demeanor under constant control, keeping her above any suspicion, as she became a perfect example of the 'communist etiquette'.

Mai went to work after a short detour to her house to bring Puppy home, while giving him a reprimand, which sounded more like a plea to stay in the house until her return and avoid showing himself up too much. Mai could leave only after she promised Puppy a little play time when coming back home and maybe even a bone from the kitchen. The concept of treats nonexistent in her country, Mai had, however, learned quickly that the 'spoiled capitalists' indulged in special delicacies for themselves and for their house pets, extravagances which seemed as an inconceivable indulgence, even when it came to pamper one's own children. But she discovered soon that a 'little something' discarded by the dining room she would bring to Puppy was rewarded with such an immeasurable joy, that she almost made a routine of it. Puppy was such a loving dog, he would meet her with enthusiastic display of love every time, treats or no treats. But Mai made a habit to wrap up a bone, a small piece of chicken or biscuit, or even a carrot or a small piece of bread, and bring them home to Puppy. Mai discovered that her happiness was complete only if she made someone else happy, and she started understanding why 'the capitalists' pushed regular necessities to 'splurge' beyond bare needs.

Hurrying to arrive to work on time, Mai caught up with her small office and gathered the lists of her activities of the day about to commence. First, she looked over the preparations in the conference room. She methodically and efficiently verified the readiness of the projectors and the screen disposition, the speaker stands and mics, and the order of the tables with the names of the attendants, papers, pencils, and water carafes.

Coming out of the conference room to invite in the guests gathered in small groups in the dining area and the lobby, Mai almost bumped into Jo. Joseph Godson was the first speaker of the day and he was looking for the seminar coordinator. He was also in charge with the counterpart of the joint American-South Korean delegation meeting with the North Korean team. Both of them trying to discreetly overcome their surprise, and after a short formal introduction, Mai verified on her guest list the name of Joseph Godson and the order of the activities of that morning. Then, she gave him a short overview of the room distribution, indicating that all was ready for him to introduce his team and start the presentations.

Before walking out again through the door left open, to call everyone in, Mai delivered the usual starched sentences she repeated by heart every time in this occasion, assuring her guest that she was "available to help at any time and do not hesitate to ask for any further assistance". She turned around and went to the first group of people to greet them, under Jo's bemused look. Having a closer sense of the communist culture, it came to him that he had to quickly adjust to such a contrasting behavior people interacted, even near to a western society present only a few miles away.

Occasionally, Mai had to meet some of the presenters before the beginnings of the conference to help the smooth enfolding of the events. During the ensuing week, Mai and Jo were to stay often in contact for the proceedings of the conference. Mai continued, as she always did in these occasions, to maintain her reserved but polite and efficient demeanor with no exception of the parleying member.

One early morning, when Mai was tiding up some papers and verifying the daily schedule, Jo came in to review with her the slide projector functioning.

"Oh, hello, I am glad to see you before we have to begin. I would like to use my 'power point' for my presentation today, would you help me to connect my computer to the projector system?"

"Good morning, I think I could take a look, it is true that our equipment is a little out of date." Then she corrected herself quickly, fearing she might have said something inappropriate. "I mean, the slide-projectors are the one usually requested by the presenters."

While exchanging these words, Jo was already swiftly checking the outlets and inserted a convertor for the connection and voltage, and managed to start his portable computer. He knew that, although only some 30 miles from the South Korean capital, Soul, he would not have central connection, but his files stored in the computer's memory were accessible for the presentation. Thus, soon he moved a little the positioning of his PC adjusting the picture, and feeling ready and relieved, turned toward Mai:

"Here we go, we even have time for a cup of coffee, if you care!"

Mai, was impressed, hiding the absence of equivalent material available at the conference center, and trying not to show her embarrassment, she excused herself blaming on her duties she still had to complete.

Being aware of the prodigious technical advancement of the South Korean people, she had been mesmerized by the description of a variety of electronics available on the other side of the border. And all this it seemed to her like a story from the children books, some magical gadget people like to brag about. And she just witnessed how easy Jo made it appear in front of her eyes.

Once Jo went out of the door of the conference room, which stayed opened at all times other than during the conference sessions, Mai continued her tasks automatically, trying to absorb what happened. She was under the magic of what Jo, without even realizing, performed in front of her; and she continued to stay in the wonder of the moment, because it seemed to her that everything about Jo was wonder.

It was not that much about his striking looks, naturally elegant body shape and handsome face with a strong jaw and uncommonly beautiful blue eyes. Not that much about his kind and unassuming manners when addressing others, although his commending knowledge he displayed in front of his audience and authority he implied interacting with its members would let anyone consider him as someone of an important position. Along with all of these considerations, Mai was aware of another, most troublesome fact: Jo made her think that there was something else to expect in life, that there was goodness and kindness, a world of a better life where magic could be expected!

The following morning, as Jo went for his run before dawn, the cold of the air was softened by the snow starting to fall. Late October 1987, winter arrived early in the Korean peninsula. Instinctively, he went around the hill behind the hotel and decide to find a track up the slop where Mai's home must be, then go down from there and make his way back to the Red Star Hotel.

Trying to get oriented, Jo was breathing hard going up, the ground covered by the soft snow and with no path to be seen, it made him meander through shrub and trees. Suddenly, he heard a laughter and a barking squeal, and looking up, he was stopped in his trucks by an image he would keep marked in his memory forever.

Mai was playing with Puppy, the two of them dancing in the snow, with the happiness of children seeing the first flakes of the year. Puppy ran in circles, making the fine white blanket blow in small sprays of white powder, while Mai bending to the ground to gather some snow in balls, was sending them in the air, making Puppy jump to catch them. All he could do was to get some cold flurries on his nose and sneeze and yelp with unexpected joy. She could not resist going out with her dog and having a few fun moments with him before leaving for work.

Gracefully twirling in the snow, her long hair waiving with her movements, her face had the expression of beauty and innocence. Looking at the sky and the flakes falling, her smile was unrestrained, her whole person enjoying this unexpected gift from the nature.

Jo's first impulse was to join in this spontaneous delight, but instinctively he stayed low and after a while, he disappeared, retracing his way back to the hotel and avoiding to attract any suspicion of his whereabout. He also realized that in this country, although a short distance keeping them apart, there were two different worlds, completely different, as though millions of miles in between. And he did not want to endanger anyone with a reckless interruption.

Half an hour later, Mai was at the Red Star Hotel, and everyone resumed their routine functions.

THE YOUNG FAMILY

Toward middle of 1990, Irvin Young's health was declining rapidly. Exhausting all conventional treatments and as a last resort, he struck a covered deal with one of the important Chinese Party's leaders, to whom he facilitated private investments in Hong Kong. In exchange, Irvin Young obtained a hash-hash introduction to secret ways of obtaining organ transplants available to powerful and rich Chinese nationals. In certain occasions, privileged Chinese transferred astronomical amounts of US dollars from their private accounts in Hong Kong to the counterpart of North Korean prelates personal and top-secret accounts kept in Hong Kong, sometimes in the same bank. Thus, covert dealings occurred frequently, serving the interests of both sides, in particular when the precious organs needed for transplants very coveted by Chinese and by people of others nations were provided by North Korea. There was no one to inquire about the provenance of these life-saving organs, as dignitaries and very influential people with end-stage medical conditions became desperate to urgently access them. Some powerful North Koreans leaders on their part, insensible about the sort of the remains of the dead or dying political prisoners, concealed their provenance and saw in it an unexpected source of private enrichment.

Irvin Young, supplying an exorbitant amount of money, was flown privately in the company of his wife and a Chinese doctor, to a landing pad serving a complex of labor camps in North Korea. They were hushed to the infirmary of the camp, while in a near-by shack, Mai, after delivering her babies, expired after a prolonged agony. Irvin was in possession of complete medical records establishing his tissue compatibility, while a blood sample had already been taken from Mai without her knowledge during her lengthy labor. Once the test was quickly processed in Seoul and compared with Irvin Young's, it had been established that this was a perfect match and, without any delay and questioning, the Youngs were at the camp's grounds.

In order to make sure that the organs were retrieved from a fresh and healthy cadaver, the Hong Kong couple, who did not have any particular trust in the communist practices, requested to see the body from which the kidneys were extracted. Irvin had obtained without much difficulty to have the two kidneys at his disposal, in order to increase his chances of a successful transplant.

When Lynn entered the shack where Mai was barely pronounced dead, she found herself in the presence of the two babies, and instantly fell in love with them. The tragic situation was so traumatic for the Young couple, that they asked to take the children and to adopt them, for additional currency. Here again, they did not encounter any opposition since the camp wardens, who would have left the newborns die anyway, grasped the opportunity, and voraciously and covertly took and split the money.

Hastily leaving the sinister site, the Youngs carried on board the priceless organs along with two newborn babies, and flew to a medical center in China. The surgical procedure was performed upon their arrival in a state-of-the-art of un undisclosed wing of a hospital, reserved to the highest political ranked members for special life-saving transplants.

After a few days, Maggie, the baby girl, developed pneumonia and was taken to a children hospital, after which Lynn was mistakenly informed that the little baby did not survive. In reality it was another baby who died, but the bureaucratic negligence did not correct the mistake. After the Youngs were long gone to Hong Kong, where Irvin was to recover in a much better equipped clinic, and nobody claiming the baby, Maggie was transferred to an orphanage in the mountains of Zichang province.

Irvin showed an exceptionally good recovery and soon Lynn felt confident enough to leave her husband regain strength during his convalescence, and followed her own plans regarding her son. She made arrangement to be flown into a private clinic in the Los Angeles vicinity and snooped her baby into a posh delivery clinic for rich foreigners. There, her son, who had barely reached the standard weight for an

American newborn baby, was declared an American citizen once the birth recorded, for Lynn was determined to take all promising precautions regarding her son's future. The upcoming handover of the Hong Kong British colony to the Chinese only a few years away, Lynn looked already into all thinkable options to protect her new son. Yes, money can buy a lot of things!

MAGGIE

The rain changed from a monsoonal shredded curtain of water, to a steady spray of steam. The small group had to leave the Jeep at the end of the muddy trail and make a final climb on foot, for there was no path large enough to yield room for a car. A young school teacher had met them at the foot of the last turn of the mountainous road, leading to a flattening of the terrain against a sheer cliff of rocks. There was, finally, the reason of this long trip initiated by an American private charity group helping to improve the conditions of the orphanages in China.

Up in the mountains, in the province of Zichang, was this modest settlement caring for up to 40 children, anywhere from a few months to the oldest of 14 years of age. As one of the many orphanages receiving foreigners, opening the doors to some agencies playing the sensitive balancing game between charity and adoption, *Lucky Children* prepared for the very first visit of some of the good-hearted donors. Children adoption from China became more accessible in the 1990s and a great number of American families open their homes to one or two children coming from faraway countries to either fulfill a dream of parenthood or simply add to their household a chance to less fortunate children.

Joseph Godson had joined the three couples adventuring in these forsaken mountains of China, far out of any westerner's comfort zone. After completing some of his assignments in the middle east, he returned to South Korea. Operating from the same military base and in contact with the American officials in place, Jo had, however, never been back to the norther side of the peninsula, since his safety had been clearly compromised during his 'affair' with Mai, tragically discovered by the communist regime goons.

In several occasions, Jo's help was solicited when semi-official groups of visitors were travelling into China and exchanges were made by students, scientists or private charities. He represented an additional layer of security to the non-military trained groups of civilians engaged in non-political missions. This time, in late October 1992, Jo met the small group of American nationals at the airport of Xi'an, and from there they traveled by train, then on a Jeep to the orphanage. They were arriving at the final segment of this exhausting trip, traveling from the United States to Beijing, China, and after a short stay in the city, they flew to Xi'an. Two of the couples were generous citizens who sponsored several orphanages around the world, this one in China, and two others in Mexico and Guatemala. They already raised their families and did not look to adopt but to see in person what were the most urgent needs for these children, some who would eventually find a forever home. The third and the younger couple, was very excited and inpatient to meet the little boy they adopted. Both future parents were accompanied, as it was promised by the agency they contacted in the United States, by their Chinese representative sent for their trip to the orphanage.

On foot and exhausted, the members of the group, after exchanging some information with the young girl coming to welcome them, climbed in silence the steep mountain trail, indicated only by occasional electric pols. The junior helper was all smiles and proudly informed them that they had recently electricity installed to the settlement. After 15-20 minutes that seemed a lot longer walking on the slippery mud, the delegation arrived to their destination, as the rain had also subsided. Suddenly the visitors faced a small assembly of 20 children and all of the personnel made of few teachers and keepers, about seven of them living at all times on the premises. They were aligned in front of the main dwelling, and were chanting and waiving small branches and miniature red flags. At first shy of how to properly react and a little disconcerted, soon children and adults approached the visitors, then children swarmed the newcomers, 'breaking the ice'.

After hugs and a few words were spoken, the children's shyness was overcome by their curiosity. For all of them this was the first time they had seen westerners and marveled at their white complexion at the ladies' blond hair, starting touching their hair and their faces. The gentlemen distributed a few candies and ball pens as they engaged in a conversation where the children addressed them with a few words of English.

Jo took a general look of the place and his heart tightened at the sight of this modest colony; there were a few small buildings made of mud bricks with tin roofs in poor condition, the floors were mostly made of hard dirt and the courtyard barren of any children play devices. There were no flowers, no swings, and no game fields. When they were invited inside, the visitors had a summary tour for there was not much to be seen; in an era of economic deprivation for the large majority of the Chinese population, there was very little left or considered needed for the 'undesirable' of the society.

The separation by age and by education degree was a loose arbitration, considering the mixture accepted by the center. The larger construction accommodated the class rooms, three altogether, another building contained the dining area leaving a small section at the end of the room for reading and free time.

The other three or four small dwellings were designated as dormitories, and although the hosts were proud to show the visitors that they had electricity and a few water faucets at the end of visible pluming pipes, it was not very clear how and when the children were taking a bath. It happened also that, when after a while, the ladies asked to use the restrooms, they were appalled to find out in what primitive conditions children and adults lived, with an isolated area containing a few holes on a cemented ground, but without flushing water and emitting the most pungent odors.

Nevertheless, the emotions were flying high when the gentlemen, Jerry, Garry and Tom, started opening a few presents the group insisted to bring in person: coloring crayons and drawing books were distributed and received with astonishing enthusiasm. Some toys were accepted as the most precious treasures, and when the older children received a few simple electronic gadgets, they were lost in the marvel of the moment. Small balls started running and jumping cords were tried right the way, but the most incredible moment came when Jerry, as the senior member of the group, lowered his backpack and cautiously extracted a small television set. The visitors knew that there was no cable reception, but they brought along a good range antenna and a large supply of videos for children.

The children had never seen a television before, although some older ones had heard about it, and the surprise and joy became indescribable. This generous present remained a source of marvel for a very longtime after the good-hearted guests had to take their leave. But the ladies, Gayle, Mitzi, and Hannah, had also great success with the little trinkets they carried along: ribbons of many colors, attractive socks and dolls, enchanted the littles girls. However, the guests were the one with the hearts filled with gratitude seeing the smiles of unrestrained happiness produced by these modest presents.

The young couple was introduced without further delay to little Cheng, the fortunate five-year old boy about to leave with his adoptive parents for never to come back. Cheng, against his tender age, understood entirely the events taking place and he went to meet his new parents. With the most natural smile and opening his arms, he hugged them like they had always been his own parents, as tears of joy were running freely and a great relief was invading the new parents, Hannah and Tom. It was fortunate that the other children were immersed in the exultation of the gift distribution, which distracted them from the sadness of being left behind, as one of them was leaving the camp.

During all this time, no one noticed a little girl, who deciding to leave the room where her little bed was close to a window and where she past most of her days and nights. At first, she timidly approached the main building, then, she entered through the back door and stopped against the wall observing the scene. She was calm and her face bore a wise expression. Unlike any of the other children, she did not jump into the frenzy of the moment and she did not ask for a present; she was rather trying to understand what was going on, what were the objects distributed around for, and who were these strange people. After a while, when nobody payed attention to her, the little girl made a decisive move; she went straight to the tall man who was smiling at a couple of teenage boys, showing them how to play with the small electronic games he brought along.

Without a word, she joined the small group, who at first did not pay attention to her, then, a few moments later she wrapped her arms around Jo's right leg and gently leaned her head against him. Absently, Jo patted her little head, continuing his demonstration. But, after a few minutes, as the little girl glided her minuscule hand into his, Jo felt a powerful jolt and stopped on his track to take a look at the child. The two of them looked at each other, with curiosity at first, then with increased intensity, like they tried to discover the other. Jo was stricken by her face, her skin of a lighter color, her delicate traits so unusual and yet, so familiar!

The little girl's eyes were large and of an intense blue hue he had never seen in this part of the world. He lowered to her level, and attempted to communicate with her with a few Chinese words, helpless in front of such a small child. The little baby girl, she must have been two years old he thought, gently took his face into her little hands and stared into his eyes puzzled, as of a faraway memory, then she softly started to caress his face with infinite gentleness. Jo was about to stand up, looking for someone to find out more about the child, when the baby put her arms around his neck, not letting go. That made Jo to slowly turn his head toward the girl, continuing to search for the right words in Chinese. He tried to tell her that "it is alright" and that he "will give her a gift too", when to his surprise, he heard the little girl speaking for the first time. Slowly and with perfect clarity she said: Pa Pa.

At the pick of his confusion, finally some help was on the way; the lady in charge with the adoption who was accompanying the group, leaving the young couple with the little boy to give them space to know each other, came attracted by the scene. After signaling to one of the associates of the orphanage to come along, she started talking to Joe. It is good to mention that the school teachers and the children, even though in these remote places, were quite good in basic English, to the surprise and the relief of the visitors. Quickly the young attendant of the orphanage reacted to the inquisitor look Jo casted toward her:

"Oh, this is our little Korean girl. She will be two next month, although she is taller than the children of her age. She is pretty, although so different from the others. That must be because she is not Chinese. And look at the color of her eyes, never seen blue eyes here!"

Jo, more and more troubled and interested, since the instructor was so eager with details, started questioning her to learn more about the toddler.

"She was abandoned in a hospital in Beijing after she had been adopted by a lady from Hong Kong. We don't know what made her change her mind, but the baby was in the ward for chronic sick children at a hospital for a while. When she was finally well, no one knew what to do with her, and they sent her to a center for abandoned children in Shanxi, after which she ended up here." Then she volunteered for more, as Jo waited for her to continue:

"Anyway, most of the children here have known parents who brought them here because they are too poor to take care of them, or because they have more than one child, as the law requests. But Maggie has no known real parents, and she is, as most of the children here, available for adoption."

Seeing that the little girl would not leave Jo for a second, and that he was also taken by this little lonely baby who until now has not been mixing with anybody, she started teasing him:

"She likes you, why don't you adopt her, it is easy to get the papers for her. And, with no known parents, no one is there to claim her later on. You should take the example of this young couple, look at them how happy they look together!"

"What is her name?", Jo asked, as to give himself time to even consider such a preposterous idea.

"Magdalena, Maggie Young. See, not a name from here, it was the name her adoptive parents gave her." And, then she added, "But you can change her name anyway, it doesn't matter."

Without realizing, the time was flying, time came for children's dinner and the visitors were invited along. It was very touching to witness the kindness of these people who had so little and made enormous efforts to show them appreciation. A few yams were cooked on a wood fire pit outside by two old women coming from a further hamlet who seemed in charge with this job regularly. A wonderful soup was also presented, made of local vegetables and seasoned with herbs from the fields, even some chicken legs, actually chicken feet, appeared on the table as a delicacy. They finished quickly the meal with a few rice cookies.

Finally, the children's bed time came up, and after many hugs and kisses exchanged generously by children and adults, the visitors' hearts completely melted by these sweet creatures, prepared to leave. Promises were made that they will come back, even though they knew that they might not be able to make again this trying voyage, but they solemnly promised to themselves that nothing was too much of an effort to improve the conditions these children lived in.

When the children were tucked in their modest beds, goodbyes said, promises made, only one child was still with the grownups. Making herself smaller than she was, Maggie did not leave Jo's lap, now her head on his chest, suckling on her thumb, and straining from falling sleep. Jo was holding her also with great care and gentleness, emotions storming inside him. There were strong feelings emerging in his heart, the heart he thought having been shattered and forever frozen. The strangeness of the story of this little girl, her unusual features, although he could not find an answer, his instincts that saved him in the most dangerous situations were telling him that he had to make quickly a decision and save this baby girl. He realized that she would be saving him as well from the despair and emptiness he was drowning in, that she might be the answer for him to go on with his life. And she chose him, amongst all people around. She came to him, as if she recognized him. And if he looked closer, she was reminding him of a face he thought friendly, a familiar face, although this little girl looked like nobody he could name at this time!

Preparing to take their leave, now the gray fog of an early evening approaching, the visitors gathered by the main room. The young couple could not wait to be on the road with their new little boy, and all of them weary after a well filled day, approached and made a circle around Jo and the little girl he was holding. A quick information came from the school intendant and the adoption representative, in a way that hardly could hide their own intentions:

"Mr. Godson found also a child he wants to adopt! They seem to just love each other."
To the puzzled look of the visitors, they anticipated their reaction saying:

"We can provide a release form issued by *Lucky Children* right the way under the article of anticipated adoption, if, after a period of trial, Mr. Godson wants to proceed to the adoption. Meanwhile he can take responsibility of the child with the affidavit that he won't take her out of the country if she is not fully adopted."

To everyone's amazement, further clarification was offered by the young official from the adoption agency:

"In certain instances, such as no known parents who can possibly reclaim the child later on, and considering the overwhelming number of abandoned children and few demands for adoption, when a claim is made after a conclusive visit of a child by an adult, the legal papers can be issued without delay. Actually, these situations are ideal, we love to work in these conditions when possible."

A little commotion seemed to take place under these unexpected circumstances; Gayle and Mitzi came closer to look at the little baby and they all fell under the charm of this little angel's innocent choice, entrusting in total faith her future to a stranger.

And shortly after, some cheerful voices started to encourage Jo to make his decision: "come on, Jo, she is absolutely adorable", "you two look great together!" and "she made a good choice for you," and so on…

Jo, realizing that he was under pressure to make a rapid decision, turned toward to the agency person:

"If things are not working out for us, can I give her back to you in Beijing?"

"It is understood, written in the temporary contract you will be provided with right now, that, if for any reason, you decide to return the child, we will accept her back. But you will see, it will never happen."

During all this time, Maggie did not move from Jo's arms, as if she never doubted the fact that she would be taken 'home' by this nice stranger. With some papers swiftly handed to Jo, standard forms where the blanks have been speedily filled in by the agent, along with a brief translation of the sentences, Jo signed them and all was summarily concluded.

Still feeling that events went way over his head, Jo inquired about the little girl's belongings, when the attendant of the orphanage seemed a little confused. Without further demand, pocketing the signed forms, this was that, and Joseph Godson became the father of a beautiful little baby girl! Then, taking off his jacket, Jo wrapped the little baby inside it and followed the other members of the group through the courtyard, then out of the *Lucky Children*'s gate.

They were all of them too excited by the events that just took place, and euphoria continued during the entire ride back to Zi'an and to Hilton Hotel, where they were to stay until the day after for their flight to Beijing, and from there, back wherever their home was.

Jo's feelings effortlessly shifted from bewilderment of his own decision, to more immediate attention to this defenseless creature that came so confidently to him, and surrendered her life to his care. Soon he was overwhelmed by an immense tenderness and desire to return to this precious candid being all the devotion he was capable of. Although he did not have any remote idea of how to take care of a toddler, he thought that with his love, that's it, because this was what he felt already for little Maggie, the love would guide him through all their needs.

It goes without saying that the ladies of the American group, Mitzi and Gayle, came enthusiastically to his rescue offering their help, all very touched by the spontaneous responsibility Jo assumed. The following morning, Jo and the two ladies went into town accompanied by the chauffer and made large purchases for little Maggie, and from that point on, the little abandoned baby was not to be deprived of anything of what a happy child should expect in this world!

MAGGIE AND JO

Special agent Joseph Godson's life changed dramatically after he adopted Maggie from an orphanage in China. Although not prepared and not looking forward to any adoption in this end of year 1992, once arrived to Seoul, South Korea, via Beijing from his China trip, he had Maggie's health checked thoroughly by the base doctors. They all found her perfectly healthy, and all Jo's friends and acquaintances marveled at the happy turn of the fate coming across the two of them.

With the adoption of his little Maggie, Jo made also adjustments regarding the directions taken by his professional commitments. Talking to his superiors, he expressed his concerns about missions that could send him away from his little daughter, along with worries about her future if he was to disappear during one of these assignments. They all convened that it would be best for Jo to return to a base in California, and have a more domestic description of his job. Once agreed upon his return, Jo was ready to leave the Korean region, too many hurtful memories haunted him there, and hoped that he would never have to see again these places that reminded him of the best and the ghastliest times in his life.

In consequence, Jo regained the United States and went to San Diego, then to San Francisco, where he trained other special force elements. His entire life started having a sense, seeing his little girl growing and becoming a happy and well-adjusted young person. Although he never remarried, not even considering the thought of it, he was happy. As happy as he could manage to be, keeping a positive attitude, devoted to his daughter, his work, and his community. Since his trips to China and other places assisting missions intended to helping the less fortunate, and especially since his visit to Zichang province, Jo discovered in his heart this sensitive string of deep compassion. He understood that his sense in life would be heightened and more balanced adding to his interests a gentler way of helping people, to his other, more violent side, requesting fulgurant strikes during special military interventions.

However, because he decided that he would always be close to his daughter, he did not travel faraway, but he found an unlimited source to help attending to the needy close to home. He assisted genuine adoption agencies in the area of his place of living, where unfortunate teenage mothers accepted to give a better chance to their children. Jo was also very keen to the acute problem of homelessness, particular of the veterans ending up on the streets of LA and San Francisco. Drugs and unemployment, disruption of a stable family life and ravages of PTSD were the main reasons of this devastating reality.

Continuing his work as a valuable instructor in the formation of a new generation for highly classified interventions, Jo built a busy life for himself as well. He remained constantly involved in his little daughter's activities, to which he added a hands-on participation to "Homes for Homeless Veterans", a nonprofit organization. As he did during other times, Jo threw himself with passion into these new pursuits, keeping his mind busy and fulfilling a more spiritual need that was maturing inside him by the day.

Growing up, Maggi became a stunning, although a more exotic kind of beauty. Following her father in many of his activities, she rescued people on the streets, fed homeless in the shelters, while bringing home all kind of pets to foster until finding them a forever home. She became also involved with centers for teenage mothers, and this at an age when she could very well be one of these troubled girls, who found themselves in a situation where the responsibilities were coming too fast, after a too short period of fun in their tender youth.

Maggie showed at an early age a surprising maturity and a profound insight considering everything in life; she would ponder deeply and come up with wise deductions in many confusing or complicated situations, and her sensibility often surprised the adults. During her visits to shelters and centers accompanying her father, Maggie began to leave or send a little note to the people she talked to and who were expressing to her their dramatic issues. At first, these notes were only words of encouragement, then she was coming up with some ideas of finding a solution to their problems.

Jo, becoming aware of Maggie's little messages to the residents of these centers, teased her, telling her that she could make an excellent psychotherapist. Maggie researched more about it and after a while decided that this was not what she really wanted to do in life. She already had started to pen down a few stories about the people she was visiting, finding every one's story more fascinating than reality. Then she thought of a leading idea behind some of these stories, concerned that the general population was largely ill-informed about most of their tragic conditions.

As her father became passionate about helping the less fortunate members of the society, Maggie found her own way of participating beyond just feeding or raising funds for them; she tried to become a voice of those who were suffering. Before her senior year in high school, Maggie made a few apparitions at the meetings of some charity organizations, then sent a few petitions to the mayor of San Francisco. With the encouragements received after a few very well delivered speeches, she forwarded a few articles to the local papers in the city and around the Bay area. She had succeeded to attract the attention for the help needed to the less fortunate. Jo was all behind Maggie's activities, very proud of her ever since he discovered her first written essays. And he was aware of the impact her articles made in their community to change many lives.

Thus, with time, Maggie pursued a journalistic career, went to college to obtain her degree, while continuing the be a rising star as a freelance columnist. She had a fierce, independent spirit, courageously adventuring in dangerous places when she felt her help was needed. Subsequently did her articles, growing bold, featuring stories about human trafficking, illegal immigrants' exploitation by their own nationals enslaving them, and even drug and gang members trapping young naïve girls into their vice.

Although Jo had moments when he, rightfully so, feared for Maggie's safety, her talent, ability to unearth poignant stories and stir the officials and private organizations attention, he resumed to discretely watching over her, considering that her work became a contribution to improving the human condition.

As Maggie bloomed from an adorable little doll, then went through different stages of becoming a young adult, at times she asked Jo about her mother, then about the place where he had found her and had decided to take her home. Watching her grow, Jo never stopped thinking that this little girl seemed so familiar to him; this feeling became even stronger as Maggie became a young lady, and gave him the impression that she looked so much like his young and long-lost wife. He associated this feeling to his promise that adopting Maggie, he would always make the little orphaned baby feel as his real child, and that she would never think otherwise.

There have been times when Maggie became aware of her father's loneliness; as a child it appeared normal that he dedicated all his free time to her. But growing up, she started noticing how handsome her father was, and followed the looks full of admiration many young and beautiful women casted on her dad. And she started teasing him that he should date one of them. When he gave her as excuses all kind of inflated motives, making her scream with laughter, he would then sheepishly lower his head and murmur:

"There is, was, only one woman for me", and with the outmost conviction he would declare, "your mother."

The questions Maggie was asking, the strange but powerful impression of belonging, made Jo in his rare moments of reverie, wonder. The resemblance, the age, all that nagged his thoughts that there may be just a slight possibility that the universe plotted for him to have their little daughter. And again, the reason was bringing him back, for him to consider all the real facts, there was no possible way that this had happened. And he was telling himself that nothing would have changed anyway, he would always consider Maggie as his little daughter no matter what.

Maggie also went to periods when, fault of asking about a person who might have been her mother, she expressed the desire to go and visit the orphanage in China. But her work was keeping her busy and the demands for her to 'investigate' new places would not leave any room for her to make a trip so far away.

MAGGIE AND TREBOR

It wasn't that she did not have a life full of excitement, but this was something to surprise even her, Maggie was thinking one night, staring at the ceiling of her comfortable room. She even had a good laugh telling her father about it, and they both had a good time. However, rerunning in her mind the same scene, she told herself that life never stops playing tricks on us.

Maggie was hurrying along to meet the head publisher of the Guardian US, to discuss one of her short stories she just pitched about a homeless person lying on a sidewalk and being literally kicked by some young thugs. She had pictures, a little video and all, and her interest in meeting with Regina was that the Guardian had an online global news network. Maggie thought that the more stories of social cruelty and injustice were made public, the more protection would be achieved for the unfortunates.

Happy that she could find a parking spot on Sacramento Street, she turned right on Mason Street, approaching the famous Fairmont Hotel. Her acute sense of observation caught on the side of her eye the silhouette of a person she knew very well; but this person seen from the back, same tall stature, long legged and feline movements, was climbing the stairs of the luxury entrance of the hotel with his right arm wrapped around a young lady's waist! They were laughing and talking joyfully.

"Dad!" she instinctively called. Then, not having an answer, she repeated "Dad", and approached the man, slightly pulling on his jacket's left sleeve.

The man, startled, turned around, wondering who was the person who grabbed him and called him "Dad". The young and beautiful lady in his company also looked at her with an amused smile.

Immediately Maggie realized her mistake; this was a much younger man, and his face, although had some striking resemblance with her father's, had feint Asian features, although his eyes were blue!

"I am so sorry, I took you for someone else, please pardon me", Maggie mumbled.

To which the young man, returned with a big grin in his face: "Oh yes, you thought I was your father!" then added, "you look like a baby girl, still, I do not think I could be your father."

"I know, it is preposterous, I beg for your forgiveness", Maggie kept on pleading, obviously very embarrassed.

But the young man did not want to let go that easily, or so she thought, because still laughing now from the heart, he was staring at her mesmerized. So was Maggie, something out of the ordinary was happening. Why this young man made her think of her father, and why had he some similar particularities she had as well? Furthermore, it was also for the first time when she, finally, encountered another person with this mixture of Asian and a blue-eyed Caucasian feature, like herself!

Then suddenly, he stretched out his hand to her:

"I am Trebor Young, pleased to meet you!"

Quickly, Maggie caught on:

"And I am Maggie, Magdalena Godson. Nice to make you acquaintance as well. "

"And this is Sam, Samantha Wallis, a good friend of mine." After handshakes were exchanged, Trebor continued. "Here is my business card. Why don't we all get together some time, I will be in town for a while", then with humor, "I can't wait to meet YOUR father!"

And taking his card, she looked at it and added: "I am sure my father will be curious to meet you as well."

Then goodbyes followed, and turning back on her track, Maggie heard Sam telling Trebor:

"Maybe not her father, but she can very well be your sister, you two have so much in common. She is so pretty!"

And fading away, Trebor's voice added: "You mean, I am 'pretty'?" and the couple burst in laughter.

Now, at night in her room, Maggie turned around and pulling up the card from her nightstand, and after lighting up her smart phone, looked at it one more time.

"Trebor Young. Financial adviser. CEO and Chairman of Young & Young Global Holdings, Hong Kong, London, New York, San Francisco, Vancouver, Paris. Very impressive, and very rich, obviously. Hey, he might want to make a nice contribution to the Homeless project, he makes a lot of money in this country, after all."

Maggie remembered her conversation with her father last night; after Jo finished his work at the training center on the north side of the Bay area, he went to drop off a whole load of blankets and bedding supplies from the military overstock to the new homeless community rearranged in the older barracks. They met close to home, tired and excited, happy to see how nicely the new settlement was turning. Since a timid idea came to Jo, who later on was presented to the base commander, there was issued an authorization to separate the older derelict buildings from the new barracks and allow them to be restored and accessible to the homeless veterans. Once the older section of the base was properly separated, volunteers could have access to the grounds and proceed to their restoration. Soon applications coming from veterans poured in, and some of them even insisted on giving a hand to make the old vacated blocks habitable again.

But there was more to it, they needed a cantina space, and they took model from the mess hall of the base. Gladly, finding a good use to outdated material, the military base provided them with their old kitchen equipment. Then, the maintenance of the new born village, its security, transportation to the medical clinic and the stores available on the base, and even leisure activities, all were needed to reintegrate and restructure the lives of these individuals who have given so much to their country and have been so unjustly and for so long outcasted. There were important efforts made to provide psychological support, proper medical care access, while members of the new community found their own ways to contribute with their skills to the good functioning of their reestablished lives. They discovered new reasons to be hopeful, encouraging and helping each other, coming out of the isolation and the rejection of a society in which they could not find a place until not so long ago.

Practically talking at the same time, Maggie and Jo had a sigh of relief when they could finally sit at a small table next to a street vendor displaying deliciously made sandwiches with baguettes and croissants. Jo was giving Maggie the latest details of the former barracks arrangements, while Maggie could not wait to tell her father about her bumping into his 'look-alike'. Then, their plates and bottles of San Pellegrino arriving, they started devouring their food with pleasure. Realizing how late they were into dinner hours and feeling better after a few bites, Jo noticed that Maggie had rosier cheeks than usual, and finally asked:

"So, what were you saying, Trebor Young… humm, Young?" and he looked as if he was trying to see if that was ringing a bell.

Then, the two of them changed conversation and only now, late at night, Maggie tried to interpret her father's reaction to her story. But she found that he did not show much of interest, absorbed by his new project. "I will talk to him in the morning and he will have to find time for us to get together, he won't be off the hook so easily", she thought, and with a smile, Maggie finally went into a deep sleep.

JO MEETS TREBOR

Well, Jo and Trebor were not to meet, not in the way Maggie intended anyway. The pressure that the United States increasingly exerted on North Korea, after the talks initiated by president Donald Trump in June of 2018 in Singapore, then the wobbly discussions following Vietnam in 2019, there were agreements that needed to be closely pursued by verification of the denuclearization promises proffered by Kim Jung Un. And the access to the sites the North Korean admitted to operate in the past, certainly weren't the only one, and even those weren't made easy to verification. Further intense deliberations and restrictions obtained from the DPRK's authorities, after countless delays, to allow an international specialized team access to these areas of interest.

Maggie was contacted by San Francisco Chronicle with a proposition for her to go along with the American representatives and to send periodically reports and pictures as their 'imbedded' journalist. Maggie was behind herself with excitement, that was a great, international break-through for her career. Talking to her father, Jo agreed at last that she would go only with the condition that he would be included into the American team as a security dispatch.

Things being worked out better than expected, soon father and daughter started planning their trip, especially since Jo was familiar from the past experience with the North Korean politics. Maggie, however, insisted to take some time prior to the beginning of her assignment dates, convincing her father to make a detour and visit the orphanage in China where she was found as a baby. Thus, Jo who could rarely refuse something to Maggie, arranged for a flight to Xi'an via Beijing, and from there to continue the trip made into the country he had known 30 years before.

Walking in the San Francisco International terminal before their flight to Beijing, Maggie and Jo were inside of one of the well-appointed stores displaying a variety of travel accessories. Maggie, very excited about her 'grand trip', contemplated all the necessary gadgets for her cameras. Stepping out of the store with her little treasures, Maggie and her father went to sit on one of those nice chairs disposed around a coffee table.

While doing this, another voyager was just standing up, ready to reach his boarding gate. At that moment, he recognized Maggie, and addressed her by her name right the way.

"Maggie, Maggie Godson, right? I thought that you will never give me a sign! And this is your real father I suppose, my 'alter ego'?"

The three of them were facing each other, and Jo was as astounded as was the younger man. Indeed, they had the same stature, slim but with an athletic built, they had the same deep blue colored eyes, and similar forehead and jaw lines. However, Trebor's cheek bones were higher and more prominent, and looking surprisingly more like Maggie's, with whom he shared some facial similarities. And a bystander could have easily thought that the three of them shared the same irresistible smile.

After only a few seconds, that seemed like minutes staring at each other, and each thinking of how much the other two looked alike, a little embarrassed, Trebor introduced himself properly to Jo and the two men made simultaneously an invitation to sit down.

"Thank you, but only for a few minutes, I have to catch my flight to Hong Kong", said Trebor. Then, with a sadder expression, he added: "I received alarming news about my mother, she is not well. Since I know her, she never complains, and I suspect it must me serious if she asked her assistant to call me".

After the appropriate and sincere concerns father and daughter readily expressed, Trebor inquired about their destination, to which Jo volunteered only: "Oh, we are going for a little tour to China, we're flying to Beijing, and we will see from there".

"That sounds exciting, I deal with the Chinese, of course, mostly from Hong Kong. Be careful, they are strong negotiators, not always easy to do business with. Well, I have to run, have a great trip, but we promise that we will get together when back in the States. I must say that it might take a while, I don't know how my mother's health really is. But we have to keep our promise this time, right Maggie?" and without thinking, he came closer and instead of a handshake, he gave her a spontaneous hug, like old acquaintances. Then, as taking hold of himself, he turned toward Jo and said:

"I am not going to hug you, don't worry!"

At that moment, Jo, who was usually keeping a cool demeanor, seeing the disarming smile on this young man's handsome face, gently pulled him into his arms and giving him a tap on his back, said:

"I really am sorry for your Mom. Have a good trip and give her our best wishes for recovery."

HONG KONG

As soon as he landed at the Chek Lap Kok, the ultra-modern airport in Hong Kong, built on the strip of land gained over the sea, Trebor felt the hot and steamy air, as during summer, although the rocky terrain was shrouded by menacing clouds and a strong wind announced the typhoon season. But Trebor's mind was galloping on high gear after reaching the exit area. With all the attention given by the transpacific Dreamliner of British Airways first-class attendants, he found little rest, shifting in and out of a troubled sleep. Trebor was accustomed to long flights and usually had no difficulty adjusting to the time zone changes and getting all his rest. But not this time. He had been unsettled since he received the news about his aging mother's condition. Then, seeing Maggie and meeting her father at the airport in San Francisco, Trebor had the impression that this only contributed to open more doors over mysterious realms, somehow making him think of the terrible dreams that occasionally visited him, disquieting his peace.

After going through the customs, Trebor spotted the sign held by one of the corporate chauffeurs sent to fetch him, and soon they were leaving the super terminal and were on the road. The limo entered Highway 8, passing in the front of Hong Kong Disneyland, then reaching Kowloon island, turned south on route 3 to Hong Kong Island, then followed Cotton Tree Road. Passing Sheung Wan and before arriving at the Arts center, the car started climbing the steep terrain at the foot of the Victoria Peak. Close to the mid-level area and not far from Dr. Sun Yat-sen Museum, they arrived at their destination after a ride that took well over 50 minutes, and seemed to Trebor lasting for hours.

In the foyer of the lavish penthouse of a skyrise building, Trebor was received by the old butler, Ting, and then by a nurse Trebor had never met before. He remembered how much he enjoyed the expanded vistas over the Victoria Harbor, never getting bored admiring the lights, but this time he did not pay attention to it, all absorbed by what he was about to find inside the residence.

Trebor hurried into his mother's bedroom, his attention drawn from the elegant decor to the bed, where he expected to see his mother. He quickly realized that she was not there, but sitting in a recliner chair he did not remember. It looked like her comfortable couch she liked to read on, landed its place to a more functional furnishing. Lynn Young was looking out, facing the bay window, and Trebor could make out only her shadow from the back of her chair. He hastened to reach her, eager to hold her in his embrace.

Lynn tried to sound cheerful and attempted to stand up, when the concerned nurse rushed to prevent her from straining. With all the enjoyment anticipated of seeing his mother, the words toned down as Trebor scrutinized her face. Lynn looked drawn, considerably thinner, while her voice quivered slightly, although her sweetness and love were all there to welcome him.

"Oh, Trebor, my darling son! I am so happy to see you", and she stretched her arms to hug him.

"Mother, how are you? You are looking good" he lied, "you scared us all!"

"Always the same charmer, don't try to flatter me, I know I look awful".

But Trebor continued and asked more about her health, to which she replied that her internist was expected any moment and he will give him a complete report.

"Now, just come and sit next to me, it has been too long... and how was your trip?"

Saying this, Lynn was getting out of breath, when the nurse came along and bringing a small portable oxygen tank, adjusted the plastic tubules to her nose, while gently scolded her:

"You know better, the doctor said you should keep your oxygen on at all times."

And, as if on cue, Doctor Jing-xen entered through the door. Although in his sixties, the doctor appeared younger than expected, moving with good strides and bringing a reassuring flow of energy with him. After expressing his pleasure seeing Trebor by his mother's side and gave him a warm hug, doctor Jing-xen addressed Lynn.

"How is my favorite patient doing today, did we have a good night? and did we take our medication as directed?" He said that addressing Lynn, but his face was turned towards the nurse, as making sure the patient 'behaved'.

"Well", the nurse started.

69

"Of course, the patient took all your recommendations to the letter", Lynn interrupted with a waving of her hand.

While Dr. Jing-xen was examining the patient, he continued to inquire, "and are we eating that good soup Mica makes for you?"

This time the nurse jumped faster with her answer, making sure that truth was told, "she took only a few sips, then turned down everything on the plate last night and this morning", and satisfied with her delivery, the nurse made a nod toward the patient.

After a few minutes, when Dr. Jing-xen made his overall review that nothing was new on Lynn's condition, he sat on the ottoman in front of her and holding her hands in his, considered his patient quietly. No words were needed, the good doctor knew Young family for a long time, since Trebor was brought in the family, over thirty years ago. Before standing up, an understanding look appeared on Lynn's face to which Dr. Jing-xen returned an acquiescent reading and made a sign to Trebor to follow him out of the room.

Dr. Jing-xen, familiar with Young's apartment, was leading the way and stopped only when they reached a further side of it, the library. Trebor seemed calm and followed all this time the doctor's reactions, with a trust he always had in him. When they sat down, Dr. Jing-xen looked him strait in the eyes, and calmly talked:

"I am not going to embellish the situation, Trebor, I respect you and your family too much for that. The sad reality is that your mother is dying, and..", at Trebor's startled reaction, he made a sign to let him continue, "Lynn was diagnosed with lymphoma, and her stage was advanced when it was found out, invading vital organs and making her condition decline rapidly. We tried a few treatments in the beginning, only to slow down the disease, but she did not tolerate them well, they were making her even more sick. At her request, we agreed to provide only support treatments and keep her comfortable."

Letting Trebor absorb the enormity and gravity of the situation, the doctor continued after a few moments:

"I entirely agree with her choices, there is not much to offer, and we respect her wishes wanting a dignifying end of her life. And I promise you that I will personally make sure she will not suffer."

Trebor seemed crushed under the gravity of the news and the doctor took his time, respecting his sorrow. After a while, Trebor slowly lifted his head and asked:

"How long?"

" You know that there is no precise answer to that, but I would not anticipate a long time, a week, maybe less...", and then he added, "but I am happy you are here, it means everything to your mother you came before she ...passed."

Leaving Trebor deep in his thoughts, Dr. Jing-xen took his leave discreetly without saying much, just that he would be back the day after. After a while, Trebor summoned all his courage and came back to his mother's room, only to find her asleep. Her nurse already lifted the lower side of the recliner to make her more comfortable, and told Trebor that she refused to go back to bed.

"Your mother does not want to alarm you staying in bed, and she wanted to make sure you will have a good breakfast prepared by Mica. Why don't you go to the kitchen and then rest a little, I will let you know when she is awake."

Moving like an automat, Trebor followed her suggestions. Later on, he woke up in his bedroom, where his body must have yielded to the fatigue and the emotions of the last days. He opened his eyes at the gentle voice of the afternoon nurse, telling him that his mother "is awake now". He quickly sat on the edge of the bed, gathering his thoughts, surprised to see that it was late afternoon. Rushing toward his mother's room, he thought that she might have had a good rest herself.

Indeed, she looked a little more rested, her face seemed at peace, the lining of age almost effaced. She lit up seeing him approaching, and with a few steps Trebor was next to her. As he sat down, he noticed that her oxygen tube was removed, lying on one of the armrests. He promptly lifted to place it on her face, but with a smile, Lynn gently pushed it aside.

"What for? We have more important things to consider, and I don't want anything to be in the way", and reaching for his hands, she took them tenderly into her tiny ones, now shaking like delicate leaves in the night breeze. "I am so happy, my darling, you came. I must set straight a few things long due. I will soon leave this life, no my love, don't cry, I am ready. I will be ready, once I fulfill the promise I made to your father before he was gone."

Trebor understood that she wanted to use all the energy she had left to convey some important matters to him, for he suppressed his desire to talk her out of her sadness. Therefore, he let his mother start her story:

"Long ago, Irvin and I wanting more than anything else in life to have children, one child would have made us more than happy. But we had given up when Irvin's health started declining. Over time, he almost lost his kidney function and only a transplant could have saved him. We were rich and he had powerful connections over the whole world, but mostly with the new rich Chinese, who, in the prospect of Hong Kong becoming part of China again, were looking at this opportunity as a big opening for their investments to the western world."

After a short break, Lynn pursued:

"And your father was one of the best placed persons for that. In short, we learned through one of very powerful businessmen, that there could be an easy and quick access to organs for transplants, without having to wait with no guarantee of ever finding one. We were desperate and...naive, and we jumped into the offer. But nothing is as easy and as wonderful as we foolishly thought. And there was no way going back."

Lynn, took a long breath, and paused for a while, looking away, lost into the world of a time that had passed. Then, she continued,

"We received a phone call and without delay we were taken, using our private jet, of course, to a place harvesting the organs. We were in possession of Irvin's full medical records with recent tests done, learning that the blood and HLA testing from the donor showed a perfect match". Lynn stopped a few seconds to catch her breath, but insisted to continue. "Crazy with hope, we rightfully thought that we were expected at some medical center in China, where the organs were brought in after an unfortunate accident, and we were given the chance for the transplant before other people."

At this point, Lynn's whole body shuddered at the vision she was about to describe to Trebor.

"No, it was not a medical center. It was a North Korean concentration camp where young and healthy prisoners were tortured or executed, and their organs were to become the subject of a sinister black market, while dignitaries found an undisclosed source of becoming rich! Irvin and I, paralyzed par the unexpected turn of events, learned that a young North Korean woman who had just given birth to twin babies, a boy and a girl, had died in labor. Somewhere, in the fog of the confusion, we've been told that nothing could be done for the mother and the babies...And, this way...Irvin being a perfect match, received a kidney of your mother, and we took you both as our babies..." Lynn managed to finish, and now both of them were holding the other, crying without retention.

It took a long time for the two of them to quiet their sobs and contemplate the facts; for the mother to re-live and open an old secret wound, sharing it with her son, who in turn, was transported by the news to this vision of a dramatic and horrifying origin of his life.

"You have to know that your father, Irvin, and I, we always loved you like our son, even more so if that can be possible. And we made the promise to your mother's soul that we will take care of you with our life. In a way, she gave a chance to Irvin to live a long and full life, and we tried, it was the least we could do, to save her babies."

Lynn, attempting to bring more air into her lungs, succeeded only to show sadness in her expression.

"Unfortunately, we lost the baby girl, your twin sister, she was taken from the hospital in Beijing, where your father had the transplant, to a children's' hospital where we learned that she passed way. I will always mourn her loss, we felt like we failed your mother."

"I tried to find out what happened, but we lost the lead, and I had to take care of you, we wanted to protect your future by making you pass for an American born child and become a US citizen"

Trebor's mind and heart were in the middle of a storm, but surprisingly, for some unknown reason he felt relieved, like a heavy weight was removed from his chest. Then suddenly, from somewhere a clarity came to him and he heard himself asking:

"Is her, was her name Maggie? Magdalena?"

Lynn almost jumped from the chair, and starting shaking violently said, "Yes, how do you know?"

"Mom, she is not dead, somehow she lived, she is alive. I met her, she has blue eyes like mine, and I think she lives with her father, in San Francisco. She seems very happy; Mom, you did not fail her, you saved her too."

Although the news sounded like a dream coming true for Lynn, she did not dare to believe that Trebor would be accepting all the heavy reality she just onloaded on him. But, observing his reactions, looking into his face, she learned that her son was taking all in the best way she could have hoped for. And in her heart was mounting this huge happiness, as she just learned that the little girl was alive and well!

"Thank God, this is the best gift a woman can ever expect in life. Now, I know that all will be fine!", Lynn was thinking, her soul filled with gratitude. Minutes later, she heard Trebor bursting, standing up:

"Then I know who my father is, I know who Jo Godson is!" and turning toward his mother, he added, "the funny thing is that Maggie saw me from behind, and thought I was her father. We have quite a few things in common actually, if we think about it" he completed with a laughter.

Seeing his mother happy and relaxed, he said" Yes, the three of us have the same eye color, and I am the same size as my...Jo. When I get back, I need to get in touch with them."

From deep inside him, emerged suddenly this overwhelming desire to know more about his mother. And Trebor started asking questions, one after another, as if scared that Joseph Godson might not know or might not want to share with him what happened more than thirty years ago.

Lynn realized that this was the least she could do for Trebor, no more secrets to be held back, and she gave him the best she could the indications about the place of her mother's last days. Trebor learned that it was somewhere on the northeast side of the communist Korea, that must be not too far from the border with China, for they quickly exited that country carrying with them the organs of the unfortunate woman. It was a labor camp where the prisoners were digging a secret nuclear base Kim Jong Il was building, she said about whispers she heard later on.

During this time, Trebor felt in his mind a surge of rage, "Bastards! I will go see where she lived and died, I'll look for her tomb, it is the least I can do!", he was saying to himself, not wanting to disturb his dying mother. For he realized, and sincerely felt for Lynn the same love he would have had for his real mother. He would not have loved Lynn any less than his own mother, and Trebor came to sit by her, tenderly.

The two of them continued to sit together for a long time, in silence, while the night was shining inside the bedroom the happy arcs of colors of the most spectacular harbor in the world. The evening nurse came in with a tray of food for Lynn and went to turn some lights on, when they stopped her after only a few corner lamps were on. Lynn refused her food, with the excuse that she will eat something later. However, she accepted to be laid on her bed for the night. Soon after, she told Trebor he needs to get some dinner and go to bed as well. He answered that he wants to stay with her for a while longer, to which closing her eyes, she smiled satisfied.

It was only in the wee hours of the early dawn that Trebor moved a little and realized he had fallen asleep in the chair by his mother's bed. Instantly he looked at her, worried. Here she was, still smiling, the same perfectly content smile. Approaching her, Trebor did not see her chest rising with a breath, and touching her hand, he felt her hand already cold. She was gone.

After looking at her for a while, Trebor felt sadness and peace at the same time, for she was so serein. Then, taking her hands, he kissed them one after the other and gently placed them on her chest. One more time he looked at her, caressed her forehead and delicately placed on it a tender kiss. Then, he went out the door and told the night nurse that it was over, that all was fine.

BACK TO THE PRESENT

Before their trip to the far east, Jo attempted to relocate the orphanage in the Zichang province, and he could not find it any longer. He had mentioned to Maggie about it, and against his conviction that his information was up to date, he promised that he would check one more time in China. Once arrived in Beijing, their information was confirmed, the *Lucky Children* orphanage existed no longer, and the two of them resumed to visiting Beijing. However, with Xi'an in their mind, they took the flight there and instead they visited the Terracotta Army. Coming back to Beijing, the pollution of the town made them so uncomfortable, they chose to take the bullet train to Badaling for the famous stretch of the Great Wall. They stayed in the area for a while, after which, feeling that they had enough of tourism, they left Beijing and resumed their voyage to the northwest side of DPRK, the destination of their assignment.

Arriving in Dandong, on the north river bank of the Yalu River, the inspections were to start with the area of the south side of the river, with Sinuiju, covering a triangle including Tongrim and Sakchu. From there, they were to continue their mission to the north border with China, up to Sonbong.

There was not much to see in these corners of south east of China, and Jo and his daughter were glad when they finally met with the representatives of the multinational team. The experts started their initial meetings getting to know each other and have a clearer definition of what everyone was expected to accomplish. There were two nuclear physicists, one American and one French, a Swedish geologist, three military engineers in weaponry technology, all Americans, two specialists in electronic logistics from Italy and Belgium, and two Chinese translators, mediating also as local guides and 'neutral party' of the commission. In addition to Jo and Maggie, other Fox News, CNN, and BBC reporters intended to make big news splashes and play a role on preventing the North Koreans from undermining the proper proceedings of the commission.

Soon, Jo realized that he was the sole member of the team assuming their security, as the only one having had the appropriate training in the past, with a little and questionable reassurance that the engineers and the journalists would make their role visible in case of necessity. To this, the two Chinese translator-guides tried to be reassuring by saying that they "will observe the Korean hosting team, supposed to provide 'complete security' to the good proceeding of the inspection."

After everyone's arrival and another two lengthy weeks of parleys, the group was informed that the inspections were to start from the opposite direction of the planned course. Well, no one was surprised at this point, since they expected the Koreans to be unpredictable. Thus, a long, tiring, and a quite somber trip ensued in order to arrive to the designated points to be examined first. The members of the team were glad to be together and keep busy, otherwise the discomfort, the unusual heat and the strict isolation from the general population, were hard to bear. After a grueling day of work, each member of the delegation continued with their specific job, writing or transmitting pictures or videos, all previously carefully censored by the North Korean authorities. The only highlights of the day happened once in a while, when they could enjoy a facetime call with family.

Jo was quite preoccupied, and, although keeping a calm demeanor, remained under an acute sense of alert. Assuming a protective watch, he continually scrutinized the surroundings where the team was operating in. Jo thought that he was probably the only one from the Americano-European team to have had an extended knowledge of the Korean social and political reality. And seeing now the country where he had spent some time in the past, was not a reassuring sight. He could not help remembering his personal experiences, most of them charged with drama. And the strongest feelings were coming to him at night, frightening images invaded him thinking of his beloved Mai, suffering and dying in atrocious conditions. Along the way, he could discern at times some detention camps, their ghostly shapes not far from the former nuclear sites, and carrying the unbearable impression that nothing had changed all these years in this forsaken country.

With all the international talks and promises coming from opposite sides of the world, it seemed to him that the real people still endure the atrocities of a ruthless totalitarian ruler, seen around the world's TV screens smiling and shaking hands with the heads of the superpower nations. "And still, nothing had changed for these poor people.

Everybody loves each other, signing treaties and having lavish dinners, and, while feeling good about themselves, nothing had changed for the general population. What a pity!" Jo kept thinking, gripped with sadness.

The international delegation carried on with the persistence matching the magnitude of their task, against the continuous hurdle exerted by the Korean counterpart. The team members tried to ignore the insidious obstacles and inconveniences they encountered constantly. They were determined to go for the long whole of their mission, until its completion, or so they thought.

LEAVING ALL BEHIND

Following Lynn's passing, the succession formalities went very straightforward for the sole legal heir of the Young family. Still suffering from the shock of a son losing his mother, event never fully expected no matter the circumstances, Trebor fulfilled all his obligations as expected. It did not take much time for the transition of the family business, since he was already the only beneficiary of the trusts and holdings, thanks to the careful preparations his father made before his death, almost five years before. It was a simple recognition, official as it was, that Trebor was now the only beneficiary of an extended fortune and at the head of a conglomerate of corporations he was already managing.

As per family wishes, Trebor followed with the traditions of obituary, flowers, and visiting obligations, against his belief that this was a macabre social constraint, along with the cremation, as it was done in the family. The day chosen to spread the ashes, this time combining the ceremony with the ashes of his father's kept until his mother's death, that day had to be postponed because of a strong storm raging in Victoria Harbor.

However, the day after the storm, under a shining sky washed by the torrential rains, Trebor was at the aft of the *Spring Song*, the family yacht, accompanied only by Dr. Jing-xen, the old butler, Ting, and another small urn. That urn contained the ashes of the old and beloved dog, Spiffy, who after a happy and a little spoiled life, decided to lead the way to Heaven a few days before Lynn.

After the boat sailed around the Hong Kong Island and found less crowded seas, the three men merged together their courage and, opening the larger urns, let the elements unite the evanescent remains of Lynn and Irvin, to which they released Spiffy's ashes to join in for an eternal company.

Coming back after the sad farewells, Trebor offered a huge memorial reception at the Hong Kong business headquarters, including all the local acquaintances they could reunite. It was a cathartic event for Trebor, staying busy and listening to his parents' friends' stories of happier times.

Soon after the funeral and spending a few very intense days at the company offices, Trebor verified the state of the enterprises and, one more time, revised the quality of their management. Trebor had a phenomenal capacity of analyzing complicated and detailed structure of the companies, with their intricate transactions and connections. He cleared a few older contracts becoming outdated and spent a few nights producing a whole volume of instructions and policies for the head managers to follow, instructions that could have impressed a team of IT specialists after months of revisions.

Then, Trebor, took care of the private family matters with the distribution of large wages to the household employees. Along with this, Trebor made sure that the old butler, the cook and Lynn's personal maid subsistence was insured for the remaining of their lives, adding regular earnings produced by comfortable stocks. Then, he released them from their work obligations.

Next, followed a brief meeting with the best rated real estate company in Hong Kong, and explaining very precisely his demands, Trebor listed the large apartment and the yacht for sale. He had decided without difficulty that he would reserve a suite at the "Upper House" when coming back in town, and he would not need to continuously maintain a property there. Although these two assets' value was extraordinary for the market prices of the area, both parties agreed that a round sum of $100 million should help to conclude a quick sale. With this prospect, Trebor gave instructions that half of the proceeds be donated to a list of orphanages in China, and the other half distributed to another selection of orphanages and shelters for women and children in the United States of America. He was aware, after all, that his choice was based on the fact that himself had been adopted, as had been his own twin sister.

In a way satisfied with his decisions, Trebor spent one last night in his parental lavish apartment. He slept very little, reflecting on his past life and on what was ahead of him, after learning about his origins and how destiny decided to give him a kind and plentiful chance in life. All this brought him a great peace and his heart was filled with gratitude for all that he had received. Early morning carried him into a restful, serein sleep. When his body was replenished, Trebor woke up and, in no hurry, took in his surroundings, for he knew that this was the last time he would see them. And he was at peace with that.

After a short while, when he was ready, he went out the building, then the chauffeur drove him one last time to the harbor. He had planned to fly to Seoul, South Korea, and from there, he did not know yet how, but he knew he would find his way to the labor camp in North Korea, where his mother died and from where he had been taken away and saved. He assumed that the camp was still there and crammed with prisoners, but he needed to see it with his own, adult eyes. Trebor wanted to know, to understand his sense in life.

LOOKING INTO THE PAST

Arriving in the Korean peninsula, although the place of his birth, a thing that Trebor did not know until a few days before, it had now become a place of deep interest for him. Trebor, observant watch tried to penetrate beyond what was visible to everyone, searching for clues, smells, sounds, language intonations, anything that could awaken some vague recognition. But there was not much coming back to him, or at least nothing that he could be sure of.

Once arrived in town, Trebor went to the American Embassy on Sejong-daero, in Seoul, obtaining a private visit with the secretary of the ambassador, to whom he explained the reason of his visit. Although properly adopted over thirty years before by a Hong Kong native, he was an American registered citizen. He wanted to find any possible link with family members that might have been imprisoned and died in one of the labor camps in North Korea.

The matter was unusual and confusing, and Trebor could have been very well dismissed politely after a few minutes of dialog, but the secretary was struck by the passion and the exceptional personality of this man, whose handsome features were as unusual as his request. After trying very hard to come with a practical solution, suddenly the embassy employee had an idea, there might be some records of secret missions no longer considered classified containing some information pointing toward the functioning of that particular camp, in the northeast side of North Korea.

Trebor thanked the secretary who made a phone call to obtain an introduction to the commander of the military base, and, without much conviction, he was on his way to the military grounds. His meeting with the commander was short, but efficient, and Trebor was directed to meet with the archivist of the base. After a quick introduction, Trebor asked the private to look back into a 30-years period, who complied entering a few keywords into a sophisticated computerized system. Seconds after, Michael, the 'geek' of the base, started punching key strokes like playing a video game, the only person so far thinking of the unusual request being just a child's play. At a 'lighting speed' he scrolled down screen after screen, Trebor wandering when he had the time to spot anything of importance among so much data, himself quite a computer wizard. Then, he heard:

"Here is something interesting, let's take a look", and the two of them got closer to the page shining on the monitor.

"There is a marriage registration by the base chaplain made on 17 of January, 1990", and as Trebor's heart jumped, he added, "it is between a Joseph Michael Godson, 28, American citizen, and Mai Lee, from North Korea, 19 years old."

"This is it!", Trebor shouted, not containing his surprise and joy at the same time. "I knew it, he must be my real father and she is my twin sister, thinking of the two people he met at the airport in San Francisco. This explains everything!"

Now it was time for the kind private to be confused. But Trebor, caught in the frenzy of excitement, pressed on to find more about the couple. Thus, Michael entered the names found and was looking for more information, as he was stating, "it must be a secret marriage, or at least not officially known by the North Korean authorities, even today such an alliance is forbidden. Good Lord, we are talking about a Noko and an American here!"

At the enormity of the revelation, Trebor slumped into a seat next to the desk, and suddenly becoming invaded with an immense sadness, murmured: "You must be right, she died in a labor camp later that year, giving birth to twins. She was my mother!"

Startled, the young man turned around and, deeply moved, said: "Just tell me what I can do." Then, shortly after he became very excited: "let's see what happened to him, to your dad."

In no time, Trebor found out that Joseph Godson was a very highly considered special force officer, that he came back to Seoul a few more times, but he never again crossed the norther border. He continued to work for the government, and he is still active in San Francisco area.

"He must work for CIA or something, or he stayed with the 'Specials', because I don't find specific military orders any longer."

After a little while, they soon exhausted all information, with the exception of Joseph Godson's address found by the computer specialist in some declassified files, at least the one he was able to provide to Trebor, which was going back to 1995.

"What are you counting to do now?", his new friend Michael, asked.

"Sincerely, I don't know, but I am sure that I want to go to the place my mother died. I will try to get in touch with my father, and from there, who knows, I will follow my instincts", then he asked, "May I have my parents' wedding certificate, would you print it for me?"

"Of course, and everything I found and is not classified", and he provided Trebor with a bundle of papers, who took them as the most precious gift he ever received.

Michael did not let Trebor leave before he escorted him to the Operations Office next door, and he introduced Trebor to his colleagues. There, Trebor made a long visit, and left only after he received a detailed briefing about the situation in Democratic People's Republic of Korea. The whole team could not give Trebor but general directions and advise him, since he was a civilian, and there was no question of accompanying him in his research. But they were adamant, Trebor needed to get closer to the northeast side of Korea going through China and approaching from there the area of his interest. Trebor had a dual residency through his adoptive parents from Hong Kong, thus Chinese citizenship, easily opening to Trebor a free access to his traveling to China mainland. Considering this plan of action, he listened to the tactical experts, who pinned on a map the points of his expedition and along with this, they gave him suggestions of how to dress and were to find shelter and food.

Filled with great hopes, soon after Trebor was ready for his perilous trip into the unknown.

CHAPTER 4 - TRIBULATIONS

LI, THE NEW FRIEND

Reaching the corner of southeast China would have required crossing a small coastal portion of Russia, which meets with North Korea along the Sea of Japan. Trebor found a way, though, with a China Airline flight from Seoul to Vladivostok connecting with Yanbian in China, without needing a visa for Russia. From Yanbian he thought renting a car and going alongside of North Korean border with China through rural areas and with less busy roads. He intended to reach Tianci Tourism Holiday Village, as a reason given to the Chinese authorities regarding his trip.

Arriving to Tianci, Trebor was planning on renting a tent or a small cabin and, avoiding to attract too much attention, he would attempt small trips on remote paths toward Heysan and Samsu on the other side of the border. Entering into the territory of his interest it was also penetrating the most dangerous sites he would visit, where labor camps were close to 'former' nuclear testing and enriching plans. Trebor hoped to find a soulful Chinese peasant, who, for a large retribution, would accompany him, or at least give him directions where he could slip through the guarded points and approach the forbidding sites of Northern Korean secret 'reeducation' camps.

It was interesting to observe how quickly Trebor had to adjust to another world as soon as he landed in Yanbian, China. Leaving Seoul, a super metropole boasting the latest electronic equipment and sophistication of an explosive economy, there was a significant transition to a more modest place such as Yanbian. Stepping out of the airplane, there was very little of the luxurious decor he had lived in most of his life. After passing through an inquisitor check at the customs, Trebor, against all his efforts to appear modestly dressed and appointed, made immediately an impression of a very affluent traveler, and he was asked to complete another form, as an excuse giving the time to the custom agents to study him a little longer. Complying with the added formality, leaning against a small table aside from the passengers' flow, Trebor pulled out a very pricy silver pen adorned with engraved designs and started filling out the form. It was a pen escaping his own security checkup before the trip and not replaced with something more modest. Soon after, he noticed the look of the young agent in front of him riveted on the silver pen, which he followed as if he were hypnotized by it.

"Do you like my pen? You can have it."

The agent shook his head like awaken from a sleep and mumbled something like a refusal.

"If not for yourself, give it to your wife, a gift from me" added Trebor with a disarming smile.

The agent looked around while he was pocketing the pen, then, taking the form Trebor was filling, crumbled it in his hand and tossed it in a paper basket under the desk.

Then, making a sign to Trebor to follow him and baring an air of self-importance, led him to the exit door. After saying a few words to the door agents, the custom agent gave a node to Trebor and turned his heels back to his post.

Trebor realized that he had just learned his first lesson of navigating the deep communist system.

Going to a modest rental car desk, a sign informed him that there were no cars available. And it was a good thing that Trebor spoke and read fluently Chinese, as a longtime resident of Hong Kong, for there were no signs written in any other foreign language either. Disappointed, Trebor went out of the unpretentious airport building, searching for a bus station or other form of transportation. He saw a few 'taxicabs' looking mostly as private-bitten down cars offering their services without much success. When an older man approached him and babbled something in a dialect he could not understand, Trebor made a sign that he was looking for a bus. Quite desperate, the old man insisted and Trebor told him gently that he was looking for the bus station for he was going far out, some 80 -100 miles out of town.

With a smile showing many missing teeth, the man looked at him: "Miles?"

"Oh, yes, some 150 -180 kilometers", Trebor answered.

The man started swaying his whole head, "I can do it, I can do it!"

There was a kindness in these supplicating eyes that Trebor decided on the spur of the moment to accept. Trebor had exchanged some Hong Kong dollars into RMB or Renminbi, more often called Yuan by the country people. Trebor, after a quick calculation for a value seven times lesser than the American dollar, and what would the conversion of $100 be in yuans, he started counting bills of 100 yuans, thinking that seven of them should be acceptable for a part of the trip. At the count of five bills, the old man reached for the money and smiling, pulled him away from the airport entrance pointing at a small van parked a little farther by the curb.

The van was an old Baojun or of similar manufactured model, but it looked like the owner had been taking good care of it, quite clean and large enough inside. As Trebor did not have any other choices, he dropped his small duffle bag on the back of the car and sat on the front passenger seat as he was directed. Soon, they were on the road, quickly leaving the outskirts of Yanbian, the view offering a nice landscape between the high hills and the wooded areas. They went south on G201 until Longjing, and although it was almost dark, Trebor insisted to continue after a brief stop to fuel and have a bowl of soup at the eatery on the side walk of the gas station. His desire was to reach Helong before resting for the night, although that would be another 50-60 kms on country roads. As his driver had no objections, they continued their ride on a deserted looking lane.

If at the beginning of their trip the two of them were silent and observing the road, after the simple meal they shared, Trebor probed the man with questions about him and his family.

"Li, Kuan Li is my name", said the driver in a slight Cantonese dialect. "My family, the Kuan family, is from the mountain area a little more south from here. I went to work on a factory close to Beijing, there was not much left in our hills to live on when the private produce selling was no longer possible. The people in the mountain and hill country already barely made it selling their meagre vegetable production, fruit from orchards, and some honey. The lucky ones had some tea rows and sold some timber, but the work on these terrains is difficult even when using a yack, usually shared by the whole family to pull the plow.

"Transportation was already slow with a few carts, but when the Cultural Revolution started in 1949, all animals were requisitioned by Chairman Mao during the collectivization. The roads are still unpracticable during the rainy season, but since late 1970s some people could save and have a bicycle, or even a motorcycle, or like me, a car."

Trebor listened quietly, trying to absorb all this information transporting him into another domain, suddenly finding himself into a completely different world from the one he had known until now. Li seemed to recognize right the way that Trebor, indeed, pertained to a place very different from his, and did not ask questions. Instead, he continued to feed Trebor with precious information, talking in shreds of simple sentences.

"When I could no longer work in the textile factory, I longed of coming back to my homeland I missed since I was a teenage boy. My parents died soon after I came back home, then we were forced to sell the land around my village including my family farm, for the electrical dam project. I had an older sister who is a teacher and who married an electrician, both living in Beijing, with no intention of coming back. So, we took the money, we had no choice, it seemed at that time a lot of money, but a pity for the price of a farm kept in the family for hundreds of years. And it happened that the dam was a mistake, the villages that weren't flooded, were buried under mudslides!"

After a long silence, Li continued:

"I had the money, all right, but no place under the sun where to live. So, I bought a car and went to a bigger city to earn a living as a taxi driver. I want to do this as long as I can, I don't want to go to the old-people's home, that's the end for anyone going there." Then Li added after a while, "There are not many things a man can do as private business in China, unless one has connections and is well up in the Party. But driving a cab is possible, it doesn't cost anything to the government and it is a needed service, only thing is that with the price of the car, of the gas, and all the rest to have a license, what am I saying, the maintenance, there is little left to make a living."

Again silence, and Trebor was thinking that Li, like many other people offering their services, had the intention to get his pity complaining about his misery. However, he asked:

"And your family, where are they, do you have a wife, children?"

Li seemed suddenly faraway in his thoughts, "Oh, I married a beautiful girl, the prettiest thing I ever laid my eyes on. But I was working all the time, so was she. We did not spend a lot of time together and she died quite young, lung disease from all the city fumes. Oh, it was terrible to see her suffocating until she could no longer take a breath. We had a boy, it's all that the Party allowed, one child. Jie is my pride, but he had an accident, he was in construction. He fell from one of the scaffoldings of these high-rise monsters and he is paralyzed, his spine broken from waist down. He is in a center, has no life, no money. I visit him when I can and bring him a few things to change his mind. I brought him a transistor radio he loves to listen to. Not long ago, I had a good deal on a CD reader and I bring him Chinese music every time I go to see him. Oh, he loves listening to that machine!", Li kept telling the story of his life with such love in his eyes.

Slowly, Trebor, moved by the tender tale Li shared with him, became aware of a deeper realization. There were people who, during their life time never had anything exciting or lavish, but they were content, very little bringing them so much satisfaction, if it were only to make another one happy for a little while.

CLOSE TO WHERE ALL BEGAN

It was already dark when Li drove his car into Helong, and traversing the sleepy town, he spotted a sign on a side country road indicating that someone offered to rent space in his home for the night. Trebor grasped the advantage of having Li with him, who was accustomed with half-hinting messages the locals tried to pass on, information that otherwise he would have completely missed.

They found a simple but modern construction, the sole bedroom furnished with two twin beds and used as source of income by the owners, who stayed in an old shack when they had customers in their house. Li and Trebor entered the main room, then next to it, they were shown with pride a simple wash room with a sink, flushing toilette, and a shower head in the corner with only cold water available, running directly on the bathroom floor.

Li seemed enchanted with the place, and after they disposed their bags for the night on the side of the beds, Trebor noticed that Li had already talked to the owners and coming back, he let him know that they were bringing some hot soup and rice for them to have supper in the lounge room. Again, Trebor was grateful for having hired Li, who, not only helped to avoid attracting too much attention over a stranger traveling on his own, he was also a valuable resource knowing the local customs.

A hot bowl of soup placed on the table by a middle-aged man and a simple brown rice wooden bowl carefully carried by his wife, seemed to restore some of the fatigue of this long day. However, they took turns for a shower, enjoying to refresh before a good restful night, Li insisting that it should do them good for the day laying ahead.

The most valuable item Trebor carried with him was a satellite telephone. Its miniaturized shape made it look like a regular cell phone, very important detail that allowed him to go through the customs without additional search or questioning. Anticipating that he would have a hard time to always find the right charging outlets, he had brought along a couple of additional lithium batteries. The phone's vast memory containing all the contacts Trebor thought necessary, had a high speed google and internet access, and most of all, a detailed GPS capability. While Li was taking his shower, Trebor checked his messages and had a brief look at the map of their location, deciding that for now, he would keep the existence of the telephone for himself.

Before falling quickly into a deep sleep, Trebor wondered if he could remember having to share his room with someone else, especially a stranger. Early risen and feeling refreshed after a simple tea coup offered by their hosts, they found the road back to their destination. The day was clear with a cool temperature, announcing a beautiful late spring weather. By the mid-day, Li pointed out to a green area, where Tianci recreational village was located, a roughly triangular park of some 30 miles each edge, with three small lakes, the larger one shared with DPRK.

As Li was feeding him with information about the area, Trebor was considering the best place to set camp, when Li came with a very ingenious idea:

"It would be good to stay close to the lake; it is nice, still quiet this time of the year and there is a running water and bathroom facility. If I don't impose too much, I can hang out for a while, you can get a car parking spot instead of a tent and we can manage to sleep in my car. I can arrange it better than you would be in the tent, and we can move during the day as we want." At last, Li dropped his real concern, "and with me, you would look less 'attractive'."

"Only if you let me compensate you the way I think is right; I really appreciate your offer and I know I am taking you away from your occupations", said Trebor, also thinking that Li was practically reading his mind; he could easily see the advantages of having a local 'guide' with him.

This said, Trebor slid a roll of banknotes into Li's palm, both having decided that it was best if Li was dealing with the payments of the camping site, food, and other immediate needs. And Li appeared to be a terrific negotiator even in Trebor's eyes, who also noticed that Li's demeanor and age called for respect. Thus, they ended up with a nice shaded camping spot close to the water, but high enough and not too far from a small concrete construction which housed toilettes and separate showers for men and women. On one side of their parking slot, which was accessible through a narrow winding alley and hidden by thick foliage, they found a flattened area with a fire pit at its center, and since there was no other parking or tent space next to theirs, it looked like it was an ideal place for them only.

Happy with their accommodations, Li had made some practical decisions while at the camp entrance, renting two folding chairs and a table, a gas lamp, and bought a large drinking water container, along with a couple of flashlights. Then, they purchased some fruit and potatoes, rice and bean cans, some plastic plates, utensils for eating and cooking, and even some toilet paper. Bringing all this to their car, Li told Trebor that in the morning he will scour a little the area to find some eggs, milk, and even some fresh produce from the small local farms. Trebor helping to load the goods in the car, whispered to Li that it would be useful to get a plan of the park and its surroundings, "just in case, not to get lost" he said, although he already had the place mapped on his phone.

Li, came back with a mischievous look in his face and handed Trebor a collection of brochures enticing the visitors to discover all the corners of the park and its hidden treasures.

Trebor thank him, then added "One more thing, I am an avid bird watcher and I need to buy a camera with long-range lenses and a simple manual with the most encountered birds in these hills", with little hope his request could be easy to fulfill.

Li was already grinning through his neglected teeth, pointing to a small booklet he had found at the welcome center filled with designs of beautiful birds. Then, he said:

"They have some cameras too, I saw in the main hall some fancy shops and a photo gallery as well."

This said, Li moved the car from the reception building closer to the side door of the shopping area, and the two of them made a tour of the place. After taking a good look at the cameras, Trebor decided for a Laika with the complete equipment that included an electronic chip instead of films, and added a couple of batteries along with a battery charger using a car cigarette lighter. With the camera bag strapped on his shoulder, now Trebor gave the impression of a regular tourist, and he adventured to enter other stores and, making a few more purchases, help boost the Chinese economy. He left with two good quality down sleeping bags, two fluffy jackets for the fresh evenings, a couple of sweat pants and shirts, rubber boots for the rain, and undergarments. Loading Li with some of the bags, Trebor grabbed a pair of woolen hats, sunglasses, and visors on his way out.

Dropping all their findings in the car, which became nicely loaded, Li could not help but act like a child on Christmas morning. Never had he known someone buying so many wonderful things in one place. He accompanied in occasion some well off tourists coming from the big cities and he always dreamed of what would be having the means to buy some of those nice goods! And now, he realized that this time he would even enjoy some of them!

After having refreshed at the water pavilion, set camp, and finished a dinner skillfully prepared by Li, and admired a quiet sunset by the lake, Trebor preferred to set his sleeping bag outdoors for the night. He was watching a starry sky while pondering about various angles of approaching his plan. They would take a tour of the lake as close as possible to the borderline with North Korea, pretending visiting and observing birds nesting in spring time. He hoped that his camera lenses and the binoculars would bring into his field of vision some of the activity on the other side of the border. Trebor thought also of fighting his impulse to rush into the North

Korean territory, now that he felt so close to the place where his mother had suffered and died giving birth to him and his sister.

According to his plan, the day after and the following day, Trebor accompanied by Li, acted as tourists appreciating the natural beauty of different sites of the park. At times, they were close to the frontier, where the Korean side seemed deserted under undeveloped brush and arid high hills. However, Trebor sighted beyond the tips of the hills some smoke raising to the sky across from the middle area of the park and sharing the central lake, while at the east and south endings of the park, the border seemed quite reinforced and well-guarded.

Li, always eager to help and show appreciation for this unexpected vacation offered by his client, made a tour of the neighboring villages with his car and came back proudly bringing fresh eggs, mushrooms, some yams and a variety of onions. During this time, Trebor rented a bicycle shortly after their arrival to the camp and combed the area, leisurely moving to different corners of the holiday village. He occasionally stopped, scrutinizing the trees and the sky with his binoculars, as if diligently studying the birds' activity. Coming back to the camp site, the add couple enjoyed pleasant meals sitting at their table facing the lake, when Trebor listened to Li's counts of his little incursions.

It was the third night when Trebor arranged his sleeping bag for another night under the stars. Li had allowed him long moments of solitude, respecting his client's privacy, and Trebor had leeway to check the terrain configuration along with the roads and constructions indicated on his GPS. He was glad his I-Satphone Pro was equipped with the ultimate combination of location and the batteries offered a duration up to one week before needing to be recharged. But tonight, he would not resist any longer the urge to explore the forbidden territory on the other side of the Chinese border. Wearing dark clothes and a black head cover, Trebor felt confident that, with the help of an overcast sky, night goggles, and the map shown in details on his GPS he engraved in his memory, he could attempt a discreet exploration.

Like a shadow, Trebor hugged the crevasses of the arid hills on his way up to the summit, where he hoped to have an open view of the area at the foot of the slops. He knew that a good 20 miles south east from there he should distinguish the lights of a city called Samjiyon. As he had seen on the GPS readings, at his feet he could make up the outline of some low concrete buildings, mostly covered with dirt and overgrown grass, and beyond that were barracks disposed on three rows along with a few other simple constructions. That site extended easily over 1-2 miles and it was lit only on a few points by ordinary poles or hanging bulbs over an entrance door here and there. But, wait a minute, there was a ray of spotlight swiping around the range encircling the barracks! Then another and another, placed at each corner of a rectangular zone and its entrance, now visibly made of barbed wires. He also noticed that the lights were oriented mostly toward the ground.

With an increased interest to find out more about the function of this compound, Trebor ventured a couple more miles into the Korean land. There was a country road winding east then reaching the main motorway and, as he could remember the diagram shown on GPS, linking Samjiyon to Pochon, some 30 miles south and very close to the border with China. Staying close to the remote road of this seemingly isolated territory, Trebor could not make much of the buildings at the foot of the mountains, almost hidden underneath, but he had little doubt of the barracks close to them, they belonged to a prisoner camp fully functioning.

Shaken by his discovery, the place that might be the one he was searching for, Trebor realized that he went well into the Korean zone. He hurried back following closely a small affluent of the Tumen River, then rounded the lake discreetly returning to China, before reaching the small incline of their camping site. He had spent most part of the night rummaging through some four miles of a hostile domain, and he realized how close he had come to being seen and apprehended at any moment. Replaying in his mind the trajectory of his incursion, his reasoning reminded him that he was not in a free world by any means, nor was he in a western country, where people on vacation could go about their hobbies and stroll as they wish at night in the mountains.

Before falling asleep, Trebor felt satisfied, he made a big step ahead into the unknown and a clearer design developed in his mind. And above all, he realized he was not afraid.

NIGHT VISITS AND OLD DREAMS

A delicious smell of fried eggs and coffee tickled Trebor's nares, making him come back into the real world and slowly open his eyes. Not far from the patch of grass where Trebor had laid his sleeping bag, Li was making breakfast, a master of bringing the fire pit alive with pots and pans simmering with his special preparations. It was well into the morning hours of this beautiful spring day, the air crisp and the surroundings serein. Besides the birds chirping merrily with Li joining in with a soft whistle, there was nobody around. Trebor, stretching as far as his lungs could fill with the fresh mountain air, joined Li, sat on a chair and smiled with anticipation at the food displayed in front of him. They shared another wonderful meal, not talking much, although Li was trying to read his friend's dealings.

"You know, I can help you if you need to go somewhere. It can make it easier for you to get around, and avoid you to get in trouble", he added with a hinting grin.

Trebor dismissed the offer without much explanation, thinking of what Li might be guessing, but determined to keep him 'out of trouble'. He felt a warm friendship growing between them, such different people, but remaining firm in his decision to avoid his friend any harm. Thus, they hanged together for the day, taking nice bike rides in the park's far side from the border, stopping at the other lakes to watch the ducklings, and finally have a quiet dinner at sunset.

Setting for an early night, Trebor planned on making another short incursion over the hills and explore more on the labor camp site. He wanted to have a clearer idea of how to penetrate the place and eventually to venture himself further into the Korean territory. Trebor, searching the web, learned that an international team was dispatched to verify that the nuclear sites in the northeast region located below and running alongside Tumen River were disabled, as Kim Jong Un had promised. He was already informed that many of the labor camps were also located in the vicinity of the 'former' enriching plutonium and testing sites for the convenient use of prisoners for digging and maintaining the nuclear plants. Trebor thought that if he could make a contact with the team of inspectors and eventually join them, it would be easier for him to approach the sites of his interest. He knew it was an enormous gamble, but he did not have many choices trying to penetrate the territory of a country notoriously isolating its population and where secrecy and fear were the routine practices maintaining the power of its dictators.

A few hours after the nightfall, Trebor, trying not to make any noise, left and disappeared into the brushes, feeling a little more confident about the configuration of the land. He found out that the underground buildings having access through heavy steel doors seemed abandoned or at least not in function. Trebor thought that the site might be closed, ready for the upcoming inspection, while patrol guards paced regularly checking the two or three entrances. Conversely, the near-by prisoner camp was patrolled more frequently by guards using flashlights, and sometimes dogs.

After taking note of the direction of the rounds and their frequency, Trebor decided it was time for him to return to the security of his sleeping bag. A little more at ease retracing his path, he was gingerly approaching the Chinese side of the lake, on its last quarter of mile of the Korean banks, when he saw the silhouette of a soldier clearly detaching against the lake. Still covered by a light brush, Trebor retrieved deeper in the wooden area, careful not to break any branches, and continued to observe the soldier. He heard him singing while relieving himself in the lake, a cigarette still burning on his lips. Then, he turned and called his patrol mate, whose answer came only a few yards away from Trebor's hiding place. The second soldier went to meet the one by the lake, where they stayed for a few minutes. Straining to take a glimpse at some activity on the other side where the visitors of the park might be, the border patrol turned around after a while and went back without hurry on the direction of the barracks. Although Trebor did not understand Korean, he picked on a few Mandarin words and had the impression that the two guards envied the Chinese who could afford vacations and such 'nice facilities'.

With his heart still thumbing widely in his chest, Trebor was elated to find his camping bag a few moments later and hide inside. "This was close! Next time watch it, buddy!", he thought before falling asleep.

In the late hours of the night, when sleep is the deepest and the sweetest, Trebor was visited again by the 'the dream', the nightmare that haunted him his entire life. The same heart-tearing cries, then mixed with his own whimper and of somebody else's wail. As the weeping became weaker, the other two increased to despair, then they gave up. Trebor woke up, pulling himself out of the terror. He knew every detail of the dream, he knew that the end of it was a terrifying silence, where no one would answer.

His breath rapid and shallow, Trebor sat up. He did not scream this time, and if in the dream there was fear, he was not frightened any longer. Because now, Trebor understood the sense of the dream: it was the story of his own birth. The crying was of his own mother, longing to hold him, them, his twin sister and him, when her life was leaving her body abandoned to bleed to death. And, as her soul was leaving her tortured physique, the soul continued to linger over the twins she just brought to life, enveloping them with her love, an immense love to follow them and to protect them for their entire life. This dream was a reminder that, through suffering and death, she was still there with them, surrounding them with her love beyond any barrier of time or space.

Trebor spent the entire day preparing for what he knew it was the new stage in his life, a very different one from what he had lived until now. Without completely understanding the reason of it, he was pulled into going to the place of his birth, it was a force bigger than his own comprehension, higher than his own desire.

During the day, Trebor continued to act as usual, while in his mind he revised his plan, more than ever resolute to pursue.

In the morning that followed, when he woke up, Li found a small zipper bag with a note on the top of it. In the note Trebor explained to Li that he went with 'some friends' he met and he wanted to explore some other parts of China. He also indicated that, if he was not returning within 72 hours not to wait for him and to return to his occupations. Li was to keep everything and not to leave anything behind, and that he will find in the bag an envelope with some money to compensate him for his kindness. When Li looked at the sum of money, he found a true fortune that would allow him not to have to work until the end of his life. Thanking him for all the good services and calling him as his real friend, Trebor added that in the bag was also a smart phone activated and this would be the way for Trebor to get in touch with him if he should need his services in the future. He insisted telling Li that he could leave without worrying about him.

CHAPTER 5 - TRANSFORMATION

40 DAYS OF FASTING

Trebor attempted to move an arm when an atrocious pain invaded his entire body. Then, he tried to take a deeper breath and a sharp sting like a lightning rod stacked on his right chest stopped him. Quietly and patiently he waited for the hurt to lessen as he did it many times lately, and started to recall where he was and reflect on what happened this time. Because this time he remained unconscious for a longer time than the others. His torturers had taken him to the water boarding, one more time as he had been brought there again and again, had a suffocating rubber cover thrown over his head, making an artificial separation from the water flowing without respite. He had been the object of sadistic jokes of these men enjoying leaving him under the jets more than any human being could have ever endured, hoping to see him break, and beg. But Trebor held on like he did not care anymore, passing out after a while and later finding himself in this cell.

At last, Trebor could move his neck to one side, slightly, for his head felt like it might explode under pressure, then he looked around. His eyes accommodated to the complete darkness and he recognized his cubicle of 8x10 feet, all concrete, including the cold slab on which he laid with no pillow, nor sheets or blankets. But he preferred this isolation cell to the cage kept continuously under a glaring light.

Trebor remembered so clearly leaving the camping place in the wee hours of the night, after cautiously placing his instructions to Li next to his sleeping bag. Crossing the frontier with North Korea it seemed easier this time, and he reached the valley next to an entrance that looked like the access to a tunnel or an underground construction. He found a hiding place above the valley and spent the entire day observing the movements at the bottom of the mountain. Then, the following night, Trebor managed to approach the labor camp from the more distant side from the hills, which appeared to be a little more isolated and the guards rounded les frequently.

Although carrying a light equipment with him, his night goggles and a pair of strong insolating gloves along with a pair of cutters, these few items allowed Trebor to enter and hide on the dark side of a small building. Trebor had noticed some activity in this block close to an enclosure that did not have a tower guard, but allowed vehicles to enter the camp without stopping through the main control. He managed to reach a shadowy spot under a window, when he stopped hearing groaning and moaning, sounds escaping from a small horizontal opening at the top of the window which allowed a small flow of fresh air to enter the room. Trebor had to calm his heart from jumping out of his chest, so much in disbelief of what he was hearing. At times, a few cries screeched through the night, to be quickly followed by silence.

Removing his night goggles, Trebor swiftly crouched to the next window finding a small dirt elevation from where he could take a peek inside the room. To his horror, Trebor saw something like a hospital room, where four beds were ranged by two against opposite walls of the room, and where a man and a woman in scrubs acted as doctor and nurse attending to patients. A summary look at the 'patients' made it clear that they were agonizing, bearing signs of corporeal torture with open wounds and black bruises, some showing limbs hanging at abnormal angles as if having been broken. With devastating revulsion, he could not help but notice that the patients were all very young, and that the medical personnel were not there to attend to them. They were talking to each other on a detached manner, ignoring the calls coming from the patients still awake. 'Doctor and nurse' moved from one bed to another making a sort of inventory, at times slowly turning or probing the unfortunate patients, causing them to shriek louder, in extreme misery.

With the head turning and feeling as getting sick at the horrific scene, Trebor exited the camp and hid on a close by brush. However, that appeared to be a good call, since a small white ambulance was approaching. Entering through a segment of the camp enclosure which opened as an emergency gate, the ambulance stayed there for a while. After about 30-40 minutes, the ambulance tech and the nurse came out from the small building, each of them carrying two big ice coolers which they quickly loaded into the ambulance. There were no more cries or screams coming from the building, and the ambulance left at high speed, leaving a sinister silence behind.

"The monsters, they still harvest organs from prisoners. They torture them until they are almost dead, then they remove their organs while they are still alive! And they make money selling organs from people they kill with all impunity."

Seething through his breath Trebor, started retching uncontrollably, then, as in a trance, he went to an isolated wooden mount to spend the night, for he would come back next evening and try to take pictures and record what is happening in the labor camps of North Korea. Trebor was determined to show to the whole world how his mother had died and how the fate of other thousands unfortunate human beings remained unchanged.

Curled up on his parka, Trebor let his body yield to the emotions and fatigue of his sinister discovery and found rest in a dreamless sleep. Strangely enough, the morning came announced by happy bird songs and the trumpet of a faraway rooster call, making believe that the rising sun shone over a peaceful world. Fully alert, Trebor first checked his surroundings, and reassured, summarily cleaned and relieved his body, almost smiling at the images of his luxurious morning routine of a life he left behind only recently. He drunk a good amount of water from his thermos and opened a power bar for his breakfast, then he relocated his observation point for a long day ahead.

And he did not have to wait for long, the doors of the barracks opened and each of them emptied in a central court, where a line formed for the regular count of the prisoners. Then, the prisoners slowly passed by a distribution window holding a small metal bowl, and with the tin canister filled, they found a place to swallow down the pasty mixture and drink some water from the same bowl filled at a simple faucet.

Soon, the line formed again, and about one hundred detainees were joined by guards. With one hand on the shoulder of the front inmate, an Indian-line exited the main gate and went directly to the closest door entering the underground structures, where they disappeared for the duration of the day. The other group of captives, looking older than the ones that just left, was directed to one of the fourth barracks, and they also stayed there until sunset. As the day went by, Trebor observed the activity in the camp, as occasionally the door of the barrack where the prisoners entered opened and barrels of laundry were pushed out, containing sheets, clothes, and other items to be hanged in the back court. In the afternoon the dried laundry was brought into another barrack, after which stacks of folded ironed items were disposed on a platform ready to be taken somewhere.

When the convicts working underground finally came back, and after they were all called to order, the same process restarted with bowls filled with some food and water drunk from the faucet. Then, a whistle was heard, and one by one the prisoners rushed to the latrines at the sound of it. It was not long after, that a strident siren gave the signal for everyone to regain their barracks, then the lights went off, with another day of the political prisoners coming to its end. But as Trebor witnessed soon after, not all of them would see another morning.

Surprisingly enough, some of the camp wardens continued their activities; two old looking trucks with their back covered with fabric tarpaulin arrived, armed soldiers dropped the tailgates, and, letting out nasty guttural hollers, started shoving down the newly arrived detainees in shackles. Their clothes were already in shreds and they had visible bruises and bleeding cuts, some of them falling when pushed by the guards. Orders that could be heard in the entire area, had the evident intention to make everyone's blood curl at the sound of the soldiers' boorish voices. And the unexpected continued, as the fresh load of prisoners were indicated the direction of the underground buildings, where they entered a side door through which they disappeared.

The night commotion did not end with the arrival of the new inmates, as Trebor continued to observe, astonished. He moved closer to the foot of the hill where the covered structures housed now new prisoners. An hour or so later, the door that was used by the workers in the morning, opened, and a few shadowy people looking very much like some of the new prisoners, came out pushing wheelbarrows. Directed by watching armed guards, they wheeled their carts to an isolated area of the camp, then tilting the barrels, dropped a dozen of dead bodies on the ground. After the corpses were covered summarily with white caustic lime, then pushed together in a shallow hole, were sprinkled with gasoline and set on fire.

"Thus, they get rid of the ones who short-lived their imprisonment. Newly arrived dispose the bodies of the ones making place for them!", thought Trebor, riveted by the horrific scene.

Then, more was to unfold, like a continuation of a living hell. Another hour into the night, more bodies were carried out, this time only four or five of them and moving. They were wheeled into the building located at the opposite side of the camp. The same building Trebor had watched the night before, where organs were removed from still alive young detainees!

After a while, summoning all his courage and determination, and before the ambulance was to come fetching their lugubrious harvest, Trebor reached the place from where he could look inside. He started taking pictures without having to worry about angles and lighting, the subject was clear as day: people suffering atrociously, then barely silenced with a gag of chloroformed gauze, their beautiful and young bodies were slashed and organs taken out in a hurry, after which they were stashed on ice buckets.

Trebor was so drown into the drama unfolding under his eyes, he almost could feel the suffering of the innocent victims, but, with tears welling down his cheeks, he continued to take pictures and at times to record the atrocities taking place. This is when he felt a slight tap on his shoulder, then a sharp stubbing on his side that took his breath away. Folding over, Trebor was in seconds covered with blows of fists and boots kicking him from everywhere and crushing him all over, then dragged by soldiers screaming and celebrating this unexpected pray to satisfy their thirst of blood and violence.

MEETING THE FATHER

Transported into his own world, to another level of consciousness from where he could review with great clarity all that had happened in this more recent part of his life, Trebor was able to completely remove himself from the limits of this miserable isolation cell. He knew that he was sequestrated in high security at the lowest level of this former nuclear enriching plutonium plant, now serving as annex to the 'Rehabilitation Camp # 12', soon after being apprehended. For some reason he was tortured and interrogated here, without being taken to the capital and making big front-page lines on the international publications. He found out that this former nuclear site had been disabled a few years earlier because of dangerous seismic movements produced by the subterranean testing explosions, followed by the collapse of some galleries risking leakage of nuclear material.

The proximity of the labor camp had shown to be useful before the gallery collapse, when manpower was necessary for the initial digging of the galleries, then their maintenance. Presently, it served as interrogation center for high security purposes, in addition to the need of constant repairs and verification of the remaining nuclear waste. The illicit trade of harvesting organs for transplants had been perpetrated here without interruption, as it has been done in many other 'rehabilitation' camps or other state prisons.

And now, Trebor was aware that his turn had come, he had been rendered useless, except for his still healthy internal organs. He understood the reason of him being kept for so long under water-boarding this last time, his tormentors expected him to fall into a coma and make easier the extraction of the 'treasures' his body contained.

What Trebor was not aware of, though, was that orders from the capital came for the site to close right the way, although temporarily, for an international commission was arriving to inspect the place. It had been found that this former nuclear site was perfect for reassuring the international security delegation, as the testing had been already suspended for a while and would only require to conceal its present utilization, interrogating high security prisoners.

Hence, Trebor was ready for the cell door to open any moment and to be carried away, rendered half-unconscious while cut open. As he was preparing himself for the last episode of his terrestrial life, he started praying, for as high as his soul emerged, the flesh it occupied recoiled like a child, defenseless and frightened.

And without knowing from where the words came, Trebor whispered: "My Father, if it be possible, let this cup pass from me; nevertheless, not as I will, but as You will." (Jesus in Gethsemane, Mathew 26:39)

Time, unmeasurable time, since Trebor had lost count of hours, days or nights, and weeks, had come and gone. He noticed that there were no more faint noises, no one had come to bring him a piece of stale rye bread or a cup of water for a while. He only smiled, telling himself "what difference would that make, anyway?", and he continued to reflect on the latest events.

During his first days of interrogation, when he was asked things making no sense to him, accused of being an American spy, of course, forcing him to agree to preposterous scenarios, at a certain moment his torturers kept his head under the bucket of dirty water for the longest. He had passed out quite a few times before, but this time it lasted so long that he was carried back into an isolation cell.

In this comatose state, Trebor's consciousness became more alive than ever, where no material limits existed. He was a living, knowledgeable energy bathing in the most beautiful, vibrant light. He had the instant recognition of it as part of our real existence, forgotten understanding of our true nature, now present along with his elevation to a higher dimension.

Reaching this new state, Trebor could see his mothers. The one who gave him birth was at his site, caressing his forehead and whispering words of love in a language he did not know, but voicing feeling he could understand.

At last, Mai could tell her son everything her infinite love had kept until the moment of their lighting. She told him that she had always been there for him, that she was very sorry she could not stay alive to care for them, but she was so very grateful she could offer her kidney to his adopting dad, Irving, allowing him to care for her son. A moment later, Mai invited Lynn Young, and Trebor could see again his adoptive mother. As Mai thank Lynn for providing her son with such a wonderful life, she also showed appreciation for her love. Then, the two of them hugged on a cloud of light, and after a while they left, as there was no need to say more.

Trebor was still in the brilliant light, advancing without effort on a path opening in front of him. Then, he saw Him, the Magnificent, the Creator of all there is. Splendor, Grace, and Love.

Because this is what Trebor felt, he was engulfed in these magnificent feelings, becoming a part of them. He felt pure joy, and he was pure Joy, Peace, and Liberation. No more pain, no more suffering, no more sadness.

"Do not fear, my son. For you are my son, as everyone else is my child. But you are a son I send with a special message for the fellow men. As I sent Jesus Christ, Buddha, Krishna, Zoroaster, and others in the past to help humanity remember of its divine origin.

"Devil humans cannot do you harm, for they have no reach over you, they have no power over you.

"The only power they have is the one that brings their own destruction."

And Trebor did not fear anymore. Every time he was hurt and tortured, then slipped into a comatose state, Trebor's soul traveled and reached complete spiritual transition. Almost every time, he met with God and asked questions about what God expected from him. And God answered to him, guided him, and He taught him.

SUNJIN

Sunjin Lee, Mai's father, miraculously survived his sentence of 20 years in the labor camp. He aged rapidly once in captivity, but against the tragedy of losing his wife and his two daughters, Sunjin endured. After a while, his tears dried out, and along with it, his body shrunk like an eucalyptus branch, and he lived on. The labor camp became his new home, then his permanent home, since he did not have another place where to go and no family waiting for him. Thus, at the end of his sentence, as the officials did not know what to do with this old man, for no one was supposed to survive past their term, the sentries allowed him to 'stick' around. Thus, Sunjin became an unofficial guard, helping with the distribution of food to the prisoners and cleaning behind the dead. For this, he received a place to stay, food, while an uniform replaced his inmate rugs.

Sunjin found a small patch of dry soil in a corner behind the barracks and cleared it up. He carried in some of the rich soil dug form the hills and started a little fresh garden. Later on, he even added a few flowers, unthinkable indulgence in these sinister grounds. The manager of the camp let him do those "thing of an old man that had lost his mind", closing his eyes and receiving regularly baskets of fresh vegetables, real luxury in these times and from such a lifeless place.

One time, Sunjin, peering through the window of the infirmary, learned that there was this special and highly unusual detainee captured. He must have been an American spy for sure, otherwise why a man possessing all his faculties would risk his life attempting to expose to the world the sinister and infamous business taking place in their sick bay. Because the camp's infirmary was not there to help the prisoners, it was to perform the most despicable actions against humanity, as it has been done, oh, so many years ago, to his beloved daughter.

For some reason not fully understood by himself, Sunjin stayed in the same camp where his wife Jia and his daughter Mai died, as if he could not leave this place, the soil containing a few flakes of their unfortunate remains. It happened that he was seen sometimes in a corner behind one of the barracks, stopping and sprinkling petals of flowers. But no one was aware that this was an older site where dead bodies were burned. No one from the new generations could remember it, as the place where their bodies had been incinerated, then buried, had changed long ago!

Against torture, suffering, deprivation of all rights and all basic needs, surviving the ugliness of humiliation and degradation, Sunjin remained a good and a decent man. Seen rather as a fixture than a prison warden, no one really paid attention as he retained quite a bit of liberty moving within the camp grounds. This peculiar status allowed him to attend, when possible, to some of the inmates in a modest and unnoticed way. A few crumbs of rotten leftovers, some fresh water, or simply a kind word had made at times the difference for somebody to give up or stay alive. During the long, harsh years of detention, Sunjin found strength within. Slowly came back to him words spoken by his priest and by his parents, in a time when people could call upon the Lord and talk about God openly. Times when a young boy like him could hope for a happy and fair future.

Although what Sunjin encountered later on had nothing to do with the words revealed in the Scriptures, he was grateful for all the gifts he considered having been graced abundantly with. He would not want anything more than the presence of his wife he had the chance to meet and share with a few years of complete happiness, to hold his two daughters and hug his grandchildren. As the time went by, Sunjin's heart filled with immense gratitude for the years of happiness granted in the past, had found in his soul the power needed to remain human. He also realized that no one could take away the moments that counted in his life, that his real power was the one of his soul, immortal, gifted to him by his Eternal Father for an eternal life over which the tyrants of this world had no command.

Sunjin thought about grandchildren, his grandchildren, for he learned that Mai gave life to two children, a boy and a girl, before leaving this Earth. He knew that someone took them and saved them from an inevitable death, and he hoped that they were well and raised by a loving family. Sunjin kept them in his heart and had them in his thoughts every single day, imagining their games, their laughter, their life. With all the longing he had of being a part of theirs, Sunjin knew that it was far better for them to be away; he had nothing to offer, but his love, and that couldn't get them anywhere from where he was! But how much, oh dear Lord, how much would he have loved to see them, to hold them, to talk to them!

With this kind of thoughts, Sunjin was shuffling toward a cell where the new prisoner was brought in, unconscious. "Dear Jesus have merci of his soul, for his head had been kept in the bucket under the water for so long! How can he even be still alive?"

Entering the cell, Sunjin stopped for a few instants to observe the young man laying without moving and his heart skipped a few beats, fearing that he might have succumbed to the evil mistreatment. Then, with immense caution and gentleness, he approached and placed a washcloth dipped in cold water over the inmate's forehead. He had almost the impression that the young man tempted to smile, and Sunjin started talking to him gentle words, soothing simple words without importance, just to give a little consolation while wiping his burning face.

The young man must have been of a very strong constitution, for he moved a little, trying to lift his head. Sunjin took advantage of it to bring to his lips a tin cup with fresh water and help the man to drink. And the young man emptied the can and sighed with great satisfaction, then opened his eyes to look at his benefactor.

"Oh, may, what a beautiful face. And his eyes are blue, how unusual!", Sunjin thought in wonder.

The young man took a few more sips of water Sunjin offered eagerly after refilling the cup. Then, seeing that the young man became very tired, he stood up and before leaving, turned and said his name: "Sunjin, my name is Sunjin."

"Trebor", was returned to him by the man before falling back on his cot.

Sunjin came later, much later in the night, just to check on the new inmate. This was awake, laying on his back, contemplating. He recognized Sunjin and seemed glad to see him, and even smiled in surprise when Sunjin started displaying food in front of him. It was all that Sunjin could scrape before the cauldrons had to be cleaned, some rice and a mixture of vegetables. But Sunjin managed to save also a few yams from his garden, he knew that they were quite nutritious, and he watched, pleased to see Trebor wolfing down every bit of the food.

"They did not give him any food since he got caught!'" thought Sunjin, angrily, and handed him a large can of water.

"Sorry" escaped from Trebor's lips, a slip of the tongue coming out in a reflex, then, "thank you", said in Chinese, when he realized he did not yet thank him. Then, "are you an angel?' came right after.

"No, No.." said Sunjin with a smile, shaking his head. Then he sat on a small crate he always carried with him when he wanted to hide stolen food. But he did not say anything more, when Trebor started talking.

"I came here to find out where my mother died. And I found the place and the way her body was used for selling her organs, instead of helping her and her children. My mother gave birth to my sister and myself, and after that she was let to bleed to death and for us to follow the same fate. And I wanted to let the whole world know what is going on within the walls of this horrible regime."

Sunjin, under the biggest shock of his life, could not speak, he could hardly breath listening to this revelation.

"Thank God, we were adopted and I grew up in a good family and my sister was eventually adopted as well."

Sunjin was trying to say something, when Trebor added again: "I am sorry, I load you with all this, but if I am to die, I would want somebody, someone kind like you, to know what happened to me too."

Finally, Sunjin muttered: "I know what happened to your mother, to my daughter. Her name is Mai, Mai Lee. And your father is Joseph Godson, and American. They married in secret and had to hide their love. What a shame!"

Trebor almost screamed, "You are talking about Mai and Joseph Godson, my parents!! Jo Godson had actually adopted Maggie, Magdalena, my sister. And he does not even know she is his real daughter!"

Mustering all his strength, Trebor stretched his arms toward Sunjin and called out: "You are my grandfather then."

Sunjin, tears finding again their way back and welling down on his parched cheeks, responded by coming to him, and wrapping his arms around his grandson he could finally hug for the first time in his life, prayed God to keep him in life a few moments longer.

"Trebor, my grand baby!"

TWO GOOD SOULS REUNITED

Thus, in the mist of suffering and tragedy, an unexpected and overwhelming joy reunited two human beings coming from such opposite worlds, but originating from the same place. Sunjin meeting his grandson in such astonishing instances, found a renewed energy, and along with it, the determination to use all his limited ways to maintain Trebor alive. His heart was filled with gratitude knowing that he had lived that long in order to be blessed seeing his grandchild.

Trebor's feelings traveled from his thirst of learning about his mother, immersing himself into what she might have been subjected to, to trying to understand, to feel the place of her last days, and, through his tortures, to share with her the unimaginable reality of such a life.

When Sunjin showed up every day and after every one of the countless punishments and tortures, Trebor received from him care, food, and words of encouragement. His words were sweet, and they were also compelling to infuse his being with strength. He told him about his mother, about the happier times when she met his father, and how much they hoped one day to be together, how courageous Mai was when she was arrested, and bitten, and humiliated. Sunjin spoke about his grandmother, Jia, and about his aunt, Sun-Hi, and how they also perished in tragic circumstances.

The two of them exchanged the images of two different experiences, two different ways of living. And along with the closeness and the love growing between grandfather and grandson, a profound abhorrence emerged for the cruel and twisted minds of a handful of people controlling the fate of so many others. While Sunjin was coming out of the torpor he lived, with his soul numbed by the loss of his family and his miserable camp existence, now fueled by the loathing of oppressive regime he lived in during his entire life, he started reflecting how to protect his grandson. Trebor was revolted by everything he had witnessed so far, by the suffering inflicted to his family, to the people of this country.

If the two of them could not prevent the hatred they had of the conditions they were inflicted to them, they could not either diminish the affection and pleasure they felt being together, the immense present destiny gifted them finding each other. And they started wondering about that. Together they searched the reason the fate reunited them.

One night, after Trebor had been carried back to his isolation cell unconscious, his face and body had been wiped and cared for by Sunjin, as usual. Trebor felt so drained and week, that after he ate a few bites and sipped some water Sunjin insisted to take, fell asleep again, almost hoping not to wake up and re-live the same days, if this was to continue on. However, in the middle of the night, Trebor regaining a little rest, woke up. Desperation mounted in his chest as a cascade and he started shouting, knowing that in this isolated place no one will hear him:

"Why, God, why all this suffering?" he let out between suffocating sobs. "And why am I here for? How can I help this people? How can I stop all this from perpetuating? And why do I have to go through this myself too?"

And the answer came. The night became a brilliant day, and his cell at the end of a tunnel resplended with the most beautiful light. The light was intense and soothing at the same time, making the cell walls disappear. There was no more darkness, no more imprisonment in a hole at the bottom of the pit. And no more pain. Instead there was love, there was hope, and there was peace.

"Why, you are asking? It is because some men forgot their divine essence they are made of. Their ego makes them think that they are gods. But, as I am their Father and their God, the divine condition is loving, understanding, forgiving, and giving. This people are the opposite of me, and because I granted them free will, they chose what is evil and they draw power from it. Only this is an illusion, a very-short lived profit they try to maintain at all cost, even if inflicting diabolic suffering."

Trebor was bathed in the glow of this luminous energy which was restoring him, caressing and holding him. The words coming to him, spoken or arising in his mind, were clear and gentle.

"You are asking why do you have to go through this yourself? As much as I resent it myself, this will be temporary and you will soon forget it, but it is necessary for you to gain the full understanding, my son."

And after a while, God added: "And, for the last 'why that'? It is because you have a mission. I give you a mission, my beloved son. And this mission is to help my people who suffer from the hurt inflicted by the ones that denied me. To stop the irrational, the evil powers spreading their destructive toil."

Trebor continued to reflect for a while on what had been said, when he realized that he was alone again. He was feeling a lot stronger, empowered, fearless. He fell asleep content, understanding that more of his questions will be answered, and that God will continue His teachings.

ENLIGHTENMENT

The life at the 'Reeducation camp #12' continued as usual for the next days, the inmates obeyed the same guards and rules, Sunjin visited and spent time with Trebor as often as he could, while Trebor was healing during the respite abated for a few days. And, when alone, in the total desolation of his donjon, he talked with God.

When Trebor asked what is life, what is the universe made of, what is everything made of, the answer came:

"Light".

"Light?"

"Yes, Light. The light is one of the forms you see of the energy making the universe and all that it contains."

After a while, the divine voice added:

"One photon, as you call the unity of the light, also contains all that is needed to recreate the whole Universe, and the one that can transport you into the next levels, to higher vibrational universes. The scientists should be happy to learn about the divine order and nature of the light, for one single photon in its complexity, the geometry of its quantum wave energetic disposition, can divide, get deeper into infinite fractal details. Light contains within and carries with it the divine matrix of all living creatures, some of its waves geometrically designed as the master cosmic mold of all DNA that is spread throughout the universe."

Then, God added: "You are light, your body is only this temporary manifestation of the energy as matter, obeying to the light vibrations flowing everywhere and assembling atoms to create this living form, you, as a living being.

"Thus, you see my son, for now, you are the 'materialization' of the light. The light and the matter emerging from the same energy, and interchanging with each other.

"And you are energy as well. You are part of this flow of energy that IS the universe, always part of it, inseparable from it."

Other times, God simply made Trebor see with his soul eyes how all this works, the beauty, the infinite perfection, the simplicity in its complexity of what this supreme energy can create.

When questioned about our physical suffering, our decay through the aging course, wonderful images flooded Trebor's mind. As God was explaining, He also showed a ray of light beaming into the cells of a malfunctioning tissue or organ. Trebor could see its waves containing the perfect genetic organization of that particular organism rearranged the molecules back to its intended structure: young, healthy, perfect.

"How sublime, how beautiful", Trebor soul uplifted with wonder, exclaimed.

"Some of your scientists and many healers know that, and some apply this knowledge, consciously or not. It is not a secret."

The following time Trebor saw God, he questioned Him about the injustice, the violence and misery present in the world. And God explained that this is the result of beings vibrating at a low level of energy, some of these vibrations measured by humans on electromagnetic, gravitational, sound, and light waves. This resonates with beings of similar levels of vibration, creating an universal law of attraction.

"Vibration waves are the result of our thoughts, feelings, words, our intentions, and our acts. The energy carried by these vibrations will attract other beings, objects, and situations representing the level of energy emitted, bringing on their manifestation. A violent act and an angry word will trigger the thirst of revenge and the return of an insult, until someone will break the cycle of destruction and hatred.

"It has been said, over and over again through human history, that one should beware of what one thinks or does, and never to curse. Sooner or later the manifestation of our acts will become our life. Humans call it karma, or judgement and punishment; it is simply the level of energy at which we choose to vibrate, bringing in return similar values. This will follow one not only for their entire life, but possibly during many of them, until the 'bad', the low energy they released during wicked acts is washed through their own experience of what they made others endure. I do not need to judge, I do not punish. People do it to themselves, they reap what they sow, the bad and the good, based on their own choices.

"The sad thing is that the one who would commit a cruel act or an injustice to another, who receives back what he already released into the universe, might be the one consciously making again the choice of a hurtful act, and not of forgiveness. Thus, generation after generation, century after century, we witness wars, barbarian acts of destruction, and violence. The arrogance of egotistic leaders attracting confrontations through occupying or enslaving other populations, clashing with other narcissistic characters responding with more brutality. And what we see is an escalade of bloodshed and cruelty."

"For how long?", Trebor whispered as for himself. "Something needs to be done about it", he finished his thought.

"Here you come, by son. My chosen one."

"Father?" Trebor turned his eyes up staring now in surprise.

"Yes, it is time for something to be done, for the chaos to end. And for man to choose once and for all."

Some time was allowed for silence, Trebor absorbing the sense of these last words. Then God continued:

" Men will have now only one chance of salvation, if they choose to raise themselves. Increasing their awareness as being part of the universal consciousness, this cosmic energy that is intelligent and keeps records of the entire history, all discoveries, creativity, of any act ever done, this living entity containing everyone's soul, will help to elevate the people of this planet to reach a higher dimension, to attain a higher density."

"This planet is approaching, along with its entire solar system, an area of the galaxy charged with much higher, denser energy levels. It was my design for the Earth to traverse this segment of the universe and it has been announced since ancient times," God explained. "This passage-through will mandate men either to rise to this higher energy level, or to perish. All inferior form of living, thinking, or acting, will be destroyed by this powerful interaction."

"But because I love man, I made it at my own image, and because I am, as I said, a loving father and not a punishing one, I want to give a chance to everyone to be saved. In the past I sent many of my sons to help human beings to evolve, to raise themselves, to be and do better. Through different times, every single one had a different mission. One of them, Jesus Christ you call him, my other Messiah, came to show man that LOVE is the way, the language, the feeling through which the universe manifests, the energy that makes the universal consciousness communicate. He came to teach Love, He showed only love when others treated him with unthinkable cruelty.

"Now, I send you to show man that they need to elevate their consciousness, to raise their energy levels and reach a higher dimension. I send you to help them reach TRANSCENDENCE."

SEEING THE END

When Sunjin made his visits to Trebor's cell these last few days, he informed him that there were changes of the schedule and activities at the camp. The work inside the former nuclear plant was suspended with the anticipation of a commission made of UN denuclearization members inspecting the ceasing of nuclear warfare production. This site being one of the places signaled in the inventory handed by the government, according to the treaty made by Kim Jung Un and USA and its allies, was part of the commission itinerary and ready to allow inspection since it was already out of order and officially 'closed' for many years.

Sunjin let Trebor know also that the prisoners incarcerated in the isolation cells had been removed and the cleaning of the collapsed tunnels has been suspended, with no detainees coming in the former plant from across, all staying for now confined in the Reeducation camp # 12. All signs of activity at this site was to be halted until new orders. Sunjin mentioned that he would probably make fewer and shorter visits to his cell, avoiding to attract anyone's suspicion. What Sunjin had abstained from mentioning was that he feared to know the fate of the tortured prisoners removed from the donjons.

With days and nights of complete solitude breached only by the rare and short visits Sunjin made to bring something to eat and drink, Trebor was left by his watchers without food or water. He had been discarded and reduced to a body barely living with no threat to them and no chances to survive.

Trebor reflected on the last time he woke up in his cell, an interval he could not define between being unconscious and the complete deprivation of his senses with passing of time. They had kept him under the water boarding for so long, as they intended to induce him into a coma, in order to remove his organs. And he was ready, he felt so emptied of breath, of life, of desire to fight, that he was ready to give up. And then, after the terror of a long waiting, a torture perhaps worse than the torture itself, he learned that he was abandoned and let to die from an even more horrific death.

It was a sure death without Sunjin coming and secretly bringing meagre sustenance to his body and his mind. And his discussions with God, the celestial Father opening his soul and filling his darkness with resplendent light.

And then, it happened! After days and nights of abandonment, Trebor was woken up by a terrible light, which for a fraction of a second burned his closed eyes, while his ears were shot down, blocked by a monstrous rumbling blast, after which his body was projected into the abyss.

IT HAPPENED

"Oh, no! He did it! The monster, he detonated his nuke!" those were the first words that came to Trebor's mind.

How long has it been since Trebor was out? no one could've said. He could not move, a massive concussion impelling his head with a bursting pain. But he could breathe! Complete silence, or was his hearing forever lost? Finally, he dared to open his eyes. And he could see! And what he was seeing was a clear blue sky and a few white clouds!

"I must be dead", Trebor concluded and closed his eyes again. After a long while, he tried again, and the sky was still there, with its clouds, and even some green tree branches shading his face. In surprise, Trebor's mind started wakening up and his thoughts rolled faster.

"So, it was not a nuclear bomb, it was an explosion of some sort and I am on the surface! I need to escape, I need to move!"

Cautiously, Trebor checked one by one his body condition, starting with moving his eyes in all directions. "Well, I am not rendered completely dumb yet, my skull hit some hard spots, but it must be a harder nut to crack!"

He probed his neck and spine, then his arms. There was soreness throughout, but no true numbness he counted down. However, his left arm was folded under him at the shoulder level, and, after a gentle attempt, he succeeded to pull it by his side. He also noticed that he could control his motion, able to unfold the shoulder and the elbow when extracting them from under his back. He could even rock slightly to the right side in a reflex movement, to make room to move his arm. "So far, so good, but boy, my elbow and left shoulder blade hurt like hell!", he thought.

Eager to check out his legs, Trebor realized that they must be covered under the ruble caused by the explosion, and had to restrained his impatience and make small wiggle movements with his toes. "What a relief, I can barely move them and feel them, but they are still there, attached to my body. Thank you, God!"

At that point, Trebor felt a surge of energy that pushed himself up, lifting his torso in a 'crunch' movement. Now he was sitting, and paused to consider his surroundings, forgetting the sharp pains making his breath shallow. It seemed to him that he had been projected on the top of the hill against an abrupt slop, turning his back away from the valley and hiding to his view where the labor camp should be. Trebor could, nevertheless, detect no sounds of any kind of activity as he took his time to assess his legs, covered with stones, branches and dirt. It was as if his lower frame went through the layers of soil at the top of the ground, coming out of the depth of the mountain, short of being covered and buried by the newly formed tomb-like mount.

After renewed efforts, Trebor dug out his legs, rubbed them to let the blood flow run through the swollen tissues, where bruises and scrapes covered them with no order, his impatience slowed down only by the stinging pain. He ripped what was left of the lower part of his inmate 'pajamas' and he smoothed off most the debris covering his legs.

"I have been run over by Orient Express, but no broken bones. I must be tougher than I considered myself. Oh, thank you again, my God", Trebor could not help murmuring these words, his heart filled with gratitude.

Feeling the urge to take a look at the valley behind him, Trebor bent his knees as much as the swelling allowed him, then softly pivoted on two quarters of turns to his right. Now, the entire area spread to his view, and he could take in the panorama.

The first impression struck him, as all around him was complete destruction, nothing survived or remained standing after a much vaster obliteration of the mountains and valleys to the north and beyond. The next impression that came to his mind was that the initial deflagration must have originated further up, growing through the underground tunnels and making them collapse. But where and what really happened was still the question.

Then, Trebor focused his attention to any minute movement he could spot, at the camp site and the former nuclear plant. He realized that it had been a complete annihilation of them both, huge boulders thrown by the explosion of the mountain over the camp with a part of the mountain rolling over the valley and leveling them, created a new geography of the site.

Assessing the situation, Trebor did not even notice that he was up and hobbling close to the edge of the collapsed cavernous side of the mountain. Confused, he looked around wondering which way to go, and he quickly thought that, if he could summon all his energy, he would be able to find his way back to the China, and reach the recreational state park. This is when he had the impression of hearing a faint moaning, not far from where he was and on the lower side of the ravine, the view of it hidden from the place he was standing on. He decided that he had to risk a look, and possibly without been seen, which appeared to be tricky, since he would have to descend a small, but a steep slop created by the blow up.

Holding onto a few branches sticking out from the side of the disfigured terrain, Trebor managed to go over the flattened part of the ridge where he had woken up just minutes ago. Now, hanging dangerously with little hold on the muddy soil breaking into small avalanches under his feet, he kept looking without seeing anybody. He found about a yard below him a contorted root offering some support to his foot, then to an arm, as he lowered himself even more along this short but new wall of the former nuclear plant.

Another moaning came from behind him and much closer this time, making him turn on a quick movement that almost caused him lose his footage. There, he could see something, not much, just a forearm dangling out the straight cliff.

Instinctively, Trebor began talking a few words of Korean, words of encouragement to whomever that person might be, telling him that he had heard him and that he was coming to his rescue, although he still not knowing if this person was a woman or a man, a friend or a foe. But with all his good intentions, once closer to the place where the arm was coming out the dirt, Trebor could not see much. The person to which the arm belonged to was completely covered and pinned under the tones of ravel. It must be of an old person, for the arm was wrinkled and darkened by age.

Once within reach, Trebor gently touched the sagging hand, triggering, along with the sound of his voice, a reaction from inside the piled mess. A long, deep sigh came out as a relief or as a statement of great pain from the one trapped under, to which Trebor addressed more words of reassurance that he would soon get him out the bowels of the mountain. His surprise made him almost lose again grip on the supporting root, when he heard a voice he recognized and spoke to him in mandarin, between lapses of hard breaths:

"Trebor, by grandchild, not to worry about me, I am too old for you to try to get me out and risk getting in trouble. If you have any force left, go, run to China and save yourself. This is my request, my demand to you."

Instead, Trebor was already prudently removing the dirt covering Sunjin, while he kept talking and asking questions:

"There is no one alive around for as far as I can see. I will get you out and the two of us will find a safe place. What on earth happened?"

"Well, the best I can put things together, at a site northeast from here, after the foreign commission had inspected, there were still some nuclear waste found and a claim was made to dispose it properly. It looks like, after the commission left and headed in our direction, Kim Jung rather decided to detonate it and with it, make all disappear, nuclear waste and inspectors, all together."

"Without regards for anyone, including for the camps around, all being considered as negligible collateral damage", Trebor thought.

"I also heard the director of our camp whispering, in the past, some concerns about inappropriately disposed nuclear material and left overs of dynamite needed for the tunnel construction of the underground plant. I think that this is what actually happened. The former nuclear plant where you were detained had already collapsed in the past, and it was the reason they had to close it, uncontrolled nuclear material having the potential to explode unwanted. But, although the site where the explosion occurred this time is far away, further breakdown of the tunnels must have followed."

While Sunjin's panting voice continued on and off, Trebor dug into the area over his head and made more room for him to breath. He asked Sunjin if he could feel his arms and legs, and Sunjin was not sure of how much he could sense. Trebor went on, slowly gaining inch after inch and opening more space around Sunjin's body, while keeping his mind occupied.

"How did you get to this side of the valley? no one seemed to have made it!"

"I was inside the plant, deep inside the tunnels."

"Mm..?"

"Yes, I came to check up on you, and since you were deep asleep, I squeezed a few drops of water on your lips. When I came out of your cell, I saw the guards coming to take you to the infirmary. After removing all the other detainees from the plant days before and left you to die alone, they must have changed their mind and thought that selling your organs should be more profitable after all, without your name added to the records and them keeping the money. Seeing them coming, I hid even deeper back in the tunnel, to the right of you cell, when the explosion happened. It must have been some explosive material left undetected at the bottom of a close by tunnel that exploded and lifted you and I up in the air. If no one is in sight, the guards must be buried in the belly of the Earth. I hope Hell swallowed them for eternity!"

It has been an excruciating task for Trebor to uncover Sunjin, and to hold him and carry him gently on a flattened place the closest he could find. He was already thinking of how to get to a source of water for both of them to regain some strength, before tempting their luck on the way to China. The hope to find the freedom for him and Sunjin, emerged again. He was already planning on his mind how to hide Sunjin across China and bring him all the way to Hong Kong, from where he could take care of him. Until then he would have to contact his friend Li.

Grimacing under increased pain, Trebor crouched by Sunjin's side to assess his condition, who, lying on his back, was obviously suffering terribly. A few instants later, Hell opened again, and a new detonation engulfed them both under its inferno.

MORE LIES

There had been a worldwide uproar in the news about the nuclear explosions occurred in North Korea during the United Nations' inspection of its supposedly closed and inactive nuclear plants. At first, Kim Jung Un vehemently denied that there has been any incident, and arrogantly released a press statement that all was another invention of the capitalist countries "plotting to undermine his good faith".

Shortly after, there were satellite images pouring in with overwhelming evidence and filling the big and smaller television screens with uncontested proofs of extended destruction at the former nuclear sites.

Only then, Kim ought to admit that there "had been 'an accident' caused by the 'inspectors snooping around', who, in their lack of qualification, prompted the explosion of old mine chargers. There was only 'limited' damage and not of a nuclear nature," the statement insisted.

Another press release issued by the central quarters of Pyongyang announced that emergency teams and equipment had been dispatched to the affected areas hastily and efficiently, and help was on the way.

The various international commissions acting for demilitarization and denuclearization passionately protested, enraged by the negligence of the government of DPRK creating an affront to the world security, and demanding that qualified multinational delegations should accompany the local rescue operations. Obviously, global fraternity and inter nation trust reigned!

FAMILY REUNION

"Here dad, there are two people under those tree roots. The last bang came from this direction!", was said in English.

"Be careful, there could be more explosives dumped and left unmarked in the tunnels underneath", came the answer in the same language.

Trebor, on and off unconscious state, thought that this time he must be, for sure, dead. This melodious voice that seemed so familiar, although he could not name the face of the person, could not belong to this world. And again, did he imagined that it had been an answer to her voice?

"Nah, if I am not dead, I must be losing my mind, to many times kept under the water and knocked on the head", bits of judgement were forming as Trebor considered which realm he belonged to this time.

For now, he could only lay there, all strength, all desire to fight for this terrestrial life had abandoned him. Other words came to him, though, and he almost repeated them aloud:

"Father, May Your will be done" (Matthew 6:10).

With great clarity other words formed in his mind:

"Fear thou not; for I am with thee: be not dismayed; for I am thy God: I will strengthen thee; yea, I will help thee; yea, I will uphold thee with the right hand of my righteousness" (Isaiah 41:10).

With no forth notice, Trebor felt his head lifted with great gentleness and water drops falling on his dried lips. His body responded as one of a child's to whom had just been given life, and he drunk, suckled the water pouring into his mouth dry as parchment. Several times the water source was stopped and restarted, allowing him to catch his breath. Again, as gently as it was lifted, his head was lowered, this time on a softer surface.

"Please, if you hear me, move a finger, a foot, anything" was said in Korean, then repeated in mandarin, then in English by the male voice.

The water ingested must have given Trebor new forces, for he lifted an arm as he finally opened his eyes.

"I hear you, and thank you" Trebor managed to whisper in English.

When the two men and the young woman faced each other, the three of them thought they must be delirious, as they recognized one another.

"Trebor Young!", father and daughter gasped in unison looking at the man laying almost dead on the ground ravaged by the series of explosions.

"Dad!" came out of Trebor's mouth without thinking.

"Dad?"

"Yes, you are my dad. My mother was Mai Lee, Mai Young, your wife and Maggie's mother. You adopted your real daughter! She gave birth to us in this concentration camp, where I came to find out more about her. And I also met her father here, Sunjin, who kept me alive. Without his help I would probably have died long ago."

There was one of these very rare moments when Jo cried, the three of them hugged and sobbed letting out waves of emotions accumulated for years, released now under the stress but also under the happiness brought about by their unexpected reunion.

For some reason, Trebor felt compelled to explain how he had been captured and kept in secrecy of the North Korean labor camps. He mentioned without giving details, that he had been interrogated and tortured, and on the verge of having his organs removed as it has been done to his own mother.

During this time Jo's mind raced sorting out the whole situation, and he soon realized that their presence there was in danger, remembering the way the North Korean regime worked. It was easy to eliminate three witnesses who experienced firsthand the activities happening in the nuclear sites and their connection with concentration camps, one of the foreign captured just being mishandled in one of them.

Trebor mentioned a recreational park on the other side of the close by border with China, which could be the quickest way out, at least for now.

Maggie had freed the older man from the entanglement of roots that kept him trapped under, but also had protected the two men from being crushed by the flying debris of the last deflagration. Sunjin, now Maggie learning who he was and what was his name, was alive, but had suffered serious injuries, blood coming out of his mouth, and reaching back into his lungs. Sunjin could not swallow water, and Jo and Maggie only managed to sweep his face from blood and dirt. Slowly, Sunjin regained some awareness, opened his eyes to see his benefactors.

Maggie let go of her retention and closed her arms around his chest, telling the old man that she was his granddaughter, then turning toward her father, she told him his father's name. A smile lit up Sunjin's face, and he made a sign of recognition toward him. Then, the three of them came close to the dying man, and understood that his last moments have been blessed by seeing his son in law one more time and holding his two grandchildren.

With a smile in his face and tears slowly running down, his dreams coming true beyond his life-long expectations, Sunjin closed his eyes for an eternal sleep. But his smile remained carved on his face, as he was now meeting again his wife and his daughters. "He died as a happy man", Jo thought, while the three of them let their tears flow freely.

CHAPTER 6 - TRANSFIGURATION

BACK TO SAFETY

Fate decided one more time to reunite what remained of a family devastated by tragedy, and soon after, the souls of the father, son, and daughter being torn between the miracle of bringing them together and abruptly losing a grandfather they met only moments before.

Joseph Godson, concerned about time running before finding safety, silently found close by a soft accumulation of dirt removed by the explosions. With his bare hands, he made a depression large enough to contain Sunjin's body, then, with great care, he lifted the light body and gently laid it on the newly made tomb. He bowed his head on prayer, joined by his children, sobbing as they were making silent farewells to Sunjin. Then, blinded by the tears, the three of them enveloped his body with the soil in which they all will, one day, be received by Mother Earth. Instead of a wooden cross, they marked the place with a small pyramid made of stones found nearby, and together they built a modest resting place for a noble soul, who, from now on would forever live in their hearts.

Jo continued to take charge of their situation, and gathered his adult children by the place where the back packs have been left on the ground, then opening them, looked for something to give them to eat. He could see that Trebor was thin and quite week after the ordeal he went through and having him to walk to safety, would be a new challenge for all of them.

Offering a few power bars, Jo always carried with him, and water from a thermos, he explained to Trebor what happened and how they came so close to this area.

"Meggie was one of the very few press reporters accompanying the delegation charged with the nuclear sites inspection. I trembled for her safety and decided that I would be with her at all times in this perilous trip. I could obtain clearance from the CIA, a passport with a slight alteration of my name and birth date. They actually found that it was a good idea to have someone trained in special missions as part of the group."

"So, you got the chance to make yourself 10 years younger, then?!", said Trebor, as Jo appreciated his sense of humor, even in these circumstances.

"No, they actually gifted me with five more years, since this would take me out of the picture from the person the Korean police might look for", Jo answered almost laughing, then he continued:

"While the commission members were doing their job, I tried to stay ahead gathering information, especially after declaring the last site visited as unsafe, my instincts remaining on alert more than ever. It is when I insisted for a temporary suspension of the mission, leaving the northeast sites from where the inspections began and decided

111

to immediately get the hell out of there. Anyway, that must have been a good call, for the two minibuses loaded with people and instruments put a good distance between us and the place where a small nuclear head must have detonated, creating the underground chain reaction of the dynamite leftovers, scattered randomly without any records properly locating them."

"However, after the explosions, I went ahead to find passages where the terrain allowed the vans to travel safely south, and from where they could be recovered by the international dispatchers. Of course, Maggie, who had her own agenda and is as stubborn as her father, followed me. She insisted on going as far as possible to see and record the extend of the explosions. I already informed Seoul, and the military, who, dressed on civilians are bringing Red Cross supplies and doctors to help the local population. Mainly, they scramble ahead to meet our team and bring them to South Korea. I also informed our friends in Seoul and the leader of the inspection team, that Maggie and I are fine and that we are making our own way to America."

Jo continued his train of thoughts without recess, all the while attentive to any movement he could detect on the surroundings.

"Now, Trebor, can you give me any indication of how far is and how can we get to the Tianci Holiday Park?"

Trebor, happy to contribute to Jo's plans, stopped chewing:

"I know pretty well the area, I visited it several times and at night. It is not far from here, maybe 30-40 minute-walk, and the lake shared with China was not very well guarded."

"But can you walk, this place has been torn upside down and 'bulldozed' by explosions. It is extremely treacherous."

Soon after, while Jo was locating the direction of the lake on his satphone and carrying their backpacks, they were moving cautiously toward China. Trebor had received a cocktail of medications including antibiotics, anti-inflammatory and pain medication, had his wounds disinfected and covered with light bandages, along with an anti-Tetanus serum. All the care he received made him feel better, many times more than he had been in a long time, after all the hardship he endured. He hobbled along, and he refused to be carried when the route was crumbling under their feet. No one was talking, though, and in less than two hours they glanced at the reflections made by the water of the lake.

A curtain of trees survived and offered a welcomed protection from the border security. However, even Jo was surprised to find out that every soldier had deserted the area. Did they take advantage of the disaster to run to the other side? That warranted for caution, even after arriving on Chinese territory.

Staying close to the edges of the lake, now it was Trebor who directed them toward the shorter distance reaching Tianci Village. When, soon after, he recognized the slight slope leading to the camping site where he stayed, he signaled it the two others with a cheering call. He thought that he was still dreaming, too many times reality had lately surpassed his reasoning. The trio arrived in no time close to the building housing the showers and toilettes, and finding them deserted, they could finally clean up, avoiding any undesired suspicion raised by their appearance.

Jo, following Trebor's directions, went to the central area to buy clothes for Trebor and all that was needed for his care, along with food and bottled water. When he showed up again, he emptied the two backpacks now full, and he joyously announced them:

"Guys, we have a small trailer rented, isolated, but a little further away from the Korean side. I could use my new passport, thankfully the visa for China was still valid." Then, handing a pair of jeans, Jo addressed his newly found son:

"Here Trebor, some decent civilian clothing for you", and he added a warm polo, tennis shoes, and a variety of accessories. "Take also the shaving cream and the razor and try to look human", Jo teased his son, his heart filled with incommensurable joy.

However, Trebor grabbed first a tooth brush, appreciating this luxury he missed since he left the same camping site.

Shortly after, they hurried to occupy their trailer, all agreeing that they would need a few days to recover, in particular Trebor, who let them know about Li and the possibility of having him coming with a car to drove them away. While Li traveled on their direction, they would appreciate the break making plans for their trip back home.

LI COMES BACK

It took Li over two good days to arrive to Tianci Tourism Holiday Village. He was startled when the smart phone left by Trebor chirped for the first time in weeks, so surprised that, at first, he looked at it perplexed. Then, a little anxious, he decided to answer. Li was so delighted to hear Trebor's voice, he began screaming, all questions coming to his mind at the same time.

"By all gods, Trebor, it has been 40 days, I was counting, I thought that you forgot about me and left for good!"

Trebor waited for his friend to cool down, telling him that he was even happier to hear Li's quivering voice. Then, he asked him if he was free and could come to the village and make a trip with him and his family.

"Of course, of course, you didn't need to ask. But you have a family with you now?"

"Yes, my dad and my sister, I will explain to you when you get here," and Trebor proceeded to indicate the trailer's position.

"I will be there before noon tomorrow, I have the map of the camping spaces in front of me, I am looking at it right now, ah here you are, I found it! Do you need me to bring anything?"

"My stuff would be nice, some of my clothing and documents, if you still have them."

Reassured by Li's answer, Trebor became impatient to be again in possession of his passport and the documents obtained at the military base in Seoul, in particular the wedding certificate of his parents. However, Li called the day after, telling them that he was at some road blocks, all traffic constantly stopped and detoured many times when approaching the border, the roads made unusable by the extensive damages done by the explosions.

At times, directed to nowhere when trying to go back to the main highway, Li learned that it had been a chain reaction of detonations extending from several underground nuclear plants, which was no longer a secret. This created a quake, shuddering the tunnels of the plants, including the ones linking different sites, for over a hundred kilometers. The Chinese government learned in dismay that some of the tunnels penetrated well into their territory, now revealed by collapsing land, roads, bridges, and destroyed villages, making the area appear like a warzone.

Learning about the magnitude of the disaster, the three escapees realized how lucky they were finding themselves at the far end of the critical zone, and staying alive.

Until Li could make his way to their place, they considered different plans for their return to the US; Jo had contacted the authorities in Seoul, and they all agreed that it was unsafe for Trebor to cross the North Korean territory again and try to come to the south. They decided to go to Beijing and present themselves to the American Embassy, who would facilitate their trip back to the US. They felt that, once in Beijing, any international airline flying to an American city will do.

And so, they did, and once Li arrived and Trebor had the time to gain a few pounds with good nourishment, the four of them packed for a long trip on the road. They loaded the car with all the necessities, Trebor again in possession of his passport and with their hopes held high, they succeeded to cover the 350 miles going south to Beijing, drove by Li in one long day. Two days later, Jo, Maggie and Trebor boarded United Airlines after saying their goodbyes to Li and compensating him generously for his company.

Once on board, where they felt on American territory, the newly reunited family relaxed with a long sigh. Comfortably resting back on their seats, the flight attendants' announcements sounded like music to their ears. "For now, the only thing to do is to enjoy the special attentions of the crew", they thought. They will have a fueling stop in Mumbai, former Bombay, India, then another one in London, UK, before landing to Newark, New Jersey, USA.

FLYING BACK HOME

Joseph Godson was looking forward to this long flight, close to 8 hours until the first stop to Mumbai, which would allow him to get to know Trebor, and learn more about his childhood he sorely missed. He had a multitude of questions and counted on the close quarters of the flight to find all the quiet time to fill the gaps of too many years apart from each other. For now, they will get some rest, they will enjoy the food and the pampering of the kind hostesses, and they will talk.

The excitement of the first hours in the plain continued with animated exchanges of the three of them, with Jo asking Trebor to start from the beginning and go as far as he could remember. Trebor was glad to answer, but he responded also with an avalanche of questions. During this time, Maggie's journalistic mind was sorting out and 'classifying' all this abundant and precious amount of information regarding the lives of the closest people she had in her life. Listening to their stories, Maggie thought that none of her editorials could ever match their tales.

Jo became more reassured learning about Trebor's adoptive parents' love and devotion, offering to his son the best conditions one could dream of succeeding in life, while Trebor could not stop asking questions about his mother.

"So, tell me again, how did you meet Mai? it was her little dog that run to you, or you have seen her first at the Red Star Hotel? When did you know that you were in love with her?", then, later on, "Incredible, you two could get married, how wonderful! but why you could not keep her with you in South Korea?" and he went on, and on with his questions.

Having learned about Mai's horrendous time in the labor camp, recently his own horrific experience, and of her ghastly death, Trebor concentrated on learning about the happy times of his parents. Jo, however, wanted to hear first-hand about the prisoners' treatment in the North Korean 'reeducation centers'.

When the lunch was lavishly served to the first-class passengers, the father and son enjoyed this time a less intense conversation, now Trebor and Maggie teasing each other, asking about their dates and personal hobbies.

The flight attendants started removing the trays, stopping and engaging in a pleasant conversation with some of the passengers. They were taking their time, since the plane was only half occupied, and with over four hours into the flight to Mumbai, the occupants would soon settle for a long nap. However, a young and pleasant flight attendant approached the trio, now Maggie sitting next to her father and Trebor behind them, looking forward to lower his seat on 'sleeping position'.

"I am sorry, Sir, Ma'am, but there is this gentleman who says that he is your friend and insisted to have a word with you", and before they could ask who that person was, they broke into a surprised laughter, for, behind the pretty stewardess, Li's face smiled from ear to ear!

"Li, sweet Mother! How in the world did you come on board?" and, "What a wonderful surprise!"

This went on a little longer, while the young attendant, reassured that there was only a friendly surprise, left them to their conversation.

Trebor asked Li to come and sit next to him, and they all spoke at the same time. Finally, they let Li manage a word or two of explanation, jumping from English to Mandarin, luckily the three others able to follow:

"Well, you must know that I no longer have a family on my own", then Li turned toward Trebor with a sad look in his face. "When you were gone, I learned that my son went to meet his mother, and he left this world. I never felt so lonely, and with you, I suddenly dreamed as having a family again. I had the hope that I belonged, somehow to yours." And shyly, he lowered his head.

The others noticed that he was trying to hold back a few tears, and they gave him the time to find his comfort in their tender silence. Finally, he continued;

"First, I met Trebor and I was amazed by his respect and generosity I've never seen before, even less being treated, me, a stranger, as someone who counted as a real person. Then, when I met you two, father and daughter, who showed to me the same kindness, I started dreaming of another life. I dared to think that I could have a family again and enjoy a place where people can be less scared and humiliated. So, when I saw you leaving and disappearing through the gate to your airplane, the sadness made me follow this desperate impulse and try my chance. I took the money you gave me, and I went to the United Airlines counter and bought a ticket to New York, like you did. Gods must have been with me, because they sold me a 'last moment' ticket with only my regular drivers' license."

"Then, I sat on the waiting area, after everyone had already boarded, and not knowing anything of these flight dealings, I was waiting. I heard the boarding agent calling several times a name, a Chinese name, and no one answered, so I went to the counter and showed my ticket. The agent, part of the American crew, obviously not reading Chinese, hurriedly checked my name and rushed with me to the plane. And after that, they closed the door behind me as soon as I was on board. A pretty agent showed me a seat and without any questions I sat down, while she quickly fastened my belt. Thank God, for that, I was getting confused, but so happy."

The Godson family was so touched and filled with joy, they wanted to cheer for Li's presence. And while Trebor and Maggie reassured Li that they would take care of him and would make everything possible for them to stay together once returning home, Jo went to talk with the person in charge of the flying crew. Joseph Godson introduced himself, and simply asked if their friend could sit next to Trebor, offering to pay for an upgrade to business class. The attendant appeased him right the way, and told him that Li could occupy that vacant seat:

"He already payed and insane amount of money for this last-minute ticket, no additional charge is needed", George said, padding Jo on the shoulder, happy to show good graces. "Just let us pamper you for the duration of the flight", and he sincerely meant to do that.

There was another cheer in order, when all seemed to settle for the best. Li was readily served with a selection of foods and tea Maggie suggested to the attendant, coming to catch up with their meal. And they continued to enjoy this unexpected turn of events for a while. Finally, all starting to slow down, everyone was ready to doze off after so many emotions and mellowed by a great meal.

The passengers resting quietly, even the flight attendants found their seats at different ends of the cabins, reading and chatting quietly.

TIBET

The quiet in the cabin lasted for a couple of more hours, passengers and crew relaxing during this uneventful flight. Then, suddenly, the plane shook, made a few vibrations, then started jerking at irregular intervals. Jo, waking up alerted, could observe that the crew exchanged a few concerned glances with each other and, trying to seem calm and reassuring, approached the cockpit for instructions from the pilots.

Then, George went to the cockpit and asked permission to enter it. He looked at the pilots and the flight technician, who were concentrating to read the instruments and stabilize the jumbo jet. Then he heard them exchanging orders and information: "all instruments are off, the same for the radar, and the ground is not responding..."

"I have no radio connection" was the flight engineer's commentary.

"Ok, let's switch to manual flight" the commander pilot announced, then to the co-pilot, "search the flight plan and locate on the map our precise location."

"We were approaching Lhasa, Tibet, and we are flying over the mountains, at 35k altitude. We are at about 10 minutes flying distance from Lhasa International."

Unexpectedly, after a few hiccups, the engines quit one after the other. The silence could be 'heard' even in the passengers' cabins.

"We will have to switch to visual flight, make a slow approach and signal distress to Lhasa tower. You see the valley, we will try to lower the plane there as much as we can, and avoid a crash", said the captain, all attention concentrated on the handles and straining to see the ground approaching fast, opening over the clouds the crests of the snowy Himalayan ridge.

Continuing to stay calm and summon his skills and attention to the dangerous situation, Captain John Samuel addressed the head flight attendant:

"Prepare passengers for emergency landing, all stay calm and follow instructions.", then turning to the co-pilot, "Lhasa is close to 12,000 feet altitude, we are descending fast but we should make it if we follow the Brahmaputra River valley, and I think I can see the east runway, please verify with the map while I sway the wings to signal the emergency landing."

For many passengers this was the most stressful time they had ever experienced in their life, and surprisingly enough, after listening to the captain reassuring voice over the intercom, they all braced for a rough landing, without screams or hysteria invading the small space.

Descending the plane, the pilots gained some speed, all masterfully controlled by the captain, who reaching the visible airport perimeter, could see the runway quickly approaching in view.

The flying crew, their nerves ready to burst under the pressure, noticed however, that there were no lights indicating the roads, runways, nor the tower, its shape detached against the sky to the right of the main runway where the airplane was dangerously heading to. "And all the airplanes are on the ground, maybe the tower notified them of the incoming emergency landing.", this thought came on a flash to the commander.

"All embrace for landing", almost shouted the captain, and a minute later the landing gear hit the asphalt, then skipped a couple of times before resuming to run stabilized on the runway alignment. Steadfastly, the captain hit the brakes and pulled back on the stick, and after a few more jiggles and wobbles, the jumbo jet came to a complete halt.

For a few seconds there was a total silence in the cabins, before an outburst of roaring cheers filled the space, everyone screaming and clapping, at the same time releasing their fears and realizing the miracle of being on the ground, and alive.

The whole crew was still on alert, some checking for any sign of fire, while the evacuation was on the way. Fortunately, it was day time since only the emergency lights battery-operated were on, and the passengers could gather their belongings carried on board. Instead of creating a chaos, they all helped each other and started exiting through the emergency door, where a sliding toboggan had been readily deployed, thanks to emergency power backup.

Captain John Samuel astonished not seeing any fire truck, nor similar emergency vehicles coming to his distressed commercial carrier, let out his concern to his team:

"Where in hell is everyone?"

"Something major must be going on. Ah, there, I see someone on bicycle coming this way!" and the copilot, pointed out to a small figure pedaling as fast as he could.

The man arriving at the jet was one of the tower air traffic controllers and, when showered with questions, the answers were not good. In fact, they were staggering.

A major argument broke between China and the north Korean leader. After angry accusation, for good reasons, made by the Chinese government against North Korea using underground tunnels for nuclear testing on Chinese territory, Kim Jung Un, already framed by the international uproar about the nuclear control commission findings, in his fury had almost lost his reason. He decided in a whim to send a nuke in high altitude, which emitting electromagnetic pulsations, EMPs, wiped out all the electronic functioning devices. And those involving practically all communications, transport by car, train or airplane, along with the electrical plants, all stopped working within minutes, creating a gigantic blackout.

"Someone at the tower found later a radio operating with transistors and captured signals from the Chinese government informing the population about the ravaging events. Good part of the eastern Asian territories is completely paralyzed by the EMPs, plunging it into a devastation of gigantic proportions", explained the tower operative.

Following a short debate between the captain and the air controller, the crew gathered the passengers, and a small crowd began moving toward the airport's main building. They all recovered their on-board luggage, but the cargo hold could not be opened manually and the storing compartment of the aircraft containing all checked in baggage had to wait for a later delivery. For now, the travelers and the crew had a long walk under a sunny afternoon sky, remaining shockingly silent over a busy international airport.

Jo and his family were glad that all their belongings were limited to carry-ons, which they pulled behind them, following the other passengers. Although some of the travelers were senior citizens, they all appeared to be in a fairly good physical condition adventuring to faraway places, and luckily, no one needed a wheelchair.

Acting nonchalantly, deciding not to reveal his special agent identity yet, Jo had approached the captain and his crew, and, after congratulating him for his extraordinary performance, he then introduced Maggie and Trebor. Maggie asked the captain permission to take some pictures of him and his crew, explaining her position as a journalist and her desire to make an editorial she would send to most publication in the US and abroad about the successful emergency landing. Maggie explained that the whole world should know about the incomparable performance of captain John Samuel, saving the life of everyone on board. Captain Samuel, not very inclined to become a celebrity, rather encouraged Jo to ask about the reason of this massive shutdown. Then addressing Maggie, captain Samuel showed some skepticism:

"Well, you are welcome to take your pictures of the crew and the airplane," captain John Samuel answered modestly, "and even write your article, but I don't think you will be able to send them anywhere yet. It has been a major EMP attack and most part of South Asia is paralyzed," then, "If you will excuse me, I have to assess the situation in the airport and make arrangement for the people of my flight."

LHASA

Jo's mind was already spinning on high gear, as he could foresee the panicked reactions of the people they might encounter in the airport, along with the very reduced solutions available for the airport personnel in these dire circumstances. Leading his siblings and Li on the side of the convoy for more privacy, he made some suggestions. First of all, they had to find a way to get to the town of Lhasa, where they would have access to food, water, and hopefully, shelter. At that time, Trebor reacted with a surprising optimism:

"Great, I always wanted to visit Tibet and Lhasa in particular! There are a few monasteries that I would love to see, and I hope the monks would be able to offer us lodging."

However, Li became quiet and made efforts not to show his anxiety, as he realized that he was far from completely leaving the Chinese territory. Jo sensed his concerns, and reminded Li that he was with them, and "under my watch, there is nothing for you to worry about, we'll all be fine."

Lhasa Gonggar Airport is at about 40 miles from the town and on one of the highest altitude airports in the world, built on the Lhasa plateau at an elevation of close to 12,000 feet. The right bank of the river Brahmaputra offering an opening, it made its construction possible after several failed attempts in the past. Still, the Airbus 330 and A 340 along with Boeing 757 aircrafts had to be operated by pilots specially trained to handle the landings and take offs on high altitude.

Jo had gathered sufficient information listening to the technical interactions and had managed to ask the tower employee how he was counting on returning home, and even if this was an option for him.

"I thought about that", he honestly answered, "I know that my car would not start and I am concerned about my family. I have a 4-month new baby, in addition to another one who is five years old. My mother lives with us also, and I worry about looters as the night will start." Then he added, "the more I think about it, the more I feel that I should make all possible to reach Lhasa. I have to see if Junko, one of the luggage handlers, is still around. He has an old three-wheel van and I have to see if he can take me home. But I will ask if he knows any other employee having some transportation to bring some of you into town. I know that the international crews stay at St. Regis Resort, it is central and close to Potala Palace, and in case of power failure, they do have some serious generators that can be activated manually and at least there should be electricity."

After learning the air controller's name, Xugang, Jo encouraged him to ask around his friends for ways to reach the town, when this inquired about Jo's situation.

"I am with my twin children, my daughter Maggie and my son Trebor, 32 years old. We only recently got to be together", Jo could not help to add, " And we have with us an old friend as well and my son went through some hardship recently." Jo intentionally omitted to specify that Li was Chinese, since he did not know how Xugang will react, Tibetans being rudely treated in the past by the Chinese occupation.

"Oh, I am so sorry."

"But how did you learn English so well? I know that the international aviation uses English as universal communication, but yours is outstanding", said Jo, trying to change the subject.

"Well, I needed to have a good level because we have direct communication with the pilots, and they must have clear orders, but I always loved America", he said looking around him making sure no Chinese people were listening. I studied with Buddhist monks, there are quite a few monasteries now open in Lhasa, the government tolerates them for the tourism is so lucrative for the government. And I think you should visit some of them, a few are within walking distance from the hotel and they are very old and interesting. Who knows, you might find enlightenment", Xugang ended with a grin.

"Captain John Samuel's performance landing in emergency the airplane at this high altitude, is truly impressive!", thought Jo, feeling himself the thin air as he observed everyone else getting short of breath and slowed down in their march. Then he approached again the crew and learned from the flight engineer, Joseph Rufus, who had flown into Lhasa a few times before, how they were going into town from the airport.

"There is an expressway, going through a tunnel under the mountain, making a shorter drive for busses and cars, but still, it takes around an hour to reach Lhasa. And we can't count on any transportation at this time. And for how long, is everybody's guess? Now that I remember correctly", he continued, "most of the flights are done in the morning because of strong winds on the plateau later during the day, and the jumbos land only a few times a week. If we are lucky, there won't be any for today, but the airport can be very busy at the peak hours. Let's hope that most of people are gone by now, it will be night in about two hours up here."

"Cover 40 miles on foot at this altitude and at night is not an option", Jo silently joked for himself: "not with Trebor's limited forces. We must find a way". Then, he addressed again Rufus, the flight tech:

"How do the locals go to town then, what are the transportations available around here?"

"There are some 'taxicabs' of a regular Chinese company, but there are also a few private drivers always looking for tourists who want to go to Lhasa, and even to hire them as guides to visit some monasteries in the region. Most of them have older cars, really, I wandered how they could even make them run with this thin air."

121

At that moment, the two of them looked at each other with a smile: "That's it! the older vehicles that work with mechanical control, not with electronic gadgets, they should be able to ride as long as they have gasoline."

"If we need it, we can syphon some from the airplane, it will have to refuel anyways to make sure we can take off on these mountains."

The Airbus 340 crew and passengers finally arrived at the two-story building of the fairly new terminal. As on many other airports, the first floor housed the checking-in and ticketing, the luggage and a visitor lounge, while the second floor contained the departure lounge, a shopping mall, restaurant, and the boarding gates. Trebor and Maggie joined Jo and Rufus on the way, and had already noticed that the 'aero-bridges' leading from the aircrafts into the building were not operating. A few airplanes were stationed by the terminal, silent and looking deserted.

"Most, if not all the flights, must be already here and with a little chance, the ones departing are already gone!" said Rufus.

Without paying attention, a small group formed by the flight crew, the air controller, Jo Godson and his party. They all exchanged concerns and ideas of what they would find inside the airport and what would be their options. The only think that was established so far was that there was no communication, no long-distance information or central directions given to the crew to follow.

Joseph Rufus was right as the flights' situation, but quite a few people were still in the building, many of them belonging to a variety of services of the airport. And if they were all ready to leave at the end of a busy day, about two hundred travelers, arrived in the last hours with short local flights, needed their attention, as things were getting out of control.

In contrast with the quiet present on the outside of the airport building, once inside, a stormy activity reigned. Everywhere could be heard complains and protests along with upset voices asking to be checked in with the 'next flight', creating a general cacophony. The captain, again taking charge of all of his flight members, guided them towards the United counter, and quickly obtained to direct everyone inside a private first-class lounge of the company, away from the chaos of the public lobby. He first inquired about the emergency lights available in the restrooms and possibly, as the night falls, in the lounge, then he made sure that his passengers are served drinks and some food was offered.

After his group settled in the private United lounge, Jo exited discreetly and met with Xugang, telling Maggie, Trebor, and Li to wait for him inside.

Xugang went to the tower control, although his shift was about to end, the airport closing at night; he found, however, some of his colleagues staying for the night, fault of transportation back to their home, some living in the villages in the vicinity of the airport, and having to come back to work in the morning. They settled for the night hoping for news and instructions to come soon, and for all to go back to normal.

Xugang was very anxious to check on his family and his mates encouraged him to go to Lhasa and make it back when this would be possible for him.

Xugang told Jo that Junko, the baggage man, confirmed that he could give him a ride home, but he also went around the luggage and employees' parking area to inquire about anyone able to give his party a ride. When Junko came back, he was not completely defeated: there were two old buses coming for some monks flying in from Kathmandu. That flight unfortunately could not take off and remained stranded there, thus, the monks' buses disposed of some forty seats. They were inclined to bring some people with them to Lhasa, and, as they were riding in front of St. Regis, they could drop off the travelers at their hotel.

Jo, wanting to show his appreciation to Xugang, offered a generous tip, but when he refused, Jo insisted that it was for the 'baby's English education'. Xugang reluctantly accepted and hurried into the trivan.

When shortly after Jo returned to the private United lounge, he made quite a sensation showing up with two monks, draped on bright orange linens. Looking for captain Samuel, they went into a corner of the large room and conferred for a few minutes. There were not enough seats for all the passengers and the crew to ride with the monks' small vans, all together making some 187 people. The captain asked for silence and then made an announcement explaining the situation, after which, families gathered together and debated over their decisions.

At the captain's request, a group formed on one side of the room with people choosing to stay at the airport, assuming that all should be in order in the morning to resume their trip. These travelers were, obviously, convinced that this was an isolated incident and it should be 'fixed' momentarily.

Some other passengers let the captain and the lounge personnel know that they intended to make plans on their own for the land transportation, not wanting to fly for a while, especially over these high mountains and after the scary landing they just experienced. Thus, they also chose to stay at the airport and take advantage of the facilities offered by the airline company.

Still, there were close to eighty people that ranged with the group wanting to go to the hotel, and maybe even 'visit' Lhasa. At this point, the monks whispered to the captain that they would try to make two trips back and forth, it might take a little more than two hours driving back to the airport, but they would do their best. The monks knew that, even in case of street troubles, their robe should be respected most of the time by the general population.

Captain Samuel announced that he remained at the airport, but he insisted that his crew should go to the hotel and get a well-deserved rest. Thus, a first assembly of forty followed the Buddhist monks.

The roads almost empty, with the exception of old motorcycles and very few vehicles, the ride to Lhasa took no more than 50 minutes, even with the eerie sensation going through the tunnel under the mountains, now lacking of lighting and the cars relying only on a few deem rays casted in front of them. The town was already getting in the dark, with clusters of people forming on the streets. Some military presence was visible, but it looked like there had not been enough time yet for the requisition of civilian vehicles, as it usually happens in time of emergency. And everywhere was present a sense of unsettlement.

During the ride to Lhasa, Jo, his twin children, and Li, entered only at the last moment the second bus and found seats close to the driver. However, Jo and Trebor engaged in a conversation with the monk sitting next to Trebor, after father and son addressed him in Mandarin. The kindness and peacefulness that the monk exuded, let Trebor feel inclined to confess to him that he had been detained in a labor camp and he was recovering. He expressed his desire to learn more about Tibet and the temples and monasteries in Lhasa. He wanted mostly to experience the spiritual connection he discovered only recently and during dramatic circumstances.

With a serein smile of understanding, the monk looked at him and said:

"My name is Lu Xiang. I am a teacher, I try to initiate young men who desire to become Buddhists. I will talk with our master, but in these exceptional times, I think he would be willing to offer the four of you to stay at our monastery. I belong to Jokhang temple, which is located in the Barkhor district, and it contains several noble houses within its walls. It is in the center of Lhasa, not far from Potala Palace. We will drop off the people going to the hotel, is on the way, and you four stay in the bus" he directed.

EAST MEETS WEST

With the night falling and a flamboyant sky hiding the sun behind the mountains, the Jokhang temple complex appeared as a spectacular site, its highly spiritual quality giving the impression that the gods were present and the temple was ascending them back into the heavens.

A small procession formed by Lu Xiang, Kuan Li, Joseph Godson and his adult children, approached the night quarters of the master at the lamas' hostel. Lu Xiang directed them through a side entrance, at the right of the main temple access, and the five of them disappeared discreetly inside, as people started massing on the main square at the front door of the temple.

Lu Xiang came back shortly after conferring in private with the temple master and led the way to the hostel reserved for the visiting monks. Then, inquiring if his new protégés were satisfied with their simple accommodations, he added that "trays with some food will be sent to you and the visit of the temple will have to wait until morning." Then, he left in a hurry.

Trebor considered the last remarks made by the monk, the entire congregation must be assembling and meditate; decisions were to be taken in the view of new calamities cast upon their city. Is there a serious risk of the population 'mobbing' in search for food and shelter, or even worse, pillage the ornate edifice? Are the monks able to secure the enclosure of the temple and even to defend it, if necessary? And mostly, are their believes in agreement with self-defense? Trebor sensed even more powerfully the need of learning more about this place and this culture, after the intense attraction he felt for this land, against the fact that they almost 'crushed' touching it.

After bringing his traveling carry-on by his bed, Trebor found his way out, in a small garden against the wall of the main temple. He sat there for a while contemplating in the quiet surroundings, admiring the dramatic color changes of the sky, as the reddish and purple shades of the clouds were making room for the stars to light up one after another.

"It must be a reason for all of this to happen", Trebor thought. "There was a reason for me to end up in a North Korean labor camp, meet my grandfather and learn about my mother. To be saved first by my parents who adopted me, my father being saved by my mother's kidney transplant. Then, Sunjin keeping me alive, afterward being rescued by my own father, and at last reunited with him and my twin sister. Then, losing my grandfather, and now facing a disaster of biblical proportions!"

If Trebor did not quite understand the reasons of why all this had to happen, he was very much aware that at this moment he only aspired for tranquility. Above all, Trebor wanted to experience this peace, learn about the mystical power of finding contentment; Trebor yearned isolating himself and finding within a new direction in his life, in the middle of these tormented times ravaging the world.

In the morning, father and his children, along with Li, were invited to the common mess hall, after a very appreciated restful night. Avoiding to interfere with the established ways of the monastery habits, the new guests resumed to only observe the monks' reactions, for they could understand very little the Tibetan language. The monks had obviously decided to continue their regular life and their manners did not testify of any agitation penetrating their surroundings.

Lu Xiang, as promised, offered to give them a tour of the monastery and the temple. Thus, Jo, Trebor, Maggie, and Li spent most part of the morning walking these six plus acres of the Jokhang temple area. If they did not venture to the outer circle, 'the pilgrims' path', where the prayer cylinders were moved by worshipers in chiming chants, they had been guided through chapels to the main shrine. Infused with a deep deference, they entered the temple where they were shown the inner sanctum with the Jowo Buddha statue, giving the name of Jokhang to the place, meaning the 'Temple of the Lord'.

Jokhang construction started when princess Gyasa married a Tibetan king and brought with her the most-revered statue, Sakyamuni Buddha chiseled as a young prince. The first temple was erected in 652 on a place indicated by a white stupa, a memorial monument replaced since then by this holiest shrine.

It is hard to imagine that, during the Cultural revolution in 1966, the most sacred place in Tibet had been closed and considered, along with many others, as a place to be destroyed. During this time, all religious activities were forbidden and during the persecution monks were killed, temples burned or desecrated by giving them ominous functions. The Red Guards were boarded in some of the sections of the temple, while other parts of the building were transformed on a pig sty and a slaughterhouse, and this until the temple was repaired and reopened in 1980.

As the discovery of this holy place continued, the four guests appeared profoundly touched by the mystery of this place out of time or human law, and they asked more questions and showed more desire to learn from this unique opportunity. Lu Xiang was secretly very pleased as well, and advancing into the afternoon hours, proposed for them to continue to walk and feel the energy surrounding the temple, while he had to attend some of his duties.

Lu Xiang had good reasons to return to its congregation, for worrisome news came regarding the situation beyond the walls of the monastery, as the crowd outside was becoming increasingly unsettled. If the monks were not to oppose a physical resistance to possible invaders, they were already getting organized for living without electrical supply and relying on their own fresh produce and water from their two wells. It has been decided, though, that the public visits would be suspended for an undetermined period of time, as they learned that the tourists were becoming frantic to leave town and sightseeing was no longer their priority.

However, the subject of possible individuals seeking refuge in the confines of the temple came up, and considering the limited means available, decisions had to be made case by case, but for now, the four foreign guests were welcome to stay.

This turn of the situation suited well Trebor and Maggie, the two of them already transported into another world opening unforeseen facets of reality, leading to a deeper awareness and search of their purpose in life. Jo, although welcoming the peacefulness of their refuge, he already located the small office of a monk operating a radio wave and asked permission to join in. He was glad to find a way to learn more about the reason and the extension of these extraordinary events, and he decided that from now on, he would stay close to this valuable source of information.

Most surprisingly, Li became suddenly aware of a reality that opened a new image over the world, a view of it that he never suspected before; he was so immersed in his own survival in the communist China, that he discovered only now other populations and cultures that had been devasted by the same regime ideology. Mostly, Li started to absorb this factual reality, while discovering the spiritual powers that guided all along the Tibetans, helping them to outlast and become even stronger under tragedy.

By the end of the day, the first at Jokhang temple of the several weeks that were to follow, Jo picked up with increased apprehension news about the spreading of an international conflict of a global magnitude. The tension between China and North Korea only continued to reach dangerous heights, and in contrast with past historical tensions, China managed to attract Japan's support against North Korean threat.

The Russian autocratic leadership was spreading thin attempting to take advantage of the political instability and promised aid to China, but also to the Iranians who menaced more than ever Israel, while contemplating regaining territories in the eastern Europe and Asia, as part of the formerly 'Great Mother Russia'.

During this time, North Korea was broadcasting to whomever wanted to hear their imminent intention to take over South Korea and to annihilate China, Japan, and even the United States of America!! Obviously the grandomaniac delirious mind of Kim Jong Un had no limits!

Jo did not need much more information to start making plans. Considering the facts, it was evident that traveling was not an option at the present time and it was important to evaluate their chances of survival in Tibet. For now, the monastery was a safe haven for them, but for how long until the mobs would to start attacking? The same goes for the authorities, soon to be overwhelmed by the problems and no longer able to prevent the anarchy taking over.

At the end of the day, obtaining some reliance on the young monk operating the radio station, and after conveying some of the worrisome data gathered so far to Lu Xiang, Joseph Godson could finally meet with the grand master.

"I am honored to be in your presence, Holy Master! First of all, I would like to express my deepest gratitude for having offered shelter to my children, Kuan Li, and myself. For this, may your soul forever enjoy a heavenly eternity", Jo started. "As a token of my appreciation, please allow me to contribute within my limited capacities to help during these trying times. What we observe here is only a very small part of the reality"

"You are right, my son, the reality, the universe is infinitely larger and more complex."

"I am humbly referring to the immediate dangers exposing this community and the survival of a legacy handed to the keepers of this temple for millennia. What it is happening at the present time in the world is affecting also this region. I could offer a few suggestions of how to prepare to resist potential attacks and take measures of survival during these cataclysmic events."

"But we are doing just that, every day and every moment, preparing for eternity and forget about the petty human turmoil creating drama everywhere and all the time!", was the reply.

"There have been times, however, if I am not mistaken, when even gods judged that it was right to fight back and defend the true principles of an orderly universe. Lord Shiva, the destroyer of evil and the transformer, with his 'trishula' as his weapon, protected and continues to protect the universe."

The revered master was in no hurry, he replayed in his mind the foundation of the Buddhist practice, as the scholars would introduce to the one seeking initiation, the steps of the 'three refuges or the three Jewels'. He started to recite them, chanting them as forms of reverence and protection:

- the Buddha, as the blessed one, the awakened with true knowledge,
- the Dharma, the practice of the Four Truths,
- the Sangha, the order of the monks, the community of the Buddha disciples to which I belong.

Then, he thought about the 'fourth refuge of the Tibetan Buddhism', the Lama, not as a place to hide, but rather to purify, uplift, and strengthen. He remembered that not so long ago the lama tradition almost disappeared, and the oldest scriptures, Salistamba Sutra, preserved in Tibetan version since the 8th-century, no longer found even in Sanskrit version, were hidden and preserved from fire and other harms in this very holy place.

After a while, the master addressed Jo, telling him that he would give an answer before long, then he retrieved in meditation. As in Tibetan Buddhism, he started with Samatha, pre-Buddha calm meditation, then to Vipassana, the insight meditation, added by Buddha. In contrast with the Samatha search for calm and tranquility, Vipassana is a pursuit for deep and critical insight. As the master completely emptied his mind into the void, he returned with clearance of his spirit as images formed distinctly in his mind eye.

This temple that was under his guidance as the Enlightened Teacher, required here and now the preservation of the past traditions to be handed to the followers in the future. It was a place to be venerated, where new generations were to learn and grow spiritually, where the sick were healed, and where the prosecuted found refuge. And the present time brought about desperate events when these principles needed to be defended if they had a chance of survival. His decision was clear, he would gather all the monks along with the four guests and use everyone's mind to finding ways of sparing Jokhang Temple and aid as many in distress as they judged safe.

PROGRESSING THROUGH ENLINGHTENMENT

Kuan Li, Joseph Godson, and his descendants once accepted by the Jokhang Temple monks, became rapidly intrinsic part of their small community. Although they expressed their desire to help in any capacity they could, they also did not want to disturb the monastic rhythm prevailing in the temple, and softly and naturally, each of them integrated to the order already established by generations of monks.

Trebor and Maggie were fascinated by everything they were seeing and learning. And there was Li, who followed them everywhere. While filtering any information he could capture through radio wave broadcast from a variety of sources and corners of the planet, Jo sorted through them to find meaningful and practical interpretation to their present situation. For a while, for any insider the monks' practices went undisturbed, although the offerings assuring the food supply coming from the worshipers and pilgrims ceased since the blackout, fault of transportation, which led to a rapid depletion of town resources.

A quick inventory of the monastery stores and needs for the 34 monks present and now 38 people with the addition of the guests, gave Jo the opportunity to assess their reserves and human capabilities; roughly, half of them were young monks with four or five of them apprentices, the other half was made of adults, and some very old monks of an age hard to determine, but commonly well over 100 years of age. However, all of them appeared strong and their condition allowed them to participate to new tasks, as tending the small garden already existing within the walls of the temple.

There was a fairly large supply of candles, incense, and oil lamps, and with the temple closed for now and most of the candles and lamps not remaining constantly lit, the monks' personal needs seemed covered for a while. However, the monks being essential vegan, the plant-based food source had to be increased and new patches of land were found around the guest houses permitting to start new cultures. Here, Jo appeared, one more time, very resourceful, and new seeds collected, bulbs saved for planting, and irrigations enlarged. He even improvised a wood burning furnace and an oven for daily rice flat pancakes, accompanying a variety of soups and other preparations.

While assuming these tasks, Joseph Godson was not only offering his help, but he enjoyed every moment of it. In the middle of a turmoil of staggering proportions, being in this serein place and enjoying the presence of his two children, Jo almost attaint a state of peace. He considered this period suspended in time as an unexpected blessing allowing him to get to know each other and to grow closer.

Li, seemed to find also some peaceful times, opening to understand other meanings of his own existence. A deeper consideration led him think that there was, for him too, a reason that life brought him along his new friends, into these secluded circumstances.

Lu Xiang continued to be a guide to Maggie and Trebor, and often to Li, making time for separate moments of mentoring, for the apprentice monks followed a more rigorous and very specific path in their initiation. As Lu Xiang did not expect the twins to join the lamas' life, he introduced them to the general principles of Buddhism, then to the meditation and prayers through chanting. Leading his two acolytes close to the areas where the monks practiced their devotion, he found a sensible way for them to experience the emotional and spiritual energy emerging from this place.

From the beginning, the great master became interested in the progress made by his 'protégés', exchanging his impressions with Lu Xiang and a few other monks. They were all very surprised, although considered that not much could amaze them, observing their very rapid and deep understanding of transcendental thinking. Humble and reverent, they only wanted to absorb knowledge and grow spiritually, a natural progression of Trebor's later transformation, while Maggie had opened a door leading to a path responding to her innermost queries. Sharing so many emotions in common with Trebor, they both discovered that, through distressed turns of fate, they continuously had to adjust to new situations. Now ascending to an elevated vision of their existence, it became natural for them to consider their own lives in context with a world going asunder.

Trebor's physical appearance, changed tremendously since his imprisonment. He had continued to mature along with these profoundly transforming experiences. His hair falling in gentle waves well below his year lobes, was dark as it was a short beard now covering most of his face. His lean body kept however the large shoulder frame and his tall stature, which was difficult to distinguish from his father's when both seen from the back. The three of them had this 'signature' eyes, with a blue-aqua shade, illuminated from inside and giving the impression of burning lasers peering through people and objects.

After having spent days and weeks in the complete dark solitude during the labor camp detention, Trebor learned how to ignore his physical barriers and, finding himself within his soul, he could expend his consciousness and connect with the divine. At Jokhang Temple, Trebor embraced the solitude offered by meditation and, in contrast with the previous forced isolation, he was entranced by the quality of this place. He immersed himself in its tranquil and beautiful surroundings, the peacefulness of the temple chambers, the dreamlike atmosphere created by the sounds of the prayer wheels, the incense burners, and the monks' chanting. This was a welcome isolation, his body healing, his soul connecting with the high powers, and his mind acquiring knowledge about this alive and intelligent universe connecting all.

Trebor welcomed also the teachings of the master, avid to discover an approach in which other cultures and faiths looked at the world, at the human presence, and its role in it. It was a new, profound mystical acknowledgement for him and Maggie, bringing a new vision of the world through this special window in time. During these soul incursions, Trebor attempted to reconnect with the celestial father, with God, his deep belief telling him that all religions tried in a variety of ways to achieve the same union with the creator.

Joseph Godson and his twin children, went through a rapid transition from an intensely lived attempt to regain the United States and reach safety, to a slow passing of hours and days, in a retreat away from the agitation of the world. It was a harder adjustment for Jo, who continued to stay in contact with the secret offices, and to learn more about the extent of the EMPs damage, in the desire to find a possible conveyance back home. He did not get discouraged when all his efforts did not produce any reassuring information.

Then, finally Jo could make a contact. The first opening came from the base in Seoul, when Jo learned that the entire Korean peninsula, along with most of south China, were completely paralyzed by the high-altitude nuclear attack. The team inspecting the nuclear sites in North Korea with him and Maggie, while in its way to South Korea, was still in the northern territory and no one had any precise information of its members' situation.

The connections were very poor and after many more trials, Jo was told that it has been taken note of his and his children's location. He finally obtained a promise for more instructions to follow as soon as possible, when an evacuation or point of meeting could be established. Then, silence followed again for days.

Volens-nolens, Jo had to go along with the community activities, increasingly astounded to observe the monks' life continuing in spite of the growing turmoil surrounding them. Li and Jo resumed to follow the twins, and found themselves absorbed in the monks' teachings, leaving into a parallel and very different world from the one just outside the temple's doors.

They learned about Buddha's life and his practices, none of them having had any previous knowledge of it. Their open minds and genuine interest of the eastern religions attracted the monks' curiosity at first, then the desire to assist them in their initiation.

Learning that Li was a Chinese citizen who took his chance to live a different life accompanying the Godson family, the Buddhist monks did not ask any questions and treated Li as any other honorable guest. Thus, Li realized the simple fact of being accepted without questions, which made him appreciate profoundly the concepts of the monks, their acceptance without judgement, their tolerance of the 'enemy', their humanity in a life dedicated to the spirit. Without difficulty, Li found his own assignment, and he coud be seen sweeping floors, changing candles and oil lamps, while stopping in front of the shrines looking deeply in thoughts. Then, timidly he begun to move his lips in prayer and stayed a little longer near the monks and, at first hesitant, joined them in their chanting.

The four guests were soon free to wander through the rooms of the vast palace, and encouraged to ask questions. During one of the quiet discussions they had with the Enlightened Master, this surprised them with an unexpected reference to old secret texts.

"Have you ever heard of Issa, the Healer and the Shepherd?"

"Issa? Never heard of him. Who was he?" came from one of the four protégés, sitting in front of the master.

"Yes, Issa, the Buddhist monk. He came from Israel at the age of 14 and studied Buddhism until he was 29. His name there was Jesus, and, at his birth, the three Magi went far away, to Bethlehem, following the new star announcing the arrival of the son of God. Then, when he came to age, Jesus followed the silk road and came to Hemis in Tibet, to perfect his education. Those were the 'lost years of Jesus'."

After a while, the master continued, amused by their puzzled interest:

"Issa, had much in common with Buddha. He thought love and pardon, and declared that we are all equal and that the world will be inherited by the meek. Like Buddha, He performed miracles, healed the sick, fed the poor with a few fish, and walked on the water. Issa, aka Jesus, was a great prophet, the first after twenty-two named Buddha. He was greater than all of the Dalai Lamas, and he represented the spirit of God, His father."

"But he died on the cross in Jerusalem!?", Trebor asked.

"Yes, he returned to Israel and he was crucified. But he came back after he had resuscitated, fleeing to the Himalayas with some Jewish settlers. Jesus remained for many more years in the Kashmir Valley, and founded a temple of Solomon. It is believed that he lived by the name of Yussasa until he was 80 years old and was buried in Roza Bal shrine in Srinagar, Kashmir. There, lives the tribe of Ben E Israel, continuing Jesus' ministry in the temple of Solomon, at a shrine that one can still visit even today."

MIRACLES

If the father, son, and daughter were deeply mystified by these astonishing revelations, so were the angles through which they looked at the world, opening new and vast considerations of a spiritual existence, beyond all the materialistic struggle they faced until recently. They were changing, and rapidly. And so was Li. And with these changes came a different way the monks and the masters looked at them, and considered them. Father and twins had a calm and quiet manner of passing through the chambers of the temple and the gardens. They always assumed a very peaceful attitude when participating to any activity and offering their help. And more changes occurred.

There was an aura emanating from the new adepts, in particular from the one called Trebor. This one, gently inquiring about simple things around the monastery, by his presence and kind ways of talking to the others, brought calm and comfort. Then, other small facts almost unnoticed, made some of the apprentices pay attention. When a monk showed to Trebor the cellars getting low on rice and flower, onions and potatoes, when he returned later, the cellars seemed replenished. If a patch of dirt in the garden became invaded by weeds and bugs, after Trebor touched them with caressing fingers, the tomatoes, carrots, bell peppers, and cabbages showed happy and fatty faces soon after.

The apprentices and some younger monks came to their superiors to tell them that there is no worry to be had regarding the monastery's supplies. However, their special guests continued to behave as though nothing was altered. That was until the following week, when the carpenter went up on the roof to repair a few wooden tiles and prevent water leaking during the monsoon season.

Suddenly, there was a big commotion in the main hall, along with unusual sharp screams and agitation from the monks gathering under the main vault of the temple. This attracted everyone to find out what was the matter. The poor old carpenter laid on the floor, his body crooked and blood coming out of his mouth. He could barely take but shallow breaths, as he tried to reach toward his left leg bent into twisted angles.

Everyone came running toward the old monk, when Jo, who had some first-aid training, approached and kneeled next to the injured man, the others stepping aside as the two tall men arrived. Instinctively, Trebor had joined his father who was carefully assessing the carpenter, avoiding to aggravate his condition by moving him too fast.

"He must have broken some ribs and pierced one of his lungs, look at this white foam stained with blood coming out his mouth", Jo whispered to himself, then sharing with Trebor his findings. "His pulse is rapid and he is clammy, he is conscious, though. Now, let's see his left leg. Oh, the poor chap, his femur is broken through and through and is twisted! It must hurt as hell. Sorry, like...well, like hell!"

Saying this, Jo unbuckled his belt and pulled it off to make a tourniquet, asking Trebor to help him. During this time, Maggie sat next to the monk with a small clay washbowl filled with water and, with extreme gentleness, she dabbed his forehead and his face with a wet cloth, all the while telling him words of encouragement as they were coming to her like a lullaby soothing a child.

Fault of a dagger or scissors close by, Jo torn the yellow wrap to have a clearer view of the monk's left thigh, then having Trebor cautiously roll him a little to the right, he could slide the belt under his upper leg, making a tight knot to stop the femoral artery hemorrhage. Jo and Trebor continued their care, placing the carpenter on his back and prudently realigning his broken bones. Then, they asked for two long splints and wraps to secure the leg.

While moving and repositioning the old monk, Trebor was instinctively murmuring prayers addressed to the Creator. Touching the injured man, he lovingly placed his hands on the chest and the left leg of the old monk, wishing to comfort him.

"Look, he is not bleeding anymore, and his breath is deeper now", some voices were heard.

"Give me a bowl with water, and add some wine if you can", Trebor asked. When the bowl was handed to him, Trebor lifted the man's head delicately and made him take a few sips of water mixed with wine.

The monk seemed swiftly appeased, and lowering his head, murmured a soft "Thank you", looking Trebor in his eyes with stunned recognition. Then, before falling into a deep sleep, he repeated: "Thank you, Lord."

"I think we can get him now to a quiet place to rest ", proposed Jo, and aided by Trebor and Maggie, lifted the tiny monk and followed the others leading the away to a close by private chapel. Maggie asked to stay with him for the first watch, letting all the others go to pray.

Next morning, when two young apprentices came to check on the injured monk, they found him up and attempting to remove the splints and bandages, bearing full weight on his left leg. The old man had a smile of comprehension on his face and not in the least sign of hurt.

A LITTLE TOUR OF LHASA

Things seemed to settle into the former routine observed in the temple, and along with it, the new addition of the persons living in the temple had found a natural way to fit into the monastic life. It was to wonder if the Great Master was not somehow aware of the periods of trouble occurring just beyond the temple's walls, in the heart of the old Lhasa's Barkhor square. For the first two weeks the unrest only grew in intensity, culminating with riots and attempts to break into the monastery perimeter. Then, as if the crowds were looking for answers to the dramatic events, the noise declined and people scrambled to find away their own solutions for survival.

One morning, when Lu Xiang met his acolytes at dawn, instead of starting with the usual morning deep breathing and meditation, he addressed the four foreigners:

"The Master thinks that you might be interested in visiting some of the other monasteries and Potala Palace here, in Lhasa. They are at a short walking reach and I could lead you there safely."

Surprised, but also filled with a sudden excitement, the four guests were ready to follow their mentor. They just realized the need to satisfy their curiosity and discover freely this fascinating place. Jo appreciated the opportunity to find out more about these disturbing incidents changing their plans and their lives, and was eager to see what was the situation beyond the monastery walls.

For now, Lu Xiang, with his brisk shuffling steps, walked them to and around the most impressive edifice of the area, Potala Palace, the residence of the Dalai Lamas. The palace sitting unoccupied, as an image of the glory of the pre-communist era, it became more recently a great tourist attraction. Even after weeks living in high altitude, the followers were still needing some adjustment to the rarefied air. Thus, enchanted but exhausted after miles of sightseeing, the four of them felt quite happy later on to regain Jokhang monastery peaceful surroundings.

The following days, Lu Xiang continued to play their guide, bringing his new protégés to other monasteries in close proximity of Lhasa. They went to Drepung Monastery, a few kilometers to the west, at the foot of Mount Gambo Utse, opening into view with its layered roofs like a heap of rice. Given the name of 'Monastery of Collecting Rice', Drepung Monastery had been in the past the largest Buddhist monastery, containing more than 10 thousand monks.

After Drepung, the following day they went south, to Tatipu Hill, the scenery offering a beautiful cradle to Sera Monastery. There, the monastery built at the beginning of the 15th Century was adorned with roses planted all around in the garden of the monastery, also called 'the court of roses', tended by the 200 remaining lamas living there. The visitors were invited to enjoy a picnic in these idyllic surroundings.

The Ganden Monastery, one of the oldest and holiest marvels of the Buddhist string of bejeweled monasteries, being situated at 50 kilometers from Lhasa, had to be reserved for a future visit. However, Lu Xiang let them know with a large grin in his face, that, like at Drepung and Sera monasteries, there too, the monks liked to get together and 'debate'. To which, Jo inquired if the monks discuss the latest events during their debate sessions, making Lu Xiang laugh: "I doubt it, but you are welcome to attend one of their debates, most of the time they don't mind foreigners. They get so inflamed, they ignore them!"

It was too much of a temptation for Jo not to use this opportunity to explore new options for reaching territories served by modern transportation, especially since his contacts with the base in South Korea remained stubbornly silent. If the other monasteries they visited seemed to manage to continue undisturbed their course of life, Jo already made notes about the limited presence of people in town, tourists almost completely gone or looking for ways to get out. Practically all stores were closed and barricaded against looters, while the locals had deserted the center town hoping to survive in the country side.

Another week went by, Trebor and Maggie immersed in their monastic life, while Jo became frustrated without any other contact after four weeks of their stay in Lhasa. Only Kuan Li, without even knowing, slowly blended into the monastery life.

Then, one day, finally the young apprentice of the radio room came out, running to fetch Jo in the garden, where he was readjusting an irrigation groove for the tomatoes. Someone was waiting on a short-length-wave line to talk in person to Joseph Godson!

MAKING CONTACT

At last, precise instructions were coming from the base in Seoul, South Korea: there was still very little progress made in the world to restore communication and travel, food and necessary supplies to the general population of a huge area of the globe, although great emphasis was made to avoid mass uprising and anarchy. However, the directions given to Jo were succinct, "he will be contacted by Jamuna, the head of a sherpa team offering tourists guided trips between Tibet and Kathmandu, Nepal, as part of one of the oldest 'Silk and Spices Routes'. They usually used Jeeps, and trips to Kathmandu were organized over 4 to 8 days, according to the number of Buddhist monasteries visited. Since the blackout, the sherpa guides regrouped and offered to bring the visitors rather to locations that could, hopefully, offer a way back home."

Well, they had to wait a little longer for the base to call back, Jo was told, until further trip itinerary could be suggested and secured, during and after the four of them would arrive in Kathmandu. "Efforts were made to find a route, or air transportation if improvement is made, and continue from Kathmandu to Delhi, India. From there, hopefully a flight will bring you to Mumbai or Karachi, where one of the military carriers sailing in the Indian Ocean rescue American citizens from India and Pakistan to bring them to the Mediterranean Sea through the Red Sea and Suez Canal. Of course, if the long-distance airline carriers were not functioning yet and a faster evacuation could not be offered."

"Anyway", the radio sentry hurried to deliver the message, "we need to get you to Kathmandu first, and out of the Chinese territory. We obtained from the Grand Master of Jokhang Temple the agreement to get the four of you to the town of Tingri, which is still an important trading post for Nepalese sherpas. This is as far as their mini bus can go, the roads and the thin air makes it difficult to ride, and the gas supply is still uncertain. There, you will meet Jamuna, who is Nepalese, trained in crossing the Himalayas and bringing regularly tourists to EBC, on their way from Lhasa to Kathmandu. But if they can't use any automotive transportation, you will have to travel out in a cart pulled by mountain oxen, then, if needed, by donkeys across the border."

"EBC? What's that?" Jo asked.

"Ah, it is the Everest Base Camp. They are actually two of them, one on each side of the mountain facing the tallest summits either from the Tibet or Nepal approach. Many tourists, who want to rough up and claim that they climbed the Mount Everest, they get to spend a night in a tent on the snow, take pictures, and earn their little trophy to brag about."

"One more thing, do not forget to bring warm clothing, for obvious reasons. Drink lots of water, melt the snow if necessary, and bring snacks, there is not much on the road, and the lodges are closed. But you may try the monasteries on the way, I heard they are magnificent. So, you might do some sightseeing after all!", ended the young man, with humor.

Before Jo had the time to bring the news to his children, to Li, and then to Lu Xiang, sherpa Khimar, an emissary of Jamuna, had already announced himself at the gate of the monastery. Introductions were made in the visitor area, and, speaking in a fairly good English, Khimar gave simple but precise information about their trip planned to start early the next morning. Once in Tingri, their group would remain limited, a Canadian from Calgary, accustomed with snowy mountains, and an Italian from Sicily, all the opposite, were to join the caravan. They would have to walk most of the time, since the carts pulled by the oxen were loaded with tents, blankets, and some basic food and water. Before the top of the mountains, they would count on the lamas' help at the monasteries on the road for shelter and food, and at times they would have to use the tents until reaching the Nepalese territory.

After Khimar left, the travelers excited and anxious at the same time, went to prepare for a new adventure. And what an adventure seemed to lay ahead! Most of the monks gathered, and the anticipation carried a new energy to the monastery, all eager to help. In no time, there was a mountain of heavy jackets, colorful hats, gloves, and fur-lined boots to be tried on. There were also jars with honey, pickled vegetable preserves, small bags of dry beans and rice, but also a couple of Dame Jeanes of rice moonshine and sweet wine. There had been added a good-sized bag with Tibetan dry tea for the strong hot Chai, and even some small pots of Tiger balm and one filled with a strange looking blubber lubricant "absolutely necessary to prevent sun burns when on the top of the mountain." Some of the lamas had even located old sunglasses, looking more like goggles than glasses.

After a good selection had been made in the middle of a flurry of excitement, it was decided that they all needed to meditate and pray for their friends' journey, then have one last good meal together, before retrieving for a restful nigh.

The time came when, one after the other, the monks made their farewells, keeping a happy mood, since they all believed in a lasting connection in an eternal world. The Great Master came too, exchanging a few words of good wishes. Then, he addressed Trebor, who was quietly witnessing this friendly agitation.

"Trebor, I wished I could spend more time with you and tell you more about our Tibetan principles and concepts."

"You did not have to talk, Great Master, for you showed them to us through your manners."

The lama looked at him with an interrogating expression.

"Yes, you showed us kindness, acceptance without judgement, compassion, and... love." Then, Trebor stepped forward and enveloped the monk with his arms into a gentle embrace: "This is all that the world needs in order to live in peace and happiness. And for this, we will forever be grateful. Thank you!"

JOURNEY ACROSS TIBET

Lu Xiang and an aspiring lama were designated to tackle the perilous mission of bringing their guests to Tingri, to that was added Khimar, who would show them the road and meet Jamuna and his team close to Tingri. After loading the equipment and provisions for the trip, they made a full tank of gas and filled four other canisters with what seemed to be most of the reserves in gasoline left at the monastery.

With a final prayer and well before dawn, the seven of them were on their way. They exited the town retracing their way in, taking the airport expressway, going south, then west. Lu Xiang made a few commentaries about driving his protégés back on the same road he brought them to Lhasa, when they met. He observed that the roads remained almost deserted, in striking contrast with the usual chaotic traffic during a regular tourist season.

Jo, asking for more details regarding their trip, learned that there was a distance of about 650 miles from Lhasa to Kathmandu, and this through the mountainous roads. First, they followed a clear path along the river to Gongga Qudesi, and attempt to cover about 360 km or some 225 miles to Shigatse in the first day. He did not mention, though, that they would ride south from Quxu, a small town about 40 miles from Lhasa, where a large prison was located and some inmates could have managed to escape during these troubled times. And the farther they would stay and the least they made themselves noticed, the better.

At this altitude, it was expected that everyone showed signs of fatigue quicker, and if there was practically little change on the 3640 m from Lhasa to Shigatse at 3840 m, the road to Gyantse through Kimpala Pass was taking the voyagers close to 5000 m, some 16,400 feet of altitude. In this early September, the weather was one of the best to travel in these regions with the clearer seasonal skies most of the time. Only close to EBC they could experience some cold temperatures, especially at night, but they should be fine with their equipment.

Well, they enjoyed somewhat the vistas during their stop by Yamdrok Lake for a picnic break, but their progress was slower than anticipated, with many road blocks controlled by the military. The passports were checked, and being in the company of the lamas was helpful, the young soldiers did not speak any English and they did not read English for that matter, and the translation in Tibetan by the monks made things more understandable. Strangely, no one payed much attention to Kuan Li, possibly his Chinese features making him less visible to his countrymen.

The soldiers were tired and undernourished, and since they already dealt with dozens of foreign tourists stranded by the EMPs attack, they were somewhat 'blasé'. Then, Jo and his keen showed their airline tickets for US, explaining that their presence in Lhasa was only an unexpected miracle to be alive. The military were also flattered to hear the three Americans speaking in mandarin, a lot more than they had seen so far. Nevertheless, at every stop their food supply was getting slimmer and slimmer, as the monks offered to the hungry looking soldiers at first liquor, then honey, and at last, a few potatoes.

Needless to say, that Karola Glacier was little admired as night was approaching and everyone was tired. However, the travelers made it to Pelkor Choede Monastery in Gyantse, after covering 230 miles south from Lhasa.

They learned that Pelkor Choede, or Chode Monastery, means "Auspicious Wheel of Joy Monastery" in Tibetan, and the travelers took the name as a promising sign for their journey. This large construction, at the foot of Dzong Hill a few hundred yards from the town of Gyantse, is surrounded on three sides by mountains. With its protection walls, a tower, and several Buddhist halls, the monastery is highly regarded for its beautiful murals: here one could admire esoteric Buddhist art with the central focus on the representation of the Mandala.

The small group quickly felt much better finding the security and the serene ambience of the monastery, and truly appreciated the simple but warm hospitality of the monks after a full day on the road. Over the supper, information was exchanged regarding the travelers' story and their itinerary, while the monks liked to boast about the beauty of their monastery. Then it was time for a good night rest, with the promise that the monks would show their guests the main hall murals before them getting on the road. They definitely would not miss such unique opportunity!

Rested and with the soul filled with beautiful images of the monastery decor, and the van restocked with some victuals, our errant group moved on to Shigatse, or the Xigaze in Chinese, almost 100 km from there, then to Tashilunpo Monastery at lunch, and hoping to arrive to Lhatse before the night. After that, they counted finding themselves some 50 miles from the town of Tingri. There, they were expected by sherpa Jamuna at the Dampapa School for Tibetan Buddhism.

JAMUNA

Reaching Tingri Lankor and Dampapa School, our group completed their traveling by the monastery van to meet the caravan led by Jamuna, and where their trekking to Everest was to start. It was an adventure so exciting that made our voyagers almost ignore that it was also a very difficult one, as they were looking forward to it with almost no reservation.

Jamuna, an experienced trekker, found ways to obtain three yak-pulling-carts which he intended to guide with the help of the other two sherpas, carrying material and food. He explained that the trail he intended to follow from Tingri to Everest Base Camp on their way to Kathmandu, would bring them from 4400m to 5300m of elevation. They were looking to accomplish over 70 km, about 43,5 miles, hopefully in four days of walking. They would encounter some of the dangers of the wild with dramatic temperature changes during day and night and even snow storms surprising them in this fall season. But on their way, they should have the chance also to admire brown bear and gazelles, and avoid wild dogs. While being careful to prevent dehydration and altitude sickness, there were plenty of moments of solitude to contemplate in front of spectacular decors of the highest mountains in the world.

After the traveling gear was transferred from the van and distributed to the carts, simple farewells were in order, when the American family was surprised to hear Lu Xiang telling them that "he is not done with them, and that he decided to continue his trip to Kathmandu and visit with lama friends at Buddhanikantha Temple. Without giving them time to react, he added that he was "eager to pursue a little longer their conversations started at Jokhang Monastery". The monk driver would make the trip back alone, having been given countless words of advice, the little gas left, and a generous compensation from the Godson family.

Well before dawn, a small caravan went into motion, Jamuna and his two helpers, Khimar and Bishnu, looking forward to regain Nepal, their homeland, and anxious to look after their own families left behind. Along came Randal Selnick from Canada and Jovanni Mira, from Italy, the Americans, Kuan Li, and the latest and unexpected addition to the group, Lu Xiang. Jamuna, without saying much, once he learned about Lu Xiang's decision to join them, went to one of the carts and shuffling a little around, came back to the monk and handed him some winter clothes.

"Here, I know you can sweat meditating on the snow, but with me, you will have to walk."

The first day required an ascension of only 150m, a good start to get adjusted to the high elevation while trekking. The group swiftly passed the Che Village, then Zhaka and entered the Ra-chu valley, where barren plains opened. Passing through Cholong Village, Jamuna let them take a break and went to a simple dwelling, coming out with what he thought to find, a small bag with barley. The villagers had a good harvest that year, even at this altitude. He had also filled a container with yak milk, one of the most nutritious natural beverages in the world. This would bring a welcome change to their dinner.

After the lunch break, the strangers kept walking with their spirits high, noticing a few herds of mountain goats far away, quietly grazing on some brownish pastures. However, they learned that, if this time of the year the sherpas would have been the busiest guiding adventurous Everest Mountains visitors, the only people seen were some isolated locals minding their own interests. They walked for about six hours and covered 12 km, stopping for lunch and for a few moments here and there to catch their breath, when they finally arrived at a beautiful site and were relieved to know that Lung Thang was also their destination to raise their night camp.

This first experience for the foreigners camping in the Himalayas, was a good preparation for harder days ahead, with longer walks and higher elevation to climb. Night came fast and surprised them with a below-zero temperature fall. The fire camp started by the sherpas, yak milk promptly warmed and offered to the travelers, created a scout-like atmosphere, that everyone seemed to enjoy. While the guests savored the simple dinner, a thick barley and vegetable soup, and getting to know each other, the sherpas mounted three small tents and laid their sleeping bags. Jo would share his tent with his daughter, Maggie, Trebor with Lu Xiang, Jovanni with Li and Randal, while the three guides were staying together by the fire.

A few more jokes and laughter could be heard as our travelers ended their meal with a sweet rice with honey and milk from the valley for dessert, when they were slowly taken by the beauty of the sky covered with millions of stars. When Maggie declared that she was setting her sleeping bag close to the camp fire, Trebor quickly joined in, then Jo, and even Randal, used to Canadian winters. Jovanni, was not so sure, and let the others take the challenge:

"I am from Sicilia, my body is hot, but I need my bed warm to get a good night sleep!"

And, indeed they needed a good rest, for tomorrow they had a long day in front of them, covering over 20 km climbing up into the mountains, and ascending 200m with an exhausting uphill towards Lamna La Pass.

REACHING HIGHER ELEVATIONS

If our improvised explorers defied the exhaustion during the strenuous climb to Lamna La Pass, 5150m, close to 16,900 feet, their efforts were rewarded with a breathtaking scenery. As they reached the pass, a spectacular sight of the four highest peaks of the Himalayas unfolded majestically in front of them as an ultimate celestial offering. Everyone could understand the efforts made by so many to experience these moments of overwhelming grandeur, where the stillness and peacefulness of the highest mountains on Earth touch the interstellar space.

One by one, the sherpas had shown Malaku and Everest peaks ahead of them to the south, then further to southwest Cho Oyu and Shishapangma peaks. Entranced, the travelers paused in awe, and even the effervescent Jovanni seemed at loss of words. And, if climbing the Everest peak was not their final destination this time, the highest summit in the world was calling their spirits to soar to its crown.

What our travelers experienced in front of Mount Everest was not only a supreme physical trial, but also this unique spiritual connection of a small, limited being, with a colossal divine creation. Lu Xiang, absorbed the vast panorama in deep contemplation for a while, then, directing his interest toward his friends, a pleasant smile came across his face.

"With all that happened lately, it looks like the Himalayas have no worries, they will be here for a long time, unchanged."

"Yes, it seems as if they were telling us that, if nothing changed for them, so should we consider our destiny, and what it was supposed to take place, it shall", softly Trebor reflected.

The group continued to walk taking a few more breaks to admire the grandiose vistas rendering their efforts worthwhile. Arriving to Zhaxizong Village, they made a longer stop, although the few shops usually selling drinks and food were closed and deserted. No one showed its face if any remained living in the village, and the primary school built in the world's highest altitude appeared closed.

An eerie atmosphere lingered in this place described by the sherpas as very animated during the visiting season, one of very few found in high elevation, where people liked to congregate, looking for equipment and provisions, and exchanging information. After finding a stand prompted against a closed barrack, they rested and had flat bread and lentils, while drinking some yak milk. Then, there were two more hours to walk and arrive to Basum Village before 4 pm, when the cold starts biting. They hoped that the guesthouse in Basum would be open, and, even if nobody was expected there to offer a meal, at least they could stay out of the cold and rest in the bunk room.

Indeed, Basum was deserted, but after a day of walking more than 8 hours, covering a distance of 21 km and ascending 200m, the convoy was ready for a good rest. The doors of the guest house were unlocked and while the sleeping bags were brought in and everyone chose the first bed available for the night, the sherpas had already started a fire in the stove placed in the middle of the room, using dry yak manure. It was not the best odor, but they were all too tired to complain.

The yaks were given feed and water from the trough near the guest house, then taken for the night into a shed where hay was left in large amount and where the three precious creatures could use the entire space. This time, no one expressed the desire to spend the night under the stars, or care if someone would be snoring. The warmth quickly filling the room, stretching on a bed and closed in the soft down of the sleeping bag, the small community found a peaceful sleep, away from any worldly hassle.

When Jo and Trebor woke up, rested and invigorated, they found out that others were already up; the sherpas were hitching the yaks to the carts, and Lu Xiang found a nice spot to make his morning prayers. Jamuna came to them and let them know that they were happy if they rested well, since the day ahead would be quite strenuous, with 8 hours of walking and another 21km expected to lay ahead. After the routine simple meal and preparations, the convoy sat in motion.

As they left Lamna La Pass area, the travelers went through a steep descent where green vegetation created a pleasant change to distract them from the difficulty of the terrain. The trail continued to show the amazing vistas of the Mount Everest, and the fields opening when the caravan entered Zommug area, although barren from any agricultural production, offered some food to the wild herds of yaks.

If the landscape continued to be spectacular, Zommug was a simple village with whitewashed walls and scarce population. One more time Jamuna could obtain some milk, the villagers relying on their livestock, some feed for the trekking yaks, but no shelter was offered by the remaining scared inhabitants. After another long day, if the group had to spend the night raising camp, at least Jamuna found a stunning site close by.

One more time, the travelers reunited around the fire camp, had dinner, and shortly after, they found their sleeping bags displayed in a tight circle. Maggie, after rubbing her feet as did the others, and exchanged a few pleasantries with Jovanni, went back to her deep considerations she had all along about the entire turn of events. As a journalist, she was capable of absorbing masses of information and retrieve it on a logical order. Since she experienced herself the depth of tragedy and learned about human suffering through her own mother's story, more recently she looked for more spiritual answers of the cosmic order of things. Maggie did not realize she was becoming more reflective and directing her conversations with her brother on the latest teachings of the Buddhist monks. She became aware of how much she enjoyed those exchanges and how welcome she felt about Lu Xiang presence during their journey. She even questioned him, during their walk today:

"Master Lu, I wish you will come with us and stay forever in our company; we will never end learning from you."

"It is true that the world we live in is changing. And it is up to you, the young ones, that it is done for the best. And, if you might learn a few things from me, I do, too, learn from you."

"Master", Joseph Godson joined in the conversation, "I feel that you, the monks I mean, live on a parallel world. Granted, an elevated spiritually, superior world, but a subliminal world. We, regular mortals, have to face the reality of a society that, if not perfect, is the one in which our families need to be taken care of, and it is not easy. We do not have only to meditate in isolation and nothing would happen to us, we have to face the harsh reality we live in", concluded Jo, a little surprised by his long monologue.

"You are right, Joseph, it seems easy for us and your sort is a continuous struggle", answered Lu Xiang, when, out of his habitude, Trebor interceded.

"In reality, we made this society we enclosed ourselves in. We are responsible of the hard times we live and we created. And we are the ones that need to change the order of things."

"Here you have the answer", Lu Xiang agreed, opening his arms.

"Yeah, I know, like it is as easy as it looks!" retorqued Jo.

"Well, if it is not easy, it is simple", echoed Trebor.

"And the lamas will allow a woman to join, as they let me sit with them in meditation", added Maggie from nowhere. They all looked at her continuing to follow through their trail.

Trebor and Jo looked at each other with a little chuckle, saying "Yes, it looks like every side needs to make some adjustments!"

EVEREST

Trebor, after watching the sky strewn with the stars so brilliant that they almost illuminated the night, send a prayer to thank the Father as he thought about their journey. He had noticed that the sherpas, when they were spending the night out camping, each one was bringing their yak next to the fire, sleeping against each other and keeping warm. Trebor was not sure if it were the fire or this kind image that made him feel so warm inside. Then, like everyone else, he fell into a deep sleep.

At first, Trebor felt warm like in the summer, and thought that he was still dreaming. But something was breathing in his neck, with a warm, "but, boy, what a bad breath!". He turned a little to get away from it, but as he moved, he heard a little growl, and felt a soft body fastened against his. Trebor feeling almost pinned by the strange embrace, started to pat gently to find out who or what was so 'enamored' of his person.

He felt fur, long hair fur, but too soft to be of a yak! And as he continued to probe, 'the creature' moved. Somehow, Trebor was not afraid, although ready to wake up Jamuna to chase away the intruder. Trebor could finally turn enough to have a look at the 'person' as it moved under his 'caress' with a sigh of satisfaction: it was a huge dog, now rolled on his back with his enormous paws held back in complete surrender!

Puzzled, Trebor tried to understand and find the right decision; he thought that it must be one of those mastiffs, the big dogs that some farmers kept around their properties, intimidating anyone to approach at the sight of those giants. Trebor did not know if they were as mean as were the wild dogs rummaging desperate for food on the high plains he saw from far away, from which he had been told to stay away.

"But this one, Trebor thought, is like a big teddy bear, he must be lost or abandoned with all that is going on. And he found us, and a place to cuddle", he almost laughed.

It could be that Trebor read the mastiffs' thoughts, or made that special connection we all do sometimes in life with another creature, when the dog felt his stare, and opened his eyes. They looked at each other for a few seconds, Trebor finding a kind and distressed plea in the eyes of the 'beast'.

Then, the dog curled up at Trebor's site, and in complete submission, looked at him as if waiting for the verdict; is he going to be chased away in the dark cold, with no place to go, and a growling tummy, or tolerated by the fire for this night only? "Please! let me stay with you", the eyes of the lonely creature seemed to implore.

But Trebor understood the dog's heart, and extracting himself from the sleeping bag, went to one of the carts. Jamuna was already alert and ready to jump, when Trebor made a quick sign with a finger to his lips: " Shuut...he is good, he only needs some food."

A little confused, Jamuna regained his senses, for he was ready to scare the dog away from the camp. But Trebor reacted swiftly as Jo was also joining the action, and awake, was looking toward them, getting out of his sleeping bag.

"Just a little food, look, he is nice, he must be lost", then added, "I will pay for him, not to worry!"

Jamuna grew up with animals, and, although he knew where each one's place was in a farm, he loved them, he understood that we can get very attached to them, for reasons he did not always grasped.

By the time Jamuna found some barley bread, while the dog was drinking with gusto some yak milk from a large bowl, everyone was awake; if at first, they had a little shock seeing the 'mammoth', soon after they relaxed, enjoying the spectacle. After picking every crump of bread and cleaning the milk bowl, the mastiff licked Jamuna's hand, then came to sit at Trebor's feet. The travelers, excited by the unexpected adventure, started asking questions about the dog's future, and, as the questions poured, Trebor found along answers:

"He will come with us, he adopted us, he is lost, he needs a family."

As everyone was wide awake, they all cheered in approval; it was settled then, the mastiff was adopted as their protector. They needed now to give him a name!

"That's easy, answered Trebor, his name is Everest!"

Cheers and applause could be heard now filling the night, and one by one the travelers came to pet their new mascot, Everest! Jamuna had even found a large piece of ox jerky and discreetly offered it to Everest. While the dog was happily chewing on his treat, the company made a few more commentaries about "how sweet Everest is, he let everyone pet him, and he seems so loving...", then they went back to sleep. If Everest felt as the luckiest and the happiest mastiff in the world, he didn't know that he already filled with love everyone's heart in that group of humans.

ALREADY GONE

"That was a good night rest!", thought Trebor, gently coming back from his reverie, and smiled even before opening his eyes. Then he stretched back an arm, searching for Everest. He did not feel his soft fleece, but he did not worry, "he must be already up and asking Jamuna for food!", then, happily he decided to get out of his sleeping bag and stretch as far as he could.

"Good morning, Jamuna, already up?"

"Well, we are only one hour behind our schedule, everyone overslept. But I would let them, we have a tricky trail ahead getting close to the picks. Our destination today is Rongbuk Monastery, we should reach it after a 15 km of trekking. Ronbuk is also our Base Camp for Mount Everest. at the foot of the Glacier Rongbuk, the world's highest monastery and the gateway to Mount Everest."

As he was giving these explanations, Jamuna laid down for Trebor some warm sweet preparation made of barley and honey boiled in yak milk, a good meal before one more day of trekking. Then, he turned to the pot set on the campfire and stirred the mixture with a wooden spoon, while adding:

"Everest Peak is only a few kilometers away from Rongbuk and offers the last station before the big climb of the highest peak for the trained, and I would say the craziest, mountain climbers in the world. But for us, Rongbuk is the most elevated place we will have to go and where we will find the best view from the north side of the mountains. But we have to hurry, after these nice and 'warm' days in these mountains, I see clouds accumulating and we don't need a blizzard!"

"A blizzard?"

"That's right, it can blow in at any time, summer or winter. We had an end of the monsoon that brought heavy rains, had a few mud slides, and although you don't see it, there is still a lot of moisture in the high-altitude valleys."

"Have you seen Everest?", Trebor changed the conversation.

"Right behind you", answered Jamuna.

"No, I mean the dog!"

"Ah, no, not seen him this morning. Just another hungry dog like many around here, he must be back at his home by now."

"I see", Trebor shook his head a little disappointed, and finished his breakfast.

As everyone woke up and started gathering around the fire camp, hungry and appreciative of the bowl of 'porridge' made by Jamuna, they all inquired about Everest and showed their regrets.

Shortly after, the yaks fed and attached to their carts by Khimar and Bishnu, Jamuna cleaned the empty bowls and covered the fire ashes, then everyone else packed, the convoy went on the trail for Ronbuk Monastery. Trebor was closing the caravan, looking a few more times back as if hoping to see Everest appearing behind, and catching up with them.

THE BLIZZARD

"Oh boy, that's cold!" was all that Maggie could think, shivering violently and assuming that the other travelers must feel the same. Their plan was to arrive at Ronbuk Monastery in the early afternoon, if not earlier, but the wind bringing heavy clouds charged with snow, caught up with them. If they were pushed ahead by the wind gusts, soon they became blinded by the icy snow slushing through their skin.

When the snow started falling in curtains shredded by hollering winds, Jamuna made a brief stop for everyone to add on more clothes and have their fur hats lowered to the eyebrows with the ear flaps down. He covered the yaks with thick pelts, and asked that they all stay close to the three carts, creating some resistance to the wind. They struggled this way two or three more hours, Jamuna coaxing them to keep going, they shouldn't be far from the monastery. Thus, they kept on shuffling through high snow, with each breath bringing in freezing air, barely seeing ahead and loosing completely notion of time.

Jamuna had a few encounters with snow during the summer season, but he did not remember the elements unleashing their ire like today. He was not even sure where they were, actually he had to recognize that they were lost in the blizzard. He silently pledged to take care of his crew and do everything necessary to keep them out of danger, for he realized that it was their lives that were at risk.

Not able to advance any further, Jamuna decided to stop and round up the caravan, then arranged the carts on a triangle aided by the other two sherpas, and placed yaks and people inside the improvised shelter. Animals and people, all together cuddled the best they could, all blankets and pelts used to keep the wind and the cold away.

The storm raged unbridled for what seemed like hours, never abating, howling winds sounding at times like rolling trains. The people inside the triangle became covered entirely by the snow, and if their courage remained strong and their faith unfailing, the cold numbed their bodies at first, then they started slowly slipping into a sleep about to make their demise quiet and peaceful.

Maggie realized that, with all the attentive protection of her father and brother shielding her on each side, she started sliding in and out consciousness. She had the impression that they were, too, fighting to stay alert, but through moments of silence, she could almost dialog with their thoughts, finding another plane where they continued to stay together and communicate. When the wind changed directions, whirling erratically, she had almost the impression that it became a powerful humm, like the ohm heard during the monk's meditation. Was the nature vibrating in unison with the background sound of the universe, claiming its uncontested supremacy? She had also the impression at times that the wind was chiming, resonating in a majestic music with the towering mountains. With these images in her mind, Maggie went to sleep.

Trebor wandered how he arrived on the top of the mountain! And not any mountain, Mountain Everest, the tallest in the world, 8848.13 meters high, or 29,029 feet, also called in Tibetan, Qomolangma, "The Third Goddess"! He must have flown, he felt so light and not tired at all, just standing on the summit covered with glowing immaculate ice, making everything around shimmer in a brilliant light.

If the sky, as far as he could see, was bathing in a brilliant glow, the majestic view below shown the splendid pageant of no less than 38 peaks raising above 7000 meters of altitude! Trebor was so absorbed in the contemplation of this magnificent natural marvel, that he noticed only after a while that he was wearing a simple tunic given by the monks, but he did not feel any cold at all.

There was complete solitude and a sense of eternal peace. Looking at the other peak close to Everest, Malaku, Trebor was lifted and started to fly in that direction, effortlessly, with immense joy.

"What a wonderful feeling", he said, and mastering the third dimension, Trebor gave free bridle to his inner child dreams, going all directions at the thought only.

CHAPTER 17 - SNOW ANGEL

After a while, in his dreams Trebor heard barking. At first it seemed as coming from faraway, but the intensity of the growling was increasing, as calling the alarm. Soon, arms were shoving things around, then grabbed him while voices shouted at him and at his companions to wake up. Suddenly, Trebor was back to reality, in the circle made by people and beasts, covered with snow, and holding each other tight. His left arm, wrapped around Maggie, along with his entire body, were numb. He, like the others, had no control of his movements, who remained frozen in a choice of crooked positions.

His mind started processing what happened, and he realized that the blizzard took hold of them and some brave souls came to their rescue. As he emerged from this numbing state, Trebor felt a warm 'thing' licking his face, and "God, this feels so good", were his next thoughts.

There was hasty activity going on around him, people were moved, shaken, and a rapid flow of concerned voices kept talking. Then a small bottle of hot tea was brought to his lips, and, recognizing the marvelous Tibetan Chai heavy in honey, he started drinking it like a baby. Trebor slowly moved his arms, then his legs and observed that everyone else started showing signs of life, Maggie complaining already that everything was hurting. Jo almost up, was helping along with the sherpas who had suffered the least from the cold, as it was for Lu Xiang and Randal, but Jovanni, as soon as he realized he was not dead, delivered all the southern Italian epithets he could remember. ("Mamma mia, Dio mio, Porca miseria", and on and on...)

"What a relief", thought Trebor going back to the creature who was licking his face and he had recognized right the way.

In the middle of the agitation, as effort were made to get the blood circulate in humans and animals, the nest was open, and a blinding sun was shining over a complete calm reigning on the Himalayas. The rescuers were no one else but the monks from Rongbuk Monastery, the caravan having missed it nearly by half a mile, not seeing it in the middle of the storm. More monks kept on coming as the news circulated back and forth, and more blankets and hot drinks were carried along with small sleighs pulled by the monks.

They started swiftly loading one by one the 10 travelers, covering them with warm furs, while others took the bridle of the yaks and walked them to the barns, where shelter and food, along with special attention was provided by eager monks to care for them.

Once inside the monastery, the newly rescued people were taken to the main hall, where to their great surprise, some nuns showed up with more blankets, hot chai and yak milk, and a large pot filled with a deliciously smelling soup. Yes, as the travelers learned then, one of the particularities of Rongbuk Monastery is that monks and nuns live there. In different buildings, but as part of the same congregation.

Soon, the bodies warmed up by the blissful heat of the fire place lit in the big hall, and with the stiffness leaving the joints, the tongues unlocked as well. The sherpas had already given the count of their adventure, and monks and nuns together, having been deprived for weeks from seeing any visitor, could not help from submerging them with motherly pampering and concern. They already reassured the guests by offering the rooms reserved for visitors, and with the excuses that these were not the most comfortable lodging rooms in the world, the hosts would compensate them by providing the best care they can manage.

Then, came the turn of the monks to tell how they found the stranded voyagers. Well, they all talked at once and in Tibetan, and Jamuna started by translating the first tale, when someone spoke in English at a slower pace.

"Actually, it was the dog, the Head Lama begun. "We were all gathered by the fire during the storm and reading some old manuscript to keep our minds away from the awful noise, when we heard barking outside. Of course, we opened the door to the poor creature, who, half-dead, entered."

Then, taking his time, added, "I see that he seems to know you. He probably hid somewhere feeling the storm coming, the mastiffs, as other animals in these mountains, know when a storm is on the way. My guess is that when he came back to look for you last night, he could not find you and followed your sent all the way here. He almost died from cold and exhaustion, but once given some warm food, he scratched at the door to be let out. I bet he went to look for you, and found you not too far from here at all, the Gods be thanked!"

The old man paused, as he enjoyed telling his story, "Not a long time went by, maybe 10 minutes? Anyways, we heard again barking, but this time the dog would not get inside, he kept running back and forth in the high snow like wanting us to follow him."

"And he found us, our snow angel!", Jovanni shouted, and all of the others started mixing in the conversation.

"Yes, he was calling us to go to your rescue! These mastiffs are very intelligent and devoted." Then, the Great Lama added with conviction, "he saved your lives, to all of you."

The big mastiff was now at the center of everyone's attention, and along with words of praise, treats, food and milk came his way without stopping. But now, as if everything was, at last, in order, sitting quietly by Trebor, the dog savored every single special reward.

"What's the dog's name?", asked the Master of Rongbuk Monastery, leaning down to pet the hero of the moment.

"He is my Everest", the answer came from Trebor.

RONGBUK MONASTERY

Outside Rongbuk Monastery the sun shone over the mountains and valleys covert with a scintillant blanket of snow, softening the contours and the angles, creating a fairytale kingdom. Peaceful, yet grandiose, it became a reminder to the monks and the voyagers that in a world ravaged by trouble, contentment and tranquility can be found after a storm.

It was a restful and needed time for recuperation, while waiting for the snow to melt and make the travel possible again, during which our voyagers discovered the beauty of the monastery and the monks enjoyed an exciting time brought about by the latest events. Groups formed initiated by common interests, at first keeping most of them indoors. The foreigners and Lu Xiang had the tour of the ceremonial halls and the library, and admired the delicate frescoes. Then, they joined in the regular prayers and meditation, at times asking for translations and the meaning of the texts and practices.

Jamuna was curious to visit the stables and cellars, and learned a new recipe or two from the monks living in such rigorous isolation. However, this was the first time he had the opportunity to enter into the sanctity of the ceremonial areas of a temple. Soon, he took the habit to stop in the back of the big hall and sit in reverence, listening to the chanting and discussions, deeply moved by the mysterious atmosphere of the place. There, stimulated by the sounds of the chimes, bells and gongs, the incents and chanting, he felt uplifted by the vibrations of a new energy, leaving behind all his worries.

Jamuna started to understand why so many had renounced the mundane world and searched for more spiritual values. Jamuna wanted to know more about the sense of his life, he wanted to learned about the master design of the whole humanity.

PEACEFUL TIMES

As the outdoors became more accessible, the foreigners accompanied by Lu Xiang and the Head Lama, went to visit the monastery grounds, then the surroundings, breathing in the crisp air and getting ready for longer walks. Everest, the big mastiff, was part of every outing Trebor made, at times playing silly in the snow, running and rolling on his back like a happy child.

Jamuna loved to follow the group and learned more about the monastery's history; Rongbuk was torn down in 1960 by the Chinese Communist regime, then rebuilt at the end of 1990, trying to recreate its dome-like buildings, the stupas, Buddhist architectural marks, and its white structures lined with red middle accents. Colorful prayer streamers, pieces of fabric imprinted with written prayers attached to a long string going all the way from the ground and reaching the top of the buildings, were floating in the wind. Ronbuk is also known as the "Sanctuary of the Birds", and there is a strict ban against killing any animal in the area.

The guests were told that they missed the Saka Dawa Festival, held in mid-April with Buddhist dancing during ceremonies lasting for three days. They would miss also another festival, at the end of the year, when monks are wearing masks during the ceremonies.

At the foot of the monastery runs the cold waters of Rongbuk River, a congregation of streams funneling from the three glaciers on the north side of Mount Everest, the biggest and the most spectacular being Rongbuk Glacier.

Maggie seemed to have found, perhaps the first time in her life, an inner peace she did not think possible. She was 'adopted' straight away by the few nuns living at the monastery, who enveloped her with constant attention and innocent curiosity. It is true that the family of three impressed everyone at first sight with their tall and elegant stature, and the unusual color of their eyes, their kind demeanor inviting to an easy interaction.

Maggie learned the humility of the nuns' practices, their craft making clothes, storing and preparing food, and organizing an entire life together, where simplicity allowed the inquiries of the spirit to become the essence of their existence.

It was also the first time when she shared quarters in feminine presence, and she indulged in this sisterly atmosphere, a new experience for her. The quiet times of the prayers and meditation, were intruded only by the chanting of the bells and prayer cylinders coming as sprinklers of harmonious showers of sounds, smoothing the stress and agitation of her mind. Maggie enjoyed also taking walks towards the glaciers, when, covered with a heavy fur coat, a hat, and soft boots, her soul eyes were filling with the sublime beauty of this unique and isolated place.

Often Trebor joined in with Everest, and their play engaged her in childish pleasures, games she and her brother never shared until now, finding out that it was never too late to build lifetime memories. Jo would show up also from nowhere surprising them with a few well casted snow balls. Caught in their games or just walking on the untouched fresh snow, exchanging ideas or just admiring the grandeur of the nature, they forgot about the outside world. They were just living in the moment, just enjoying life, completely immersed in the now.

The purity found in this elevated part of the world was washing out sorrow, traumas, and worries, it re-energized them for the times to come.

TREASURE IN A GRANGE

Jo, fully enjoying the sacred energy of this place, was taking the time to reflect on the events of the last days. Eager to help around Rongbuk Monastery until the weather conditions would allow them to be back on the road safely, one day he accompanied Jamuna to the stables. Jamuna had a fatherly watch over the yaks, who appreciated their 'forced vacation', gaining a few pounds and finding plenty of rest.

As the two of them dug into the hay bales to feed the livestock, Jo noticed some material buried under the mountain of straws. He became interested at once, and soon they uncovered a couple of old Jeeps, obviously abandoned there for some unknown reason. They appeared to be of a model from the 90s or even older, and Jo wondered if he could make them function again.

Going straight to the Head Lama, Jo inquired about the presence and the future plans of the Jeeps, when the master tried to remember:

"Well, I am not so sure. I think that after the earthquake in 2015, a mission of international aid was allowed to come to Tibet. Probably the Americans or other westerners used old machinery left in their own military bases, and at the end of their mission, some were so excited to be close to the Mount Everest, that they went back to Nepal escalading from the north side. Then, arrived on the Nepalese side, they abandoned most of their equipment here and went on, back to their own countries."

"Is anyone using the Jeeps?", Jo asked, knowing that the answer was obvious, they were left for years in the granges and forgotten.

"You know, we rarely take a voyage. The sherpas are bringing us what we can't make here. Their trucks drive the few tourists coming so far, and then, they use yaks or donkeys for carrying the material going up to the top of the mountain, where they make the trip on foot." Then, he continued:

"I learned that, after the nuclear explosion when all modern life stopped, Jamuna and his helpers found themselves in Tingri with their trucks. They had to leave their vehicles there and use yaks to come here, thus, they would have to get back the same way. Let's hope that things calmed down and they can find some work before the end of the season, there are left at the most 3-4 weeks for tourists venturing so far. As I understand, most of the sherpas are Nepalese, and they wouldn't want to spend winter in Tibet, far from their family. They all depend on what they earn during tourist season, and they can't leave wives and children alone during the winter."

During all this time, Jo waited patiently for the Grand Lama's details, learning a little more of the local habits, working in his mind a solution for his own family.

"Grand Lama, may I kindly ask your permission to repair one of the Jeeps? It would be large enough for us, the foreigners, to go to Kathmandu. I will compensate you, I mean, the monastery, for this favor", then Jo looked at the master with the most hopeful anticipation.

"Of course, go along and help your family. And we do not need anything. The trucks were staying there, buried with no use, anyway", the master of Rongbuk replied with a smile.

"Oh, thank you, thank you Grand Master, and all blessings be upon you", Jo answered, filled with gratitude, and suddenly a wave of excitement was swiping through him at the thought of finding the means to reach Kathmandu, one step closer to home.

"We will need all the prayers, in particular yours, to get the engines to work!"

"Well, we will all pray for you, son", was the answer as the master turn to leave the room.

Jo, who was retrieving, eager to go back to the stables before the night, saw the Grand Lama turning to address him one more time:

"You know, I got to like your presence here. And your children's. You are very special people, your light shines very high, I've seen it in my meditation. You should know that, but much is expected from you."

Going back to the stables, Jo started tinkering with the jeeps, once he removed and dusted them from the hay the best he could. Then Jamuna came along and he appeared to be of a great help, for he already gathered a variety of scattered tools besides the toolbox he took from one of their carts, and obtained to bring a gasoline canister from the monastery garage. "Take as much as you want, our bus will not get started, all controls have been shut down, for now we will have to stay here", he was told by the monk in charge with driving and maintaining the monastery minibus.

Eventually, Jo managed to make one of the Jeeps run, the mechanics were in good condition and he bypassed the automatic controls, restricting to use only the manual drive. It took him a full day, but it was a miracle of ingenuity, with additional spare tires and another canister of gasoline. It was a mid 80s model, and it could transport 8 to10 people comfortably, albeit in a rustic interior. But the heating worked, and the suspensions, breaks, and transmission, seemed reliable.

As the preparations for the departure were on the way, a new fever spread, shaking all from the somnolence felt during the last few days. Jo consulted a map and selected the shortest way to the capital of Nepal, limiting possible complications on the way. Going first to Shegar, then hoping for good road conditions to reach Nylam, then to arrive to Zhangmu, the Chinese border town. Once crossing the border, they should reach the Nepalese equivalent, Kodari, losing 2500m altitude on the way and another 1200m while reaching Kathmandu. Jo thought that keeping up their optimism and a good speed, the 240 km, about 150 miles distance, should take a whole day, aware that some segments of the road could be muddy and treacherous. And this, if there was no trouble with the Chinese authorities.

Once the Jeep was ready for the trip, the time of departure came faster than anyone expected; the traveling group was decided, the five foreigners, then Lu Xiang on his way to Bouddhanath Stupa, Kuan Li and Jamuna. Against all desire Trebor had to take Everest with him, this appeared almost impossible to travel that far during these uncertain times, and he would have to consent leaving him in the good care of the monks. Jamuna expressed the desire to go back home with his clients, as he was familiar with the route. His two helpers were to return to Tingri, bringing back the yaks and the carts, where they hoped to regain their trucks. Then, if all possible, find a few clients before the end of the season and their return to Kathmandu to their families.

The Head Lama insisted on a last dinner together, when the monks expressed their good wishes to their guests, who planned to discreetly go on the road during the monks' morning prayers. As they all were regaining their simple quarters, Jo and Trebor entered their guest dorm room, when the two of them stopped on their track, then Jo plunged towards his backpack. His telephone was ringing!! After over two weeks, there was, finally, a sign that connected them with the outside world!

"Hello, Jo spoke on the receiver, incredulously. Joseph Godson speaking", aware that his number was shared only with people who knew him.

"Mister Godson, we're happy to have you on the phone and give you some new information. Your phone's GPS tells us that you are in Rongbuk. Ah, you are about to pass the border and arrive in Kathmandu? That's good! We want you and your children to go to the American Embassy, where further arrangements will be taking you to Mumbai, India, then to Dubai, the United Arab Emirates. An official pass will be issued for the three of you to embark on a military airplane of the EIPC (Enhanced International Peacekeeping Capabilities) working with Nepali military teams to bring you to Mumbai, where a navy carrier is repatriating American families to north America", the official from the base continued with his explanations.

Although the messenger was pressured to contact other stranded citizens, he continued a little longer giving news. At this time, only the official and military personnel had re-established electronic connections and communications. If the super power authorities scrambled to assume some control over the international situation, it appeared that some of the countries with recently acquired nuclear capabilities were inclined to enter into a psychological power-play as well. This is why it was paramount for them to regain their homes, and some of the military vessels were deployed to secure the American families out of harms' way.

Then, the conversation went on for a while covering further details, when Trebor's attention was caught by their conversation:

"I understand that there are possibly other people traying to regain west, an Italian, a Canadian, and you said a Chinese? You will have to check with the evacuation team once arrived in Kathmandu. But I know that there will be a few other foreigners we would like to help repatriate."

Then, the technician became quite interested in the Himalayan experience and asked a few more questions about a possible visit, but recognized that it would have to wait for better times. Then, becoming quite friendly, he wondered:

"You have a dog, you say, and want to take him with you to the States? the voice on the receptor could be heard. Well, let me see what we can do for him". Then laughing, "It is a Himalayan mastiff? I heard that they are beautiful! I have a dog myself, I wouldn't want to leave him behind. No way."

Trebor' heart filled with gratitude for his father, went to Everest and petting his dark-red lion head said:

"It looks like you might become an American citizen, after all."

ON THE ROAD TO KATHMANDU

If the roads going to the border with Nepal through Nylam and crossing in Zhangmu were not in the best condition, they were at least quasi empty, fewer people having the means to travel after a blackout that paralyzed the country for many weeks. It also appeared to be a good decision, even though a further road crossing at Gyirong Port was a much better way using the Sino-Nepal Highway and the Friendship Bridge, but since they were busier, they were also more controlled by the Chinese authorities.

The 5 foreigners, Kuan Li, Lu Xiang, Jamuna, and the dog found a raggedy terrain in Zhangmu, made worse under a torrential rain surprising our travelers from nowhere, and abating over them without relent for several hours. The border patrols, either called to other more critical situations or having sought temporarily shelter from the rain, were nowhere in sight. The rain, after all, enabled our travelers to cross the border without any questioning, making them shout with relief once arrived to the other side of the Sino-Nepalese border, Kodari. There, the road became even more difficult and at times the younger men had to push the car over the muddy runs over the asphalt. However, by the end of the afternoon they made it to Bouddhanath Stupa, on the outskirts of Kathmandu, one of the largest Buddhist edifices in the world. A little village of monasteries formed around the Bouddhanath Stupa, where many Tibetan monks found refuge during the Chinese oppression. This is where Lu Xiang was expected, along with Kuan Li and his American friends, while Jamuna went to his family and their Italian and Canadian companions, once arrived in Kathmandu, parted for their respective embassy or consulate.

After presenting themselves at the American Embassy, Jo and his two siblings met Lu Xiang and Kuan Li at the monastery, choosing to stay with them. It was another exceptional experience, while waiting for the transfer out of the country to take place, which allowed them to discover the amazing architecture of the monuments of this incomparable city. The American family, attuned to the Buddhist monastery life, joined in naturally and continued their query about this ancient otherworldly approach to life, that had transformed them so profoundly. Moreover, after paying a long visit to Bouddhanath Stupa, they ventured around the town fascinated by such wealth of spiritual atmosphere, and taking advantage of quiet strolls on the squares empty from the usual crowds.

Joseph Godson walked at a leisurely pace through the famous Kathmandu Durbar Square, where a multitude of old palaces displayed the magnificence of Nepalese history and architecture. It had been a light rain, announcing the rain season soon to come in this side of the Himalayas. The place glistened with a special glow, uncommonly deserted by tourists for this time of the year, only seen back in 2015, after the earthquake damaging many old structures.

Trebor and Maggie trailed behind, admiring one of the most coveted sites in the world, regardless of anyone's culture or religious believes. Earlier, they started their day by climbing on the high hill where the Swayambhunath Pagoda, one of the holiest Buddhist temples, looked down at the city. And now in Durbar Square, as they passed from one edifice more impressive than the previous, they laughed a little at the idea that they were playing tourists in the least expected personal and worldly times.

They continued to wander for a while, when a much-expected call from the Embassy chimed in, telling them that an airplane was ready to take them early in the morning from the airbase and fly them to India.

CHAPTER 7 - TRANSCENDENCE

GOING TO MUMBAI

Looking out the window of the military cargo aircraft approaching the runaway in Mumbai, refugees and military kept silent, granted the roar of the engines made any conversation worthless. Trebor, alike Maggie and Jo, was absorbed in his thoughts, each of them reviewing in their own way their life events moving lately so unexpectedly and so dramatically.

Boarding the Boeing C-17 Globemaster III in one of the military bases near Kathmandu was facilitated by the United States Pacific Commander in collaboration with the Office of Defense Cooperation with Nepali military. A few American families stranded in Kathmandu, along with an Australian, had joined our trio in their trip to the States, along with Kuan Li, as part of the Godson party. To them were added Jovanni Mira, the Italian, and Randal Selnick, the Canadian, who informed their respective consulates about the friends who found a way to leave the area. This ensued a special request to the American Embassy for additional folks to be accepted for upcoming evacuation, and luckily, it had been granted.

Trebor smiled when he thought about an interesting turn of events, when Jamuna and Lu Xiang became part of the trip as well. Jamuna, who was usually very much in control when directing a full team through the most difficult mountains in the world, timidly approached his three American friends confessing that his dream had always been to come to America. He explained that he was helping his mother to raise his two younger brothers after their father was buried under an avalanche when he was very young. Now, that the brothers were married and had a family and children on their own, they could take care of their mother. That would allow him to explore and learn about the world and come to America.

Lu Xiang, on his special way, wanted to travel the world as well. When he heard from his 'protégés' that an airplane would bring them to Mumbai, he told his new acolytes that there was one of the most important Hindu temples. Lu Xiang went on to say that Siddhivinayak Temple was erected in honor of Lord Ganesh, the most beloved god in India, and he finally admitted to his friends his desire to visit it, insisting for them to do it as well. Lu Xiang feeling quite a genuine attachment to his new friends, let them understand that he would love to stay together while continuing his teachings to the three of them.

Overall, perhaps as a result of uncommon circumstances, formalities for all of them were made without difficulty and they were all flying together. Trebor turned a little around to watch his new companions, while patting Everest's head. Everest, who took two full seats next to him and was resting his head on Trebor's lap, looked completely oblivious to the noise and the activity of the air travel.

"He must be the coolest dog in the world, he doesn't care about the cars and the traffic, and has no fear of flying!", then, looking at him, he took his head into his hands, rubbing his ears. "Hey, buddy, we're going to have a great trip together."

Everest, as if he understood his new master, moved closer and gave him a sloppy kiss, then sighed a little and went back to the comfort of his berth.

RAJ

Mumbai was hot, crowded and noisy. It was not clear to which extend the EMP attack disrupted its usual activities to a person taking a new look at the city; the street bustle seemed undisturbed, swarming with people moving everywhere and in all directions, on foot, bikes, scooters, and buggies.

Arriving at the US Consulate, Jo and his family were informed that the navy carrier had a delay for reasons not clearly understood, and they would have to wait there until their continuation to US becomes possible. Meanwhile, they should visit the sites and allow the office take care of the necessary formalities for Jamuna, Li, and Everest. It was not yet decided what would happen to Lu Xiang, but when Jo implied that it would be a good idea to have a visa for him too to enter the USA, the employees smiled at the idea of a Tibetan monk being part of the rescue directory.

Once the small group settled in the improvised quarters offered by the Consulate, the American family connected their telephones to the foreign services of the embassy in order to remain in contact at all times. Then, they hired a double rickshaw which transported them around the closer areas of the town, so they could visit the Siddhivinayak Temple.

During the time the group of six spent inside the Hindu temple, after being welcomed with the customary "Karo Shri Ganesh", it became easier to understand why Lord Ganesh is the most loved god in India. And learning that Ganesh is also the remover of all obstacles, they found that this was the right place and time to address their heartfelt prayers.

Filled with a new energy and luminous new images received during their meditation in the temple, our friends found themselves on the banks of the Mithi River, close to the Consulate. Jo and his children decided to take a walk back to the Consulate building, which was not far from there and let go of their rickshaw, after telling their friends to continue back to their living quarters without them.

This did not appear to be the best idea, since our travelers became quickly spotted by the people on the busy road. Many of them without a job or a home, kept begging while tagging along.

The American trio was struck by the shocking poverty and the extend of horrendous conditions these people 'lived' in. Most of them were young, some children accompanied them, but all of them showed signs of early aging and poor health. Some older ones, staying away from the others, were disregarded even by the poorest; they were the true 'untouchables', perhaps the most discriminated cast in the world.

Maggie in particular felt ill at the scenes of entire families living on the streets, while the passersby ignored them and considered them as part of the natural local decor. The atrocious state of insanitation, the lack of food and clothing, were strikingly contrasting with the ones of a few privileged. Some of them held and protected by personal attendants, kept on passing through, unmindful of this considerable mass of social outcasts. Jo, Maggie, and Trebor could not help stopping and at time staring, having a hard time advancing through the crowd and wanting to regain their place, no longer enjoying their city tour.

It was about time, the change they carried with them almost all distributed, they needed to find their way back; Trebor, however, trailed behind, for he had noticed someone lying on the side walk, not moving and even less coming close to them to beg. He had learned that many lived and died on the street, and this one was arriving at his end, all around him letting him be without any further concern. In a country where fatality is accepted as a way of living, the only hope is to reincarnate into a luckier existence next time around. But this was not enough of a consideration for Trebor and he went to kneel next to the man, and gently touching his shoulder, he asked if he could be of any assistance.

Maggie had joined Trebor, and waited for an answer from the man who had his body turned, facing the sewer. Getting no response, they feared he might have already expired, when Jo, who had been exposed to unfortunate situations and had to assess injured people, did a brief examination.

"No, he is only very week, probably from starvation and dehydration. And he must be also ill, he is burning with fever", he concluded.

While the two men stayed close to the homeless person, Maggie, very decisive had already looked and found a street stand with food and beverages. She swiftly came back with a bottle of water, a container with a thick soup and a big bottle of orange juice. On her way back, she had grabbed a rag, and without saying anything, she sat by the poor man, and in a soothing voice, she explained what she was doing. She started spoon-feeding him, holding his head on her lap. The man regaining some of his forces, began taking the food with increased appetite, then drunk the orange juice like a divine manna. Maggie, pouring some water from the bottle she bought, attempted to clean his face and mouth with the rag, when the man straightened a little and holding his hands, opened them to bring some water to his face and started washing it with great pleasure.

During this time, some people walking close to them had their own reactions:

"Do not touch him! He an untouchable, he is not pure."

"Let him die, it is his sort. It has been decided by the gods."

Maggie, her brother, and her father, entirely ignoring those remarks, were surprised hearing the man saying: "Thank you, thank you very much."

Maggie, all excited to see that the man came to life, started asking questions:

"What is your name, where do you live, how can we get you to your family?!"

"My name is Raj. I don't have a family, I don't have a home. The street is my home and its people my family."

Raj spoke on a clear, beautiful voice, his English of a person who had some education.

They learned that Raj, name meaning royalty, used to have a family that lived in a rural area close to the big city. He went to sell some of the produce of his farm to a market in the city, when a catastrophic storm came and dropped an unusual amount of rain after an already strong monsoon season, which created a flood never seen before. They were not rich, but all disappeared along with his family, all was taken by the waters, people, homes, cattle. When he could finally go back, there was no longer a home, nor villages, only shambles of ruins mixed with branches and mud left behind by the giant lake brought about by the flood.

With his heart broken and beyond despair, Raj returned to the city, thinking to dedicate his life helping others, since he had not been able to help his own family. After a few years of living in the harsh conditions of a city without pity, a sense of failure slowly took hold of him, and, through illness and dejection, he gave up.

Maggie, along with the other two, asked Raj how she could help him. Raj replied that they had already did more than one like him could ever expect. When the others dismissed doing any particular favor, they left him after making sure he would have enough money for food and pay for a bed in a neighboring home. And they promised to come back and see him the day after.

Regaining the safety of the Consulate surroundings, although simple, these seemed sumptuous compared with the place they just left. There, one of the secretaries of the visa services came to meet them. She was holding Everest by his strong leash, although he seemed to follow her without any worry.

"Is there any problem?", Trebor asked right the way, concerned.

"No problem at all", the young lady answered with a big smile. "After Everest received his 'physical' and his regular shots by the quarantine veterinarian, we needed to take his picture for his passport. When I went to get him, I admit, I was terrified, but the vet and his assistant were fussing all over him already, and as it happened to them, I fell in love with him too."

As she handed Everest's end of his harness to Trebor, she added:

"That must be what we call 'love at first sight!", and she laughed with all the others.

"Now we have his passport and all the other papers ready for his trip to the US. And the vet declared that he is the picture of health."

While our friends were out, visiting the city, behind the windows of the visa offices of the Consulate, the employees were delighted to find a new distraction from their boring routine, and competed on their attentions to their new mascot. "If you need to go to town until your transportation is ready, you can leave Everest with us any time", they announced.

FROM DUST TO FRIENDSHIP

When Maggie woke up the next morning, she had only one thing on her mind, take the short walk to the Mithi River banks and check on Raj. Leaving Lu Xiang to his morning prayers and meditation, Jamuna and Li to complete their immigration papers, and Jo to track their chances to continue their trip, Maggie and Trebor left shortly after their breakfast. They walked gingerly exchanging their impressions, a little anxious of what to anticipate from Raj after their encounter the day before.

Maggie and Trebor, busy talking, arrived in no time to the place they had left Raj and started looking for him. After a while, not seeing him, they kept watching as far as they could, their tall stature helping them take a good glance over the head level of most of the people on the street. When feeling almost defeated, they heard a melodious voice behind them, a voice they recognized at once:

"Good day, Miss, Sir. How are you this morning?"

They turned quickly to see Raj, but when they did not see him, they looked around again.

"Good morning", the same voice repeated.

This time the voice was of this man in front of them, this handsome, clean and cultivated looking person, who added:

"I am Raj!"

"Raj!", the two of them said in surprise, having a hard time recognizing him.

As if he attempted to avoid any discomfort from his new friends, Raj tried to explain:

"I went back to the temple I used to go when I could wash and get clean clothes", he said pointing towards a building farther down the river banks. "With the money you gave me I went to the drift shop, and then washed and changed at the owner's back shop. I could get inside the temple where I spent the night, as I did in the past, when I came from my village. Then, I lived hiding inside for a while and learned a lot. I always wanted to get an education. That was until I run out of all means of keeping clean and decent, and, too ashamed to stay there, I ended up on the street."

161

Then, Raj looked very touched when Maggie spontaneously went to him and gave him a hug, while Trebor shaking his hand, gave him a friendly tap on the back.

Maggie and Trebor were so relieved seeing Raj and enthralled by his transformation, they asked him if he had anything to eat that morning. When this told them with a smile, that he is happy when he had a meal a day, they directed him to a close by café and they all sat at a table to order a true continental breakfast.

There, the three of them sharing a meal together, enjoyed the happy energy of this new change. After allowing some time for Raj to savour and replenish with more proper food, they discovered that all of them were vegans.

They also learned that, during his time at the Hindu temple, Raj acquired quite an extensive knowledge and education. The pujaris expected the devotees to follow a rigorous path, and encouraged Raj and educated him in Bhagavad Gita, Ramayana and Mahabharata. Secretly, Raj had hoped to become on day, if not a pujari himself, at least become a part of the brahmin group. He loved to observe the daily pujas, prayers, and mantras performed by the pujaris during the ritual washing of the deities with milk and water, and offerings of food to the devotees.

Above all, Raj wanted to express his gratitude to his friends for 'saving' him form dying miserably on the street. He was not afraid of dying, as any other Hindu, there was nothing to fear in the after-life, but he had been abused and maltreated by some other homeless thugs addicted to drugs when he became too weak to defend himself, and thought that this was his destiny. In fact, he was looking forward to seeing his family again, on the other side.

The newly formed trio was so engaged in their conversation that they ignored the time slipping toward the afternoon hours. There was a deep connection forming between these three people of the same generation, yet from such different worlds. Surprisingly, Maggie and Trebor felt admiration for Raj, for his desire to learn, to rise above his condition. And admiration was the last thing that Raj would have expected from the brother and sister, for whom he sensed already so much appreciation. If his heart was filled with admiration for them, there was also a nascent desire to spend his life around these beings who spontaneously cared for him and showed unconditional love to a total stranger.

Amongst some of the things that Raj had said, there was this image that struck Trebor, coming back to his mind again and again: after the terrible tragedy taking away his family and, along with it, destroyed all the reasons to carry on with his life, however, Raj came to the city to help others.

Trebor had achieved the ability to retrieve far out into his higher self, even if in a crowded place, and reviewed his own stage in life for the time being; until now, he followed a path of inner discovery, of personal spiritual growth. He was aware of what was asked to achieve for himself, the Father had told him: Transcendence.

However, the story of Raj, his whole presence created this vision in him, along with a powerful blossoming aspiration. He had just discovered what he wanted to do in the future: he wanted to help others. Trebor understood that he could transform himself, transcend to a higher, more noble level of resonance only helping others as well. Along with this realization, Trebor felt this incommensurable happiness. And finding his real purpose in life, brought in another thought that made him almost laugh: "I feel selfish, caring for people makes me so happy, it is like I do it for myself."

"Why are you laughing?", Maggie and Raj asked in unison.

Trebor, coming back from his reverie, answered to their astonishment.

"I thought that it would be wonderful if Raj could join our group and come to the States! He could teach us how to help others."

DETOUR

It appeared that the military carrier expected to transfer the group of refugees from Mumbai had to change course and new arrangements had to be made. The Boeing C-17 Globemaster III that brought them from Kathmandu to Mumbai was called again to offer its help in the evacuation mission. It was their only hope for now, and the Consulate offices pushed for the departure of the growing crowd, as more were expected to be in need to find a way back to the United Sates.

Jo, a little more privy to the intel coming in, took notice of some decisions regarding their routing, the best way to London, England. From there, it remained to be decided. The pilots went back and forth considering either a straight flight above the Arabic desert with a stop to Alexandria for fueling at the American military base, then continue to England, versus several shorter segments with halts to Qatar, Jordan, Italy and England.

However, soon the decision was made for them, the Middle East was getting unstable by the day after the recent attacks in Asia. There was increased fear of a coalition involving Iran and Syria, even Iraq and Russia, against Israel, and indirectly, against the USA. The crew opted for a speedy departure flying over the Arabic peninsula and the Red Sea, looking to reach the more clement waters of the Mediterranean Sea.

With passports and visas ready, a group formed at the foot of the ladder of the aircraft, ready to board, all having in common a light luggage and a strong desire to reach the US. Interestingly, the entire group counted less than 20 people, although other parties who were eager to leave Mumbai until then, decided against travelling by airplane. Instead of a shorter fare, they wanted to 'stick to the plan' and wait for the large military ship to bring them directly home.

Besides the technical crew of three, there were two members of the Consulate, Amanda and Sonia, who were going back home, now assuming the role of improvised flight attendants. Jo's 'family' also grew in size, along with Maggie and Trebor, there were added Lu Xiang, Jamuna, Li, and Raj, not to forget Everest, who, remaining in his best behavior, showed nevertheless quite a bit of excitement for new adventures.

Two other couples were aligned along with our travelers, while Randall and Jovanni followed the special offer kindly offered by the American Embassy in Kathmandu. Finally, the group was ready for a long-anticipated flight, soon to take off.

The airplane, once in the air, gained a good altitude of 32,000 feet, since the cabin was pressurized, and everyone settled into a long, tiring and an uneventful trip. A few jokes were made in order to ease off the stress regarding the four non-Americans that had little or never flown before. Raj eyes were becoming even bigger as he watched the ground disappear under the wings, and Jamuna, bracing himself, tried to remain brave for his second flight experience, not looking out or saying something. Li did not want to show his terror and even though he should consider himself un 'experienced frequent flyer' for this third flight exploit, however, after the forced landing in Lhasa, he was now slowly sliding in his chair almost to the floor, keeping a mask-like smile all along. Only Lu Xiang had surprisingly felt a rush of delight as the airplane became air born.

"Who would've believed, a Buddhist monk thrilled to fly!"

"That must be their ability to levitation."

"Yeah, now he is training for the high altitude!"

"Jamuna, Raj, Li, get ready for the group levitation", and so on, everyone participated to lessen the apprehension of their friends' flight adventure.

Raj, after the first bouts of motion sickness and laying down for a while on a row of seats, let go of the fear and later on joined the others.

During the long stretch of the flight over the Arabian Sea, a meal was served. If this was not by the international refined standards a first class spread, a large amount of simple foods and snacks was offered at all times. Along with the monotonous rumble of the engines, came the quiet relaxation, almost all of them ceding to its hypnotic effect. Lu Xiang seemed to meditate, the two couples started a game of carts, and everyone else stretched for a good nap.

Jo felt rested after a deep sleep, and after making a visual tour of the cabin, was reassured to see that all the passengers were resting. He grabbed his satphone hoping for a connection, when he was approached by Amanda, the young secretary now flight attendant, who discreetly told him that the captain asked if he could come to the cockpit. Jo entered the flight quarters seconds later and when he attempted to introduce himself, captain Scott Hunt addressed him:

"We know who you are, Mister Godson. Very nice to meet you, I am Captain Hunt and this is my crew: Phillipe Prior, co-pilot, and Andy McLean, the flight engineer. Jo, fine we will call you Jo, I go by Scotti", then he continued, "Andy received an urgent message from the admiral of the South China-Indian Ocean division, and we are now also in contact with the Qatar division commander about some unfortunate developments playing somewhere not far from the area over which we should be flying soon. Someone from the Central Intel knew that you are on board of the craft and wanted you to confer with us as well."

Captain Scotti handing over the airplane controls to Phillipe Prior, came around the cabin, now an operating center.

Jo was hastily briefed about the events taking place, learning that pirates made of a group of Yemeni and Somali had managed to attack a small village school on the shores of northern Ethiopia, kidnaping young girls with the intention to sell them as sex slaves. However, the pirates could not reach their boat with their pray and retrieved deeper into the north Eritrea, staying away from the capital Mek'ele, where they could encounter reinforced police resistance. The local authorities were not sure of their precise location, the satellite transmissions remaining limited and in poor condition.

However, the Ethiopian government reached out to all the help they could obtain, in particular the American military, and this was the reason the C-17 Globemaster's crew was contacted. The Central Intelligence Agency combining the international forces with the military in the region, considered as a lucky coincidence that Joseph Godson was also there. If the orders did not contain precise details yet, they were clear, they would have to momentarily detour the direction of their flight and assist with the rescue mission of the kidnapped girls. And if there was a public exposure of the shocking occurrence and the world waited in anger, the operation undertaken had to remain secret in order to ensure its success.

Basically, the airplane would have to land as close as feasible to the area where the girls were detained, and where the military crew and Jo meeting with the local police, the other passengers would have to remain behind and in security. They would receive instruction each step at a time while reporting their own observations and findings.

Thus, when Scotti announced that they were approaching the Gulf of Eden, then the Bab-el-Mandeb Strait to enter the Red Sea, they notified the central command that they were in view of the Yemeni coast to the north and Somalia to the south. As they were instructed to descend to barely 3,000 feet altitude, they were also told to use caution since they could be shot down by ISIS rockets based on Yemen territory. Surely enough and as on command, plumes of missiles firing could be seen below by the crew.

"Time to gain a little altitude and move northwest fast!", the captain reported.

"You are less than 200 km from the base close to Mek'ele and we are connecting you with the tower and with Police Chef who is waiting for you."

The last 20 minutes prior to the landing were used for the preparation of the civilians to the new changes, the crew giving reassurance that no one was in any danger. Jo learned a little more of the situation on land, there was a suspicion that the kidnapers were hiding in the vicinity of the ancient city of Aksum, on the Axum Plateau.

More information and directions were given to the quickly formed committee of four within the minutes preceding their arrival. Their stop on Mek'ele was cut short to the time necessary to take on board Chef Beshadu and his aide, and to refuel; following a brief debate of the conditions in Aksum, the airplane then continued to Aksum Airport, located northeast from the ancient city.

While on the ground at the base in Mek'ele and introductions were made with Chef Beshadu and his assistant, Addisu, Jo remained glued to his satphone as the gasoline truck was connected to the airplane's tank for refueling, and some ammunition and military equipment were subtly loaded in the back of the cabin. During the short flight to Aksum, arrangements were made for the travelers to stay in a hostel managed by Christian nuns, who lived in a monastery close to the town center. It was the time of the year approaching the peak season for the pilgrimage, and appeared that the already simple hosting conditions of the city were even more reduced.

As he continued his conversations on the phone, Jo was considering Trebor's position in this operation, he did not quite want to expose his son to danger, but he could see the help he might give with the communication between the civilians and the actual operating team. He could take care of the civilians and then bring them back to the airplane once all was over, hopefully on a happy note for the girls and their families, as for the entire world watching the events.

AKSUM

The task force team including Jo Godson, the technical aviation crew, the Police chief, Beshadu, and his assistant, along with a local police representative and an investigator, remained at Aksum Airport and settled summarily their quarters in the control tower, hopefully permitting them to maintain the best communication with the international assistance. Although the local police had little experience with criminal investigations and even less with kidnaping matters, Aksum being the holiest place in Ethiopia and a peaceful destination, Teru, the head of the police, had a good knowledge of the area.

The mapping of the region and the study of the topography of the plateau displayed on a wall of the meeting room came under intense scrutiny. Jo had the reflex to retain Jamuna with them and use his tracking instinct, and Trebor, who had insisted to stay with the group offering his help, both followed Jo's explanations of the terrain configuration. At Jo's insistence, Jamuna also received a telephone to connect him with all the others, while Trebor had long before synced his phone to his father's coordinates.

During the briefings received after their landing in Aksum, the newly arrived learned about the pirates and their barbarian practices, terrorizing the region and attacking indiscriminately cargo and cruise ships, as well as the African neighboring countries. All this was confirmed by the local police.

The other civilians of the group, upon their arrival to Arbatu Ensessa Monastery, received a warm attention from the nuns, who, striving to hide their trouble regarding the recent events, started by making them comfortable within their simple accommodations. Then, used to frequent visitors and attempting to divert their attention from the unfolding drama, introduced them to the rich history of Aksum.

Interacting with the nuns and later on, during their visits wondering in the old and rustic town, they discovered its amazing sites and a history going back to biblical times. Aksum or Axum, is the original capital of the former Kingdom of Aksum, one of the oldest remaining inhabited cities in Africa situated in the north of Ethiopia, a region that still retained the name of Eritrea. With its unique written language, Ge'ez, the Kingdom of Aksum developed an architectural style erecting giant obelisks, also called stele, the oldest one believed to date before 3,000 BC, while the buildings were made of stones fitting tightly together without the need of mortar.

Aksum flourished even during the pre-Roman era, established as an important trade center along the silk road, with a large maritime port on the Red Sea, Adulis, destroyed by Islamic invaders in the 8th century. Today, the sites visited are considered as one of the most sacred in the world, mainly thanks to the Church of Our Lady of Zion. According to the Ethiopian Orthodox Tewahedo Church, it is believed that here is housed the Ark of the Covenant, which contains the stone tablets carved with the Ten Commandments.

The city of Aksum was, like the entire country, in turmoil since the news of the kidnaping of the school girls. Hence, there were very few tourists walking the dusty roads of the old town, observed by kind and unobtrusive locals. But our little group wandering around the main historical sites could easily be spotted, making some of them smile at the unusual sight of an orange wrap flowing ahead of the group, climbing and descending the ruins with a youthful energy. A Buddhist monk visiting was not the most common event even in these sought-after places!

"Would you believe it, this is Queen of Sheba's palace, and a little north from here there is a pool, Queen of Sheba's bath!", an excited Lu Xiang delivered his impressions. "She even went to Jerusalem where the great King Solomon fell under her spell; he was the seduced one! Coming back, she had their son, Menelik, whom she raised here, alone."

Then he continued: "Arrived at the forming age for a man, Menelik went to live with his father, King Solomon, and stayed in Jerusalem for a while, then returned to Ethiopia. But not with empty hands, he stole and brought in secret nothing else but the Ark of the Covenant containing the stone tablets engraved with the Ten Commandments!"

"That would explain why the Ethiopian church claims that the Ark is still in Aksum, for which the Church of Our Lady Mary of Zion was built!", Maggie replied.

Back to Arbatu Ensessa Monastery, their lodging place, they admired the beautiful edifice built like a fortress, with beautiful Byzantine arches. And since Arbatu Ensessa complex is not too far from the Chapel of the Tablet, it was easy for one of the younger nuns to lead the way, eager to give more explanations:

"At the height of the Aksumite Kingdom, King Ezana converted to Christianity and was baptized in 356, AD, by the Byzantine King, Frumentius. He built the first church in honor of Virgin Mary, Our Lady Mary of Zion, or Tsion. Eventually the first church burned in 1500 AD in the war with the Abyssinians, but it was rebuilt later. It is still as one of the structures, see, in front of us there are two Cathedrals side by side. The newer one was dedicated by Emperor Haile Selassie as a pledge to St. Mary for the liberation of Ethiopia from the fascist occupation."

"Between the two cathedrals, which are open to the public and site of ceremonial processions, there, see? That's the Chapel of the Tablet! But the Chapel does not allow anybody anywhere close, even the head of the Orthodox Church, the Ethiopian Patriarch, is not permitted inside. It is under the strict protection of a single monk who lives inside the premises until his death, and he is the one to name his own successor", the kindhearted nun continued tutoring them.

"Then, the only one who ever sees the Arc of the Covenant is the monk?" they reacted together. "How one would know that it is still in there? It must be someone else!"

"No one, but the monk." then, after a pause, she added: "It is a matter of faith!"

After Aksum converted to Christianity, its power declined, being rejected by Islam which predominated in Africa. However, in the years 600, when Muhammad faced oppression from the Quraysh clan, he sent his daughter and son in law to the Kingdom of Aksum for protection, and since then, the two religions kept a friendly tolerance.

BARBARIANS

"Wake up, you swine!", yelled Qutaybah, rattling the cages with the butt of his riffle. "Lucky you, you'll get some water. We don't want you to die before receiving other kind of attention from our rich friends", then he smiled with a sarcastic grimace on his face, taking a good look at each one of the terrified little girls locked up in a cage.

Because there they were, the 12 little kidnapped girls, stocked in individual cages usually transporting cattle, inside two medium size trucks and tightly covered with a canvas. This was their second night spent in there, after the brutal attack during the after-class study. Their quiet attention was removed from their homework by sudden screams of the old cleaning lady who was sweeping the corridor, waiting for the last students to leave for the day. Then, her cry ended with the sound of a thud as she hit the floor when pushed down by the intruders, followed by the detonation of a shooting gun. The next second, their classroom door was blown open by five man, holding guns and having their turbans wrapped to leave room only for their eyes to see.

Entering into the classroom, Mutaa shouted a few orders, although most of the girls present, stunned by the invasion, could not move, only a few started screaming hysterically. Mujaahid and Fahad joined Mutaa and started grabbing the girls, who under the shock, seemed not to understand their orders. The aging supervisor intervened with authority and courage to defend the students, when Husaam turned around and, lifting his arm, aimed to her forehead and shot her between her eyes without flinching, and not even looking at the unfortunate lady sprawled on the desk with her brains splashed on the blackboard, he said:

"This is to serve you as example. You will be shot at the first sign of defiance."

The five men were well prepared, all experienced already in a lifelong piracy. They opened a bag of tissues and socked them summarily with chloroform and covered the girls' nose and mouth, rendering them limp and easy to remove without any resistance or sound.

Their plan was simple, although desperate, they operated in close association with ISIS, not that much for religious allegiance, for they were the children of no one and they obeyed to no laws, but ISIS provided them with good quality ammunition, while they did not need training nor support while robbing and killing the infidel. However, the pirates were individualistic and thrived in anarchic situations, notoriously impulsive and undisciplined, their survival aided by the unpredictability and cruelty of their attacks. The large loot accumulated plundering ships and defenseless populations do not seemed to add up with their dissipated lifestyle, and their group of five was in dire need for cash.

Others had kidnapped young Christian girls and converted them to Islam, the few of them determined to resist having been raped and hanged close to their parents' home, after having had inflicted horrible mutilations and tree branches inserted inside their vaginas.

But these pirates would not waste this precious cargo, as "they will get good money selling them to brothels in Cairo, even Tunis or Casablanca. They will let the rich government prelates, even some of those pervert mullahs 'play' with the little Christians, knowing that they would not survive for long their 'converting' treatment." The pirates learned long before that, with all the respectability they put forth, the rulers had no better morals, they were only more hypocritical. Before going to a brothel or visiting a prostitute they believed that making a solemn mental denial of their marriage three times, their sins were pardoned. Then, they only had to come back to their obedient wife or wives, who had no say to this parody, claiming all prerogatives solely resulting from being born as a man.

True, they would have to choose the prettiest ones amongst these young females, and get rid of the less 'fortunate' ones. After raping those, they would kill them, for they were no saints, never pretended to be, and it has been too long since they had seen a woman with no clothes on.

Hanna and Zhara who were the oldest, 12 years old, whispered words of encouragement to the younger ones waking up after the anesthetic worn out, and prayed aloud for them. Elene and Aster could not stop shaking, and all the others muffled their sobs, terrorized. Rekik only 8 years old, laid glued to the cage wall connected to the one of Leilit, who managed to slide an arm inside and hold the little one all night long.

When the canvas was removed, Wubit, her name meaning Beautiful, the youngest one, only five years old and who suffered from asthma, entered into a severe spell, triggered by the fright.

Qutaybah let his bad temper take over him and hollering, started looking in the direction of the distressed heaving, searching who was the one already creating them problems. He was ready to grab the girl by her hair and pull her out of the cage, to finish her, when the others came around to see what was the matter.

"She will die anyway on the road, we don't have time to waste with her, and she can attract attention with her whooping."

The pirates started arguing for a while, each one shouting over the other, when they stopped short, in disbelief, the trucks were moving! Someone must have jumped on the driver seats in unison taking advantage of their quarrel and drove away with their merchandise!

The confusion was reigning during which the trucks gained distance, then the pirates started running and cursing behind, fuming with rage. At first, the girls already traumatized, held on the bars, as the cages shook in all direction. Then, realizing that they might be getting away from their captors, after a few timid calls, they started cheering with hope.

It appeared that the team made of Jo Godson, Jamuna, Chief Beshadu, Aksum Police chief, Teru, and Trebor tracked the location of the kidnapers, who found refuge for the night north of Aksum, by the kings Kaleb and Gebre Meskal tombs. In this isolated place on the Tigray plateau, there is a small wooded area giving good coverage to the kidnapers.

After running out of breath, the pirates realizing that they were not able to catch the trucks, even on these rugged trails, went back to seize some of their fire power left next to their improvised night berth. Faakhir was their leader and the only one who did not intervene during the quarrel and the skirmish, during which he was deep in the wood for a nature call.

Once armed and regaining some control, the bandits running after the trucks, attempted to cut their way across the brush, all the while shooting blindly. Although they got dangerously close, they had to duck the bullets fired over them. The two trucks took advantage and increased their distance separating them from their attackers, and before long, they were on the main road.

Soon, the girls, liberated and surrounded with loving attention at **Arbatu Ensessa Monastery**, became the center of animated concern, as all of them were properly attended and reassured. The youngest of the girls, Wubit, went spontaneously to Maggie, who became her designated caregiver. Security was placed and all entrances quickly closed and guarded, while the parents were informed about the rescue of their children, putting an end to the worse nightmare a parent could ever go through.

This is when the task force team noticed that Jo was missing.

CAPTURED

Jo, who was in charge with the rescue operation, and, as the well-trained senior of the group, had decided to be the one closing behind the trucks the surprise attack, in order to insure the success of this daring mission. He was still crouched low on the bushes behind the last truck, when he noticed one of the pirates coming from the woods hurriedly buttoning his trousers. In a flash, he decided to apprehend the man and make him a prisoner, increasing the chances to free the girls.

He was ready to make a quick leap to catch Faakhir, when at the corner of his eye saw something moving with a sizzling noise, he had disturbed a carpet viper nest! Venomous, the Kenyan carpet vipers are unfortunately endemic in these areas, and one of them was sitting on a small pile of white eggs, not pleased by the intrusion. She attacked and bit Jo on his leg, luckily the venom not penetrating the skin, protected by the thickness of his camouflage pants. But this was enough to make him muffle a scream and jump, revealing his presence.

In no time Faakhir took advantage of the situation, a rush of adrenaline veering his furious deception into intense instinct of revenge. He had someone he could blame on and torture for the losing battle he could forth see, his mates already coming back, defeated. And he could show off his authority in front of all of them. Few minutes later, the other pirates alerted by Faakhir hollering, run towards him, all attention now concentrated on their new pray.

RANSOM

Chiefs Beshadu and Teru came into the monastery hall, looking for Trebor and Maggie, Beshadu holding his phone to his ear. He made a discreet sign with his hand toward the two siblings to follow him next door. The four of them entered a small office and closed the door behind them, then Beshadu turned his telephone's speaker on.

"We have your man, turn on your face-time for you to see in what a good shape he is!', a beasty voice barked.

Maggie, even though encountered so much in her young life, had the hardest time to contain her distress, as they were looking at Jo, brutally pushed on the ground, covered with bruises, blood dripping from a corner of his mouth, his arms tight behind his back.

"Here are our conditions, and we are not negotiating: we want our trucks back with the load of girls and $50,000 in cash as penalty for your annoyance. This is if you ever want to see your friend back. The exchange will be done at dawn at a place you will be notified a few minutes before. There will be no other calls before that."

It took a great deal of strength to Beshadu to reply;

"Don't even bother, our government do not negotiate with pirates and kidnappers, under any circumstances. There will be no exchange and no further discussion!"

"Oh yes, there it will be!", Faakhir continued talking on the phone he had taken from Jo, "you only saw your penalty raise to $200,000! Cause, otherwise you will see Mr. Godson here, receiving the treatment ISIS reserves for special agents: it will be a public decapitation if you refuse to obey our demands!" and the phone went silent.

Maggie could no longer retain a long cry coming out of her chest, as Trebor came closer to her and they were supporting each other from falling under the blow, a vise tightening their breath.

Beshadu was already pacing and searing under his breath, "they must be still somewhere close by, otherwise could not ask for an exchange early in the morning. We have to find them."

Jamuna, who came in the office to find out what was the reason they all left the hall, had listened to the entire conversation, and without saying much, he left the room. He knew what he had to do, he would put to use more than ever his life long experience and instincts to find out where Jo was detained.

PRAYERS

It was still dark and cool when Beshadu's phone rung an hour before the sunrise. He let it ring, he didn't have to answer. He knew who the caller was, and mostly, where him and the others were. And if he let the ring chime for a while, was only to verify one more time that their coordinates were correct.

Jamuna came back to Arbatu Ensessa Monastery around midnight and went straight to the meeting room. He was not coming emptyhanded, he had found where the bandits had set camp and he explained the plan he had in mind. With renewed hope, the entire team entered into an effervescent activity, hovering over the maps. They reviewed the tracking possibilities available, the GPS satellites were still very limited on signals and could not be completely reliable, and if they disposed of a small drone, its presence could only attract attention and ruin their chances. However, Jamuna had gathered enough information and he was almost sure that the place the pirates backed up by ISIS planned the execution: the platform in front of the Great Obelisk. In their boldness, the kidnappers decided to give a lesson to the world! And this time their arrogance knowing no limits, they wanted to do it on a public place.

Beshadu and Teru, the local police Chief, who knew like their hands the ancient ruin site, came quickly with a strategic plan to position their forces, all the while avoiding to collide with the hiding places of the bandits. After that, aided by night vision goggles and earbuds communication, they went with their assistants to the archeological site, situated a little north from Our Lady Mary of Zion. Between the uneven grounds made by the ruins and clusters of trees, they placed the best officers the town had available. Meanwhile, they asked Maggie and Trebor to wait at the monastery for their further orders.

Jamuna had mentioned that he left Everest hidden at the left edge of the open area. He also said that he noticed some preparations at the foot of the Obelisk, and Teru commented that they would probably have a camera getting ready for a 'live' execution on the platform in the front of the monument.

On their way out, Jamuna and the locals ran into Lu Xiang. This had been in contemplation and prayers since the dramatic news of Jo's capture.

"Your holiness, let's pray all together, and give us all the good energy you can ask from the above", said Beshadu.

And for a few minutes, they all prayed together, regardless their religion: Maggie and Trebor, the Tibetan monk, the sherpa from Nepal, the Ethiopian police officers, and the abbess of the Christian monastery. At the end of their silent reflection, in a calm voice Lu Xiang concluded:

"They are aloof and blinded by revenge, but they are desperate and ill prepared. If they believe for a second that their cruelty will keep them safe, they don't know that they isolated themselves in their own trap", then he went back to pray in a secluded corner of the monastery.

Maggie and Trebor followed him instinctively in his meditation, they would pray with all their ardor until they would have a signal from Beshadu. However, Maggie, her eyes filled with tears, could not help asking Lu Xiang:

"But, Master Lu, they might get apprehended, but before that, my father could be...be...beheaded", and she let out a heart tearing cry.

"That's the one up there to decide", Lu said, pointing his index toward heavens. "Let's pray!"

EXECUTION ANCIENT STYLE

Minutes before dawn, shadows began moving silently between the ruins and the ancient obelisks. They were dragging and pushing Jo without merci, and, once arrived on the platform of the Great Obelisk, they removed the black hood covering his head. Although no one payed attention to their prisoner's feelings, Jo's eyes expressed determination and courage. His country and his children will have, more than ever, the proof of his commitment to defending the noble rights to freedom and justice of any human being of this planet. He did not flinch in front of the enemy, and he was ready to die with pride.

The bandits' preparations did not take long, a simple iPad was placed on a stone in front of Faakhir, who appeared to assume the role of the bourreau. Connected with Al Jazeera, BBC, NBC and Fox News, the tablet was ready to start broadcasting on voice command. Then, all the other bandits left to hide behind the closest stele, only their chief remaining on the platform, holding the object of execution: a sword!

Jo, hands tied behind his back and rammed down on his knees, was praying thinking of his children. His prayers were more ardent than ever, he was asking God only for forgiveness for himself, and implored Him for the protection and grace for his children. After a while, he looked around and wandered:

"A sword, ancient pirates' style! But what are they waiting for? Ah, the sun rise. Almost there!"

All of sudden the voice once heard on the telephone became live and started shouting in front of the camera, making a theatrical oration:

"Glory be given to Allah! The Western world fallen under depravation and sin, beware! The Infidels will be destroyed and Islam will pardon only the repentant, and the ones that resist us will die from our hand, like this white dog in front of you today!", and he reached for the sword.

"Stop" a voice shouted, making Faakhir look at the figure that appeared behind the camera in the middle of the field facing the Obelisk. "Take me, I will follow you and serve you, but let go of my father", "He is old, his death will not bring you anything." Faakhir, still under the shock of this apparition, strained to see the face of the silhouette protected and surrounded by the aura of a glorious sunrise behind it.

"No, take me, I am stronger, she is only a woman", Trebor's voice shouted as his figure appeared next to Maggie, the two siblings shrouded by the intense rays casted by the sun.

Joseph Godson, who had already summoned all his strength to face these last suffering moments of his life, felt his heart melt under so much love witnessing his children's devotion. With tears of gratitude welling down his face, he was ready to die in complete peace.

Faakhir was thinking rapidly, he probably should accept the offer "those two idiots" made, and take them too prisoners, his chances of getting richer increasing by the moment, his greed getting a strong hold of him. He opened his mouth to talk again, but this time he let out a horrific screech piercing the air, as he arched backwards.

Jamuna had come behind the Grand Obelisk swiftly as a mountain lion, and profiting from this unexpected distraction, he threw with a masterful precision his pickaxe into the back of Faakhir. He had used the metal gripping power of the pickaxe many times during high altitude glacier climbing, saving lives as a guide. But this was the first time he used this harpoon to kill someone. In no time, another shadow appeared next to Faakhir, pinning him to the ground, even though he could no longer be of any danger, Everest had flown to the rescue, and his massive frame towered over the pirate.

This happened in seconds, and at the moment Jamuna casted his tool, the other pirates, their positions easily spotted near to the central execution area, had been immobilized by the agents coming from behind. The irony was that some of the pirates, the real 'idiots' wanting to have personal memories from the event and eventually post them in You Tube, were busy making their own recordings using their smart phones. Their guards dropped, they became easy to apprehend by the agents surrounding the place.

Maggie and Trebor leapt toward their father and in no time, Jo was freed and held on each side by his children, carried to a police car appearing around the corner. Jamuna, Raj, and Lu Xiang, joined them, leaving to the local authorities to deal with the kidnappers.

Collecting Faakhir, who was dying, Beshadu noticed the iPad that had continued to broadcast the entire scene, and before turning it off, addressed the stupefied audience:

"All is under control. Thank you for watching!"

WHY?

Maggie and Trebor stood on a pew in the magnificent old monastery. Their father, who was found stable after being examined by the local emergency physician, was now resting in a hostel room of the complex, after been given a sedative. Feeling the impulse to recollect themselves, they followed the footsteps of their other friends, who retrieved into quite corners of the monastery in search of clarity and peace.

Maggie had already had a long conversation with her twin brother about the troublesome events they traversed recently; with each exchange they uncovered the depth of their connection, able to read each other's feelings without need for words, the unique closeness they shared uniting them. They both realized that they would never feel lonely again.

Together, they tried to sort out reasons, or better, the irrationality of the tragedies they encountered, and the precise motive for them to be thrown in the middle of this gigantic whirlpool. Was it an actual purpose of these dramatic changes in the world, and consequently, in their lives?

Deep in their thoughts, everyone in the basilica felt suddenly uplifted by the divine and majestic vibrations of voices chanting. Pure intonations of the nuns' angelic interlacing harmonies singing 'a Capella', without instrumental accompaniment, filled the entire space with beauty and renewed hope. While the nuns were liberating their passion through their singing, they simply followed their usual life rituals, and with it, perpetuated the sanctity of these godly chosen places in the world.

Trebor felt inspired and addressed his questions to God; more than ever he felt that it was time for him to unburden his heavy heart from the revulsion and resentment gripping at times his thoughts when facing the lowliness of human acts.

"Why, Father, why people would do such horrible things to each other? and how long are you going to tolerate this?", Trebor kept on repeating.

The sounds of the music became words in his mind, as God was talking to his heart:

"My dear son, you know the answer, this is the 'free will', the gift I granted to every one of my children. It is up to them to choose how high or how low they want to stand in the stages of the Universe. You are asking why there is, more than ever, this turmoil in the world? This magnificent planet Earth, this little Eden I offered to humans to live in, in order to complete their education and their spiritual growth, is going through a periodic transition to higher levels of energy. Men's individual energies, good or bad, or in terms of frequency, high or low, will determine their destiny, based on their own choices. One will run into its own destruction or reach higher realms and everlasting happiness."

"But it is not as simple as that, it appears that there is no justice in this world!"

"There is justice. Justice comes with people's own choices, they decide of their own punishment, disappearing forever, or embracing love and kindness, and eternally live in my house. It is as simple as that."

"Meanwhile, Father, you ask for forgiveness, for tolerance. And this does not seem to discourage the vile minds from perpetrating evil acts", Trebor interjected, confused.

"I mentioned to you about one of my special sons, Jesus Christ. The mission I gave him was to let the world know that LOVE is my law. He lived and 'died' showing love, beyond all cruelty and injustice inflicted to him, Himself the embodiment of the unconditional love I have for my children."

"Still, for many, all the love in the world was not enough from preventing them to take advantage of the others incline to forgive!", Trebor expressed his impression.

"Now comes my special message to you: you are to show how, through love and forgiveness, one can be saved. I want you to show the humanity that it is time for TRANSCENDENCE, if one wants to exist."

After a while, God continued:

"I understand you saying that many, once forgiven, think that this is an infinite source granted to continue on the same path, no remorse, no repent, whatever they do, they will be forgiven. Well, I say into you, that one should not accept abuse, nor tolerate to be victimized. There is no abuser and victim designated, all my children are equal!"

"Trebor, my beloved son, you are on Earth to land a hand and help one stand and raise himself to become the one I initially made. But you are NOT to be dragged down to their low level. Show them the way, forgive, and if they don't change, wish them well and let them go wherever they choose. As some say, forgiveness is not enabling."

"Thank you, Father, now it all became clear!"

The sound of Trebor's whisper made Maggie turn and look at him. She saw his face raised toward the heavens and eyes closed, irradiating with a great peace.

LEAVING AKSUM

One more time, Captain Scotti Hunt verified his flight manifest and scrolled down the check list with his co-pilot, Phillipe Prior, before the take off. A few days after the drama unfolding in Aksum and Joseph Godson regaining his physical condition, he received the green-light to continue their repatriation trip. Captain Scotti was ready to complete his mission and leave these troubled lands behind. He even held a private wish that, once arrived to their Mediterranean destination, he would take his long-due leave and go back to the States for a while.

Scotti Hunt did not have much time to reflect on his own feelings besides his work duties, caught like everyone else into the whirlwind of stressful international events. But for some reason, he felt this strong interest to know more about the family of three, the father and the twins. He noticed how the other people who started following them, Trebor in particular, and coming from such different extractions, showed the son so much devotion. There was something very magnetic about this person, although he was not talking much, but during their discussions he was expressing the vision of a new world, a world that their latest friends, along with his sister and father, were willing to discover together.

During their last dinner offered by the nuns at the monastery, Captain Scotti recalled Trebor's answers when asked about traditional and modern ways of living. He emphasized the urgent need of respecting the nature, the source of our riches, returning to using them wisely. Regarding the future of humanity, Trebor talked about the need for peace and harmony, every one attempting to reach a higher level of understanding of our divine origin and our unlimited possibilities of our being as a light soul. He insisted even on our ability to overcome the modern technology if we bring our energy to vibrate at higher harmonics. And if science shows us how the universe works, the sacred spiritual traditions teaches us how to use the universal energy to work for us, even if it is not always said how is done.

Scotti remembered Trebor talking of transcendence! Yes, he said that if we achieve the power of harmonizing our energetic level to the divine cosmic energy, we can transition from the material density of this existential entrapment and become free spirits. Keeping all the essence of our person, with all the memories, talents and aptitudes, feelings and experiences of the present and all past lives, becoming pure light, we can communicate with all beings, here on Earth, or anywhere in the Universe. We can be free from gadgets and devices, be present at any moment anywhere in the Universe, experiencing permanent love and complete bliss, as an individual expression of oneness.

"Wouldn't that be awesome?", captain Scotti Hunt thought, climbing into the cockpit for the last preparations before their incoming flight.

BESHADU AND WUBIT

The passengers filled the cabin, the same travelers who arrived unexpectedly in this historical land, naturally choosing the same seats they occupied before. Then, Captain Scotti Hunt had to add to his surprise, Beshadu to the flight manifest. Profoundly troubled by the drama that just unfolded, the Police chief invoked the changes brought about by these unusual times, and requested to be excused from his duties for a while. Beshadu desired to travel the world, however, the deeper reason was linked to the realization that his soul had been moved to the depth of its fibers by the presence of Joseph and Maggie, and in particular by Trebor.

Thus, Beshadu thought that here was the best opportunity for him to further his knowledge about the mysteries contained in Aksum and follow his call to go along with the three Americans visiting new places. And now, there he was, cheerful like a child on vacation, Beshadu could not contain his excitement of being in the company of so many, granted so diverse, people seeking like himself, enlightenment. There were Lu Xiang, Jamuna, Raj, Li, and along with Jovanni and Randal, they all were looking for a better understanding of the reasons shaking the world.

There were also a young couple, Deborah and Joshua McClain, and a more mature couple, Rebekah and Dr. David Anderson, part of the initial passenger list. To them were added the two secretaries from Mumbai Consulate, Amanda and Sonia, who resumed with joy, their 'new job' as flight attendants. In preparation for the takeoff, the two of them took a quick tour of the cabin alley, and smiling, they checked that all passengers were comfortably seated and that their belts were fastened. The jumbo jet was taxying along, when one of the improvised stewardesses looked to the back of the cabin and had the impression that something was moving under the seat; and it was not Everest, who had already, occupied a double space on the bench next to Trebor!

"What do we have here?", and bending over, Amanda, the young attendant, pulled from under the last bench a little girl.

Wubit, trembling with her entire small frame, started imploring, her plie hard to understand between Ethiopian and English, words hardly heard in the middle of her sobs. Then, slipping past Amanda, Wubit run toward Maggie, who promptly standing up, was coming toward them to see what was the commotion. Wubit wrapped her little arms around Maggie's knees, and looking up into her eyes, implored:

"Please, don't leave me here. I don't have a place to go, I don't have a family, my parents are dead, I am an orphan!"

Maggie, lowering to the little girl's level and wiping her tears, was talking to her on a soothing voice. She quickly learned that the little girl lived around the school, where she was given some food, handed out some clothes, and sometimes offered a place to sleep. Wubit was accepted, as others like her, to be an orphan growing on its own, at the pity of the community, let to flourish like a wild plant.

Without delay, Captain Scotti's voice made an overhead announcement that they were aligned for the takeoff, and Maggie gently grabbed the little orphan, and turning toward her seat, placed Wubit next to her. Then, Maggie fastened their belts, and hugging the beautiful child, whispered to her ear:

"You will see, you will love flying."

With this said, Wubit, the little orphan girl had a family! And nothing could compensate the joy brought into Maggie's heart as these immense black eyes filled with tears of gratitude looked into hers.

As the C-17 Globemaster containing a growing crowd kept reaching altitude over the Ethiopian Easter border, a joyful ambiance expanded enveloping everyone on board. Soon, they were flying over the Red Sea, and in preparation of a meal to be served, a variety of beverages and snacks had already been generously distributed.

Maggie was entirely taken by her new occupation as a designated foster mother, and she enjoyed every minute of it. Giving reassurance and comfort to little Wubit during the beginning of the flight, then introducing the orphan girl to the novelty of air travel, absorbed Maggie's attention and desire to make all of this a great experience for her new protégée.

At a certain time, Maggie and Wubit exchanged seats, and the little girl moved to the window, while Maggie commented on the clouds and the sea below. Wubit, after an initial apprehension, was so immersed on the exhilaration of seeing things from so far high, her sweet squeals and her little hands clapping with enchantment attracted every one's attention. Young and old passengers smiled and relaxed under the cathartic effect of this pure and innocent young presence.

It seemed as though Wubit was placed on their path as an answer to their search for healing, finding a new energy needed to continue their journey back home.

After a while, Captain Scotti allowed his co-pilot Phillipe take over the controls and he could, finally, appreciate a short meal break, while periodically shifting his attention to the dashboard and the horizon beyond. After their lunch, the three crew members commented about the good weather with a perfectly blue sky, and the three hours left out of the four-hour flying time before reaching their destination, Alexandria, Egypt. They even commented on the fact that, after fueling, they would be in good shape to continue to Heathrow, London, and not to linger any longer until securing from there a direct flight to the United States. Things were starting to look a lot better as the road became a little closer to home!

CHAPTER 8 - REFUGEES

DETOUR

"Do not go to Alexandria! This is an order. I repeat, do not go to Alexandria. Change direction of your flight going north and avoid Egyptian territory, stay over the Red Sea until new orders! Over", suddenly an alerting voice broke the quiet of the cockpit.

Startled, the flight crew jumped into action for the changes to their flight plan, and verified that they were staying over the international water lines. All the while, they wandered what was the cause of this urgent announcement coming from the Indian Ocean Military Division that followed their voyage. It did not take long, minutes later Jo asked permission to enter the cockpit, obviously having himself details of outmost importance.

"I have news from the Intelligence Headquarters, some extreme Muslim factions had formed a coalition against Israel, after years of conspiracy. Since the US is an ally of Israel, any American craft flying over, or approaching the Egyptian territory, is considered as a national violation and shut down. That goes for Libya, Tunis, Algeria, and most of the Middle Eastern countries, including Turkey. All American flights and military vessels are ordered to keep away from these territories and out of confrontation", Jo delivered the latest facts he was just been made privy.

"They know we have enough fuel to fly for four hours but we've been in air for close to two hours now and they scramble to give us a port of landing."

"What a mess!", Scotti Hunt said in frustration. "At least we know what is going on," and the they proceeded to consulting the area map, preparing for major changes of their plans. A decision was made quickly for now, though, not to alarm anyone in the main cabin, including the new 'flight attendants'.

"Bravo-Gulf-Mike, do you copy?", suddenly the microphone crackled and came to life, "We have clearance for you to touch ground. Go northeast and tune to 21d 25' 59" North, 40d 0' 0" East, this is Makkah airport in Saudi Arabia, you are approved for landing. Just identify yourself. You are 25 minutes away at this altitude and speed. Any questions? Over."

"We don't think so, thank you. Over."

"You will be contacted after your landing and given further instructions to your passengers, but it looks like you will have to notify the American Consulate in Jeddah, on the east coast of the Red sea upon your arrival. Over."

"Roger that, thanks. Over."

Shortly after, Captain Scotti had to make an announcement:

"Here is Captain Scotti Hunt again. I hope that you are all enjoying the flight, and since it looks like everyone is having a good time, we will add to our entertainment a short detour to Mecca."

As he could hear the surprised reaction to his broadcast, he added:

"Just joking! We have been requested to make a stop in Saudi Arabia before reaching our final destination. Nothing out of the ordinary, just verification of the passengers", said Scotti, making his message sound as mild as possible. "And since we are not transporting any terrorist group, we have nothing to be concerned about. We will be landing momentarily and let the festivities continue", he concluded.

A little surprised, the passengers took, nevertheless, the captain's message as a benign interruption. They started gathering some of their belongings, verifying their papers. Maggie, however, exchanging a glance with her brother who occupied the bench across from her, and, getting up together, they went toward the cockpit to meet their father.

The only person not paying attention to the action, was Wubit. When, a while ago Maggie went to get a cup of tea from the gulley, Everest stood up at once and went straight to the little girl and getting comfortable, put his head on her lap and took a long sigh of contentment. Wubit, delighted to make another friend, caressed his thick fur, and after a while, the two of them fell asleep. Now they were the perfect picture of contentment, ignoring all commotion around them.

Maggie, for good reason, was concerned about the lack of legal documents for Wubit, which should be requested at their arrival. Jo stopped her in her tracks reassuring her that he had already asked for an official addition of the little girl to the passengers' list. He expanded his information though, telling Maggie and Trebor, that, since Wubit did not probably have a last name as it is common in Ethiopia, he told his superiors the whole story and suggested a name for her:

"For now, she is Wubit Godson!"

MECCA

"Are we going to visit Mecca? How extraordinary, I always wanted to go to the place of birth of Prophet Mohammed!", Rebekah exclaimed almost in unison with her husband, doctor David Anderson, one of the couples being repatriated. Their faces beamed with enthusiasm matching the feelings of other travelers joining in the conversation.

"Not really, only Muslims are allowed into the holly city", came a quick response from Jo, who regained the cabin for the imminent landing.

"We will circle the town without entering it, and we will go to Jeddah. The only view we will have of the Al Haram Mosque with the Kaaba at its center, will be from the air", continued Jo. "It is impressive, though, the larger mosque in the world. But even if you were allowed to visit it, you might want to consider this overcrowded place, many perished in stampedes of daunting proportions in the past."

Just before the final approach, more information was coming from Captain Scotti:

"In a few moments we will be on the ground at Makkah Airport. Our destination for now is to reach Jeddah, and present ourselves to the Consulate General of the United States", the captain's voice tried to be as reassuring as possible. "I know, the King Abdul Aziz International Airport is only 12 miles north of Jeddah, but is the busiest airport in Saudi Arabia, and the air traffic control could not give us clearance to land there at this time. But not to worry, there are only 75 miles from where we will land and the town, and we should arrive to the consulate in about two hours ride. Now, all relax and enjoy the spectacle below, I reserved for you a little 'peek' of Mecca before landing!"

Once on the ground, the Boeing C-17 Globemaster was directed to taxi to one of the British Airways cargo hangars provided for private use of the non-Muslim nations providing goods during the Haji period. They were not to enter the premises of the actual airport terminals. After their discreet reception when the captain handed the list of the passengers, everyone was hurried into a waiting space, providing limited air conditioning. Being served some non-alcoholic beverages while waiting for the luggage to be transferred to a minibus, the travelers understood that this must be their ride to Jeddah, and wondered what to expect next.

Scotti Hunt appreciated that he became partner with Joseph Godson from now on, as he had been informed by the military authorities in agreement with the Central Intelligence; at least he would have someone who was versed on international administration, besides somebody like him, only with air flight expertise. He realized that his 'mission' changed constantly according to this 'crazy' international situation, but he was still, nevertheless, in charge with his passengers' safety. At least for now, he had some help coming from Jo. And Scotti liked him and started appreciating Jo's presence and personality by the day, as he was most impressed with his family and the way they all conducted themselves.

Sipping on a well appreciated icy cold tea, Scotti took a general view of the crowd, all part of his traveling manifest. He counted a little over 20 of them, including Phillipe Prior, his flight assistants, Amanda and Sonia, the newly improvised flight attendants, then the Godson family, now counting five with Wubit and Everest. Because Everest, even though he was a dog, everyone considered him as a real person and fully occupying the space of a human being.

He counted the other initial travelers, Jovanni and Randal, the two couples, Rebekah and Dr. David Anderson, and Deborah and Joshua McClain. Joining the group that kept growing and formed a kaleidoscope of nations and religions around the initial American trio, came Kuan Li, Lu Xiang, Jamuna, Raj, and most recently, Beshadu.

Then, Scotti joined Jo and the two of them debated on the situation of the airplane, the need for its safety and maintenance. Captain Scotti, along with his technical crew, had to secure the aircraft inside of the hangar, but the orders were still not clear as far as their next move: they have been told that British Airways serving Jeddah were overwhelmed by their own repatriation long list and there was no American Airline coming to Jeddah, even during normal times. What remained available for their trip continuation was only their airplane, which would lift off sometimes soon from either Makkah or King Abdul Aziz International, if he had to come fetching the passengers for their flight to London.

Captain Scotti was about to let out his frustration, in a "what a mess", short sigh, when Jo's smart phone started chirping. Scotti observed Jo listening intensely for a while, then turning off his phone after saying: "We will follow your instructions, sir. Yes sir, good night to you too, sir", after which, Jo turned toward Scotti:

"It seems that you will remain here with the two other crew members and make sure that all is ready for a flight possibly in the following days. You will have rooms available at the hotel where the British Airways' crew stays usually. I am in charge to accompany the passengers to Jeddah and we will have later on orders for our trip continuation. "

"Good," answered quickly Scotti, "I will enjoy a fresh shower while you will be still on the road."

"Not to worry, my friend, it doesn't look like you are getting rid of us so easily. I bet there won't be any other transportation available until London than this old coocoo", replied Jo, giving Scotti a tap on the shoulder. "We will continue the party together."

ON THE WAY TO JEDDAH

For once, the remainder of the day proceeded almost uneventfully; after the group's arrival at the consulate, passports were verified for the American citizens and all other formalities simplified and cleared to all the people accompanied by Jo.

It goes without saying that, after a precipitated but full of hope departure from Aksum, some of the extremist Islamic governments overtly turned against the western world, another reason forcing the airplane to land in Saudi Arabia.

Even without knowing how these explosive events would evolve, the unplanned landing made our travelers conspicuous during their ride to Jeddah. However, their driver, Idris, was polite and cheerful, accustomed to many visitors coming to the holiest city of Islam. Prepared well ahead, he offered to all the ladies of the group proper head covers, as requested by the Saudi laws.

Idris, after closing the doors of his Mercedes van and checking that everyone was sitting comfortably, was eager to explain that his name was the equivalent of Hebrew Enoch, after the seventh prediluvian prophet. Taking the route 4029 south, he then turned east on route 301 and made a circle to south avoiding Mecca. Riding on the 'Christian Cutoff', he pointed out, however, at the Qur'an Gate, presenting a gigantic open book design, raised as a boundary keeping the non-Muslim out of the holy city. After a turn on Highway 80 leading all the way to Jeddah, some two hours later they arrived at Al Andalus and Falastin block, where the American Consulate General of the United States is located within the diplomatic district.

During the ride to Jeddah, Idris took the opportunity to give a brilliant performance describing the best he could what the visitors missed from entering Mecca. He explained that all Muslims are to visit this place at least once in their life time, and there were about 15 million people visiting Mecca each year, with several millions during the few days of the annual Haji celebrations. Muhammad, or Mohammed, was born in Mecca in year 570 AD, but the city is believed to go back to the time of Abraham (Ibrahim) who built Kaaba helped by his elder son, Ishmael, around year 2000 BC.

At his death, in year 632, Mohamed achieved a large expansion of the Islam religion with pilgrimages to Mecca becoming with time part of a strong religious tradition.

In 1924 there was a Battle of Mecca when the Sharif of Mecca was overthrown by the Saudi family and Mecca became part of the Saudi Arabia. Idris expressed regrets while commenting on the fact that since 1985 under the Saudi rule, close to 95% of historical monuments have been neglected, some dating over thousand years old. This included five out of seven most sacred mosques built by Muhammad's daughter.

Idris, keeping his enthusiasm high all along the trip, told his new audience that there are in reality two pilgrimages to Mecca, the mandatory one, the grand pilgrimage Haji, and a lesser one, not mandatory, Umrah. During the Haji, the devotees approach Kaaba, which is covered with a black cloth and situated in the middle of the square of the Great Mosque Al Harami. They have to circle it seven times making prayers to Allah. When home, during their prayers five times a day, the Muslims always turn toward the direction of Mecca.

Before arriving to the Consulate, Idris found the time to add that Mecca, being a place of massive crowds coming from all around the world creating a very cosmopolitan center, it also favors the exchange of a variety of ideas. Thus, Mecca has become a

185

'center of liberalism', an oasis within the Islamic world, promoting opposition to the rising of extremist Islamic discourse.

Maggie asked playfully if there were any exceptions to the non-Muslim visitors to Mecca, to which Idris laughed, but he was happy to show his knowledge in the matter,

"Oh, funny that you asked, no, nobody as far as we know could 'sneak' in the recent times. It is reported, though, that a certain Ludovico di Varthema of Bologna, Italy, managed to pass the city guards in 1503!"

QUICK STOP IN JEDDAH

Jo felt relieved as he joined his group at a long table in the dining room of the cafeteria inside the consulate complex. He was thrilled with the outstanding help given by the consulate administrative personnel. Whether every diplomatic service present in the Muslim countries scrambled to repatriate the citizens and to facilitate their transfers out of the politically inflamed regions, or they wanted to expedite their work as the volume of paperwork was piling up, everyone at the immigration/repatriation office was efficient and kind.

For the group that Jo and his siblings tried to obtain temporary permission to enter the US, Jo Godson seemed to have been granted larger authority than he suspected, allowing him almost 'carte blanche' for the names added to his list. He could arrive to agreements with the employees to choose accordingly between the Humanitarian & Special Situations, or Religious Worker visas. Thus, every one of his new friends had been swiftly taken pictures, finger-printed, and issued an official document that enabled them to travel to America in all legality.

Even Everest passed with flying colors his paper check, having already his physical and vaccinations completed recently in Mumbai; sitting at Trebor and Maggie's feet, he was just enjoying his milk bone treat, totally oblivious at the idea that someone could have found him 'delinquent' under any respect.

AISHA AND FARID

Aisha came out of the American Consulate immigration office content. Belonging to a prominent Saudi family, she had a permanent UK visa and she came only to ask a favor for boarding the American aircraft going to London. As a matter of fact, she asked a favor for herself and for Farid, her chauffeur and the man she was in love with, to be permitted to fly together to London as passengers of the C-17 Globemaster. In London, she possessed a lavish flat in Chelsea, in addition to several properties owned by her family as residential dwellings or investment buildings all over the world. Aisha had already informed her parents that she desired to take another trip there, as she liked to do regularly.

This time, though, Aisha had a bold plan, she would be accompanied by Farid and marry him, against her family's previous refusals. She was the youngest of three other girls and two boys, and she learned how to have things her way since she was a baby. Although she would expect a complete opposition from her family marrying outside her social class, having lived for half of her life in the west and attending the best European boarding schools, Aisha mindset molded into an emancipated western woman. She was convinced that, once she would announce her marriage with Farid to her parents, they would understand and at the end approve of it, seeing how much they loved each other and how happy she was.

The American Consulate had only to make a request of two additional people to be added to the passenger manifest of the C-17 Globemaster, which had been granted in view of these troubled times. In reality, Aisha intended to avoid boarding British Airways or any of the Saudi airlines servicing London, in order to shun any suspicion of flying with Farid, using the airlines in which she was a frequent flyer.

As usual, Farid was to drive her to the airport, but this time, after parking the car at the usual spot, he would leave the keys at the security gate. Then, he would accompany Aisha to the airplane, without having to go through the airport security and terminals. For Aisha was aware of a simpler formality checking everyone's documents before the boarding on the military American airplane, contrary to the commercial flights, where the passengers must pass several public checking points before the boarding.

LEAVING ARABIA

One more time, the C-17 Globemaster voyagers and its crew met at the foot of their 'bird'. Captain Scotti and his mates made a short 'jump' from Makkah Airport to Jeddah King Abdul Aziz International to meet the passengers, avoiding them another road trip back to Mecca. During the two days spent in the British Airways hangar in Makkah, Captain Scotti hooked up with the ground mechanical team and managed to obtain a full and greatly appreciated inspection and maintenance of the aircraft, since the technicians were FAA qualified and had all the necessary equipment.

With the international conflict sparking randomly but reducing drastically the leisure travels, the Brits were half-busy compared to their schedule from a few weeks before, and getting bored. A couple of oversized Wild Turkey Bourbon Whiskey bottles aiding as after-hours cocktail time, the mechanics were happy to get to work. While the Boeing crew gave them a hand, they worked together exchanging jokes and striking a friendly detente, after days of stress. Although the fees for the services were quite steep, the captain was happy to take care of his 'baby', and the ground team compensated them largely with additional maintenance and help not shown in the invoice. The only thing they had to worry about was the liquor, although even here it was tolerated, as long as they were drinking privately and appearances were saved.

Fall was gently slipping into late October, and the trip to Heathrow Airport, should last some seven hours, but this time of the year, there was a light-saving time change in Saudi Arabia, not followed by the United Kindom, setting London time three hours back. Thus, even leaving Jeddah in the middle of the morning, they should reach England before the sunset.

All on board, with introductions made spontaneously between the former travelers and the Saudi couple, everyone was looking forward to their destination to England. And from there, God willing, a whole new group would cross the Ocean to their old or new home. Most of the people regained spontaneously their former seats, while the Saudi couple preferred more privacy choosing to go to the back of the plane. Wubit, however, who took a huge liking of Everest, chose a place to sit together, while Trebor and Maggie occupied the bench across form them, on the other side of the emergency exit.

Before taking off and one last time the checklist of the main cabin completed, Amanda told Joseph Godson that the captain invited him to travel in the cockpit along with the flight crew.

CHAPTER 9 - ARMAGEDDON

THE SAND STORM

A typical flight from Jeddah to London would follow a general northwestern direction over a part of central Egypt, then through the northern side of Libya and, once over the Mediterranean Sea, would fly over some Greek and Italian islands. Then, the plane should arrive over France, before starting its descend once reaching the English Channel for the Heathrow Airport final approach. However, another possibility was to continue north until meeting the Mediterranean Sea, then turn northwest all the way to England.

And this was the route recommended by the military North African Division and approved by the tower in Jeddah. The Globemaster was in the air in no time, and soon over the arid regions of northwest Saudi peninsula. They kept a couple of hundred miles inside the land, staying off the Egyptian firing range, just in case.

They were cruising for over two hours, crew and passengers making the best of the time bringing them closer to their destination. However, for no particular reason, the aircraft jerked a few times, as they run into some air turbulences, 'air bubbles' making the airplane 'slam down' with no warning under a clear sky. This caught captain Scotti's attention, who verified their position and the weather radar.

Nothing abnormal. But looking at the horizon line ahead, Scotti was intrigued by the haziness seen far before them. Minutes later, he understood what was the problem, a sandstorm of enormous proportions begun as from nowhere! Anticipating to run into it shortly, Scotti asked permission to gain another 2,500 feet of altitude. That was all the elevation they could afford keeping within the safety parameters.

The shaking and bouncing did not get any better once reaching the claimed altitude, and, while they were climbing, the sandstorm had already engulfed the aircraft, and the pilots struggled to stay on track against the swirling winds. In the main cabin the passengers had been instructed to keep tightly fastened at all times, while in the cockpit the crew scrambled to reroute the trip out of the storm. The captain gave orders to contact the ground in Tabuk while strived to keep the airplane steady.

"We don't have an answer", Andy, the radio operator said, swearing in his beard. And after a few long minutes of unsuccessful attempts, "I will contact the Mediterranean fleet, see if they know anything", then he turned on the speakerphone.

"Bravo-Gulf-Mike, we read you. Do not fly over the Red Sea and stay off the Egyptian territory. Copy that? Try to fight the storm and continue north, over."

"We are over 20 people on board, passengers and crew included. The sandstorm reached uncharted altitude, we cannot go above it and the turbines are choking under the sand. We don't have a ground contact and we are running into an emergency situation. I need to have clearance to bring my people to the ground safely. Please advise. Over", captain Scotti intervened.

Again, silence seemed to last forever. Then, finally a voice was heard:

"The Saudi and Jordan are not answering. You will have to stretch to Ben Gurion, close to Tel Aviv. We will patch you through, stay firm, over."

"Copied."

Still nothing after 20 minutes of going through complete obliteration of the visibility, the engines starting coughing and all attempts to obtain ground control response, any response, failing. To improve the engines' performance, they must find clear air but with suffocating motors, it was not possible to ask for more effort and reach higher altitude.

"This is crazy, never seen or heard of sandstorm at over 25,000 feet of altitude, and covering so much land", a frustrated Phillipe complained, feeling powerless.

A few crackles on the mike startled them with hope.

"Bravo-Gulf-Mike, state your position for verification."

Scotti did, all the while raising his brows of not having a connection with Ben Gurion yet.

"Ben Gurion seems to have their own problems, sensible information. We managed to get an answer from their Security Division and obtain an OK for an emergency arrival. You are 25 minutes from the landing time, from now you will remain in constant contact with them", then, "we will be in touch with you later, have a safe 'day trip' through the storm! Copy?"

"Roger, thank you!"

"Here they are, so long!"

Then, there was a change of voice on the mike:

"Shalom, captain Scotti, I am Ivar. We are going to guide you to the landing strip reserved to the military", then proceeded to giving the coordinates for the flight, after stating that they would be communicating on special frequencies scrambled against undesirable ears.

The flight crew arrived at the short segment crossing over Jordan, the only way to avoid Egypt coming straight from Saudi Arabia, and the atmosphere was still clouded by the thick floating sand. The crew was concerned about the plane making it to Israel, the engines now skipping, engorged with dust. At last, the air cleared a little, and suddenly they were flying under a blue sky! A cheer could be heard all the way to the cockpit coming from the cabin and it was time to inform the passengers about their unexpected landing.

"Simple maintenance and check of the engines, that's all to be said, no need for panic on board", decided captain Scotti.

There was another 15 minutes flight descending toward Tel Aviv that kept the flying team's full attention, and finally the designated landing strip in view, they were urged to touch down.

THE HOLY LAND

The C-17 Globemaster did arrive to the tarmac, when it was indicated to pull on the side of the taxiway, close to a military building covered with camouflage painting. A surprisingly young military personnel made of two men and a woman came into view and requested to stop the engines at once. Then, each soldier went to each one of the airplane's exits. After a polite but careful documents verification, everyone was rushed into an office inside the military building.

However, while the passengers were directed indoors and all documents reviewed, the flying crew was allowed to return to the cockpit and restart the engines to get closer to a hangar where they have been asked to park the aircraft under cover. Both turbines, damaged by the sandstorm, barely whimpered chocked by the dust infiltrating the rotors and ducts. The airplane could be moved, however, for a few hundred feet to the entrance of the hangar, then, the turbines completing faithfully their duty, stopped with a whine. At least, the Globemaster could be rapidly howled inside where hopefully expert hands would be able to repair the damages.

During these last maneuvers, Scotti Hunt was taking notes of a few unusual details catching his attention. He could remember, now that he was thinking back a few hours, that his clearance for the take off in Jeddah took no more time than on a rural air flying club. As he was clearing the airport surroundings with a swift semicircle and reaching altitude, there was no other activity in the air, coming either from the commercial or private flights, highly unlikely for a busy international airport.

Getting close to Ben Gurion, although absorbed with the airplane conditions while landing with failing engines, here again, there was absolutely no activity on the ground at the large civilian airport perimeter. Along with the three other members of his team, now Jo considered as one of them besides Phillipe and

Andy, stepping out of the airplane, captain Scotti went to the person coming toward him, possibly the head mechanic as he was wearing work overalls and sweeping the grease off his hands on a piece of rug.

"Shalom, Captain Scotti Hunt I suppose? I am Sam and we will secure your bird here for now, until it will be able to fly again", he said, trying to sound reassuring, but not giving any further details. "You are expected to join your group at the office next door", and leading the four members of the crew to the large exit door, he indicated the place without any other commentaries.

The four of them walked the hundred yards separating the buildings and entered the door marked as 'Security Office', where they met all the other members of their group. They have been accommodated with chairs and bottles of water and Jaffa orange juice, during which they were provided with neck-hanging badges showing their picture ID and names, looking like passes of some sort. After a quick glance around the room to verify that the passengers were fine, Scotti followed Ivar, who had made a discreet sign to the four members of the crew, to follow him inside a small office.

Ivar seemed very much in control, but somewhat in a hurry, as he apologized for getting straight to the core of the matter:

"Four hours ago, Israel has been attacked by a newly formed Islamic International Coalition! We are at war and the highest levels of security and emergency have been declared". Then, letting all this set in, Ivar added, "The airport has been attacked, but suffered limited harm", then almost choking, Ivar barely managed to say: "but Jerusalem is completely destroyed, or so we have been informed."

The four Americans were stunned; the insanity was spreading instead of being contained, and spreading at a lightning speed. First North Korea, then China, now the Arabic world, then what or who else, Russia, Venezuela?

It was evident that the Islamic Brotherhood stroke an alliance with Iran, Syria, and whatever faction of North African nations including Algeria, Tunisia, Libya, Egypt, along with African and Middle Eastern Isis militants from Yemen, Senegal, or others.

"The world is marching toward its own auto-destruction!", Jo thought.

"We have orders to bring the civil population, including foreigners, to the train tunnel. We have an electrified train going from Tel Aviv to Jerusalem, and there is an access to it at terminal 3 of the Airport. We must bring all of you there, the tunnel reaches 100 feet underground and it is doubled as nuclear shelter."

"Do you have family in Jerusalem, are they OK?", Jo Godson could not help but to ask.

"Yes, we all have, and thank you for asking, but no news from them", at which point Ivar, trying to overcome his emotion, he forced his quivering voice to raise: "It must be Armageddon! And where is the New Messiah, when is he coming?"

NEW DIRECTIONS

Scotti and his companions came out from the small conference room and, gathering the members of his group around, explained the best he could the devastating situation. Jo went close to his children, then addressed the group with a short briefing. Trying to prevent the beginning of a panic, Joseph encouraged all of them to concentrate by taking one step at a time, one minute, one hour at a time. Somewhat, Jo, Trebor and Scotti had taken the leading positions directing their moves out this situation.

During the updating of the passengers, the ground people brought inside the luggage recovered from the Globemaster, and they all had a sticker marking them as checked by the security. The members of the group were then asked to quickly verify and take possession of their property, then to board on the three electric carts parked for them in the front of the building. They would be driven to Terminal 3, then inside of the train station.

If there was confusion on the travelers' minds, they showed no panic, they all applied themselves to comply with the instructions given, realizing that they were all looking to find safety during catastrophic events which had only began.

The electric carts in motion, the security employees rode them thinking that, if for now the bombing subsided, it could restart at any time, and rushed to get to the train station entrance as fast as possible, riding under the buildings cover.

If people did not talk much, they were all, regardless nation or religion, addressing ardent prayers to God. And at the same time for the New Messiah to come. And, where was he hiding?

INSIDE THE TUNNEL

Our travelers followed the directions given with little time to react to the overwhelming reality. Now, they were in the tunnel drilled under the rocky terrain at Ben Gurion Airport Railway Station, and where other people removed from the airport terminals had been gathered. It was a fairly new construction with a price tag of $2 billion, an electrified rail bringing voyagers either to Tel Aviv in 28 minutes or, taking the opposite direction for a 20 minutes ride, to Jerusalem.

Since this was a double railroad and people were packed in the wagons going in both directions, as orders were to remove as many people as possible from the vicinity of the airport, in the fear that more heavy bombing could be expected at any moment. However serious damages have been done to the capital, Tel Aviv, and to Jerusalem as far as some were aware of.

The group arriving from Jeddah were shown a line to follow, while they received a small bag containing two bottles of water and some basic food under cellophane. They slowly advanced behind others people who boarded a wagon. Shortly after getting seated, their coach went into motion; it looked like most of the people stranded in the airport had been already evacuated and our friends were among the last ones to depart. The overhead speaker made a brief announcement in Hebrew, then in English, recommending that they all be seated and keep calm, and that the train was going in the direction of Jerusalem. If under normal circumstances the train runs at a speed easily exceeding 150 km/hr., over 92 miles/hour, this time it moved slowly, showing a surprisingly cheerful modern and well-lit tunnel. Nevertheless, they all kept silent, absorbing the notion of these serious and scary times, making many wonder, if this was only the beginning of a mondial conflict that caught them in the middle, and, for how long the new war would last?

Jo and Maggie Godson, Trebor Young, and the flight crew had succeeded to place everyone from their group together, the little Wubit never leaving Maggie's hand and Everest Trebor's side. Trebor also tried to give some explanations to Kuan Li, Lu Xiang, Raj, Jamuna, and Beshadu, who were so much de-rooted from their surroundings, while Scotti and his helpers opened a conversation with the two couples, then Jovanni and Randal, well-traveled folks, all assessing their options. Aisha and Farid, the Saudi couple who chose so far to remain isolated, joined the others, Farid offering his help to the alliance that started forming among men, while Aisha came naturally toward Maggie.

While the train advanced at a slow speed for 5-6 minutes then made frequent pauses, Trebor and Jo congregated at the edge of their group and quietly debated, reviewing the situation.

"I don't have any contact, yet. I do not have any reception in this tunnel either, so I hope that once close to Jerusalem and on the surface, I will get intel", said Jo, straight to the point.

"But Jerusalem is destroyed, I heard. What if this is correct? I don't understand why we even go in that direction?"

"It could very well be to bring underground as many of the remaining population as possible. There could also be some shelters prepared for the Jerusalem's inhabitants", Jo tried to find some reason to the train motion.

One more stop and the speakerphone could be again heard:

"The train will stop here for now. Everyone is welcome to stay inside and more instructions will follow as we have more information. You understand that this is a situation of extreme emergency and food and water supply must be conserved, in the eventuality that you must remain underground for an extended period of time. Please remain calm and courteous."

After a short pause, as if someone had managed to ask some questions, the voice in the speakerphone added:

"We are a mile and a half from Ha Uma Train Station in Jerusalem. The entrances and exits to the station had been obliterated by the attack. From this train to the end of the tunnel, we aligned other carts with people from the airport and the city of Jerusalem. Please do not attempt to go out. Here you are safe", then the voice went silent.

Hours went by and the people waiting in the tunnel felt unsettled, under a cover of a genuine effort to control their emotions and their growing fear. Jo teaming with Scotti, and Trebor with Jamuna, decided it was time to explore the situation and the security of their location. They split going to opposite directions, Jo and Scotti going west, back on the direction of Ben Gurion and Tel Aviv, while Trebor and Jamuna were to evaluate the possibility of exiting the tunnel and, possibly have a look at the city of Jerusalem, and maybe beyond that.

Men and women were aware that the tunnel offered protection from aerial attacks, the temperature was constant and pleasant this time of the year and at this depth. Thankfully, there was power and the toilets functioned, so far. This gave a little reassurance to the four men leaving the others behind for a few hours. However, they were concerned by the short supply in water and food, and they needed to find a way to sustain the needs of their group.

Jo and Scotti kept walking northwest for a long time, they had covered some 10 km, when they had to accept their bad luck, as they could not find any opening to the surface. There was no food or water supply, and the lights were shot off at a point, making them stop, for beyond that, they could see only a peach dark hole like the mouth of a monster ready to swallow anyone adventuring further down.

Just when they became disappointed and decided to turn around and come back, a side door at the limit of the area lit by the LED tubes, opened, and a couple of uniformed young men showed up. They quickly understood that Jo and Scotti were some stranded people form the train, and after a short exchange of information, they learned that the situation above ground was becoming disastrous by the moment. They were pushing a cart filled with food and water supply that would fit the rails and was intended to bring it to the people massed underground. That was all that could be done for now, and probably for a longtime.

Jo and Scotti learned also that the railroad was emptied all the way to the airport, where the traffic was stopped and travelers evacuated in the cars assembled close to Tel Aviv, offering cover also to the population of the neighboring towns, similar to the portion close to Jerusalem.

Jo, reacting promptly, offered to push the cart secured on the tracks, and bring the provisions to the train, thus sparing the young men the trip back and forth. Assuring them that they were more useful back with their comrades, Jo and Scotti promised that they would take good care of the goods provided.

During this time, Trebor and Jamuna arrived to the end of the tunnel on Jerusalem side. However, they had to tell Everest several times to go back: after a few yards on their way, the two friends found out that Everest had decided to come along. Trebor had to take a little time to coax the giant mastiff to keep "an eye on Wubit and Maggie, and all the 'girls, for that matter", until their return. The closer they got to the network of escalators where the tunnels brought the travelers down to the trains or up to the surface, more destruction was visible. Some conveyers and smaller corridors were filled with ruble, and possible with people buried underneath.

Thankfully, they could not detect any injured people, and went to explore some of the tunnels that allowed enough room for them to pass. They came back and forth many times, even stopped at one point to memorize the configuration of the train station and avoid to get lost, trapped in its labyrinth.

Finally, an opening to the surface was possible, although deserted, and the two of them risked to take a peek outdoors. The desolation was beyond belief, nothing seemed to have remained standing. It looked like at some point, in the beginning of the raid, ambulances came to the train station, which apparently was one of the intended targets. But even the emergency cars had been hit and many laid unusable, the first responders suffering casualties in the process of rescuing injured people as well.

Dominated by strong and new emotions, Trebor and Jamuna, were taking in all the information without saying a word. Trebor's mind worked feverishly, a plan building as they looked around, where an eerie decor showed massive destruction and very little sign of life. He was even surprised that the power in the tunnel was still working, as a miracle of Israeli engineering.

Going back and forth and exploring the areas still accessible inside the train station, Trebor found the janitorial work stations and pulled out some of the large containers. He started filling them with everything he could find in the distributing machines, breaking the windows with one of the pick hammers taken from a fire box. At last, he could gather a few train station employees still alive and very frightened, barricaded in a small concrete room. In a way, relieved to learn that the attack was over, at least for now, and having lost all notion of the time that had past, they were happy to be mobilized by Trebor and help the stranded people.

Trebor seemed to bring hope and a new motivation to these people who were still under the shock and thought that there was not much to expect for their rescue. They started following eagerly Trebor's directions, and assembled every item that could find to increase their survival chances. All the food, water, flashlights, blankets, cleaning supplies, disinfectants, rugs and plastic bags were piled in the wheeled containers.

Then, Trebor went one more time to the surface to look for medical supplies he could find in the damaged ambulances. He found in one of the vehicles under the owning of the train station that the chauffer was still alive with minor lacerations and an EMT agent cared for him. The EMT himself had laid on the ground for a while with a commotion after being blown away from the open door when he was loading an injured pedestrian. Unfortunately, after the EMT regained consciousness, the pedestrian could no longer be helped. The nurse working in the same emergency vehicle went inside the station to assist some voyagers by the rotating gates. This was only to face the shocking reality not finding anyone alive; there were adults, a few children and a baby, all killed by the last bombs. Now, she was sitting on the curbside crying desperately, overwhelmed by the feeling of a powerless guilt.

Trebor went to her, and gently offered her his handkerchief, without saying anything. Aleezah's chest opened like a dam under the flow of tears, and she let her torment wail her sorrow out to the world. After a while, she turned toward Trebor and faced him. Something strange and powerful happened to her, this time feeling hope in the middle of this calamity of biblical proportions, and, standing up, she bowed and addressed Trebor before he could talk:

"Pardon me, Seigneur. Where have you been? What do you want me to do?"

"My name is Trebor, and I try to gather as many people as I can to bring help to the one in need. There are many underground and Tobias, the EMT, and Manuel, the chauffer. We will gather medical supplies and you will come with me to assist the ones that might need medical attention."

Thus, after a few hours, Trebor and Jamuna were returning back to the train pushing containers and started distributing, as fairly as they could, food and beverages. They finally reached the end of the train where their group waited for them, and, as Jo and Scotti showed up practically at the same time, there was almost a little sensation of celebration brought about by this spark of hope.

CLOSING INTO THE BIBLICAL PLACES

Trebor opened his eyes and contemplated for a few moments the low ceiling of the train car above him. It had been a long time since he had a nightmare and he needed to clear his mind and understand the meaning of this dream.

It had been a long rest of the day, wearing them all down with uncertainty of what the next moment would bring along. Trebor had helped, along with many others, distributed food, medical care, and other necessities available to the people settled in the wagons of the Express Railroad, waiting for better times to be announced, hopefully soon. Jo continued incessantly to try make contact with the military and intelligence agency, without any connection still possible.

The emergency rescuers had joined the underground crowd, fault of better choices found outside. And now, everyone slowed down for a much-needed rest, groups forming, or like our group of travelers, just remained together and comforting each other.

Trebor had a hard time before his body found the quiet and allowed the Greek god's wand, Morpheus, to transport him into the dreamland. And now, after a few hours of an agitated on and off sleep, he contemplated the images that visited him. They were simple but very powerful; he was back in his labor camp dark cell, constricted within the bare walls of a small space. Water was running on the walls filling the room with a humid penetrating cold. Trebor experienced again the atrocious desperation that invaded his being at the beginning of his incarceration, and he cried again for his celestial father, for God, to hear his prayer.

Shortly after, Trebor saw the walls of the prison fade away, as he was raising above them in a surge of light. He found himself in the middle of an abandoned city, destroyed, with old buildings laying shattered, in complete devastation. As the decor changed, so did his feelings, going from pain to surprise and confusion. But there was also the reassurance that God was there all along, a loving, compassionate presence taking away all fear. It was as if Trebor had to be there, to do something.

Since he had left his secure and comfortable life behind and traversed a world ravaged by tragedy, something in his heart was telling him that he had to find himself in the middle of this vast confusion and chaos.

As his mind transitioned form dream to reality, Trebor sensed that there was a message in his dream; no more traumatizing traps controlling his consciousness, or at least his sub-conscious mind, but freedom. Liberating and empowering freedom. He could do something about the dramatic events exploding everywhere, he was expected to do something.

"But what?", Trebor thought getting up, cautiously, trying not to awaken his companions. Then, although it was still long before dawn, he decided to go out. Giving Everest a little sign, Trebor and his faithful companion by his side, went to the surface.

JERUSALEM

"What an earie silence above this cataclysmic scene!", as far as Trebor's eyes could strain through the pale eastern light, in front of him laid the enormous ruins of what not long ago had been a very special city. A holy city chosen by God. And now men had annihilated it!

Even the fires and the broken water hydrants had completed their rage. And no signs of life seemed to show their presence.

Trebor's heart felt as shattered looking at what had been buildings, monuments, and streets. His throat tight, chocking under the fumes and dust, but also from sobs and screams he tried to repress, Trebor was contemplating the epical devastation expanding as far as he could see, not aware that his eyes were letting tears pour down his face. He started walking without direction, stumbling at each step on the gravel and ruble, unable to recognize much of what was left of former places. He wandered for a long time, the only living soul in this desolation, when finally, he could distinguish some contours. This must have been Jaffa Gate, not much of the old city walls were still there, sad, but still majestic remnants of the most venerated sites in the world.

Trebor, overwhelmed by the disturbing display opening as an ultimate evidence of injuries inflicted to the city, let go of his grief without retention. He started shouting, crying and sobbing in despair:

"Oh, God! What have we done? Where is the Church of the Holy Sepulcher? and the streets of the Via Dolorosa walked on by Jesus Christ? And the Wailing Wall? here must have been the Temple Mount built by King Solomon, on the altar of King David! And there, is that what is left of the golden pride of the Dome of the Rock, from where Mohammed ascended to Heaven?"

Trebor went on, walking and touching the precious remains of the ruins, lost proof of thousands of years of sacred history.

"Oh, Father, what happened with this place that was supposed to cradle and unify three major religions? Three major ways to show our love to You, our same and only God? Why can't we live in peace and harmony?", Trebor lamented aloud.

ISHMAEL

"Stop, hold your hands over your head, or you are a dead man", a voice behind him shouted in English, with strong Arabic inflections.

Turning around, Trebor saw a little boy, who must have been not older than 7 or 8 years old, holding a riffle pointed at him. But the riffle looked real, kind of hard to say.

"With this baby face? I don't think you will shoot me", Trebor returned and, calmly, started walking toward the little boy.

"Stop! I am going to shoot!", and, as if he were searching for the right words in English, the little boy added: "Don't come closer, leave me alone!", and he continued to hold the riffle as children do when playing, not really knowing the right way to hold it.

"Come on, angel, give me this riffle and I will give you a chocolate bar!", kept on saying Trebor, and once next to him, gently took the arm from the boy's trembling hands.

"My name is not Angel! I am Ishmael", the child said, trying to keep a serious voice, but he almost snatched the chocolate bar out of Trebor's hand and hungrily took a good bite at it.

"Where are your parents, where do you live?", Trebor inquired.

At first, Ishmael sat on a broken stone and wolfed down the chocolate. Without saying anything, Trebor handed him a small bottle of orange juice, which was emptied in no time at all.

Then, the little boy looked down, as if the weight of the whole world was a too heavy load for his little shoulders.

"I don't know where my parents are. I went out to play soccer with my friends and all of a sudden, I was thrown up in the air. When I woke up, all was gone. I couldn't find my family. My parents, my two sisters, my grandparents, all gone! The explosions covert everything. I looked everywhere, I couldn't find anybody! O couldn't recognize anything!", and getting up, Ishmael leaped the few steps separating him from Trebor and threw his arms around his waist, crying.

"I am alone, everyone is gone. Don't leave me, I don't know where to go!"

"Another little child alone in this vast wide world!" taught Trebor, thinking of the little 5-year-old Wubit, and now, of Ishmael. Then, he addressed the little boy: "Of course, I won't abandon you. Walk with me and we will go find you some new friends, maybe a new little sister. How old are you?"

Strangely, Everest had kept at a slight distance during this interaction between the man and the child, as if he understood not to scare the little boy. But now, he decided that it was the right time to get closer, and while Trebor talked words of consolation, Everest joined them, and licked Ishmael's face, wiping off his tears.

Trebor's heart melted when Ishmael, with all the natural instincts and innocence of a child, took his hand and placed the other one around the dog's neck, ready to leave this place and go together to a better one.

"Thank you, Father!", murmured Trebor almost aloud, looking up, to the braising sky, where the sun rose, announcing a brilliant day. Tears came back to Trebor's eyes, but this time they were tears of hope, tears of gratitude that something good happened in the middle of so much tragedy.

BRINGING IN A NEW FRIEND

Trebor returned to the train track and made his way to the car where his friends were waking up. Jo had noticed his absence, and before he could say anything, Trebor greeted him with a big smile:

"Look what we found! This is Ishmael, he is seven and no longer homeless."

Maggie and Jo came close to them, and introductions were made. Then, almost in unison, the three of them looked for Wubit. A perfect harmony of their thoughts was expressed in the few words Maggie spoke, reading their minds:

"We think Wubit has now a brother!"

"And I am the lucky Grand Pa of a growing family! Christmas will cost me a lot of money from now on!", added Jo, with a huge grin on his face.

Quickly enough, reality called them to order to face the urgency of their situation; the supplies in food and water were very limited, as were the medical resources, and no messages could go through, nor could they receive the ones transmitted by the local authorities.

Trebor confirmed, after his tour on the surface, that Jerusalem was completely destroyed and no signs of any activity were present either. Although it has been a respite of the bombing, Israeli forces seemed concentrating on different points of the country to resist against the aggression. It was an enormous task, since attacks could come from all directions surrounding the small state of Israel, presently facing a massive coalition.

With little hope for success, Jo started walking on the quay along the cars of their train, and looked for a controller operating the train, as he considered it was a must for a place always on the edge of a military conflict. Indeed, he rapidly identified one in a cabin displaying the latest hi-tech design. Jo introduced himself to Jibril, who, enclosed alone in his cubicle and feeling the need to unload the pressure mounting for the last 24 hours, offered an open collaboration.

"I am not to engage in any communication with civilians, but those are not regular times we are living, and you are a special allied force. Maybe we can find a solution together", Jibril volunteered in a whim.

"Let's get inside your cabin and see what quality of satellite connection I can get", said Jo, who went into action right the way.

It took the two of them what seemed a long time, but Jo managed to gather some idea of the situation, his mind searching for an opening out of it. After a short debate with Jibril, he went straight to Trebor and together sorted out their options.

"It looks like Tel Aviv is preparing for an imminent attack, but there are also counteroffensive plans with the allies. I am not aware of what those plans are, but I proposed to Jibril, the train engineer, to bring us back to the airport and see what we can do from there. We might have to get closer to the shore, possibly Ashdod Port, and find a boat if our airplane is still not functional, which probably is the case."

"I think that the other carts should be going toward a station in the direction of Tel Aviv, where the population might find refuge in the areas or shelters still operational; nobody could last for too long here without food and water anyways. They might get evacuated out of Israel to European countries. I am going to see what the people from the other cars decide, while you talk with our folks", Trebor proposed.

It was not very difficult for Jo to obtain the approval of his comrades to shift again directions and go northwest. However, Trebor's task was more delicate, since in the four other train carts some 120 people came from a variety of situations: some just tourists reaching Jerusalem, some businessmen from many corners of the world deposited at Ben Gurion International, others from the capital, Tel Aviv. If most of the people travelling, including the older ones, were in a relatively stable health condition, some local commuters became concerned about running out of their medications.

Going to meet these people, Trebor introduced himself and informed the travelers that the train operator agreed to move them back toward the capital. He explained that they hoped to obtain assistance from the local authorities offering them proper shelter, and, hopefully, a safer way to be evacuated to a more peaceful location.

It was easy to understand that, fault of any other solution, and until now no one offering any plan of action to their complete isolation, small groups debated for a few minutes only, then, people begun to gather around Trebor looking for a leader in these confusing and scary times.

"Alright then, we will go back to our places in the train. But I will recommend that you introduce yourselves to your neighbors and find in your heart words of encouragement and assistance for each other. We all need to keep our calm and help our group according to our abilities and knowledge."

And explaining that nobody could know at this point for how long they would have electricity, food, and water supplies, Trebor added:

"Please find in your generous hearts and fairness of your minds the willingness to share with others our meager reserves. May our celestial Father watch over us all, and keep His arms around us, His children. And we all may open to the higher powers to receive their divine inspiration for a lasting peace in this world!", concluded Trebor, speaking words coming to him effortlessly.

The little crowd appeared moved by these words, words unifying them in the desire to see this prayer fulfilled and their lives uplifted, and lowering their heads, a murmur traversed the attendance:

"Amen", was heard from someone, then others joined in, and the crowd made of so many strangers, blended in unison in the universal conclusion of their prayer. Then, some approached Trebor embracing him and thanking him for the hope he inspired to them.

Gently, Trebor led them by small groups into the train, and with a last wave of his hand, went to his own cart. It was about time, they were all ready to move, new hope filling everyone's thoughts.

CHAPTER 10 - EXODUS

PREPARING TO LEAVE ISRAEL

Close to one hundred and fifty people, their souls filled with hope, found their seats as the train went into motion, at first with a slow vibration, then the smooth mechanics gained more speed. The train engineer continued with caution at a lesser speed than usual, however, the train glided flawlessly through the tube marked only by the regular punctuations of the LED lights. Few minutes later, they encountered the section that was in the dark, and the powerful head lights of the train help to advance, the rail condition looking intact. Ten minutes at a speed of 50 km/hr., there was light again, and they finally slowed down and stopped at the quay indicating the airport arrival.

Here, when the train stopped, the convoy was received by several guardsmen, and a quick delegation formed to represent the civilians. Jibril, the train mechanic, Jo, Trebor, and Scotti went to meet the military, eager to learn more about the situation in general, and about their chances of escaping from there, in particular. The military people listen very carefully to the introductions made, then the small delegation was invited to follow to a side office where they disappeared for a while, deliberating.

The news remained critical and delivered in scarce amount. Most importantly, it appeared that Israeli government and the administration were well prepared and went into emergency action very efficiently. Years of preparation and frequent drills rendered the response to attacks better chances of defense of this small country, newly formed but claiming such an ancient history linked to this land.

For over 24 hours since the attack, the railroad and the train stations had been swiftly transformed into a solid and gigantic shelter, offering additional large spaces equipped with all necessities for large number of people to survive for days or weeks. Thus, the orders were clear and simple, the train occupants were summoned to be distributed to one of the shelters remained intact, opening at regular intervals once past the dangerously exposed airport surroundings.

The travelers have been given the choice, though, for the ones living in the country to stay at a shelter mid distance to Tel Aviv, from where they would be able to regain their own hometown when the order was reestablished, others could gain the train shelters close to the capital, if they were domiciliated in Tel Aviv. As soon as they were out of danger, they could even reach the town and enter one of the well protected shelters of the city, as they were impatient to check into their families.

A more sensitive position was presented by the American group, their intention being to return to the US, which required finding a way to leave the state of Israel without delay. Surprisingly enough, even this eventuality was part of a list of possibilities, and Jo had been connected with a dispatcher to look into exiting the country. At the present moment the conditions were not safe for the foreigners to be directed to a specific port of exit, but there was a real desire on the part of the administration to see the non-Israeli citizens let out of the territory of Israel, avoiding to deal with additional international pressure.

Jo, familiar with delicate negotiations while on foreign land, had learned long before that it was best to have at hand a practical solution to offer; he expressed the idea that he would like to explore the possibilities available at one of the entrance ports, Ashdod or others. As soon as a ferry or a larger embarkation, commercial or for leisure could accommodate 25 or more passengers, Jo asked the authorities for assistance to escort them safely there and allow their group to leave the territory of Israel.

Once the travelers informed of their choices and reaching a decision, eventually the train continued the ride. The passengers were unloading for shelters of their choice, as fortunately, all the ones away from Jerusalem remained intact. Jo, Trebor and Scotti informed their group of their plan to reach the coastline in the hope of finding an embarkation that would take them out of this endangered area. For this, they would need to reach a shelter close to Tel Aviv.

Soon arriving to the terminus and after exiting the railroad, a simple bus drove the Americans and their group on route 20, the roads cleared for the access to Wolfson Medical Center. The activity around the hospital was harried but not hectic, the Israeli used to live under constant threat, acted just like during a regular work day. A few miles south, every one disembarked and the group was promptly allocated to a bunker south of Holon and near Rishon Le Tsiyon.

It was fortunate that the Jewish government was so well prepared for an aggression against its small territory; the newly arrived migrants received a load of basic clothing and could access hot showers they fully enjoyed. Food was also offered in a small but well-organized cafeteria with bottles of fresh water always available. Compact food packages displayed, if not competing for a 'cordon bleu' quality, proved to be of a highly nutritious content.

Eliezer, the liaison person that had promised to arrange before long their transportation to the maritime area, explained that Ashdod was at less than 15 miles south from there. Jo, remained in contact with Eliezer, anxiously waiting for his call, hopefully without much delay.

UNDERGROUND DREAMS

Jamuna allowed his eyelids to slowly close, hoping to bring into his dreams these gentler images, to capture inside the serein beauty of the face he was contemplating. Fighting a little longer from falling asleep, he wanted to feel the spell of this moment, the secret intimacy of being the only one observing this graceful silhouette abandoned to rest. His gaze caressed her perfect profile, the high cheeks and the slope of her eyes, which he knew that, even closed, were hiding a liquid azure he had never seen before. Jamuna did not linger over the flower design of her full lips, he could not bear the profound ache he suppressed so many times, refusing to even recognize the reason of it. Still touched by the almost child-like jaw line, he admired the long, silky dark mane, tossed naturally on her pillow, making Maggie look even more attractive.

Their group, counting now over twenty travelers, had arrived at the shelter and settled casually for a stay they all hoped to be very provisory. Coming out of the massive concrete cover of the train tunnel, some communications could be established using Jo's and Trebor's satellite telephones. This is how Jovanni Mira, after insisting to search for his uncle's marine freight and cruise company, 'Stella Mare', could actually connect with Giorgio Montovani, his uncle and owner of the company.

At the great and unexpected surprise to all of them, there was an opening of opportunity with one of the company's small vessels just coming out of one of the shipyards. Getting ready to regain Naples and continue to charter small trips around Italy and the Greek Islands, captain Montovani was impatient to leave at once these troubled shores. He previously had decided to fly from Naples and watch over the repairs and personally ensure the good return of *Syrena*, a 187-foot yacht. *Syrena* was one of Giorgio's favorites 'babies', and could accommodate at her best times 24 guests in 12 pleasantly sized state rooms, along with the captain front quarters, besides a crew of 12 attending to all desires and needs of demanding voyagers.

Although the ship was in good condition to sail off, there was no cabin service offered, and the crew was furbished only for the navigation back home with a limited crew of four during the relocation of the ship. The only food available was the reserves left in the freezers, although there was still plenty of good wine and other liquor, and some of the ship hands loved to fish and supplied their meals with fresh seafood.

Giorgio, a bon vivant, responded with an explosive joy to Jovanni's phone call, then, after the situation was presented to him and was asked to help bring the whole group out of the war zone, he did not think for long:

"I, myself, can't wait to get out of here, and now that the ship is fixed, we won't stick around any longer. And if you all can take care of yourselves without room service for a few days, then 'mia casa, sua casa'", he ended with a débonnaire tone.

It was decided that a military truck would dispatch their group to Ashdod early in the morning, and now they were all resting after long moments of intense expectation to return home. Everyone felt the thrill of high hopes, as their exodus seemed to continue through a new opening ahead of them.

Jamuna, had observed how close Jo and his two siblings were. This particular evening, gathered in a corner of the shelter, with Ishmael and Wubit next to them and Everest lying at their feet, Jo talked about Mai, his twin children's mother. Trebor and Maggie were always hungry for more details of the time their parents shared, and Jo complied in this reminiscence of happy and touching stories. To Jo's children, the now 'surrogate grandchildren', Wubit and Ishmael, joined in with an even more fervent curiosity.

They must have continued this way for quite a while, and succumbed to the fatigue and the emotions, now sleeping before their early morning trip. Wubit had found Maggie's arms, and since she came into her life, Wubit never had enough of Maggie's motherly comforting embrace. The same for Ishmael, when sleep time arrived, he naturally cuddled like a small child between Trebor and Everest. Even Jo found a way of lying next to them against the furry back of the mountain dog.

Jamuna however, his entire life lived practically in the large spaces of the highest summits, and after these days spent in the bowels of the tunnel, needed to breath fresh air. He took great risks to venture outside, but his tracker practice made him almost invisible, and he could watch the scintillant stars in the night. His instincts were telling him also that this calm was filled with troubled anticipations of menacing times ready to strike. And he returned as discretely as he went out. He had also been concerned lately about Lu Xiang health. Far away from the places he could meditate and interact with other monks, this world he met lately must appear to him as of an inhospitable foreign planet.

Once inside, Jamuna checked on his old friend, and he was happy to find Lu Xiang resting in a calm sleep. Then looking for a cot he could stretch on, he found one in front of the Godson family, and as he sat his back against the wall, his eyes fell on this perfect picture of a happy family reunited in a restful truce.

LEAVING THE HOLY SHORES

On a swift and discreet retreat, our errant group moved out of the bunker before the crack of dawn. They were directed to climb into the back of a regular military truck, nothing that could provide special protection, but this was all Eliezer could obtain for their short ride to Ashdod. The truck was driving fast through the almost empty road, trying to keep an average of 70 m/hr., and to return to more pressing activities close to the hospital. Jo noticed that the Route 20 was not lit, as the main roads in Israel usually are, providing a superb clear night vision of the highways to the drivers. It was fortunate, though, that the day light filtered now from the eastern horizon. And all seemed so calm, as the promise of a marvelous day ahead.

Ashdod Port presented with a frantic activity, small and large ships, foreign tanks, and a few cruise liners, private leisure vessels, all in the fever of preparations for leaving the Holly Land's shores, while the Jewish military ships had obviously received orders to take position to strategic places at a defensive distance from the coast.

Once the Italian flag was spotted and *Syrena* appeared on sight lengthwise a quay, the truck pulled along and the group was swiftly deposited next to the ship. Quick greetings and thanks were exchanged, after which, the driver and the two military personnel left in a hurry with a sharp screech of the wheels.

Giorgio Montovani showed up on the bridgeway without delay, his warm reception trying to hide his concerned expression:

"Welcome, welcome on board! Please hurry up, we are ready to sail off. We will try to accommodate you the best we can, we should reach Italy in not more than one week, with God's will. We have filled our fuel tanks, and found some spared drinking water jars, although we have a desalination station, we usually reserve it for washing", and he continued to shake hands, then to direct the people inside the ship.

With kindness and concern, Giorgio took notice of the frail Lu Xiang, and he helped him gently to walk the gangway and personally found him a comfortable cabin close to the common hall. Lu Xiang tried to protest, his broad smile telling him that his monastic life style was not accustomed to such luxurious quarters.

"Nonsense, nonsense, let me spoil you a little, in our Catholic way", said Giorgio with a friendly laughter.

Two other young and handsome Italian mates directed all the others, who were happy to realize that they would all have a nice stateroom if they formed small groups of two or three to include a child. The two good-looking sailors had instantaneously eyed Maggie and the two young secretaries, Amanda and Sonia, and made sure they would enjoy their stay on board of the ship. Thus, Maggie was to stay with Wubit, Jo and Trebor would occupy a good size suite next to hers with two double beds, to include Ishmael and Everest. Eventually, all made their choice of roommates if single, very satisfied with these unexpected accommodations.

As some were still admiring the elegant ship, not believing their chance, and begun to take possession of their rooms or timidly taking a walk to discover the ship, Jo was on the main deck with captain Giorgio. The departure was on the way, two of the sailors on the quay, already detaching the ropes and preparing to jump on the ship.

At that precise moment, Jo noticed some shadows approaching very fast the quay where *Syrena* was moored; immediately he called out with a sharp whistle catching the attention of the sailors making signs to the two of them to jump on board without any delay. Jo's trained eyes had swiped the entire view and realized that there were small groups spread around the port attacking and attempting to disable all embarkations they could reach. This did not seem to him as an operation made by outsiders, but rather as a domestic insurgent outbreak taking advantage of the disarray created by the anti-Semitic coalition.

Indeed, further away, there were voices of attackers approaching the quays where a variety of vessels were anchored, shouting angrily:

"Allaku Akbar! Ash-hadu!", "No other God but Allah!"

Shortly after, explosions could be heard and seconds after a few ships ignited in flames. Some attackers were approaching *Syrena* running fast, beginning to fire blindly in the direction of the yacht. Jo, reaching over the railing of the lower deck, started pulling inward one by one the seamen. Giorgio, with a stern voice, ordered the departure on full throttle, against the no-wake rules of the port. Their attackers kept firing and even throwing haphazardly small hand grenades in their direction, fortunately only to fall in the water, the ship now gaining distance from the quay.

Suddenly sirens filled the air with their sinister sounds giving the alarm of an imminent air attack. Seconds after, explosions lighted the sky farther to the east in the direction of Jerusalem and a squadron of bombers approached slowly, carpet bombing on a systematic and evil destruction of all that was existing below.

The fleeing *Syrena* desperately ran away, pushed by the twin powerful engines. She quickly gained some distance from the shore, as the dark cloud of the messengers of Death made their ominous approach, with deafening sounds of continuous blasts accompanied by the flames engulfing everything into its inferno. Giorgio, Jo, and his men, quickly joined by Trebor, Scotti, Phillipe, Raj, and Jamuna, rushed to check on potential damages made to the vessel. Fortunately, they escaped almost unscathed, with a few chipped side boards but nothing else more worrisome. Even the gangway could be saved and pulled at the last moment on the lower deck.

As the ship achieved to exit the harbor, the last images showed the total destruction of ships and embarkations left behind, making an almost continuous line of fire along the shore. Then the other members of the group came on deck, all distraught by the dramatic escape. Wubit was crying, her face hidden in Maggie's chest, while Ishmael was sobbing and screaming, addressing the sky:

"Why? Why can we live in peace?", repeating the almost same words Trebor had said when he found him in the ruins of Jerusalem.

The vessel gaining speed, advanced at a good distance from the land, eerily flowing over the waters. Along with a few others, hands gripping the rails, Jo was watching one more time the furnace left behind. And he was thinking," even the insurgents could not escape to the destruction, they perished by the hand of their own", when he heard Trebor saying to him:

"So, the predictions are fulfilled, and Armageddon is real!"

SAILING WITH *SYRENA*

Captain Giorgio Montovani planned initially to move northwest, toward Cyprus, and avoid Egyptian presence around Port Said. After their precipitated departure from Ashdod and suspecting very much a possible impending attack against Israel coming from the sea, he realized that he would have to take the risk and continue west. Slowing to a speed of around 20 nautical miles per hour, although *Syrena* was able to easily sail at 35nm/hr., he thought making a short stop in Paphos, a coastal port of Cyprus, for additional provisions, where the captain hoped to arrive by midnight.

Late in the afternoon, when the travelers started to feel more relaxed and out of immediate danger, Giorgio learned from the port commander in Paphos that there, too, were serious concerns. The Turkish ethnic population occupying mostly the north side of the island, took advantage of the international unsettlement and begun organizing mobs, intending to take over the Greek side of Cyprus. Thus, Captain Giorgio informed Trebor and Jo that they won't stop on Cyprus, and would have to continue west for another day to reach Crete, a Greek island, where they would, hopefully be able to make a stop and refuel.

The seas were clement until *Syrena* arrived in view of Crete, then continued to Heraklion, the capital of the island, situated on the north side of the legendary Island. This permitted the travelers, fitting the true description of refugees, to become a tightly knit group of people, who, even though pertaining to contrasting provenances, were nevertheless reunited by the same desire to find a friendlier place to live. They all tried to know and understand each other, exchange their experiences, while offering their capacities to participate on their personal way to the small community they had already formed.

The magic of the blue expansion of the Mediterranean waters had a calming effect on everyone and this allowed an improvement on the moral of the people on board. Captain Giorgio was happy to confer with his new 'headquarter' surrounding him at the command center formed by Jo, Scotti, Phillipe, and Andy, all experts in a variety of areas very much appreciated by the captain.

Other members of the group gathered in smaller circles directed by their inclinations. Aisha and Farid came out of their isolation and blended with the other well-traveled couples, Rebekah and David, and Debbie and Josh, who, having already acquired the ropes of modern approach of connecting with the locals, could spontaneously adjust to new cultures through their past voyage experiences. Aisha, more used to a shielded life style, even though she had been exposed to the style of the western women, and Farid's job bringing him close to the wealthiest of this world, soon became attracted by the natural manners of their new friends. They discovered that their worlds have been years apart concerning their expectations and realization of personal goals.

Gradually, the young Americans and the Arabic couple discovered their differences in the ways they have been raised, while in their young hearts they were so much alike. Aisha and Farid were mostly surprised to find out how rigid they have been judging the others and how inflexible their upbringing had been, designating their social status for life. The other two couples were talking about the Universe, and they heard Trebor speaking of a loving, non-judgmental, the universal only-one God. Now, they were discovering how at ease they felt in their friends' presence, simply interested in exchanging ideas and trying to understand their emotions. What a different and full of promises concept of looking at life this was!

While Amanda was timidly approached for a while by Raj, fascinated by her milky complexion, her angelic curls and the eyes of the palest color of the sky, Paolo, one of the ship mates, was less shy to show his interest in Sonia. Amanda was reserved and kind, although professional, while Sonia's contagious laughter and tendency to talk fast and address everyone in a familiar manner, made the two secretaries become inseparable friends. The latest circumstances shaking their worlds, only brought them closer, and they knew that they would remain friends for life. And now, as they became the object of attention of two young males, only reminded them that they were young and attractive and that life would go on no matter what the circumstances.

Paolo looked for their company every time he got a chance, and an almost vacation atmosphere spread on board, as he explained:

"You see, we entered the Dodecanese Islands, in the east side of the Aegean Sea. This is the sea between Greece and Asia minor, Turkey of today if you want. And Dodecanese, meaning twelve in Greek, comes from the number of islands forming the archipelago, which they actually are 15, and not 12. Soon we will enter the Sea of Crete, north of the island with the same name. And it is a shame we won't stop to Santorini, another beautiful island, located north from Crete."

Paolo continued on with his description as they were sailing along the beautiful blue waters.

"Too bad we won't have the time to visit Crete either. It is amazing what the Minoan culture left behind; Knossos, the old capital, dates from the bronze age, and the town could contain ten thousand inhabitants. It had an advanced water supply using hot and cold water and sewer systems with flushing toilets. And the ladies dressed following very modern and elegant fashion designs."

Then he added, "of course, the ancient Greeks believed that Crete is the birthplace of Zeus, the boss man for the Greek gods!"

As Paolo was getting very excited when it came to challenging the Roman culture with the Greek one, practically everyone on board was attracted and joined him on the deck at the stern of the boat, to enjoy a good debate: " But Crete is different", he considered, "She is so old, even the Greeks were mystified."

Paolo was so animated and witty, he even rushed to his cabin and came back with his iPad and started showing pictures he took during previous trips *Syrena* floated between the Greek and Italian islands not so long ago, when entertaining happy and fortunate vacationers.

"Oh, the ancients knew, as we knew ourselves, how to live back then", Paolo said, with a voice sounding so old, making his audience burst into laughter and call out:

"Was it that long ago, I wonder? but it does seem like centuries since people had a normal life!", said Jamuna, thinking of how much his own life had changed lately.

"Are we tracking Ulysses' tribulations?" asked Trebor with a change of the subject, referring to Homer's epic hero from his 'Odyssey'. "Having explored these regions and after his desire for adventure quenched, Ulysses was desperately trying to find his way back to his wife, Penelope, in the isle of Ithaca."

"Did he find her?", Ishmael asked, caught in the story.

"Of course, he was the King of Ithaca and his people and his wife were waiting for him, although there were many suitors swarming to obtain her favors. It took him 20 years to get back, though!"

"I hope it won't take us that long", Ishmael replied, with a face of discomfiture that triggered another chorus of merriment.

Upon this, the captain and his 'adjoints' met them, wondering what was the reason of so much enjoyment. Then Captain Giorgio made a few announcements, letting everyone know that they would arrive at sunset in Heraklion, where they could get off the ship if they wished. His intention was to refresh their stocks on food and water, fill again the tanks with fuel, and leave early in the morning.

After that, they would enter the Ionian Sea, west of Greece, hoping to reach Sicily in a couple of days. There, they would make another stop at Reggio di Calabria, Italy, tucked inside a pass between the tip of the boot and northeast corner of the Island of Sicily. And hopefully soon after that, they would follow a direction toward Naples, Stella Mare's home.

"But, if you want to continue the trip with me, you will have to be back on board by dinner time, at 20:00 hours, or 8:00 pm", he warned his passengers.

HERAKLION, CRETE

Syrena's arrival and reception in Heraklion unfolded as a regular coming of a tourist vessel visiting the island, and its business appreciated during the low season. Captain Giorgio's concerns faded away once on shore and meeting the harbor master. Here the situation seemed to remain untouched by the recent events that shook the world, and for the moment the Cretans went untroubled to their regular occupations. The harbor master acting as a casual authority, admitted that the news they captured weren't very encouraging, but he reacted to it with philosophy, in the old Greek tradition:

"We are only an island with no particular riches except for the antique treasures made of old ruins and broken pottery, and the only interested people are the tourists enjoying our food and wine. Many things happened in the world for the last millennia and we are still here, and we hope to 'sail' through this as during other countless times before", he concluded, sounding as reassuring as he could, adding that the majority of the population was even less aware of what he had learned so far.

Captain Giorgio thought wise to do the same, and he proceeded to loading up with provisions and filling the tanks with fuel, then he was ready to relax at one of the restaurants on the docks of the port and have dinner admiring the sunset.

During this time, Jo followed Giorgio's advice to go on shore, "relax and leave the fever of contacts for later, they will have time enough to worry us, now it is time for a few moments of normal life ", he said. Thus, Jo walked leisurely with his friends and caught up with Trebor, Maggie, Jamuna, Li, and even Lu Xiang, while the children jumped up and down on the quay of the harbor along with Everest, all happy to enjoy the 'terra ferma' feeling.

Other couples had already formed and strolled happily on shore, Aisha and Farid along with the two American couples with who they became friends, experiencing a freedom they never felt before, simply visiting, stopping by some stores and walking without a specific program. They were followed not far behind by Amanda and Raj, and Sonia and Paolo, who played a little longer the guide for all of them.

Then, they eventually all regrouped by a large open terrace of a restaurant and followed the example of a few locals watching the sunset and having an Uzo, Resinato, or another aperitif.

"What did you see so far?" Jo addressed his children and his 'grandchildren'.

"We had ice cream!", a chorus of little voices answered together.

"Ice cream before dinner?" Jo eyed them, faking an admonishing look. But Wubit and Ishmael continued their exciting squeals:

"Even Everest had some! Wubit dropped her first cone, she got scared by the cold, and yap! Everest got it!", Ishmael kept on screaming and laughing, while Wubit protested:

"I did not get scared by the ice cream!"

"You did, too"

"I did not", and they continued to tease each other, joyfully, while Everest kept jumping around them, happy to be with the children, and hoping for more ice cream to drop his way.

Jo, turned toward Trebor, leaving the children to their play, happy to see that they adjusted so easily to their age occupations, and Everest played such a good nanny for them.

"I got a pair of double-bee earrings from Trebor, like the queen of Crete! You can find the original in the museum, look daddy!", and a very pleased Maggie, gave a gentle dangle to one of them to show her present. Both father and brother were moved to realize how feminine and adorable Maggie looked at that moment, bringing them together in a magic moment, far from the world's worries. Jo came closer and gave a tender kiss on his daughter's cheek, and if there was still this deep hurt inside his heart, he also knew with outmost certitude that Mai was there, with all of them, enjoying together what a family moment was meant to be.

"Oh, let me see", Aisha and Sonia approached, curious to look at the beautiful golden earrings.

To this, Farid sprung up to his feet, happy to find something that Aisha liked and it happened that she did not have, and asked Trebor where the shop was.

"Is the jeweler on the corner, off that street. I guess that if you hurry, you might find it open", and pointed in the direction of the store.

Farid started walking following the directions, soon joined by Paolo, Raj, Joshua, Jamuna, and David. It was almost hilarious to watch them walking like on a mission, serious and resolute to arrive to the store before the closing. But Raj was the most concerned, since his meager funds were only some savings out of the donations he received from Maggie and Trebor, back in India. Did he hear Trebor whispering to Farid that the shop was not that expensive?

Back at the restaurant, a long table was set for all of them, including Giorgio with his crew coming along, and a variety of beverages were ordered. The children were discovering one more time the pleasure of lemonade made locally, as Everest was very satisfied with a large bowl of fresh water. It was offered by a pretty young server, who came to take orders and carried water for the dog without even being asked. She proposed for dinner to bring typical Greek appetizers, the 'catch of the day' and Greek salad, roasted new potatoes, and other vegetables, all from local gardens. They all agreed to leave it to the owner's menu and have a true Cretan experience. The nice waitress reassured them that they "will all be pleased, including the dog, and after I bring him some juicy bones and meat, he will decide to stay in the island, with us."

Joyful voices were heard making toasts of happy travels, and everyone was delighted by the food, the unique decor enhanced by a dramatic sunset and the company of the new group of friends they formed. And indeed, this evening remained a wonderful experience for all of them.

NIKY'S STORY

It was the middle of the night and the Island of Crete was shrouded in the quiet of a pleasant stillness. The air carried a crisp quality, a slight hunch to the approaching cold season, while an isolated barking or the homey smell of a wooden fire place, would remind one of the closeness of the land.

Maggie found a soft place on a bench at the aft of the ship and let her spirit wander, observing the contours of the hills, trees and houses projecting against the sky studded with stars. Her entire being delighted in those blessed moments of peacefulness and happy expectations. The closer they were getting to home, the stronger the anticipation of returning to a life that changed her forever, an existence she would fully appreciate, although it would never be the same. It was the middle of the night, when she left her room after she was sure that Wubit found a deep sleep.

Jamuna and Raj were meandering on the decks, finding little rest in their cabins, then giving up staring at the ceiling. They started talking and their steps brought them close to the aft of the boat. Jamuna spotted first a little glitter, coming from Maggie's earrings, and made a swift movement to quietly retrieve on their tracks, but Raj kept talking and gave them up.

"I see we are not the only one not sleeping around here ", exclaimed Raj approaching Maggie.

"Sorry, I thought that the night is too beautiful to stay in the cabin. And we had to take care of baby problems", she added with a change of the tone in a jokingly maternal voice. "Wubit had a tummy ache after eating moussaka on the top of ice cream, followed with a few baklawas. But now, she is fine, I can say she is 'sleeping like a baby'! Hard to believe how much these little ones can eat and get away with it."

"Raj and I were talking about this incredible story that happened this evening and right here. Raj, start again from the beginning", Jamuna insisted.

"Well, I followed the other young men to the jewelry shop, although I could not buy much at all. I followed my heart, looking for a little present for Amanda", he said shily, then he continued his story.

When the six men entered the jewelry store as a little procession all excited with the anticipation of finding something, they wondered, clueless about what to look for. The young owner was closing the cash register, while the last employee was stashing the better pieces in the vault.

Nikos Ioannidis, going by Niky, the owner of the store, let the men hover a little over the glass cases, then offered his help:

"You must be from the *Syrena*, the ship that just anchored! I didn't know that she was bringing with her some beautiful young ladies that would look even more beautiful adorned with our rare museum-quality reproductions. Any specific request?", he continued, in a perfect British accent.

"I was thinking of a pair of earrings, the double-bee copy, perhaps", Paolo ventured, the most accustomed with traveling and bartering in touristic harbors.

"We have a connoisseur here, I see! Yes, we do have different sizes of those, and pendants as well. But here are some nice rings with precious stones, rubies, sapphires, diamonds...You can even get engaged with the ones from this case", he added, going behind the next display.

"Well, some are already married, and for the others, is too early to say", Paolo continued, maintaining the dialog.

During this time, Raj stood a little apart, observing the others and daring a few glances at the precious trinkets, and, although there were no prices attached to them, he had concluded that there was nothing he could afford.

"And you, sir, what do you have in mind for your lady?", Raj heard Niky addressing him.

"Oh, nothing,", said Raj, blushing through his olive skin, "only window shopping as they say."

"May I see this bracelet with mermaid charms?", suddenly Joshua became attracted by something he could offer to Deborah. "I think Deb will love this one, she likes to giggle those charms and call on their good fortune."

Then, the others found a little something to content the person of their interest. Paolo spotted the earrings similar to the ones Maggie received, and he already could hear Sonia delighted with surprise, then David found a neckless with Greek geometrical design for Rebekah, while Farid went for the whole package with the 'queen's double-bee' earrings and neckless.

Nikos let his assistant, now back in the store, make pretty wrappings for the presents, and went again toward Raj, who stayed aside, only watching the others.

"You look like an old friend of mine from India. Are you from there?", asked Niky.

"Yes, I am from Mumbai, former Bombay. Now I follow my friend Trebor and his family to America", was Raj's answer.

"And you don't have anybody that you would like to present with a souvenir from Crete?"

"Of course, I would love to buy her something, but I have to wait until I get on my own feet in America, and then, I will fulfill her smallest wishes."

"I see, America looks like your land of opportunity. I wish you well, my friend." But Niky did not shed away and continued. "Years ago, I wasn't doing so hot. I came from Athens, where my family is from, after investing my savings in a 'promising venture' with two others. We were supposed to start a charter business, and at my arrival here I expected to board the 18-meter brand new Sea Rays I paid for on the continent. Once arrived to Crete, I found out I was 'taken for a ride' by the two others, who never showed up in Crete."

Raj became interested in Niky's sad story, urging him to continue.

"After a few days, starving and desperate, I needed to make some money to get back to Athens, although ashamed to face my parents, who would have probably given me the 'I told you so' routine. I entered this shop in a whim, after being rejected everywhere else. Here was this old Indian, who, after I told him the straight truth, took me to the back room, gave me a plate of curry and some lemonade, then asked me if I would like to learn the trade. As shocked as I was, I thought that anything would be better than hearing my father jeering, and I accepted."

Niky took a little break, lost in his thoughts, then continued: "he told me later that he had a son and a wife back in India and that he had lost contact after a revolt that followed the liberation of India. Sadly, things did not get any better later on and he could never get in touch with them, against all his efforts. He thought me all the 'tricks' of the business and treated me like his own son. A few years later, he died from a brain tumor and left me all his possessions. He gave me a chance and he changed my life, and I will always be grateful for that", he continued deep into these special memories. Then, he was brought back by an idea:

"I would like you to choose something very special from here. This neckless is a copy of one worn by the Queen Pasiphae, wife of King Minos, and is made of precious stones and the purest gold with beautiful designs of birds of paradise. Please accept it, it is in the memory of Sharma. I promised him that I will give a chance to others as well, every time I would be able to", and without listening to a word of protest from Raj, he laid the superb neckless in an elegant box, and pressed it into his hands. Then, he gave a hug to Raj who could not talk, his throat strangled with emotion, his eyes filled with tears.

Niky put Raj at ease turning toward his employee, and said aloud to cover the others' voices:

"Everyone is my guest tonight, my treat. Everybody, have something from Niky Ioannidis!" and have a glass of Uzo to celebrate it."

After all of them left the store elated and filled with appreciation, Niky, who proceeded to closing the shatters, shouted toward them:

"And do not forget to give a big hug to your ladies on my behalf! Mine is going to pout, I will be late for supper, and I will have to grab something for her too", they kept hearing Niky's voice fade away with a laugh.

"What an extraordinary and beautiful story, Raj!", Maggie exclaimed with excitement. "Let me see the neckless."

"I put it away, for a more suitable time, but I will show it to you, it is a beauty."

Jamuna moved a little like he had something to say,

"Since everybody got to choose a gift, I thought that you might like this. It is a lot more modest than the one Raj got, but it will match your earrings you have from Trebor", and saying this, he timidly approached Maggie and handed her a rectangular velvet box.

Maggie took the box and with her hands trembling a little, she opened it, then she gasped when she saw the present. It was a neckless with a large and beautifully crafted double-bee motive in the middle of it, the gold shining in the clear night. Then she turned, spontaneously lifting her mass of flowing hair and discovering her neck, she asked Jamuna if he could attach the clasp for her. Now, it was Jamuna's turn to have shaking hands fumbling with the chain. Fortunately, she had her back turned and was too excited to discover Jamuna's own emotions. Then, Maggie touched her throat and felt with delicate fingers the beautiful jewel, when she realized that she did not thank Jamuna for his wonderful and unexpected attention.

"Thank you, thank you so much, Jamuna! You and Trebor are the best brothers I ever had", then she jumped to hug him and give him a kiss on each cheek, European way.

ORGANIZING LIFE ON BOARD

After a welcomed stopover in Crete, *Syrena* left anchor in a crisp morning breeze, all on board feeling restored and confident. This time, captain Giorgio thought wise to recruit all hands available to assume a variety of useful tasks around the ship. He realized that his passengers became his new mission, and he vowed to bring them to a safe port, even though the times became precarious and the final destination was still uncertain.

Therefore, captain Giorgio invited all young men to meet with him and the four crew members on the command deck where he exposed them his plan. He did not hide that there were real concerns regarding the deterioration of all European countries' stability along with the inability of their governments to insure the general population with the basic means of existence when military priorities were taking over. As Israel had just suffered a series of sustained attacks from anti-Semitic coalition, now Europe faced preemptive raids from the Chinese, Russians, and Koreans, from East, along with the Islamic league from the south and east, intending to occupy this small continent. These bursts of attacks, expecting to confuse and destabilize the European countries, were so far sporadic, but they spread like wild fires cutting off EU forces from building a resistance forefront.

Giorgio explained to his new assistance that he was aware that the travelers on board needed to ultimately reach the United States of America and he informed them that he had already changed his initial plans and now he intended to make all possible for them to connect with one of the vessels or airplanes organized by the US for the repatriation of its citizens. This would be possible at some points in west Europe, as they continue to receive more specific information of these locations. He also admitted that he did not know what it would happen to his crew and with himself after that, but, for now at least, his desire was to help his passengers.

Then, Giorgio exposed to the men, who unanimously adhered to his projects, that there were further needs for a good function on board of the ship and how they could help. Following an imperative debate, tasks were distributed, shifts were established, and even a review of defense capabilities of the ship were considered. Jo proposed to train everyone on armed or martial arts tactics, and with a detached tone, he let them know that much can be done with simple means found around, and that they had the obligation to protect the women, children, and their older friends, referring to Lu Xiang, the oldest and the most pacifist person around.

The ladies did not wait for long to offer their contribution to render the conditions on board efficient and agreeable; they organized their own teams rotating for the gully duties, rooms and common quarters cleaning and maintenance, while Maggie suggested even finding time for the children's education. She sensed the need for Wubit and Ishmael to open up and discuss with a grown person their feelings. They went through so much trauma at a tender age, Wubit almost 6 and Ishmael almost 8, with times ahead remaining uncertain, with no one able to anticipate what laid ahead for them until their life would become more stable.

Maggie had been approached by Lu Xiang, eager to propose teaching classes, and if they might not follow a more conventional practice, the long tradition of an old culture could have a great appeal to the young minds. Looking in depth at the world and the meaning of the planet itself at a cosmic scale, as well as acquiring self-control and inner peace, indisputably could prepare them for life in a more fundamental way.

Thus, in no time, a new routine was established on board of *Syrena*, and everyone seemed content to join efforts, as they gained distance and, having a solid plan, hoped to arrive to safe port. The atmosphere was almost joyful, good humor and best intentions making the travelers become a tight community, a large family where everyone received help and gave all its potential and efforts in return.

Lu Xiang became an attraction with his classes held in quiet places of the ship, and no one was surprised to see the children and adults mixed together on deep meditation, well received breaks during demanding activities. There were also debates, unexpectedly initiated at first by the children, who had un uninterrupted flow of questions. Then the others, coming from a variety of cultural upbringings and religions, challenged their own believes against the Buddhist monk creeds.

As *Syrena* sailed without stopping, taking advantage of clement weather conditions, the captain pushing forward aided by his new large and dedicated crew, an optimistic stance reigned on board. Once the chores completed, the 'sailors' found time to appreciate the beauty and the magic of the liquid azure surrounding them. Passing at times an island profiling on the horizon, watching the constant change of the light and the color of the sea and the sky, transitioning from the sunrise through the sunset, all created this special feeling that they were living unique moments, having them forever engraved in their memory.

REFLECTIONS AND CHANGES

If a distant observer would have noticed subtle or dramatic changes in practically every member of the errant group, as the most unusual situations brought them together and, somehow, made them harmonize their own thinking and interactions with each other, Trebor was the one who incurred most of the changes.

From a successful and immensely wealthy young man, immersed in a frantic and industrious life style, through drama and suffering, Trebor found the deep essence of his soul, discovering the sense of his destiny here, on Earth. His nature had always been of an honest and generous person, and, if he had enjoyed the advantage of a privileged life, he never abused the high social status he belonged to.

Trebor participated with the other young men to every task assigned to him, no matter how difficult or modest. However, he found himself, in his personal times, thinking about the more profound reasons of their trials and tribulations, their connections with the world turmoil and their presence in these particular places. Mostly, he tried to look beyond these events, and see the direction the world was taking and where his own path needed to follow.

While in deep meditation, Trebor renewed his conversations with God, his Creator. He had the confirmation, without having to ask, that the whole world had undergone supreme transformations. At times Trebor sought out Lu Xiang's company, they shared moments of meditation and prayer, when no words were needed to be exchanged. In occasion, Trebor searched for his mentor's wise reflections, continuing to admire and to learn from his detachment he could withhold from the stark agitation surrounding them.

There were instances when Trebor went through moments of total isolation finding quiet corners of the ship, when he became completely oblivious of the world around him. Since there was not a place where one could stay lonely for long, he was found by the children at first. Then his closest new friends were attracted, as before, by his presence. Jamuna, Raj, Beshadu, Li, but also Jovani, Randal, and Scotti were drawn by his magnetism, the peaceful and promising feelings felt in his presence. Just sitting by his side when Trebor was lost in one of his trance-like moments, they were filled with hope and expectations, and they felt encouraged and protected. But above all, they were filled with love. A love that brought them reassurance and peace in the middle of the tempest.

"Abu Trebor, how long the bad people are going to attack us?", Ishmael asked searching for an answer, but in reality, looking for reassurance.

"Well, they might continue to think that they can control the world and gain power over every one", Trebor said, making room for Ishmael to sit next to him. "There will always be this fierce confrontation between the good and the evil, the love and the hatred. And this will continue as long as people from this planet do not understand that there is everything one can desire in this universe, and even more than one can ever want. For there is an infinite supply of riches and no one could ever run empty. Hence, no one should want to take anything from another, all belongs to everyone, and no one has the right over anyone."

It did not take long at all for a regular rhythm to be established on board, and at the end of the work days, when everything had been cleaned, polished, washed, or cooked, and when the navigation plans followed their established course, many came silently to join the times of reflection with Trebor. Maggie and the children absorbed his words and his interactions with Lu Xiang like fresh water from the fountain. In no time, each one became attracted to sit around this inner group, and many times questions fused between these friends, thirsty for answers, for knowledge.

Since his escape from North Korea, Trebor kept his long hair and the beard that had grown during his captivity in the concentration camp. The change in his physical appearance reflected the transformation taking place at a more spiritual height, this new stage in his life bringing maturity, but also elevating his personal concerns to a more global level. Trebor was preoccupied in finding answers and solutions to the devastating conflicts spreading all over the world, in a desire to suggest ideas transforming the general order into a more noble and loving place for all.

"Is this Armageddon, swiping all over the planet?", David asked in one of these moments sitting together.

"Yes, is this the world getting to an end, as it has been predicted by the Bible, the Mayans, and other religions?", joined in Phillipe, the flight engineer.

"And why God allows this? Or is that other civilizations would want us to disappear?", Sonia's voice raised her question.

"These confrontations happening around the world are ours only, no one has the intention to destroy us, but ourselves", came the response from Trebor.

"I don't want to die!", a little voice protested, with the determination a child can express against limited power, triggering some laughter and distending the seriousness of the subject.

"No one wants you to die, and no one wants to die. You see," continued Trebor, "the world will be destroyed and its order, this civilization we built over millennia, will come to an end, one way or the other."

"So, we are doomed!", Jovanni almost shouted, as Trebor let his words sink in.

"We always have a choice, but this time the choice is of the humankind."

"And what is this choice?", Jovanni continued, almost angrily.

"We must understand that, we, humans of this planet, function at a quite limited level of energy, keeping us in a dimension of low density, subjects of the matter limitations. We can, if we make the right choices, transition, advance to a higher dimension and access a world of new possibilities, a world of supreme peace, love, and prosperity."

"But how?", Beshadu joined the heat of the conversation.

"Understanding that we are not alone, that our world, our civilization is not the only creation of our Father God, the Supreme Creator. And that God's creation contains many levels of existences, where beings achieved long ago complete happiness, knowledge, and uplifted they spiritual, intellectual, and emotional levels to the highest energetic vibration. This ascension can elevate us, reaching a blissful harmony."

Since his new acolytes waited for more, Trebor continued: "It is also important to know, that we are offered at this time, when our planet traverses a highly energy charged galactic passage, to make a leap of faith and transition directly to higher vibration level and save ourselves."

Then, he added: "But this powerful energy we entering and traversing now, is not without stirring a gigantic clash between the forces of the good and the bad, pushing everyone to the extreme of their choices. No matter what, this planet will cleanse itself from the evil powers that lasted for too long, and only the good will survive through an intense purification set off by this higher energy."

"And it only takes to do good, that's it, to choose to be good and be with God?", Wubit stated, surprising all, as she understood the simplicity of the salvation.

They all looked toward the youngest member of their community, as one more time, the truth came from an innocent mouth.

"Yes, my sweet child, you see how simple that can be? Just do good and look for the high guidance of our celestial Father, calling Him the way you have been raised to do, for He is the same God, the only One."

"But if somebody wants to harm you, you just let it do it?', Wubit, remembering her recent atrocious experience, almost revolted.

"No, this time the Father is not asking to show the other cheek. This time He wants you to defend yourself and defend the other suffering an injustice. But remember, never harm, just defend. No more abuse, no more lies, no more greed."

This initiated passionate exchanges, when the beehive-like humming coming from the friends' conversation paused to hear one more time Trebor's voice, as a conclusion: "This time is to do our best, to ascend higher dimensions. As hard as this might appear to be, one must see these harsh times as a blessing for transformation, as an opportunity to transcend our limitations and fulfill our divine potential."

MARIO

With a little bit of luck and cutting back some of the gasoline consumption, *Syrena* should cover the 600 some miles distance from Heraklion, Crete, to Reggio Calabria, Italy, in 4 to 5 days. The weather continued to hang on to a late 'Indian summer', and the winds were good in this late November. Sirocco, the hot wind form north Africa, was quiet and did not bring its gale force rains moving north, nor hammered on people's nerves like on a drum, while Bora, usually blowing from the Northern Adriatic, did not send high gusts to surprise the ship with strong and unpredictable swells. Only Maestro, late in the season, lingered, continuing to bring a gentle breeze from the Balkans.

During their time on board, people adjusted to their small community in no time and in good humor; chores and gatherings rendered them closer and more understanding of their differences. Their curiosity allowed them to discover each ones' aptitudes and talents, and appreciate and learn from one another. Above all, they found out that they coexisted in perfect harmony, even in a small place.

One's objective became theirs, since the migrants had to resume to the fact that they were all looking for a safe place to go, and that only together they would succeed. They also had the advantage of having mystical teachers on board, guiding them through this exodus and helping them to grow spiritually. Thus, the voyage across the Mediterranean Sea allowed our refugees to benefit from this truce, restoring them physically and emotionally, while filling their souls with a strong faith on higher powers help and protection.

When, on a clear morning, the high hills of the southern Sicily profiled on the horizon, Captain Giorgio climbed at the command post full of excitement. He had sailed around the Sicilian waters many times and this was one of his dearest places on earth. He maintained true friendships with many of the local port of call patrons, always greeting each other on a boisterous manner. He could not wait to see Mario, the Commercial Dock director and tell him about his, their adventure. Giorgio was sure to obtain all the necessary help, more accurate information about the real situation in Europe, but above all, Giorgio was happy to get closer to home, the city of Naples, just a day of sailing away.

Invigorated by the fresh morning breeze, Giorgio hovered over the maps and supervised from above the approaching maneuvers, then keeping the proper distance with the coast. However, Giorgio could not help noticing that there were less vessels, cargos, small and large commercial and leisure embarkations, which were usually zipping over the blue waters of the Ionian Sea.

Entering the strait between the nose of Sicily and the tip of the Italian boot by mid-day, Syrena finally docked against a large space of the main quay, close to the buildings of the Marine Officers.

Once the ship was safely fastened to the quay and the engines silenced completely after almost a week of continuous rumble, Giorgio was impatient to walk down the gangway and make his first steps on solid land. Mario showed up, coming ahead to welcome Giorgio, his booming voice calling from afar. After a few strong taps on the back and hugs of recognition, Giorgio noticed, however, that Mario was not as flamboyant as he always remembered him.

After a few words exchanged, Mario hinted to Giorgio the need of a private conversation, to which Mario let know that he wished to have his 'headquarter' members included. Making a sign to his operating team, Giorgio introduced them to Mario and, shortly after, their group was directed toward the harbor master's office.

Behind the closed doors of the observation tower, operating also as a conference room, Mario could not contain himself and almost blared:

"The world is going crazy, Italy is on fire, Hell had opened loose!", then, catching his breath, he tried to explain, "terrorists allied with some of the internal factions of legal and illegal immigrants in one hand, but also receiving Russian support from abroad, are taking advantages of our instability to infiltrate Europe. Rome is destroyed, worse than after the fall of the Roman Empire, the Vatican had just been blown up by the Muslim terrorists, who want to make Rome, and in particular the Vatican, the European center of Islam!"

Then, without letting much time for questions, he continued:

"Everywhere reigns complete chaos. Looters and bandits, criminals escaped from jails and psychos from mental asylums, are free to attack and terrorize the population. No one is safe any longer!"

"But, what are the United Nations doing, is there anything underway?', Jo inquired. "it must be started an opposition front."

"Yes, I followed the shortwave radio transmission coming from the official channels for the defense of the ports, airports, and train stations. But there is a lot of talking, meanwhile we don't see much coming to our rescue", concluded a very frustrated Mario.

Joseph Godson, keeping his cool as usual, asked permission to use the radio station in order to enter in communication with his agency. While the other group members continued to converse over the situation, Jo came back shortly after with some new information.

"There is a massive operation creating a western block of resistance against the Russian forces on the east, all the way to the Baltics, and another preventing the North African and middle Eastern takeover from the south and southeast. The radical Islamic infiltration in Europe growing over the years, though, is well organized and intrinsic part of the society, making everything complicated. There is not only an enemy from outside to fight, but this time, there is also the one from within."

"That's all good to know, but meanwhile we got to get organized ourselves before the thugs come to take over the whole society", Giorgio said, in the light of what he just learned.

"Regarding our repatriation" Jo continued, "the American government had already initiated an extensive procedure to remove the American citizens out of harms' way. There is a coalition between Americans, French, and British coordinating a base in Normandy, where they gather all American civilians arriving from all corners of Europe or even farther out. There are points of contact over many countries in Europe, and allied forces are trying to bring the refugees to Calais, in France, and other places close to the English Channel. From there, any available American floating embarkation is used to bring people to the US", concluded Jo, glad to have a specific information regarding their repatriation.

However, Jo and the others noticed that Mario wanted to say more, but was a little hesitant. When he felt an encouraging look from the others, he opened up:

"I know that you arrived at the worse times in our country, but you also arrived as a blessing and an answer to my prayers". Then, he continued, seeing everyone's interest, "there is an imperative message to be delivered to the Pope, his life on depends, and only the one that knows where his secret shelter exists can deliver it to His Holiness."

Then Mario continued: "I was in charge for many years with the secrecy of transmitting messages, in case of emergency, between the Orthodox Patriarch in Athens, that receives messages from the Christians in Jerusalem via Mount Athos, and the pope. A small delegation of monks from the Hilandar Monastery in Mount Athos arrived recently to Athens and from there the message must be forwarded to our Holy Father. But in these circumstances, I cannot leave my post and I have to entrust you to be the messengers."

After letting this peculiar declaration sink in, Mario went into more details:

"Although I can't go to the Vatican myself, I came up with a plan. As I told Giorgio, I will stock *Syrena* with all that is needed and even more for the trip to Ostia, one of the closest sea ports, while sailing to Rome. That should take two days at most. Giorgio should keep the ship at good distance from the shore, out of the view of smaller desperate boats or pirates that will try to attack *Syrena* and steal your goods. And they might even want to take over the yacht. Giorgio told me that you know how to defend yourselves and I will add some guns and ammunition to the cargo as well."

Then Mario continued with his plan, all enflamed with the hope that he might be able to have the crucial message finally delivered:

"Once arrived to Ostia, only a small group should go on shore. I think that Jo and this gentleman here, Trebor? Yes, he has something that inspires me confidence. Ah, he is Jo's son? Then, it makes all the sense. Anyways, I think that Jovanni, Giorgio's nephew should accompany the two of you to Rome, he knows the city and speaks Italian."

"During this time, the captain and his assistants should wait on board and ensure the security of the ship and of everyone's else on board. From there, it is up to you to decide what to do, whether the roads are safe enough to continue to France across the land, or all of you would be safer sailing. Marseilles, perhaps? it will take about 3 days to get there from Rome, and I will make enough provisions of everything for you to survive the trip", then Mario, finally became silent, looking at his new friends with pleading eyes.

STROLLING IN REGGIO CALABRIA

While captain Giorgio and his new staff debated with Mario, the port master, the remaining travelers went on shore to explore the beautiful surroundings of Reggio Calabria. Maggie, although she remembered having had an assignment in Sicily years ago, she did not get the chance to cross into the southernmost part of Italy. The young couples began strolling nonchalantly on the quay, and even Lu Xiang and Kuan Li went on shore to admire the decor while warming up sitting on a bench. Wubit and Ishmael skipped and ran playing with Everest for a while, then they became impatient to see more.

Maggie had consulted the maps and some brochures displayed on shore, and read about a few unique attractions: the old roman baths, many museums, palazzos, and churches. And if they would not have the time, nor the access to visit any of them, she started to explain to the children a little about the history of this place. Maggie pointed toward its magnificent architectural style of the buildings, reminding of many edifices and private villas found all over South Europe; she even told them about the Planetarium Pythagoras, taking the time to explain what a planetarium was.

As the visitors wandered and enjoyed the chance to walk without having to keep a sailor foot, Maggie was taking pictures of the place, of the children and her friends, a strong professional habit pressing her to keep a chronicle of their journey. However, she directed her steps toward a pizzeria-gelateria she spotted for a while, where they might have a light lunch with fresh authentic Italian ingredients, to the delight of all, including Everest.

This is where the more senior of the group found them, sitting at the outside tables moved close to each other, marveling at the tempting choices offered. Wubit and Ishmael talked at the same time, asking to know what all these chanting words in the menu meant, and acclaiming every single one as their final choice. Obviously, just reading the menu there was enough to make one hungry! Without delay, freshly squeezed orange juices were served, some divinely tasting simple tomatoes salads seasoned with local olive oil, herbs, cured olives and round scoops of Mozzarella cheese were passed around, along with freshly baked brioches. This somewhat sweetened the news Jo and the captain shared with their friends.

Mario, who had come along with the group, helped decide what would be the best time for them to lift anchor. He suggested that taking the day off and having a good night sleep would prepare them for the uncertain times ahead and would give him the necessary time for the preparations on board before the continuation of their trip.

Thus, at dawn *Syrena* left the shore behind one more time, and progressed north through the Strait of Messina, offering a spectacular vista that many did not want to miss. This passage reminded Giorgio of the long Strait of Dardanelles, between the Sea of Marmara and the Aegean Sea, separating Asia and Europe, as Bosphorus gives passage between the two continents from the Black Sea and Marmara Sea, cutting through the large town of Istanbul.

The ship made a good time sailing northwest once exiting the Strait of Messina, now enjoying the waters somehow protected of the Tyrrhenian Sea, with Italy to the East, Corsica and Sardinia aligning on the west, leaving Sicily to the South. The winds of Bora from the north, or Sirocco from the south, rarely could do much of damage. And, as the Mistral blowing from southern France could not reach that far, these mild conditions allowed *Syrena* a steady and pleasant cruising.

Giorgio had to make a big effort to resist the temptation of getting too close to Naples, his home town, the blessed Napolitan shores that have been sang by all Italian tenors. Unfortunately, their destination had changed and he could not risk to face any additional trouble that could have affected the region. However, squinting through his binoculars, there were other travelers who also wanted to have a glimpse at the vertiginously steep Amalfi coast, the picturesque town of Sorrento and the Isle of Capri as they entered the Gulf of Naples.

This, persuaded the captain to slow down the engines and all had a look at the area for a while, as he shown them Pompei, then Naples, profiling tucked inside the cove-like shape of the Gulf of Naples. Then, sailing around the Island of Ischia, he sighed a silent 'arrivederci' to his beloved motherland. Before Giorgio could pick up the speed again, Jo and Jovanni, sensing the captain's disappointment, started to sing together 'O sole mio', the famous Napolitan canzone.

And since neither of them was Caruso, nor Pavarotti, Giorgio started laughing, asking them to "shut up". But no success there either, everyone around started shouting and singing in a complete cacophony; it did not matter, they succeeded to change the captain's mood.

DINNER AT SEA

Night was getting close, and, with a flamboyant sky transformed on a braze by the setting sun, they left Napoli area behind. Giorgio decided to reduce the ship advancement to throttle and proposed all to have dinner on the mid-deck by the gully and revel in the exceptional spectacle. He kept thinking that the safest way to approach Rome, within which resided the smallest sovereign country in the world, the State of Vatican, was to travel to Ostia, their next destination. The best would be to eventually moor at Ostia Antica by the middle of next night, and avoid attracting any attention.

While tables were arranged on the deck for dinner, the captain paced along and discussed his plans with Jo, Trebor, and Jovanni. He did not hide that once arrived in Ostia, the best was to play by ear their options. The easiest way to reach Rome and the Vatican at its center, was riding the Tiber River with their Zodiac, the inflatable dingy all yachts have on board. That would be if they could advance Syrena up to Ostia Antica, well inside the mouth of the Tiber River. From there, the Zodiac could bring them close to Piazza San Pietro, San Peter Square, some 20 miles up the river.

On these premises, they joined the others to share another meal on a relaxed ambiance like a big, happy family.

Trebor was asked to say the blessings, while the ship continued to float smoothly on a light enveloping everything in its changing colors. At first, all was immersed in soft pink sun rays, then, more intense hues were diffused in the sky, the sea, and the occasional clouds. Blending with the gentle gliding of time approaching evening hours, the colors transitioned to red, fuscia, and lastly, to indigo. The sea, however, held a little longer on the opal and silver shades, creating a decor of an immense and fantasque production. This ethereal vision absorbed Trebor's thoughts into the beauty of the moment, and the image of the little box given to him earlier, stayed with him.

Just before leaving Mario's office, this went to a back room and returned shortly after with a carboard box. Then, placing it on the conference table, he opened it.

"The instructions I received are to ensure that the content of this box is placed directly and uniquely into the hands of His Holy See, Pope Francis I." Mario said this lifting gently and showing a dark reddish leather box, about three inches by six.

"I was not told or shown what is enclosed in it, and I was untrusted to keep the secrecy of the mission, which I am entirely committed to respect."

Then, to the surprise of all present, he handed it to Trebor:

"I have been told that there is a message inside explaining everything to His Holiness."

Trebor instinctively touched the side of his docker pants where the box was from now with him at all times.

THE VATICAN

"We are here to deliver a message to His Holy See, but all that we have in front of us is a mountain of ruble", declared Trebor, astonished.

Trebor accompanied by his father, Joseph Godson, and Jovanni Mira, staggered through broken stones, glass, bricks, and whatever had been streets, buildings, and objects of all kind of designation. In front of them it was a gigantic pile of what had been a glorious city, now pulverized, reduced to total ruin.

Syrena sailed on clement seas until the port of Ostia, and found her way, silently, in the early hours of this day approaching December, through the opening of the Tiber River, to Ostia Antica. There, Raffaele Antonioni, a friend of Mario and alerted by him, came ahead to meet Captain Giorgio. Raffaele helped himself *Syrena*'s crew to attach her on a side docking, offering little visibility from the water, or from the road. They worked fast and quietly, and once the ship was safety fastened, Raffaele advised the captain to turn off the lights and leave only the minimum necessary on. Then, he warned Giorgio:

"The unthinkable happened. The city of Rome has been attacked by the new coalition formed between ISIS, Al-Qaida, Hezbollah and the Muslim Brotherhood, under the name of Sa-Tan Order, helped by the local Islamic extremists, to which they provided heavy ammunition." Then, taking a little breath, Raffaele let out:

"Would you believe it? The same people we welcomed and offered a chance for a life they would have never dreamed of in their own country!" Raffaele continued appalled, everyone listening, no questions needed.

"They formed cells and provided safe houses for terrorists infiltrating through Turkey, some riding small embarkations to Greece, or even to south Italy. The government said little about the rumors and the movements traced in the country, seemingly not to scare the population, thus, very few were cautious. And very few took it seriously, and almost no one prepared; we all like to ignore the warnings, we've seen so many attacks already, and it was more convenient to show a bravado face, or bury our heads in the sand!"

Somehow, Giorgio and the other three charged with the secret mission, had the impression that Raffaele was aware that their arrival was important, although he did not say or asked any insinuating question. However, after finishing his discourse, Raffaele proposed straight forward his own water taxi for the trip up the river to Rome.

"My boat is old, but dependable with dual 300 HP Yamaha engines, all new. As a water taxi we won't look too suspicious, and I will drive you there, I know every nook and cranny of the river. And I will keep the lights off in the dark most of the time."

Rapidly the things were settled, no arguments were raised against this generous offer. Trebor and Jo were secretly very touched by the kindness they found in Italians, all along the encounters with them. In no time Jovanni, Jo and Trebor found their place in the rustic, but comfortable water taxi after the quick brotherly 'good luck' hugs Giorgio generously distributed as sign of encouragement. Raffaele jumped on board and started the engines, then he navigated at the limit of no wake speed, efficiently and confidently.

Reaching the middle of the river, he did not try to cover the sound of the engines shouting, but pointed out places that could be seen close to the river banks, fires continuing to consume what remained after massive explosions. Later, they learned that a few roads left manageable between Fiumicino, Rome International Airport, and the city of Rome, where the National Guards were swiftly ordered to assume control, had been confronted by groups of militia riding military trucks. Armed with automatic and assault weaponry, they had the intention to take control of the area, although the authorities were trying to alert everyone and watch for any rebel group showing unexpectedly.

Some 50 minutes later, Raffaele pulled against the quay under the Ponte Vittorio Emanuele II, on the right bank of the river, a few blocks away from the Vatican City. Raffaele handed Trebor a brochure with a map of the Vatican, and as they climbed out of the boat, he said a silent 'Ave' for their success.

As soon as Trebor turned toward west, he started looking for the large avenues converging toward Borgo Santo Spirito leading to the famous Piazza San Pietro. This should open in front of San Pietro Basilica, burial site of Saint Peter, the mother of the Catholic church, the largest church of the Christendom, and the cathedra of the popes. And to the left of it is where he should present himself to the Papal residence.

However, there was nothing left standing up!

ANNIHILATION

The apocalyptic vision unfolding in front of their eyes was even more ghostly, since it did not look like anything had survived, and all was shrouded in an unnatural silence. Trebor and his companions advanced, desperately searching for some clues to direct their steps. If behind them, on the other side of Ponte

Vittorio Emanuele II on the left bank of Tiber River, sinister sounds of sirens of all kind of the emergency interventions could be heard, rescuing hundreds of people injured or trapped under the collapsed buildings, extinguishing fires and preventing new explosions from the broken gas pipelines, the Vatican City had suffered a complete and fatal blow.

The attacks against one of the most remarkable cultural contribution to humankind over thousands of years of a splendid continuation in this exceptional country, appeared horribly well coordinated. The wounds inflicted to this beautiful Italian homeland were vicious and heinous, even more sinister since the people of this beautiful country are genuinely kind and generous.

As Trebor kept on wandering, stumbling on chunks of mingled stone, bricks and distorted iron rods, his heart was racked with pain, and his eyes, no longer containing the flow of tears, blurred his eyesight. This reminded him of another saint place they just left behind, reduced to ruin and desolation, Jerusalem. Trebor felt that his heart could not bear another tragic annihilation of such biblical proportions.

In the lugubrious light announcing this winter dawn, casting shadows over a sinister decor coming out from Dante's 'Inferno', Trebor continued to advance without knowing where to go, nor what to expect ahead. In a strong impulse he addressed, one more time, his celestial father. As his distress overflowed him, he suddenly felt a deep sense of peace taking hold of him, enveloping his whole being on an embrace of complete love and ...hope.

Then, discerning some reality coming back, he heard a voice calling to him. Trebor turned in the direction of the whispering, and understood that someone was traying to catch his attention. Not far from where he was standing, to his left was a mound of ruble, a sad caricature of what had been a palace, walls, windows and doors angled in disarray, like a house in papier mâché crumbled by a giant hand.

Trebor approached the closest wall, where he could hear the sounds coming from a doorway, half off the hinges. Behind the door slightly cracked open, a hand appeared and made a sign to get closer, then someone struggled to squeeze through the opening to get out. Trebor grabbed the thick door pulling on it with his two hands, and was finally able to give enough space for a slender human frame to slip into the open.

"Ave, Grazie", were the first words that the young priest spoke. His cassock covered with dirt and cement dust, was torn at the knee level. But Father Marcello, sweeping lightly his garment from debris, continued to address the man that helped to extract himself from the fallen building:

"You must be Trebor Young. I was waiting for you, our Holy Father is waiting for you", then he tried to explain, "Pope Francis received a warning short time before the attack had started, and we had the time to get him to Castello Sant Angelo through the underground tunnel. There is where he is waiting for you."

"Waiting for me?", Trebor asked, in disbelief. "I have a message to deliver to him, but I did not know that His Holiness was expecting me. This will render my task much easier."

Father Marcello had a light, almost jumping step, like a goat making his way through the mess left by the explosions. He did not show much of a surprise being introduced to Jo and Jovanni, and continuing to explain, he directed all of them back toward the Tiber River.

"The tunnel leading to Castello Sant Angelo had collapsed under most part of the Vatican, there is left only a shorter segment usable past Museo Leonardo da Vinci. We will take that route, and afterwards, you can return to your boat through an exit of the Castello that brings you straight to the quay, close to Ponte Vittorio Emanuele."

Thus, the trio followed Father Marcello, eager to have a guide giving precise directions to complete their mission. Arrived at the opening into the tunnel, Father Marcello showed them a narrow hole in the ground, hard to imagine going anywhere, if not led by a knowledgeable person. They entered the tunnel through a precarious descent, and eventually the place opened up soon, giving way to an underground walkway, where surprisingly, small LED lights turned on, activated by their motion. There must have been some autonomous electrical system powering the lights and the air filtering, now our messengers able to walk and breathe easier.

Once everyone felt their nerves distending a little, Father Marcello gave more explanations:

"It is clear that this attack was a direct assault against Christianity, aiming precisely at the heart of the Holy Catholic Church. This has been declared before and after the strikes by the extremist Islamists of Sa-Tan Order, who claimed the aggression. Gloating victory, Sa-Tan proclaimed this as a new takeover of Christianity by Islam, where they intend to instate an Islamic European outpost. They are determined to convert the whole world and to make it obey to Allah and the Koran, as the only way God can be worshiped." Then, the father continued:

"Now, the bombing of Rome and many other cities all over Italy and other countries, might have different origins, but they seem coordinated with local cells created by fanatic immigrants. I heard that Russians, the Chinese, and others, taking advantage of these attacks, are ready to crush Europe and move toward the Americas. God Have pity of all of us", he concluded with a sigh, crossing himself.

Half of a kilometer later, the little procession was inside the fortress, and walking through, Father Marcello turned into an erudite guide, explaining the history and the designation of the structures as they encountered them. Initially a tomb for Emperor Hadrian and his family build in the 2d century AD, Castel Sant Angelo continued to be the burial place for the Roman emperors, until the papacy acquired the castle in 1277.

With time, this had undergone many changes and additions, including the prison on the lower levels, where Giordano Bruno was detained for six years, and the action of La Tosca, the main character of the opera by Puccini, took place. Then, our group climbed out to the surface, walking amid beautiful gardens, which suffered some damages from the bombings. But looking at the glorious statue of the Archangel Michael above the round tower, defending the city from the plague of the 13th Century, this seemed untouched and determined to continue to protect the Holy City.

The group finally reached the upper levels, where most of the sumptuous papal apartments remained intact.

"We moved His Holiness' chambers in this area, where the Castello is still in relatively good condition", brother Marcello had added, "but we don't know for how much longer, for we have been informed that more attacks are on the way."

MEETING THE POPE

The man sitting in front of him was old, tired, and... wounded. Trebor had been hushed through a large loggia covered with exquisite frescoes and lined with monumental doors on one side and windows on the opposite side. Then, Father Marcello and the Pope's secretary, Father Seraphim, who joined them on their way, finally stopped in front of a door at the end of the loggia.

Trebor was allowed to take in the scenery only for short time, but he could get a quick glimpse at his surroundings; if everything he had seen on the way through the papal apartments was magnificent, this room, although of fine proportions, was simple, almost austere. The wall in front of him making also the back of the chamber, was lined with shelves filled with books up to the ceilings, living room only for a large desk covered with documents and papers. On a side of the room was a modest cot holding fresh marks on the pillow and the unadorned cover of someone having laid on it recently. The only valuable object appeared to be a beautiful prayer stool at the foot of the bed.

Trebor heard the Pontiff, who, sitting on a large armchair, was addressing him in English:

"Come closer, my son. I am happy to finally meet you", the Holy Father said in a soft and kind voice. Then, as his Chamberlain and the new arrived group tempted to leave and allow His Holiness some privacy, this made sign that he wanted to have them staying.

Trebor, remembering vaguely some ecclesiastic protocol he had seen in the movies, approached, made a deep bow, and before he could be stopped, kissed the papal ring he had noticed on the Pontiff's right hand.

"Your Holy See, it is an honor beyond my words could expressed", managed Trebor to articulate, filled with emotion.

Then, remembering the precious box he was carrying, he fumbled to open the pocket on the lower hip side of his dockers:

"We are begging your indulgence for our incorrect appearance", he added, realizing how dirty and rough they must look. Then, he simply handed the little box to His Holiness.

The Pope nodded, and before opening it, made a sign for his secretary and the Chamberlain to accommodate his guests with seats, and a few folding chairs appeared from a side room. Then, Pope Francis I opened the box and studied its contains, after which he extracted a roll of parchment, unfolded it, and started reading it with intense concentration.

The pope's expression became deeply affected by the significance of the message. Without saying a word, after he read several times the letter, he slowly went to his prayer stand and went into a profound meditation. Everyone in the room lowered their head in respect, but they almost heard some sniffs coming from the Pontiff's direction. Or, were they sobs they've heard?

REVELATIONS

At last, His Holiness looked at his Chamberlain for help. Once back on his chair, the Pope addressed Trebor.

"The box contains a message from the last Templar Knights' Great Master, Jacques de Moley, and it was intended to arrive in these trying times. After fleeing Jerusalem in 1291, following the attack by the Mamluks, the Grand Master went and stayed in Cyprus until 1306, when he went back to France and confided this box in complete secrecy to the Patriarch of Cyprus. Then, the box was entrusted to the head of the Orthodox church, the Patriarch of Athens, who kept it since then in Mount Athos."

Reflecting on this choice, Pope Francis I tried to find his own conclusions:

"Jacques de Moley did not have much trust on the head of the Holy Catholic Church of his time, Pope Clement V. And this prove later to be for good reasons, for the pope plotted with the King of France, Phillipe IV, also interested in the vast wealth of the Knights Templars and concerned by the increasing power of their order. All the Templars of France were arrested and imprisoned in 1307, included de Moley, and accused of heresy. After enduring seven years of horrible tortures, Jacques de Moley was burned at stake in 1314."

As His Holiness spoke, everyone listened captivated by the mysterious account, giving all the time to the Pope, whose breathing became increasingly labored.

"The Grand Master placed in this box one of the most precious objects found hidden under the Temple of King Solomon's ruins, during the excavations the Templar Knights underwent while in Jerusalem during the crusades. It is a small vial containing myrrh that Jesus used a few times for the anointment of his disciples. He chose this vial as a secret symbol needed in the future times. The Grand Master also wrote a prophetic message, which he added along with the content of the box."

"Jacques de Moley talks about a new Messiah who will come on times of calamity announcing the end of this order on Earth. The prior of the monastery in Athos had strong visions recently signifying that it was now the time for the secret to be delivered, when the last judgment is near. He insisted upon the Patriarch of Athens to do the necessary and have the box handed to the Pope, as he believed that I would know when a new Son of God will appear. For He is the one who will establish the New Era."

"Forgive me, Your Holiness, but what is the New Era?", Father Seraphim, his secretary asked.

"In a simple way, it is the time when war and hatred, fight and injustice had ended on Earth, and we all live in peace with each other", the Pope answered.

"That would be wonderful, and the ideal path for mankind. But how can we live in harmony with each other when we just witnessed the barbarian and evil intentions of fanatic groups to destroy all we believe in, religion, freedom, respect, fairness...", Joseph Godson's voice raised the question.

"God is the creator of all that is, and he would not let anyone take over the people who express their faith in Him. Even if their manner of practicing their faith is different from others. No one is better than the other, and we all must respect our traditions. Our Celestial Father wants us to treat the other the way we want to be treated, to love each other. '"This is my commandment, That ye love one another, as I have loved you', John 15:12-13."

"What is happening now is not what God's intention is, and it has never been. We do not have to submit to any false idols, as our Lord never asked anyone to sacrifice his own children or wife and have them commit suicide in the name of any religion.", the Pontiff concluded.

"You mean we have to fight the evil forces, to defend ourselves", it was a statement, not a question coming from Joseph Godson.

"Conquer and enslave in the name of any doctrine is the result of personal purpose, of enormous ego some individuals exhibit. They damn themselves for eternity by using God's name for evil ambitions", the Holy Father declared in a stronger voice, an effort that had almost taken away all his force.

"But what about poverty, people coming into more economical developed countries, who are welcomed with open heart by its citizens, helped, fed and offered shelter, and then, the ones arriving want to take over, change the country's traditions, religion, and hate the hosts' way of living? Some come with an open agenda to destroy the values of the country that offered them a chance for a better life, and in return they bring in drugs, traffic young girls into sex slavery...", Jo could not resist from having the opportunity to ask those questions to the highest authority in morality and in what loving the other meant in real life.

"Education, coming out of the ignorance. The wealthier countries must help and show the way to overcome poverty and corruption to the ones less fortunate in their own countries. Coming into another country and not embracing that culture, refusing to respect and appreciate the help, but instead trying to destroy someone's else's culture, is not the answer. Each nation should follow their own cultural inheritance and learn from each one's differences, and not try to impose or change the other."

THE NEW MESSIAH

There was a little pause, as it seemed that the guests exchanged a few glances and nods of agreement. Then, Trebor made an attempt to signal to his father and Jovanni, now that the message had been delivered, it was time for them to hurry back to the ship.

However, His Holiness, although visibly fighting exhaustion, had more to say. With immense gentleness and reverence, he reached inside the little box and took out the vial into his palm, then he addressed Trebor:

"Trebor, my son, allow me the highest honor to anoint you. You are the Chosen One, the Harbinger of the New Era", and the pope stretched his shaking arms toward Trebor.

Everyone's eyes were riveted in the person holding such an incredible call. Trebor, stood up, and slowly advanced toward the Holy Father. And everyone was struck by the aura emanating from this young man's entire persona. Tall and thinned by a long year of trials, with deep blue magnetic eyes, his long hair and a short beard not entirely covering an expression of ultimate kindness, Trebor radiated an indescribable serein and loving energy.

Although Trebor was deeply touched, astonished by the words of His Holiness, the Pontiff seemed to be the most moved, when, succeeding to open the saint vial, he approached it to Trebor's head.

"I anoint you, in the name of The Father, the Son, and the Holly Spirit, as the New Messiah! You are to establish the New Era, to fulfill the prophecy of God Son's return!"

The special people present in one of the most austere rooms of the Castelo still under the mystical power of this unrivaled moment, remained spellbound under one of the most touching experiences of their life. The visitors spent a few more, unique moments in the presence of His Holy See. They learned about his intention to remain close to the foundation of St. Peter Basilica and to ensure the rebuilding of the old established holy site.

Pope Francis I was aware of his declining health, and he was just informed of more, imminent attacks to be expected, while remaining determined to lead the local resistance and to rebuild the Catholic Church on new bases.

"I see this as an opportunity to raise an even more magnificent basilica, and reform our practices referring to the models left at the foundation of Christianity."

Before Trebor, his father, and Jovanni took leave, the Pope insisted for a collation to share together and give some sustenance to the travelers before going back into the unpredictable streets and waters of Rome. During this time, the Pontiff confided in Trebor a few more secrets he rarely unveiled. Thus, Trebor learned that within the thick walls of the caves of the Castelo, where the old prison existed, the priceless documents of the Library of the Vatican had been transferred in the past, and secured in volts able to sustain a nuclear attack.

The Pope let him also know that the treasures of the Library of Alexandria, founded by Alexander the Great have been rescued well before the devastating fire put out by the Moslem Caliph Omar in 640 AD, and those precious manuscripts were included as well. Pope Francis insisted that these facts have been kept secret and preserved for future benefit of humanity.

At last, came the time for their farewells, deeply emotional, all aware that they were not to meet again, but in exchange they were filled with a sense of renewal and expectation of great forthcoming events. And, if Trebor was elated by the last events of his new life, he was also imbued with a profound humility and apprehension in face of his new responsibilities.

AGOSTINO

This time Father Marcello guided the messengers out of the Castel Sant Angelo's boundaries through the southwest tower, which exit faces the Tiber quay in the direction of the Ponte Vittorio Emanuele. This is where Raffaele must be anxiously waiting for them.

Once out of the Castello's walls, the three visitors contemplated for a few instants the grey dreariness of the morning, which even if approaching midday, remained mourning the tragedy afflicting the Eternal City. The air was musty, filled with dust and smoke, but also with the siren sounds, attesting of the continuous need for help. Then, they walked in the direction of the Ponte Vittorio Emanuele II, seen at some 500 feet away.

The three voyagers did not advance more than 20 feet, when they saw in front of them, at the beginning of the Ponte, a couple of black birds chasing down a flock of pigeons. The common pigeons, cohabitants of many European cities as fully entitled co-citizens, landed on a small elevation offered by the base of the right column marking the beginning of the bridge. Our travelers stopped, startled to observe the strange scene, when the landing of the birds triggered an explosion. The column and part of the bridge blew up in the air, then the stones fell scattered everywhere. The visitor trio was fortunately still at a good distance away and the explosion did not harm them. However, the birds, aggressors and fugitives, were all victims of the explosion.

"It must have been a delayed explosion", Jo said, "these birds saved our lives, so sorry for them, though!" Then, he quickly realized that they were cut off from reaching the boat.

As if he were reading his thoughts, Jovanni intervened:

"We need to turn around toward Ponte Sant Angelo. Raffaele could come and fetch us at the foot of it. Hopefully he is OK, but it looks from here that only the street and one side of the 'Ponte' entrance was damaged", then he turned around and pointed to the Castelo Sant Angelo Bridge about 300 feet behind them.

While Jo was busy with his satellite phone to contact Raffaele, Jovanni and Trebor looked at their new direction, were one could admire the beautiful angelic statues aligned on the ramp and adorning each pillar of the bridge. Once there, they would have to take the stairs leading to the base of the bridge, and reaching down the Tiber River quay by the massive food of the second pillar, they would have to wait for Raffaele to come with the boat.

"Dio mio, perdone mi!", 'My God, pardon me', a voice implored, between sobbing moans.

The sadness of the plea tearing apart anyone's heart, stopped Trebor on his track, as he was ready to take the first step down the stairs from the bridge to the lower part of the river's banks. He looked in the direction of the crying sounds, but he could not see anyone. Then, there he was, a human form up on the ramp of the bridge, next to the third column, making him blend with the statue.

"Oh, My God, he is ready to jump", Trebor thought at once. In no time, Trebor managed to approach the column and, reaching from behind the man, wrapped his arms around man's legs without difficulty, the ledge of the bridge arriving at his waist level.

"Please, don't jump", Trebor almost shouted, but the tone of his voice was filled with kindness.

"Io sono un' miserabile persona, io merito morire,", and the man bent over shaken by uncontrollable sobs.

"No one deserves to die, you will be fine, everything will be fine. You'll see, everything can be changed."

"No one can save me", the man attempted to speak in English.

"Why don't you step down next to me and we will sort this out together".

The man shriveled even more into a crouch, and cried harder: "I am so ashamed, I wasted my life, and the end is here, I cannot expect absolution", he added.

Gently, Trebor succeeded to lower the man to the ground level, who, so lost in his desperation, did not resist any longer, and holding onto Trebor's shoulders, cried with his face buried on his chest.

Trebor allowed the man all the time needed to empty his flow of tears, softly stroking his back and whispering words of comfort.

After a while, the man started confessing, between wails and moans, bringing out all the sorrow his heart contained, the tragic story of his life.

"I am a drug addict. Heroin!", and a new cry ripped his chest. "Mi chiamo Agostino, my name is Agostino. When I saw the attack against Rome and the Vatican I realized it is too late for redemption for me. I wanted to inject an overdose and finish my misery. But I had no more money for drugs, and I was ready to jump. You don't want to have anything to do with an abject failure like me."

"Agostino, my brother, it is never too late for anyone to find his way back to our Heavenly Father. There is always something good in all of us, and I am sure that He gifted you too with some special talents."

Trebor's soothing words made Agostino open up, and he said, "I was an artist! A painter, and a good one. I was asked to renovate paintings in the Vatican. I even helped with the Sistine Chapel's ceiling frescos by Michelangelo! But then, all was destroyed when tragedy struck."

As Trebor showed patience and waited for Agostino to unload his sorrow, he continued:

"Only a few years back all was going well for me, I was married, very happy, to the most beautiful girl in Rome. Any artist wanted to paint her, my Monalisa! We had a little girl, Agostina, the light of my life. One day, her beloved cat escaped, and ran off on the roof from our second-floor apartment. Agostina tried to catch her kitty from the balcony and... she fell to her death."

The souvenir of his little girl made Agostino sink again into despair.

"Oh, angelo mio, I miss you so much! After she was gone, I could no longer work, think, sleep. I lost my job, my wife left me, so did my friends. I became a vagabondo, a homeless, and I lost my soul in drugs." Then he concluded, "There is no future for me."

Trebor kept listening the sad Agostino's story, when he noticed that his father and Jovanni came to the top of the stairs looking for him, and now were making signs for him to come down.

"Well, Agostino, I think I see a future for you, but you have to trust me and come with me."

It was the first time when Agostino looked Trebor in the face and the two of them could discover each other. Trebor saw a disheveled man with unkept hair and a week-old beard, but there was a depth of intelligence and honesty in his eyes, although the sad expression concealed most of it.

Above all, Agostino's demeanor changed suddenly once he looked at his savior. Agostino had seen images of saints and prophets in the art of the famous Italian masters, he even repaired some of their work, but this time he was seeing one of them in flesh and blood! Agostino got up and bowed to the man standing in front of him:

"Master, I will follow you anywhere you go!"

LEAVING OSTIA

Bringing along a new follower, a desperate soul in need for salvation, the water taxi and its travelers found the way back to *Syrena*. Their friends on board received them with great relief, thankful for their accomplished mission through this frightening wreckage. It was no time to waste before retracing their route out of the Tiber River, and reaching the high seas. However, the heartbreaking images of the beautiful Italian peninsula devastation remained with them, as it was the regret of leaving a new friend behind. But Raffaele prove to be a strong character, courageous and energetic organizing already defense operations in his beloved country. However, after escorting *Syrena* out of the river, Raffaele turned around waiving, while the two ships let sound a siren salute for best wishes, then, they went on to face their own destiny.

On board of *Syrena*, Captain Giorgio took charge of the navigation and directions needed for their safety. He spontaneously made the decision to continue their exodus sailing, after the sad encounter with the dramatic situation on land, and he did not hesitate a minute before offering again his ship to transport the refugees to safety. Giorgio conveyed to his 'headquarter' members the general dispositions for their trip, and they all were very grateful for Mario's generosity and forethought having provided *Syrena* with well appreciated provisions.

Leaving Ostia, *Syrena* went west about 100 miles, regaining the deep seas and keeping a good distance from the shore. They cruised at a steady speed of 25 nots per hour, and, although most of them were tired, the security watch was increased, doubling the number of people staying on during the shifts. Towards the end of the day, making a good time and distance from Rome, they took a northwest direction, sailing parallel to the shoreline. Giorgio hoped to approach the north tip of Corsica and have a good view of Bastia, cruising on the west side of the Corsican capital and the isle of Elba to the east. By the middle of the following day, as he directed the ship mid distance between those two famous Islands, captain Giorgio reflected on how these islands were linked to the life of Napoleon Buonaparte, before slowly leaving them behind.

Then, Giorgio, pointing to his crew their position on the map, explained changing direction straight west, toward France, in order to save time. If Raffaele, in his generosity, had fueled the tanks to full capacity, Giorgio had good hopes to expand their destination to the mouth of the River Rhone, which meant they would avoid all together the French Riviera Coast, aiming rather the south tip of Provence.

From there, Giorgio intended to take all his chances to arrive to Camargue, about 50 miles west from Marseilles, and possibly to engage into the Rhone River, as much as their fuel reserves would allow. His intention was to advance going north on the river, in the direction of Lyon. From there, the options were open, and entirely relying on the situation they would find in France. But they all knew that there should find a way to contact the repatriation points established by the Allied Forces.

However, as a seaman, Giorgio mentioned a few possibilities using the rich canal and river network present in France, where barges could transport merchandise and voyagers practically everywhere. That opened the possibility to take the direction north, and eventually arrive to Calais, on the English Channel, or possibly opt for a western direction from Lyon, and find a ride on the Loire River to Nantes, then Sant Nazaire, and finally to the Atlantic Coast.

Two more days at sea, and our travelers found an improved moral as they were sailing, following the captain's plan, along the south of France. The old routine was almost restored, with times for conversation, existential debates along with spiritual teachings, and work alternating with meals shared together.

They finally had a glimpse at Toulon, and it was time to move a little north, as they had another half day of sailing before Camargue. But before that and with a little chance, the large port of Marseille should start profiling along the coast. Joseph Godson, continuing his leads on the international state of affairs, remained in a tight contact with the Agency and passed on to captain Giorgio the news, which became more worrisome by the day. The attacks taking place recently in Italy mirrored similar upheaval of the extremists organizing terrorist attacks and open rebellion in France, along with most of the other countries of Europe. Thus, Jo was advised not to stop in Marseilles, since some members of the large Muslim population created havoc in the city and the streets were unsafe.

The local citizen barricaded themselves in their apartments and homes, hoping to find protection from the gigantic mayhem present in town, where the National Guards were overwhelmed by the extend of the troubles and could barely contain the riots. For *Syrena* the only choice was to continue and reach the Rhone River as they anticipated. Hopefully, it would be possible to sail north and arrive close to a contact point of the American repatriation teams.

It was regretful, though, that the ship could not stop in Marseilles, since, to complicate things, a big storm was announced, and the crew had to start preparing for it. The Mistral decided to blow its winterly anger into the sea, and, gathering air moving from the plateau of the Massif Central, it created a current channeling south through the Rhone Valley, gaining speed, and spewing its anger on the Mediterranean waters.

Soon, the crew had a hard time not to bump into the railing and superior structures, as huge swells formed, bouncing the ship dangerously off balance. The captain made a quick announcement to inform everyone on board regarding safety precautions and bring some reassurance that they still had sufficient reserves in fuel and victuals to continue their route.

Maggie and Trebor were already in full rush to instruct the children and organize the other passengers, not part of the ship crew, to remain inside the vessel and wear the safety jackets at all times. They also recommended reading or watching a movie, while Trebor initiated a meditation session.

As *Syrena* continued her progress toward Camargue fighting the fury of the unchained sea, the night was falling rapidly, heavy clouds casting their darkness over anything that could give some visibility to a sight navigation. The captain and the crew, all on duty, nerves strung under the pressure, kept all the attention steering through un unexpected and horrific storm.

THE STORM

Captain Giorgio and his crew were living a nightmare, not sure how much the other travelers were aware of it. Little by little they were at the mercy of unleashed natural forces, the sea lashing out all the ire mounted against humans for having disturbed its natural course. First, they lost the control of their rudder, freezing its movements after one of the cables broke. It could have been when the captain tried desperately to maintain the ship from veering out of control under the assault of gigantic waves. The steering wheel activated by powerful electronic systems, forcing the helm to pull the cables, made one of them give way under pressure. Now, they were drifting without direction, the engines stopped since there was a real risk of the ship smashing against a 'falaise', a steep rocky shore emerging from that side of the Mediterranean coastline.

Then, a huge lighting fell on the main mast, and travelling through the middle of the ship, created a massive short and the electric transformer exploded into flames. The crew intervened promptly and managed to extinguish them before the fire spread on board. But the rage of the storm did not let out. Most of the travelers had no or very little experience with sea faring, making them so sick, they no longer cared whether they would die from their sickness, or being swallowed by the sea.

Captain Giorgio summoned all his concentration and abilities to maintain the ship at flow; considering the time they were at sea, and the direction of the wind that pushed them to southeast, he thought they must be somewhere back in the middle of the Mediterranean Sea! He called his helpers, Jo, Scotti, Phillipe, Jovanni, Randal, and Trebor, to inform them about the gravity of the situation. He told them that it was not about losing his ship, but he was concerned of how long they would be able to endure the horrendous conditions they were facing.

"Until the storm won't slow down, we cannot have a clear idea of the extend of the damages, and try to fix them, or at least, reach some port", captain Giorgio admitted. "Our radar is out and we have no GPS connection."

Some aides stayed with the captain in the wheelhouse, others went along to help the mates, while Trebor found himself at the bow, facing the elements.

Time and time again, monstrous waves, raising mountains of water above the upper deck, curled the crests of the swell under the wrath of the Mistral, and for long moments swallowed the ship under its twisting tunnel. *Syrena*, as everyone on board, was at the mercy of the elements, and it felt as though powerful undertow currents were sucking her toward some unbeknownst direction.

Trebor gripped hid hands tight around the railing of the bow, and, fronting the sea, was drenched by the curtains of the water fallen with packed force. And he started praying. Ignoring the incessant salty whipping, he prayed for the salvation of the precious cargo of the ship, for the salvation of all the desperate beings hoping for a safe place to live and enjoy the Father's creation.

The majestic figure of this erect man, standing tall and proud, showed no defiance, but an ardent imploration. Trebor became a magnificent apparition, and if the lightnings profiled his handsome features for a few seconds, one could have had the impression that he had become himself a glowing presence in the dark. He started praying aloud, talking to the Creator and his energy feeding from the storm, harmonized with higher realms. Trebor transcended to a higher dimension in the attempt to approach God, bringing together this world, swept my terrible human and natural storms, close with the divinity.

And what happened next was nothing short of a miracle: without warning, the cyclone abated. The winds fell to a whisper, the waves became a gentle ripple, the sky open to starry spaces between clouds, and everything looked like there has never been any trouble in the world. Only the ship drifted without lights, nor navigation gear.

Giorgio and Jo had approached the stern for a little while, inspecting the condition of the frontage, and praying that this would hold for a little longer, the risk of all drowning not quite gone. They run into Lu Xiang, who apparently tried to reach the upper deck as well. He was serein and appeared as though he just emerged from deep meditation, not surprised that all entered into calm. Giorgio and Jo had observed Trebor and without need for words, they were both awestruck by what they had witnessed.

Suddenly, *Syrena* came to a halt with a whoosh, as if landing on a bank of sand, then gently leaned to the right.

"This is it", thought the captain, we hit a shoal, "at least we are not sinking, but how far are we from the shore, can anyone see us?", and he asked Jo to check if his satellite telephone gives him any indication.

People came on the deck, breaking the earie silence felt after the storm. They were all shaking and disoriented, their footing unsure after all the bouncing like ping pong balls just minutes before. After a while, in the dark and in the cold, the captain and his team sent them back, with reassuring words and promises, to get some rest in the comfort of their cabins.

Trebor and all the other men stayed on the deck to spend what was left of the night, some blankets were distributed, and soon, they all fell into a deep sleep.

LAGOONS OF CAMARGUE

Rays of sunlight came through his eyelashes, as he felt a familiar nibbling on his neck, then a little lick of the ears and face, and finally, a hard sneeze, close enough to make him move away from the too friendly 'beast'. Trebor ruffled Everest's dense fur on the top of his head while smiling out of his dreamless repose. He almost thought that Everest was ready for a playful morning start. Then, in a flash, he returned to the alarming reality.

In seconds he was standing up scrutinizing his surroundings. *Syrena* felt steady under his feet, her decks leveled with the horizon, and Trebor noticed that Giorgio must have been up for a little longer than him, and had already stabilized the ship lowering the anchor. The sound of the chains free falling must have awaken the men and they quickly gathered on the main deck.

The landscape, or better defined as the waterscape, was stunning in its surreal beauty; after the horrifying storm during the day and part of the last night, a bright raising sun was illuminating a blue sky and green waters. However, in all directions, scattered sections of lowland could be fathomed through the lifting morning mist. Somehow, the ship had been carried by huge waves over the banks of sandy shores into the middle of swampy lagoons.

As many of the crew members wondered where they were, Jo came along, looking at his satellite telephone and showed the captain the precise location indicated on his GPS.

"We wreaked next to Saintes-Maries-de-la-Mer. We ended up on the Etang des Launes, the Launes Lagoon", announced Giorgio. "About 10 miles south from Lagoon of Vaccares, and maybe 20 miles east from the River Rhone", Giorgio added.

The activity on board gained the lower levels of the ship, and everyone showed up, eager to learn that the storm was replaced by a shiny morning. As the travelers were enquiring where they were, Trebor offered some enlightenment:

"This ancient town at the confluence of the River Rhone with the Mediterranean Sea, was named after three biblical Maries. According to the legend, their boat drifted on these lowlands of the Camargue, during a storm, as it happened to us. Joseph of Arimathea accompanied to Egypt the three

Maries after Jesus crucifixion, from where they sailed to escape the persecution."

"The village was named initially **Nôtre** Dame de Ratis, Our Lady of the Boat, and was changed much later to Saintes-Maries-de-la-Mer, Saint-Maries-of-the-Sea. The roman catholic church built in the 9th century, served as Fortress and refuge, and it is said to contain relics of Marie Jacobée, Marie Salomé and Marie Magdalene."

As they all strained to see the tower of the cathedral, Trebor fed them with more 'exotic' facts:

"In May and October, up to 40,000 gypsies arriving from far away, gather in an impressive pilgrimage. They celebrate Saint Sara, a dark-skinned woman to whom some attributed the role of servant from Egypt to the three Maries, while the locals maintain that she was a pesante who rescued the three refugees."

"It is quite a spectacle to watch the large crowds of Roma entering the waters of the sea with their horses, sending flowers and seeking purification in these holy waves. Then, they leave in a rush of shouts, taking their horses on a cavalcade into the setting sun."

"Emaye a, mother", Wubit addressed Maggie, "I am hungry. Can you make oatmeal, please?", her beautiful little face looking up at her.

The sweet voice of the child brought all of them back to the more concrete facts of life, and small groups broke up and hurried to assess their losses and reconsider their options.

"I will make you a bowl of cereals, we don't have a stove working right now. Is it OK with you?", said Maggie, with one child in each side advancing toward the stairs. "But I bet we can find some jelly and bread too!", and Wubit and Ishmael followed their new mother, already forgetting all their worries at the thought of a good breakfast.

Half an hour later, Giorgio had already made a tour of the boat inspecting her condition, then inquired about their provisions, after which he finally led his helpers to the observation deck.

"*Syrena* is not operational at this time, alas! With the rudder broke we have no direction, and the electrical controls are fried by the lightning. Without radar, nor depth scanner, we can't go anywhere", the captain explained, with sadness read on his face.

"We have only the flashlights to go under the deck to the cabins, but soon the cold and dampness will start penetrating everyone to the bone. We still have water reserves, but the desalinations station and the pumps are not functioning, so the toilets will be plugged, if they are not already, and there is no pressure to the faucets. To make things worse, the refrigeration is out and we are about to lose our food supply within the next 24 hours."

Taking a deep breath, captain Giorgio took his time to make his announcement:

"We have to abandon the ship", then, looking into his friends' eyes, he continued, "a few of us will take the Zodiac and go into town and see if we can bring every on shore and to a safe place to stay until we can find a way to continue our trip."

After captain's concise overview of the situation, Giorgio appreciated to see that they understood and he was surrounded by a group of reliable friends. Then, he attempted to lighten up the mood and said:

"Hey, we made it that far and we are in France now. We only need to arrive to a port with a naval base and get shipped to America!" Then, changing the tone again, he went on, "I speak a decent French, and I know that Jo does too. How about you, Trebor?"

Instants later the Zodiac was lowered on the water, and they convened that Giorgio, Jo, and Trebor would go on shore to Saint Maries-de-la-Mer. They were also taking along Maggie, since Trebor told the captain that she spoke French beautifully. Captain Giorgio thought it was a terrific idea and having a woman with them could help against unwanted suspicion.

Thus, the other members of the group were informed of the next plan of action, and would start sorting out the remaining food in good condition for the time they remained on board. They would also gather their most precious belongings, ready to evacuate the ship when possible. Words of encouragement were shared, Wubit and Ishmael left under the supervision of Sonia and Amanda, although Aisha and the other two ladies on board volunteered on the spot for the child care position.

In no time Maggie and the three others were in the Zodiac, ready to follow the directions indicated on the marine map Giorgio took with him, and if they were at less than three miles from the town, the treacherous wetland configuration needed special attention. However, the Zodiac was a quite good way of traveling, since the inflatable embarkation offered a flat bottom.

As the captain was looking at the map, Jo already scrolling every bit of information he could access via the satellite, and Maggie continued to give directions to the two little ones, only Trebor saw the big dog coming in full speed and without hesitancy, jumping into the boat. Everest almost reversed Trebor on his back, and they all had a very hard time to make Everest go back on the ship. There he stayed, his head on his front paws, yelping and watching the boat carrying his master away.

SAINTES - MARIES - DE - LA - MER

"We will go straight to the Canal des Launes, it runs practically along the entire west side of Saintes-Maries-de-la-Mer. We should look for a place where we can tie the boat and then walk into the town", explained Giorgio to Trebor, who was navigating while Jo was studying the satellite images on the screen of his phone.

Maggie seemed captivated by the unique scenery, still looking at the lagoon across the sliver of land separating it from the canal. As the foggy vails dissipated into the air, she discovered a new and unexpected ecosystem created by the Rhone River delta. If the pink clouds of the flamingoes were gone for the winter to the Nile delta, Maggie marveled at the worriless play of the wild horses of Camargue. Further away, huge black bulls advanced slowly through the marshlands, grazing on the lush greenery of the seaweed, and further down were sheep chewing on the high grasses, infusing their meat with a slightly salty taste from the 'marées salantes', the salty tides, of these pastures.

The oyster season must've been at its pick, for some simple fishing shacks in front of the shallow oyster plants disposed simple wooden tables over the water. There, people would be served loads of oysters freshly scooped in front of them, "The best and the freshest oysters one can ever sample in their lives", the owners would claim.

"Here, I see a parking lot we can reach on foot, and there is a road", said Jo, interrupting Maggie's day dreaming. "And the canal is lined with small barks fastened at this dock."

While they spotted an opening and secured the Zodiac at one of the poles, Jo continued to read the map scrolled on his telephone:

"This road will become the Avenue de la Plage, Beach Avenue, and it brings us in the heart of the town. There, about a mile to the west we can turn north on the Route de Cacharel, then a hundred yards to the right we will find the Hotel de Ville, the City Hall."

Walking in the town, as in all places in Europe is a natural thing to do, our friends did not look out of the place. Especially under a brilliant morning sun, tourists would be showing up any time of the year to enjoy the nature, the food, a boat ride, or a more spiritual experience of the local atmosphere. But so far, the four travelers were the only one on the road. Approaching the more populated area of the town, they noticed that instead of opening the shops and businesses, some cars were parked in the front of the houses and people were loading them, and looking preoccupied, were getting ready to leave.

"Maybe the storm scared them and they are taking a break from the biting of the winds", Jo remarked. "Anyways, here we are, let's see the mayor if we can", and he showed the entrance of the City Hall, without saying that the agency had already sent a message to the mayor and that he was expecting them with new information.

MAYOR BERTRAND

"Enchanté Madame, Messieurs. Very pleased, lady and gentlemen. You all speak beautifully French! This will make our conversation easier. Your boat suffered damages? I am truly sorry. Many of our fishermen left to bring their crafts to the north side of Vaccares. Still, the Mistral got terribly upset those last two days!"

"But the most upsetting is that", continued Jean-Marie Bertrand, the Mayor of Saintes-Maries-de-la-Mer, " there are troubles in the South, gaining control over the most peaceful of our southern territories. We expect some insurgent crowds coming our way, and we try to prepare the best we can. I already announced my jurisdiction to secure their property and, if they can, leave the area."

Jean-Marie Bertrand continued for a while to inform the visitors, all the while expressing his own concerns. And, if he were aware of allied forces helping to repatriate the foreigners, mostly Americans, his most pressing obligations were pulling him to find solutions for his own town.

The visitors learned that Marseille was literally on fire, and the fact that the storm brought them to west of it could be considered as another blessing. It appeared that the local Arabic sympathizers having united with the new waves of immigrants, and after slowly growing an immense resentment toward the country that opened new opportunities to them, they fueled an unjustified hatred toward it. The refined culture and sophistication of the Frenchmen were interpreted as arrogance, and they felt humiliated, although the social advantages provided them with a departure into a new life never dreamed before, and at the expense of heavy taxes for the French nationals.

Starting at first with small skirmishes, the clashes between the French population and the minor ethnicities took a more religious turn, the newly arrived infusing more radical ideas claiming a worldwide takeover by Islam. Over the years, extremist cells had already become organized and there had been increasingly terrorist attacks over Europe. With time, this became a well-coordinated network spreading across France and the entire Western Europe. And now it seemed that Armageddon had reached far out Middle East.

"I was informed that Paris, and in general most cities in the country, are facing the same situation: everywhere Christian population is assaulted, women raped if they dare to leave their house, stores are looted and put on fire, as are cars, public buildings, museums, churches, etc.

"If anyone adventures underground to the metro, it is at the risk of its own life, for all public transportation had been invaded by gangs and hooligans. A curfew had been instituted and the National Guards have been deployed, but they are overwhelmed by the extent of their task."

Abruptly, the Mayor of Saintes-Maries-of-the-Sea, looked at his guests startled:

"Je suis désolé, I am very sorry, please excuse me, I forgot my hospitality. You must be starving and tired. Allow me to invite you to a 'French petit déjeuner". Then Jean-Marie Bertrand disappeared next door for a few minutes.

Coming back, the mayor continued the thread of the conversation:

"While the café is brewing, let me tell you that a plan for your evacuation was discussed with American authorities. I arranged a transportation for your group using one of commercial barges riding the **Rhône** River north, up to Lyon. I do not have much to offer after that, but I would not recommend you to continue toward Paris, but rather circumvent the entire north side of the country and go west, to the Atlantic coast." And the mayor went to point out several options taking the travelers in the direction of La Rochelle, where there is an American Navy base, and either Saint Nazaire or Brest, if going further north.

After sharing a typical French breakfast with croissants, local apricot jelly and butter, and invigorated with a strong coffee, the visitors took their leave from Mayor Jean-Marie Bertrand, who resumed his urgent assignments. They would momentarily return to *Syrena*, take at least half a day for the captain and his crew to secure whatever possible on board with the hope that, one day, he would return and try to have her sailing again. Everyone else would have to prepare to come on shore and, with the compliments of the mayor, a city bus would transfer them to the **Rhône** River, then embark a barge south of Arles, at the end of this vast natural preserve of La Camargue.

SARA

Having a precise plan to follow and after thanking profusely Mayor Bertrand for his help and hospitality, the visitors retraced their steps back to the inflatable boat, all the while animated by the perspective of their trip ahead. They arrived at the parking lot next to the decking of the small boats, and started crossing the parking, now empty from other visitors. All of sudden, they were swarmed by a group of gypsies, surrounding them with no warning and no indication from where they were coming from.

An old woman, ostensibly showing a longtime practice, addressed Maggie, her tongue all honey:

"Let me tell your future, my princess! Let me read the lines of your hand, ma jolie. I see in your eyes that there is a man who loves you very much", and, as Maggie essayed to escape her touching, the old gypsy pulled even harder. "Don't be shy, ma belle, I can make your man love you even more. Give me your gold neckless and I will give you my special potion, he will be under your spell forever. And you will have lots of kids!", the old Gypsy went on.

The others gypsies, mostly children or teens, were begging the men for money, with watering eyes and showing their clothes in rugs and lamenting of hunger. Maggie and the others, realized that they would get rid of the gypsies only if they were giving them some money. She started speaking in French, to make them believe that they were not foreigners and setting them as an even easier prey. And she was right, as soon as a few bills came out of their pockets, they were swiftly snatched from their hands after which the youth took off in a hurry.

Trebor, who had been pushed back by the running rascals, noticed a slender figure, wrapped in a dark cape and with the hood lifted over the head, approaching Maggie from the back and slipping a hand in her pocket where Maggie had placed back her wallet.

"Hey, arrêtes! Stop that", Trebor shouted and attracted Jo's attention, who was besides Maggie.

In a fraction of a second, Jo's reflexes kicked in, and grabbing the figure's hand holding Maggie's wallet, he restrained it hard, and with a little twist, the person covered with the cape was on the ground, immobilized. All the other pickpockets vanished to wherever they came from, as though they never existed.

Trebor, rushed also toward the scoundrel, "You should just ask for more money, don't have to steal", and father and son slowly lifted the form that was no longer opposing any resistance.

The hood slid from the thief's head, making the other four stop and look agape at the person standing trembling in front of them. They thought they had never seen anything so beautiful and so unexpected: it was a young girl, the hood freeing a cascade of blond curls, around an angelic face, with the fairest complexion one can see only in the Scandinavian countries. She was so young and she looked so innocent, no one could've ever thought of her being able to bring harm to someone.

She started sobbing, her eyes of the purest blue imploring for forgiveness:

"Je vous demande pardon! Je suis désolée. I am so ashamed, I did not want to steal from you", and her voice strangled under a wail.

As she was shaken with sobs, the cape fell from her shoulders, and they had another gasp of surprise, the young girl was on an advanced state of pregnancy!

Their hearts melted and, guiding the soon to be mother young girl toward a bench on the dock nearby, they made her sit, comforting her. And, as she slowly felt in confidence, she started telling them, in a perfect English, her astonishing story:

"My name is Sara. I am from Sweden and I am 16. My grandparents raised me since I was six after my parents died in a car accident. They were hit by a truck losing control on an icy road. When I was 13 and entering the high school, I begged my grands to let me go on a summer school trip to France. It was my dream, but it was also when I was kidnapped by a group of gypsies in front of Nôtre Dame Cathedral in Paris. They surrounded me, I learned later they were quite experts at this, and no one could see as they dragged me to a derelict mini bus. They 'chloroformed' me and when I woke up, I was tied and locked up in a cage in a place far from Paris. I was beaten, starved, drugged up, until the nomads 'broke' me and forced me to steal from tourists in the places they wandered."

Every one listened, spellbound by Sara's story.

"My kidnappers were laughing and saying that because of my being blonde and looking like a westerner, I could rob people easier, no one would suspect me. They even made me carry their own loot so they could escape the police." Then, Sara seemed almost crushed with despair.

"The gypsy chef, Dracu, raped me one night. I was defenseless, no one came to my rescue. His wife, though, became enraged and hit me merciless, thinking that her husband gives me more attention than to her. My life became a nightmare, Dracu would come during the night and force himself in me, and his wife covered me with bruises daytime. They slowed down since I discovered I was pregnant, though. No one examined me, but I am pretty sure I am due in less than a month."

At the end of her confession, Sara glided and curled on the ground, bending her head on the dirt, her chest heaving with anguish.

"I don't want to live like this! I don't want my baby to come into a world like mine. I want the best for her, for I know, I feel it, it is a girl that I carry."

Thus, under desperate supplication not to leave her there, as it was the first time that Sara found herself alone amongst strangers, away from her fellow gypsies, Trebor took her hand and caressing it gently, reassured Sara that she would never go back to the miserable life she just left behind.

"We will take you with us if you want. We will take good care of you and we will make sure you and the baby will never lack of anything. But you need to know that we are going to a place that is very far from here", said Trebor looking deeply into Sara's eyes, to make sure she understood.

"The further, the better", Sara answered and threw herself to Trebor's neck.

It was the first time they saw her smile, and it was as if the sun rose a second time that day.

LEAVING *SYRENA*

Once back on board of *Syrena*, preparations for the travelers' departure were on the way, although everyone was quite sad having to abandon her. The adults expressed their gratitude for the floating quarters *Syrena* offered so timely, keeping them out of danger for many days and bringing them so close to their final destination. But the most touching was to see Wubit and Ishmael going around the ship, touching her walls, masts and benches. Sometimes they stopped and gave kisses and thanks, reassuring *Syrena* that "we will come back and we will fix you and take you with us to America!"

Maggie, Trebor, and Lu Xiang observing the children with tender eyes, when Jamuna's voice was heard behind them:

"Their pure hearts know that objects have feelings. They have their own history and connection with us, as everything is connected in this world". Then, he added, "I hope too, that one day I will see *Syrena* again... Never been at sea before, always in the snow of the high mountains, but I am indebted to her for the new world she opened to me."

Maggie, hearing Jamuna talking behind them, turned to bring him closer, and continuing to watch the children, she wrapped her left arm around Trebor and brought Jamuna closer with the right.

"And we had such unique times all together, some scary ones, but mostly wonderful moments creating a large family all together."

"May God keep it this way", agreed Jamuna, with a deep sigh of secret hopes in his heart.

Slowly, Maggie detached herself and went to check on Sara, who had been received and surrounded with love and concern by everyone at their arrival back on board. It seemed that the whole little community was committed to compensate Sara for her suffering and fill her new life with love and caring, while showing her another face of humanity.

It was interesting to see that Lu Xiang came along and discreetly encouraged Sara to open her heart. In his wisdom, he sensed that she was ready to unload her bad memories, and he thought that, perhaps, this would be the beginning toward her healing.

For the first time, Sara telling her dramatic tally, faced the demons that tortured her for the last three years. Once liberated from them, in the presence of warm and concerned people, her young age could allow her a speedy recovery, and hopefully, regain trust in the goodness shown by some.

"You would not know how many children, even babies, disappear, kidnapped to be used as beggars and cause pity. They did not make me beg because they knew I did not look anywhere close to a gypsy, only made me rob tourists in the crowds, always one of them watching so I could not escape. And if one day the booty was meager, I would not get food and sometimes they would chain me to a pol outside, like a dog in the cold, to teach me a lesson."

"Some children are sold for human trafficking, I would have probably been sold for prostitution for a good amount of money as well if Dracu, our chef, would not want me, at least for a while, for himself. But I feared every day that his wife would sell me without him knowing", and with a sad look on her face, Sara added, "would you believe it? I would consider myself lucky as long as he would keep me with them?"

Originally from Asia, and centuries ago migrating from India, gypsies liked their freedom and even in the modern time European countries were aware of their errant life and allowed them free passage and some documents for them to easily go across borders.

They lived relying on small jobs offered by the local population and most of them attracted sympathy from the regular inhabitants. And they were, by definition, honest people, only living by different rules. They were masters on horseback riding, hoofing and making harnesses, trading silver jewelry, even guns. But with time, some fell into the greed of earning easy money stealing and robbing tourists and locals. When apprehended, they were given a small allowance and sent back to the country that had registered them, mostly western Russia and Easter Europe. But they would come right back, and the cycle would recommence over again.

"I am so sorry they've been so bad to you, and you were without your family. I know how hard that must be", the little Wubit said, sitting by Sara's side and caressing her arm.

"But don't you worry, now you are with my family and we will love you forever", Wubit concluded with a sisterly hug.

One more time, Sara broke into tears, but this time, after a very longtime, these falling tears were tears of happiness.

BREAKING BREAD WITH LOCALS

"Bonjour! Is captain Ricardo there?". The voices were coming from below, next to the ship. Several men and women bent over the railing on the port side of the boat to see who was calling.

"Bonjour a vous aussi, good day to you too, I am Captain Ricardo, what is the matter?", answered the captain, looking down.

There were three small fishing embarkations, each of them containing two people on board.

"Ah, capitaine, je suis François Dubois, my name is François Dubois, and with my friends here we came to give you a ride to the shore for your bus. We thought that you might have a hard time making several trips to bring the people and whatever you need to transport. And you might not have enough gasoline for your dingy."

"Oh, thank you very much, all this is true and your help is very much appreciated. Especially with everything in town closed, I didn't know if I would find a gas station and be able to go back and forth several times. But please, come on board", and an overboard ladder was lowered, and, as François jumped on the deck, he warmly shook hands with Giorgio. He was a young man, with long white-blond hair almost touching his shoulders, and his face battered by the sea salt and the sun.

"Jean-Marie, the mayor, is my cousin. He told me about you and with my fellow fishermen we already noticed your ship stuck on the banks of the 'Étang'. We won't leave the town like many others from around here, we live on the other side of Vaccares and our shacks are not visible from strode places. And anyway, we don't have much to attract those 'crazies'. But, how can we assist you?"

Soon after, people were distributed evenly on the three fishing boats, the captain and his helpers made a last tour of the yacht, looking for anything that could be secured, and with a last good bye, they detached from the hull, riding back to Saintes-Maries-de-la-Mer. The distraction caused by the arrival of François and his friends helped to lessen the feeling of abandoning *Syrena*.

However, François added:

"Not to worry, we'll be watching over her and we'll make sure no one will loot or damage anything. And we'll be looking for your return, Captain, and we will have a big 'fête' then!"

The convoy went smoothly to the docking area where the Zodiac was attached earlier, and the travelers walked toward the parking lot, this time not completely empty. There was a mid-sized city bus designated for the transport to the banks of the **Rhône** River. But there were also several villagers form around the lagoons, some women and children, and they had displayed on folding tables a small, but delicious feast for the stranded people. If all was simple and the villagers, having the habit to come to town on the days of the market with their produce and fish, this time they were sharing a meal with friends that would continue their adventure and that they might never see again.

Children and adults exchanged their stories and ate together, dogs sniffed each other and as part of the family, enjoyed chicken legs and pieces of cheese. If Everest triggered some surprised exclamations from them, being compared to a dog from the Pyrenees and not from the Himalayas', soon the children and dogs enjoyed a few plays and laughter together. Obviously, Everest knew how to make friends everywhere.

Delicious loafs of bread, soft and dry cheeses from sheep and goat, **pâtés** and tartes were tried and declared tasting as "out of this world." Children delighted with orange juices and thick hot chocolat from thermos containers, while the adults discovered the divine flavors of some **Côtes du Rhône** wines, never exported abroad, the local production remaining small and limited for the local consumption, a well-kept secret even from the richest connoisseurs.

Conversations became animated, and some of the travelers, like Aisha and Farid, even Beshadu, took a sip or two, eager to comply with the general request to 'discover' this local production. But most of the success went to Lu Xiang, who came along and claimed his "own right to new experiences".

Sara, however, kept on sending quick glimpses beyond the parking lot, and remained constantly close to the Godson trio. Soon, Sara attracted the warmest sympathy from the ladies, who, once they noticed her condition, started offering the future mother huge plates loaded with the best selections of food. As usual, the feminine spirit united them in a deep visceral connection, bringing special attention to the young expecting mothers and their precious creature growing in the womb. Under so much affection, Sara lessened her fear of being observed by her former captors, and savoring with increased delight the best food she had in years, began to empty one plate after another.

"La faim vient en mangeant, appetite comes while eating", the ladies smiled, tenderly watching Sara.

After feeling properly 'stuffed', then playing soccer on a patch of grass, the children took a break and sat down. One of the teens, brought up the conversation about the storm lasting for almost two days.

"It was terrible, we thought that we will all die!"

"I was not scared", a little voice said.

"Of course, you weren't, you were sleeping like a log!"

"The wind was so strong, we thought it will lift the house with all of us inside", said another.

And a heated conversation started, all giving a more frightening description than the other of the cyclone. Finally, one of them concluded:

"But thanks to the Holy Father, the storm ended, all of a sudden, like it never started!"

Ishmael entered the conversation:

"I know, it was my father who stopped the storm!"

"As I said, it was our Heavenly Father who did it."

"No, it was MY father!", Ishmael insisted, vehemently.

"And who is YOUR father, then?", Denis asked.

"He is my father", said Ishmael, pointing out to Trebor. "I saw it with my own eyes. We were in the middle of the sea and I was sure we were about to die."

Now, all the kids' eyes were on Trebor, and Denis considered him with the outmost attention.

"C'est vrais, il a l'air magnifique; It is true, he looks magnificent!"

Then, the children were called back, for it was time to make their farewells.

Children and adults made a final tour to the facilities next to the docks washing hands and using the toilets. Sara discreetly whispered to Maggie to accompany her there too, who reassured her that she would never let her go anywhere without being accompanied at all times.

Names and addresses were exchanged, along with wishes for safe and peaceful times ahead, sealed with kisses on both cheeks, making them forever friends. Then, our travelers climbed the bus for the 25 some miles across the lowlands of the National Park of Camargue to reach the barge taking them to Lyon. They carried the belongings they could save, but they've been also loaded by the villagers with the remainder of the food, who were not sure when their next meal would come along.

The last rays of a beautiful and unusual sunset accompanied the bus ride through one of the most spectacular and mysterious natural preserves found in Europe. This time of the year the nature retracts into a wise hibernation. All slows down, taming colors and activities in preparation for the spring renewal.

Satiated by the good food and drained by the emotions of this long day, the travelers watched in silence the calming decor scrolling before their eyes. Transported into a dreamland, the children and Sara fell asleep. Ishmael, lucky to have Trebor on one side and Everest on the other, would make one wonder who was holding who?

With a sleepy voice, Ishmael murmured, "I love you, dad."

Moved of being called 'dad' for the first time, Trebor answered:

"I love you too, son. I love you with all my heart."

Everest lifted his head from Trebor's lap and called out: "Woof?"

"And I love you too" Trebor said with a little chuckle, and gave a little kiss to the top of their heads.

Maggie was the most overwhelmed, with Wubit finding her favorite place on her lap, and Sara on the other side, slowly leaning her head on Maggie's shoulder. Able to feel secure and relax at long last, Sara was the image of an innocent and angelic figure. Maggie smiled, caressing the two little heads, one with tight dark curls, the other one letting a flow of blond ringlets run down her arm. Maggie almost laughed aloud when a flashing thought came to her, "How would a red ribbon bow look in Sara's hair, like the one Wubit is wearing?".

Then, her heart filled with love, allowed the sweetness of the moment to transport her also into a world of beautiful dreams.

LA FILLE DU MIDI (THE GIRL OF THE SOUTH)

A still sleepy assembly of now 26 people approached an unpretentious quay, once the bus driver could locate the barge the US embassy succeeded to reserve for their group. It was a barge owned by a local company offering rather rustic, but charming river cruises to tourists, since riding a 'peniche', a barge, it has been a long tradition in the European countries. France counting a dense canal system connecting most of the major waterways, it has been said that "one could float from Paris to Moscow without setting a foot on land".

Now, with the low season, most of the companies closed their business for the winter and proceeded to repairs and upgrades of their embarkations. However, once maintenance and revisions done, some barges remained available and they were sought out by many French families who thought using them for fleeing the unsettled areas. In these troubled times, the use of barges offered safer means of transportation, with more secluded ways of traveling, even though at a slower pace than using highways or major routes through big cities.

La Fille du Midi, The Girl of the South, offered 15 cabins, to include the voyagers and the crew. And if the cabins had basic commodities, there were simple quarters for dinning along with a small deck at the aft of the ship for limited lounging, mostly housing the bicycles the tourists usually liked to ride around the rural areas. Since the French landscaping was a spectacle on its own, there were no showrooms and only an informal bar. Because of the low season, there were retained on board only the captain and his mate, one cook and his sous-chef, while the cleaning lady liked to double in the evenings as a singer entertaining the audience at dinner time.

However, after warm introduction, Giorgio readily offered his and his own crew help, and some others, naturally inclined to continue their routine established on *Syrena*, proposed their assistance. Maggie wanted to be amongst the first to assist in the kitchen, when Chef **Stéphane** introduced himself as a true 'cordon bleu'!

The river boat captain, Pierre Launier, was greatly relieved by this unexpected 'work forces' joining into their adventure, and declared:

"I promise you then an epic trip across the most beautiful countryside you've ever seen! Welcome on board, soyez les bienvenus", he proudly made his reception.

The travelers took possession of their cabins quickly, instinctively keeping their arrangements they had on board of *Syrena*. And without much fuss, many were asleep, cradled by the gentle movements of the boat, bringing them back to their recent habits taken up while at sea.

A few, however, returned to stay with Pierre, who was in a hurry to 'get on the road'.

"I will make the trip to Calais, fortunately in 10-12 days, as I promised to your folks. We will have to run the engines most of the time though, with exception of the time we are going through the locks, and this if we don't encounter trouble on the way. Sorry you won't be able to fully take advantage of the superb sites we are going through, the castles, the monuments and their history, the wineries and the local cuisine. But we hope that all this is not going to be destroyed by the time you will be able to come back one day."

Before drawing a plan for the new members of the crew, Pierre gave a general idea of their trip:

"We will navigate on the Rhone River for most of the part until Lyon, close to 150 miles, and it should take us less than 48 hours. From Lyon to Dijon, the capital of Burgundy, we will float on the River Soane to Auxerre, then to Montereau on the Yonne River. From Montereau will sail on the River Seine all the way to Paris. and finally, from Paris to Calais we will cover about 300kms, 185 miles, and navigate on the Oise River and the Canal du Nord to

Calais. But don't try to retain all this, there are many other alternate canals or small rivers if need is for us to follow."

When Pierre indicated taking the first night shift, for the Rhône River was large there and allowed them a fast advance, Giorgio offered his company. The two captains stroke a spontaneous friendship, facilitated by the fact that Giorgio spoke quite a good French.

When the next morning came and everyone gathered in the dining room and looked out the windows, they were all seized by a quite different view. They were floating, but in a slower and gentle way, and they could admire a different landscape from each window. It was a calming decor that invited to reverie.

French crew and passengers interacted creating an easy-going atmosphere. They learned that a few hours ago they passed Arles region, the 'pays of Van Gogh' and its inspiring site for the 'Café terrace at Night', amongst other places where he placed his easel to paint. Danielle mentioned that Arles offered an exceptional quality of light not only to the impressionist artists, but long before, when the Ligurians came along around 800 BC, then the Celtics and the Phoenicians, followed by the Romans, who, in year 123 BC established the province of Gallia.

"There still in place beautiful ruins of the Amphitheatre, the Roman Circus and the Theater, and of a massive high-arched aqueduct. Roman emperors established the headquarters for their Praetorian Guards when in Gallia, and liked to relax in the Roman baths. Arelate, the Roman name of Arles, is the favorite place of the Emperor Constantine I, and his son, Constantine II was born there. Constantine III, in his attempt to become the Emperor of the West Roman Empire, established the capital in Arles in 408." Thus, Danielle went on, proud to distract the travelers' attention to more pleasant subjects.

"This land witnessed many other invaders coming attracted by the pleasant climate, rich soil, and water springs. The Cathars, came in the 5 and 6 centuries, followed by Saracens in the 8th century, along with the Vikings during all these years. Arles continued to be a city linked to political and economic interests, where The Holy Roman Emperor Frederick Barbarossa, in 12th Century, then the kings of France, signed various important treaties."

Therefore, Danielle volunteered spontaneously to become the guide for the travelers; so many times in the past had she heard the certified guides giving details of the sites and their history to other groups. And now, she was thrilled to elevate her designation on board from maid, to 'historian'. At the end of her 'exposé', Danielle announced that in the afternoon they should arrive near Avignon, another important city in the history and cultural life of France.

She briefly reminded them about the Palais des Papes, the Palace of the Popes, the residence of seven Roman Catholic popes from 1309 until 1377. The palace is still a site of interest for visitors, and Danielle started singing the famous popular children song 'Sur le Pont d'Avignon', 'On the bridge of Avignon', enticing the young and the old to join into a dancing circle.

Later on, Danielle pointed out south of Avignon the River Durance going east to traverse Vaucluse-Bouches du Rhône, when she announced that a few miles past Avignon, they were 'missing' Chateauneuf du Pape, the land of one of the most prized vineyards in the world.

Then, only a few miles from there, they went west to Orange, a flourishing town since the Roman time, although named after Arausio, a god from Gallia. A triumphal arch still stands in all its splendor, in honor of Julius Caesar. Also dating from the first century BC, one of the best-preserved theaters in the ancient world built by emperor Augustus, contains in a niche on the back stage wall the impressive statue of the emperor. The arena, with a stage and semicircular tiers of seats, can contain 9,000 spectators! This creates perfect settings for some of the most spectacular operas and concert productions one can ever experience, even nowadays, during the Summer Orange Festival.

"There is a similar summer festival in Avignon, where I've seen last year a beautiful ballet production in the Palais des Papes courtyard", added Danielle with enthusiasm.

CRUISING THE RIVERS OF FRANCE

Captain Pierre and his extended helping hands, including Jovanni, Jo, Trebor, Scotti, Phillipe, and even Jamuna and Agostino, kept a vigilant watch for any unusual movements they could notice on the river banks and the towns they passed along. The teams formed on board were welcomed to helping with the chores, while enhancing the shifts alertness at all times. And everyone was happy to learn about this type of navigation, discover the charm of these unique places, and even keep their mind busy from the boredom of inactivity.

Since the Rhône River offered large waterways and no locks slowed down the trip until Lyon, their good progression up the river was favorable. Along with a nice weather with crisp temperatures and clear skies offering views stretching well beyond the rives, the travelers actually enjoyed a wonderful trip. Against the close quarters, the spectacular vistas chased away any feeling of enclosure, as *La Fille du Midi* carried her passengers in an appeasing journey, away from a tormented world nearby.

Thus, during these few days, the people on board could turn their attention to the enchanted moments of a trip that was promised, against the dramatic circumstances, to remain as an unforgettable encounter. Montélimar and Valence, went by, then Vienne, and on the morning of the third day, the boat came close to the south edges of Lyon.

Danielle, assuming with all her passion the role of the historian of the voyage, had already introduced with great pride her home town, Lyon. For half of the previous day she bragged about Lyon's architecture, its history, long tradition, and contribution to the French cuisine and fashion.

During this time, the group formed by the captain, gathered by the 'wheel room' to share the latest on the situation in Lyon; the riots started there by the wild insurgency of the extremist factions, showed already signs of bringing the beautiful country of France to the edge of anarchy. One more time, the newly formed headquarter realized that avoiding to travel on land, this would give them a better chance to minimize the risk of becoming a target to the anarchists. *La Fille du Midi* was cautiously blending with some other embarkations going their ways, while in town, the large institutions, markets, and stores remained an easy prey to the blind fury of heartless and mindless mobs. The captain was glad having anticipated a steady continuation of their trip; the ample provisions of food and fuel being secured before Vienne with the best quality of simple and natural food found in the countryside, allowed him to avoid stopping in dangerous areas.

However, as long as Captain Pierre directed the barge circumventing the large town of Lyon, and intended to follow his plan to reach Dijon, via the Soane River and the Burgundy Canal, he nonchalantly used his charm to entice the other passengers, particularly the women and children, to stay inside, suggesting a cooking contest. This put Stéphane, the chef, into his best mood, proposing a 'scrumptious menu', and having the contribution of everyone, including the children. Soon, after finishing their breakfast, the tables were emptied leaving room for small groups to form and share new tasks. Shortly after, a joyous activity occupied them entirely; here were chopped some beautiful carrots, turnips and shallots, there were pealed some nice red potatoes or were cleaned trumpet mushrooms, bell peppers, and leaks. Even the children had been entrusted with whipping white eggs or making the real Mayonnaise 'from scratch'.

When, later on came lunch time, *La Fille du Midi* was already flowing on the waters of the Soane River, well to the north of Lyon. Pierre came, as promised, to check on the contest results, and everyone was invited to share an animated debate between the aspiring gourmet chefs. As everyone claimed to have done the best job, Pierre continued to supervise the safe advance of the ship, keeping the travelers inside as he did when going through the dense area surrounding Lyon and avoiding to be 'spotted' by unfriendly eyes. He did not have any difficulty to do so, the passengers continued for a while their testing and retesting, laughing and joining in innocent lies, claiming having prepared the best dish or desert of all.

Tired of their 'hard work', too much eating and having too much fun, most of our friends decided for a cozy winterly nap. This left even more peace of mind to the captain to operate the ship without attracting any unwanted attention. And if for once everything outside the boat was quiet, inside the squeaky voiced of the children continued a little longer; this time Wubit wanting to nap with Everest as well, and Ishmael had to make room for her also next to their soft and tender 'teddy'. When Maggie and Trebor came to check on them a few minutes later, they could hear them even from outside the cabin door, but this time there was a snoring contest going on between the three of them.

They distributed a few kisses nevertheless, and then Maggie, closing the door behind them, looked at her brother and whispered:

"Everest won the contest this time, no question about", and the two of them breaking into a giggle, pushed each other away from the door, not to wake up the sleepy angels.

GENTLE RIDE ON *LA FILLE DU MIDI*

With two boat captains minding the navigation of their new home, along with a vigilant scrutiny kept by the other leaders of the group over the local and general events development, a semblance of security and retreat slowly took shape on board of *La File du Midi*. And along with this, a routine was established, modelled over the more recent one, shared on *Syrena*.

If the children restarted an exciting open class continuation of their basic academic curriculum, to this was added ancient masters' teachings, opening a larger understanding of the world. Sara, after important years in her education being neglected, spontaneously joined the others, and showed probably the most interest for the opportunity to further her education. She absorbed with passion every bit of information heard, amazed to realize how much she had missed, but proud to effortlessly follow every discussion.

Aisha and Farid, as well as the other couples and single men and women, sat together in an intellectual communion and exchange of cultural and spiritual ideas. They learned from Trebor, Maggie, Lu Xiang, and they learned from each other. Danielle became herself an unexpected and very appreciated addition to the group as she introduced them to the rich history and culture of the places traversed, setting a superb decor for a trip that could have otherwise been another horrid experience.

The next few days became a time capsule, *La Fille du Midi* protecting and carrying its precious cargo on a gentle passage through the Saône River. Like a string of precious pearls one would wear close to its heart, the travelers admired one after the other picturesque places passing by, leaving behind Mâcon, Chalon-sur-Saône, Beaune, arriving in Auxonne, from where they followed the Burgundy Canal on the east of Dijon.

Through the Burgundy Canal, they had a glimpse at Dijon, the cherished capital of Burgundy, proud of the rich terroir production of worldwide known wines, mustard, and unique cuisine, but beyond the epicurean pleasures, boasting a valuable cultural record. Then, Captain Pierre, choosing the shortest ways to Paris, at Auxerre he followed the River Yonne, then at Montereau the waters of the Seine River, planning to cover in less than three days the distance from Dijon to Paris.

"And then, from Paris, three more days, and we will be in Calais, if all goes as I hope", he sighed.

Indeed, Captain Pierre steered the barge with care and devotion during a mission that offered the travelers not only a secure, but also a marvelous ride, making the best of their voyage. He was getting excited as he approached the south side of Ile de France, the area surrounding Paris. There, the River Seine was making many turns, snaking leisurely through the France heartland, then through Paris, separating the city into two well defined sectors on each river bank, all the while adding small and picturesque island formations.

Pierre, could not hide his concerns about what he might find in Paris and its burgs, places well populated by minorities and immigrant population, often clashing over religious and cultural matters. He already learned that serious riots and street fights went on, but he was still not sure of the extend of the danger going through the city following the river. Thus, Pierre pondered whether to continue their trip as planned, or he would have to consider a different strategy and use some of the smaller canals, covering the town like a web.

No matter which waterways was his final decision, Captain Pierre though prudent to make the crossing through Paris during the night hours.

A CHILD'S QUESTIONS

"Why are people and all these countries fighting? We had to flee one place after another, why abbi?', Ishmael addressed Trebor with insistence, during one afternoon gatherings.

"Yes, papa, why some people are so mean and harm even children?", Wubit joined Ishmael in the conversation.

"Is this ever going to end?", this time Sara entered the dialog.

All eyes of the children and the older ones were now on Trebor, as he had become their spiritual leader. In spite of his gentleness, the people following Trebor and his family in this exodus for a safer land, each one developed a true reverence toward this radiant figure. They all thought "isn't he who stopped the storm? and before that, in Ethiopia, faced the bandits that almost killed his father and kidnapped little girls?'

"I don't know why there is so much cruelty and hatred in the world, and when this is going to end, Trebor began his answer, finding a place to sit among the audience. His voice was harmonious, his demeanor humble, and his answers honest. "But I can tell you with assurance that all the evil acts will soon come to an end, and a period of endless happiness and harmony will reign on Earth for you to enjoy."

In the silence covered only by the rumbling of the engines, bright eyes filled with expectation invited him to continue.

"You see, above all this, there are higher powers watching over us, and when the time will come, all the suffering of the human kind will be abolished. For God, the Supreme Power, the Supreme Knowledge, Universal Energy, the Life Essence, or whatever you want to call Him or Her, created this Universe and this planet as he created everything that is, everything that breathes". Then, trying to see if the children follow, he asked: "You know about the Universe, this one where our galaxy and billions of others are contained, as there are many other universes coexisting and interacting with this one, right?"

"Yes, emaye Maggie told us, and even she showed us on her laptop", Wubit answered with pride.

"Great, then you understand that there is this unaltered wisdom that governs them. And you know what unifies them all?'

"God, of course!' someone tempted to give an answer.

"The good angels", a child voice rose from the attendance.

"Yes, all of this, but the way everything manifests is the Universal Energy. An intelligent field of vibrations acting as an unlimited and perfect consciousness, uniting everything, containing all knowledge, recording all the history, depository of all creativity, inventions, and above all, of our actions."

"I told you that Santa can see everything!", Ishmael turned toward Wubit, easing up the ambiance with a laughter.

"That's true, and any bad action will no longer be tolerated without punishment. This is called karma, or whatever name you want to give to 'justice'." Then after a pause, Trebor added, "it is important for you to know that our own consciousness can be united with this Universal Consciousness if we elevate ourselves to the level of its high vibrations and resonate with them."

"What is consciousness?", Amanda asked, for once less shy.

"But how can we be part of it?", someone else asked in the same time.

"Consciousness is what defines us as a person. It is more than our mind, our thoughts, and our feelings. It is the essence of who we really are. It is our soul, immortal and created by God, perfect and at its image. It is what makes us aware that we exist beyond the biological and above our purely physical functions."

"In order to be reunited with the divine field of energy representing the Universal Consciousness, we must elevate our own consciousness through good and loving actions and thoughts. This is what will bring our vibrations to higher levels, allowing our consciousness to become part of this energy, as we remain connected with our higher self, or our consciousness elevated to its highest vibrations."

Trebor made a gesture to get up, thinking that the others wanted time to ponder over these ideas, when more questions rose as a protest.

"Well, on the other hand, when someone does something bad, harms somebody, its vibrations become literally, measurably lower. To the point that conscious malice will bring someone down, disconnected with its higher self, 'losing its soul', as we say. He or she will become a falling person, possibly even a falling angel, an evil person like Lucifer."

"What we witness in the present times is a ferocious confrontation of global proportions between the forces of the good and the evil. And this will decide whether one would rise transcending to another higher dimension, or will be destroyed."

"Is it like in the scriptures, last days before the Final Judgement?", a voice was heard from the group.

"It looks very much like that, and as it has been announced by other mystical prophecies. We are traversing through a section of very high energy in space and time, and only the vibrations at high energetic levels could subsist, the lower ones will be burned like in a solar flash. Thus, the bad energies, the bad people will be wiped out. This will bring this planet and the inhabitants who could elevate their consciousness to this new level, to a higher and blissful existence."

Trebor stood up, bringing his intervention to a conclusion:

"The universal consciousness is inviting us to recognize and act on its divine principles: unconditional love, compassion, gratitude, appreciation, care for each other. And it is summoning us, during our life on Earth, to recognize our purpose and fulfill our divine potential."

"I already told you, just do good and everything will be fine!", Wubit calling the final point, made everybody laugh.

Instants later, Pierre poked his head through the door:

"On mange? I am hungry, when is dinner?", and happy that chef Stéphane was ready for them, Pierre sat at a table and invited everyone else to join for another gourmet dinner.

CHAPTER 11 - APOCALYPSE

PARIS, THE CITY OF LIGHT AND LOVE

The uprising in Paris continued to grow, from unrest and street demonstrations, the hostilities built up between young generations of immigrants and minorities, extended to the older, more traditional French population, all the while reaching insurgence proportions. The newly arrived, most of them coming to the European safe harbors for political freedom and/or trying to escape poverty, pushed to the limits the local population patience and resources, which started to consider it as an invasion, bringing along increased trouble and insecurity. Brought about by a hidden agenda of rebellious extreme elements, based on religious beliefs that their destiny is to change the established society and take control over it, it became a visible danger to the cultural values, the ways of living of the French ethnicity, and their survival.

Initially presenting as isolated terrorist attacks, these acts were regarded as minor differences of political and social views, with no clear agreement of opinion even between the French citizens themselves. Some younger sympathizers proclaimed full acceptance of the political refugees of everybody and anybody under the auspices of freedom and open immigration, while the more conservative ones were deemed as outdated in their concepts. However, the degradation of the quality and the conditions of living, public safety, or respect for women aggressed overtly in any place and circumstances, all this slowly brought together different sections of the French society to resist the revolution started by foreign nationals on their own streets.

Since the international unsettlement and the adjoint social movements ravaging Europe, in Paris the curfew was instituted. But this was not respected in many areas of the city, particularly on the outskirts of the town, where the Muslim population was dense. Like in London, Berlin, Marseilles, and practically all major cities in Europe, Martial Law was declared, but poorly reinforced, since the authorities were overwhelmed and the National Guards being called everywhere, could cover only limited areas.

On the main avenues and boulevards, one could see barricades made of cars, buses, and whatever the insurgents could bring on the streets, furniture from elegant showrooms, hotels and restaurants, used now to set up fires. The most worrisome fact was that the terrorist factions were well organized and supplied by foreign powers having interest on destabilizing the West, who manipulated these militants for deeper reasons. Thus, these factions had at their disposal scores of assaults weaponry and ammunition, even hand rockets and missiles, along with large quantities of explosives.

For the past week, the Parisian population had witnessed an unprecedented fury of destruction; the insurgents, after blocking all access to the Metro or any other public transportation, commonly used in Europe, they went on with systematic explosions of the historic monuments, museums, and churches.

Most of the television and radio stations had been devastated, since there was no resistance from the pacific employees with no means of defense. It had been said that the Louvre Museum was blown up room by room, as it has been done in the past with the museums in Bagdad, and priceless and irreplaceable art work and artifacts were forever destroyed. Even the Palais Elysees, the president's official residence, had been attacked and the president had to seek protection in an undisclosed location.

Practically everything in the path of the mob had been ransacked, smashed, or vandalized. The fires started, spread easily through the gas pipes exploding and fueling the blazing inferno.

Tragic scenes took place in many areas, where defenseless older citizens, revolted at the sight of their cars and apartments plundered or torched, went on the street to confront the assailants, desperately attempting to reason with them. Unfortunately, they became an easy victim in front of bloodthirsty mobsters, long before brainwashed against any humane feelings. Other family members watched powerlessly when mothers, fathers, daughters, or sons were stubbed or crushed with metal bars, then thrown in the fire or even dismembered.

And now, Parisians witnessed an escalade of violence and desire for vengeance which degenerated beyond control, Hell breaking loose in the City of Light.

"It got a lot worse than I expected", Pierre addressed his close headquarter team formed since the beginning of the barge ride. "I hoped to make it across Paris during the night hours, and I still do, now, that in winter the nights a longer. But I have to refuel, and this became tricky", then looking at Jo, Pierre continued, "we might have to see with your Embassy if they can offer you another way to go to Calais."

"I already checked with them. The Embassy is under siege, the personnel had been evacuated days ago and nobody is accepted inside until safety is warranted again. The compound, located close to the Place de la Concord, where huge manifestations are held, is under heinous attacks and can barely resist the assaults. I am afraid we have to continue until Calais."

Pierre and the others expressed their concern and disappointment, when Jo added:

"On a positive note, the Allied Forced are ready for a massive 2d D-Day, a second debarkation since World War II is underway. The Navy is already taking position on the English Channel and is supporting the NATO forces in the Baltic and the Mediterranean Sea, while is reinforcing other strategic positions. We should be protected and find a way home once in Calais, Dunkerque, or Boulogne-sur-Mer."

What Jo had omitted to mention, was that even in the United States troubles had begun on both coastal cities of the USA.

"Al right, then", said Pierre. I will find a way, I will contact a body of mine in Isle Saint Louis, a little island in the heart of the old Paris. We will have to be very careful, though, and stay on the west side of the Island, facing Nôtre Dame de Paris. And avoid the south side looking across at the Rive Gauche, the Left Bank, where demonstrators are everywhere."

'MAY THAY WILL BE DONE'

"Music! how beautiful!"

Trebor, deep in prayer, a state of meditation transporting him to realms where his vision reached clarity and profound existential questions were debated, heard coming from faraway the sounds of organ music. Someone was playing on a gigantic organ with powerful, uplifting cords, and with an unrestrained passion. The formidable waves of vibrations enveloped the entire area, resonating in the approaching dawn over the spectral ruins of what had been only recently one of the most beautiful cathedrals in the world.

Trebor, instantly drawn by the compelling sounds, understood the poignant statement, the crushing emotions contained inside this impressive musical declaration. He left the boat moored last night under the cover of older house-barges, where everyone was sleeping. Then, he went like a shadow over the Pont Saint Louis, the only bridge connecting the two islands at the heart of Paris, Isle de la Cité and Isle Saint Louis.

Pierre Launier had found safe to 'hide' his embarkation for the night along the small waterway connecting the arms of the Seine River surrounding these two islands, considered the cradle of Paris. Trebor took the direction of the miniscule but romantic square lounging the south side of the Nôtre Dame de Paris Cathedral.

The only problem was that, arrived on the Isle de la Cité, the Island of the City, the cathedral no longer existed.

Street fights and blood thirsty destruction of anything representing the West, and in particular the Christian religion, became the target of hatred, the object of systematic and symbolic eradication of the values that it represented. The mob could easily be manipulated and inflamed under false pretexts, as most of people had some personal grudges to solve and found an outlet to their frustrations joining the riots on the streets. Once anger escaladed, the crowds blindly lashed in a hysterical, unstoppable paroxysm. On blind moments of fury, judgement was lost and only primitive instincts prevailed in a lust of a celebratory drunkenness of destruction.

In these early morning hours, when Trebor contemplated the wraithlike sight where used to be an ancient cathedral, built upon layers of other shrines, drawn by the sacred power of this holy place, he shivered and, one more time, called upon his Celestial Father. A few buttresses subsided along with a few residual walls on the north stairs of the tower, but the stain glass windows and the front entrance with its famous Rose window above, had been shattered. Statues dismembered and blown in all directions mingled with pews scattered without order.

Strong emotions storming through the core of his being, Trebor experienced, in a trance, the 'deja-vu' of his previous encounters of devastation in places representing important sites of humanity, Jerusalem and the Vatican. Again, tears streamed along his face as he asked one more time about the reason of this violence and destruction, although he already knew the answer:

"It is part of the confrontation of the good and the evil. It is about the freedom of choice man has been endowed. The change is taking place right now, and what you see is part of this change that must befall. And based on the choices made, many will perish and other will ascend to a higher layer of Heaven."

Trebor bowed his head in recognition and acceptance: "May Thy will be done, Father."

"I understand your sorrow, my beloved son, for your heart is good and tender. And I will give you the strength you need for the changes ahead, and a great deal of accomplishments will happen, and many good deeds you will accomplish in my name."

Trebor, his heart filled with beatitude, acquiesced again: "May Thy will be done."

GABRIEL

The majestic flow of sounds of Bach's Toccata and Fugue in D filled the daunting place, and Trebor began to distinguish in the dark the tips of organ pipes. Rising as clarions, proudly resisting the damage inflicted to the organ masterpiece constructed by Francois Thierry in the 1730s, it looked like the organ loft had landed in the middle of what once has been the nave. Some of the electrical connections and the sunken high-pressure pneumatic transmissions must have subsisted, since fierce harmonies raised their voices in protest.

Although the beauty and the power of the music enveloped everything around, Trebor thought with regret that this was not the time of the regularly scheduled concerts offered freely and so graciously to the public. With a few more steps taken in the direction of the music he noticed a figure moving frenetically over the keyboards, and at the same time, Trebor could discern desperate wails accompanying the music. It was a young man, a priest, who had found the only thing left in the church that could, still, express his desperation. And now, he was shouting and playing for the whole world to hear it.

Before he was able to get any closer, Trebor stopped on his track. Behind the organ player, moving shadows were approaching, hiding behind pillars and rubble. He quickly understood that those black forms had no friendly intentions, and were about to silence this defenseless protest. On a leapt, Trebor stepped in front of the assailants, between the musician on his left and the attackers on the far right.

"Don't come any further and go away! you have done enough destruction."

"We will kill the infidel playing this cursed music, and you too", came the answer in a north-African accent.

"Do not lose your soul in anger and hatred! He is only a kid, playing the organ. Just sit down and let your soul be washed in this beautiful music", Trebor pleaded, in a calm voice.

Now, Trebor could notice three short figures, dressed all in black, including their faces covered by ski masks. In a flash, he saw that one of them was kneeled and supporting his elbows on a block of stones, as he was taking aim at him; the two others were just behind the one crouching, standing and holding something in their hands. Then one shouted:

"You shut up! And your music. We will make sure that there is nothing left of it!"

At that moment, Trebor caught the glimpse of one of the men standing behind, pulling on the top of an object, a grenade obviously, and, as he bent backwards lifting to throw it, he stumbled on debris and lost his balance falling on the other one standing in front of him. This one on its turn, also lost control and fell on the top of the squatted man below him.

It took only a fraction of a second before Trebor felt a gush of air pushing him closer to the organ. The explosion of the grenade occurred when the attacker was still holding it in his hand, triggering the second grenade to detonate in two successive murderous fireworks. Moments later, a sinister silence confirmed what happened, for all there were only human remains left, mingled with more broken stones, the three mobsters practically buried under the object of their own rage.

Still dazed by the shock of the deflagration, Trebor staggered toward the place of the explosion, only to realize that there was nothing he could do, nothing was left of the three men. And as he returned to the young priest, he heard him taking his anger on his direction:

"Why did you have to get in the middle? It was none of your business, you should let them shoot me. I am a worthless, insignificant aspiring priest, can't fight all this madness! It is a lost cause."

Trebor allowed the troubled young man spew out all his helpless frustration, then he tempted a few words of encouragement:

"No one is worthless, and we all can resist and overcome evil. What you see is only the agony of desperate people of a lost cause."

The young man seemed oblivious to Trebor's words, and in a new wave of desolation, fell on his knees, imploring between sobs:

"Father, all I had and all I hoped for, is gone. I have no one left. Tell me what to do, tell me where to go! Please, Father."

"You can come with me. There is much to do, and it is only the beginning of a new era. And you can help to build it!"

The lost man, as if coming out of a daze and becoming aware of Trebor's presence next to him, turned and wrapped his arms around his legs, sobbing harder.

"Please, don't leave me. And, please, forgive me, you are my only salvation."

Trebor gently pulled the young man to stand up, and, giving him a hug, asked him:

"What is your name, my friend?"

"Gabriel, my name would have been Father Gabriel once ordained."

"Well Gabriel, we have to hurry now, there are other people, other friends of yours, waiting for us."

LEAVING PARIS

It was about time, Pierre, Ricardo, and everyone who had noticed Trebor's absence, started wondering and worrying. Then, Jo recognized his son's figure walking on the bridge. Hurrying along was a smaller person wearing the robe of a priest, and they all felt relieved. *La Fille du Midi* was ready to get back on the large river and leave Paris as quickly as possible, things were getting out of control, and fast.

Once covering a great deal of water leagues, *La Fille du Midi* left behind Paris and its troubles, heading north. First loop of the Seine River took her west of Paris and, rounding Bois de Boulogne, the forested area helped camouflage the river traffic. A few hours later, at Conflans-Sainte-Honorine, she borrowed the waters of the River Oise, and stayed on it until the night fall, passing the charming small towns and villages scattered on the hills and inclines of the river banks, reestablishing the peaceful, sleepy feeling of the winter rhythm bore by the French countryside.

The routine of the life on board was needed as the only 'stable grounds' everyone could count on, and the arrival of Gabriel, and not so long ago of Agostino and Sara, was desired for their integration into the migrant group. That evening, everyone carried on with their best efforts to create a warm and pleasant atmosphere, Stéphane taking his guests into another culinary exposé of the areas they were traversing along.

After a welcomed quiet and restful night, Joseph Godson woke up with the urgent gut feeling of contacting his agency for an update of developing events, when his sat-tel rung. After conferring with the agent, who asked to have Pierre and Scotti close by, they learned that the allied debarkation being under way in Calais, all resources were concentrated for that operation. Two major navy carriers were stationed there after bringing 10 thousand troupes, while some airplane fighters were patrolling the area. It became evident that the refugees going on the opposite direction, would interfere with the military logistics. Thus, two small frigates scheduled to cross back the

Atlantic, were expecting them and other groups at Boulogne-sur-Mer, some 20 miles south from Calais, for their repatriation to the United States.

Pierre, went right the way to consult his charts and find an alternate route. He would use a labyrinth of canals from Beauvais to Amiens, then the River Somme and River Liane to Boulogne-sur-Mer. He calculated that this could be covered in a little over two days. Then, going to meet his travelers in the dining area, he announced the new directions of their trip.

Pierre was happy to accompany the news presenting the travelers with a place and a date for the conclusion of their tribulations. Then, he added:

"I will be missing you, but let's make the best of the time we have left together."

"I will miss you too, Pierre", little Wubit spontaneously came to give Pierre a hug. "Me and my family love you very much".

The youngest member of the group unprompted gesture attracted all the others to come close in a collective embrace.

DOCTOR ON BOARD

Rebekah and David, a couple from Colorado who recently retired and decided to enjoy their new freedom with a long-anticipated trip to the Far East, had watched discreetly over Sara's condition. David, had enjoyed a successful career as an orthopedic surgeon specializing on sports trauma, his practice established for a long time in Denver, Colorado, and at a close location to the mountain sports. With time, Dr. David Anderson grew his practice to a larger group, as there was a continuous stream of patients committed to serious competitive activities. Along with an increased interest in extreme sports, so was the diversity of the injuries, challenging the surgeons to adapt to the latest technologies and procedures. Because Dr. Anderson was in reality a trauma doctor, he did not have any experience in obstetrics since his internship. Thus, he began searching and refreshing his basic education through internet med websites, when accessible, in the eventuality of a baby delivery.

Rebekah, who also retired with her husband, David, was a nurse, and fortunately a pediatric nurse. She had already examined Wubit and Ismael when they came into their group, and fortunately, after getting proper nourishment, both appeared to be in excellent health. When Sara came on board, only a little less than two weeks ago, Rebekah gained the young girl's confidence and did a summary examination at first. After a few days, Sara trusted Rebekah well enough to allow the nurse to follow closely her condition.

With all the experience Rebekah had in treating children, she had her concerns regarding an imminent delivery, and if she was a little more at ease with the condition of young mothers, she tried her best to hide her anxiety in front of Sara, who needed rather a midwife and a neonatal nurse. However, Rebekah was quite pleased to see how well her young 'patient' was doing, leaving behind the stress and the unspeakable life she had been a victim of until recently. But now, able to sleep and eat properly, surrounded with love and attention, Sara was blooming into a beautiful, glowing expecting teen, healthy and joyous for the baby she would soon hold in her arms.

Maggie and the other ladies showed Sara great attention and tenderness, and they all started preparing for the birth of a new baby; knitting and crocheting became a preferred occupation, exchanging ideas and patterns animated their conversations and everyone inquired about the future mother's needs and plans. It was understood that Sara would stay with the American repatriation group and Joseph Godson had initiated a research to contact Sara's grandparents. Nevertheless, for now Sara remained under the protection of Godson's family, as they had been granted custody of the minor Sara. It was a real pleasure to see the young girl gaining a rounded girth, looking happy, and singing while crocheting.

A few times, Maggie had managed to go on shore when the ship was refueling and new provisions were made at the close-by fresh markets. Searching in the country stores for what was needed for a new born baby, Maggie came back elated with her finds, a 'bassinette', a portable baby basket, bottles, formulas, outfits and blankets, and even a musical angel, for the baby's peaceful sleep. All this happy effervescence helped tremendously the mood on board, often succeeding to diffuse the stress of the outworld reality.

USS INDEPENDENCE

The river boat reached the Opal Coast and arrived near Boulogne-sur-Mer, a little south of Calais, a beach stretching along the English Channel and facing England, at the closest distance between the two countries.

To our travelers, on the path of this long exodus, it appeared almost hard to believe they were now boarding this navy ship. Once presenting at the harbor, they were swiftly directed to the office provided for the repatriation to the US, run by American administrative personnel. Then, after being cleared by both authorities, French and American, they were ready to be 'shipped' back home. The travelers did not have time to learn much about the history of the place, that Boulogne-sur-Mer is still considered one of the largest fishing ports in France, nor did they stop at the memorial places of past war tragedies, such as the Wimereux Cemetery and its Commonwealth War Graves. In these dramatic times, no one would look forward to the sight of other unfortunate confirmations that history repeats its self.

USS Independence, the lead-ship of littoral combat ships, is a small corvette used for various operations in the littoral zone. Although able to provide self-defense to some extent, it is mostly a platform for command and control, moving at high speed and accompanying larger ships, such as destroyers or air wing carrier war ships.

Capable to fulfill independent scouting and protection for commercial and troupes' transportation, alike a frigate, *USS Independence* has a more modern and more performant profile, with a sizable interior volume for large mission containers and a side access ramp for vehicles loading from a dock. In addition, the top deck provides a platform for H-60 helicopters airlift and rescue, along with anti-submarine and anti-ship torpedoes and missiles.

Once arrived on the Atlantic coast of France, *Independence* and her sister *Freedom*, unloaded Humvees, armament, and combatants, along with modules of electronic equipment. Then, the two sister ships underwent promptly adjustments for civilian transportation, and efforts were made to ensure the transfer of as many people as possible.

The under-decks cargo spaces emptied, the areas were filled with cots and tent-like separations, as for temporary emergency shelters, this time anticipated for close to 200 refugees, housed on two levels during the 5 days of the Atlantic Ocean traverse. Routing from Boulogne-sur-Mer to a new docking area close to New York City and Long Island, the two ships were expected to fulfill their mission bringing back civilians and some official liaison persons to the United States. Then, justifying their corvette designation by crossing back the Atlantic to Europe, they would continue to bring more troupes and warfare material to the second allied debarkation site.

The precipitated farewells when leaving *La Fille du Midi* were nevertheless filled with emotion, strong bonds having been made with friends sharing times of intense dangers, which surprisingly brought them forever closer.

Pierre Launier, the river boat captain, depositing his guests at their destination and happy to successfully complete his mission, had expected to find a place out of the harms' way and wait for warmer and more peaceful times to come. However, he was immediately found very useful to contribute to semi-military operations, bringing refugees from distressed zones to safer ones, helping with evacuations of foreign citizens relocation, and even of natives inside France. It appeared that navigating the calm and secrete water passages became an effective resource of transportation, which remained available across vast distances.

Chef Stéphane found himself on board of *Independence*, after he mentioned that he could help with the meal preparation. In truth, he bragged a little about being able to make a feast out a few potatoes and carrots, but for the military crew all was more attractive than the pre-prepared rations. Thus, Stéphane was cleared to go to the US and fulfill his dream of visiting the American territory.

The living quarters allocated to our migrant group were a pair of adjacent 'tents', one for women and one for men. In the middle of a multitude of other rescued families, they recognized themselves as a growing assembly, forming their own extended family. Maggie assumed her role that fate attributed her as a mother for Wubit, and to a certain extent, to Sara, while Trebor watched over Ishmael like a father, and Jo kept a responsible, yet a tender guard over all of them.

The errant family counted now also Ricardo Montovani, the unlucky captain of *Syrena*'s, lost in the storm at Saintes-Maries-de-la Mer, along with two of his helpers.

277

Jamuna, Beshadu, Raj, Randal, Li, Jovanni, Captain Scotti Hunt, Phillipe Prior, and Andy Foster, continued along their journey. To them were added Agostino and Gabriel, while the eldest of the group, Lu-Xiang, showed an extraordinary resilience all along.

Aisha and Farid chose to stay with the group, turning down the opportunity to make the leap over the English Channel and go to London. They were ready to start a new life on their own. Part of the group were also Dr. David Anderson and his wife, Rebekah, as there were Deborah and Joshua McClain, along with Amanda and Sonia.

Ishmael, shortly after settling one more time on his new quarters, followed Trebor and Joseph Godson on the deck as they sailed away. He went close to Trebor, and he slipped his hand in his with a natural gesture:

"Abbi, papa, where are we going?", then he tried to explain, "I see everybody happy."

"We are going to America, my son, we are going home."

"It is like going to Jerusalem?", Ishmael asked, thinking of his place of origin.

"Yes, we are going to find a New Jerusalem."

SAILING TO AMERICA

It took less than 48 hours for the passengers on board of *USS Independence* to adjust to the life of improvised military transportation; and if this was not a cruise line vacation, the anticipation of seeing soon their home and family, made everyone do the best to comply with the restricted living quarters. The 34 military crew remained on board assuming the safe return of the civilians, promptly instating a schedule and the routine of the shifts, for a smooth functioning on board.

Families and small circles of friends kept close to their assigned areas at first, then people started interacting and 'visiting', all eager to create a jovial atmosphere and make the best of the trip. Since they were now getting close to Christmas, recreating the spirit of holidays greatly improved everyone's mood. The two ministers that happened to be among the passengers, one catholic and the other Greek orthodox, initiated the advent and a few religious gatherings. Along with them, people of other faiths felt the need to reflect on the approaching holy celebration, the recent events bringing deeper meanings and reasons to show gratitude.

Some suggested even making a few touches of Christmas decor, and with the help of the crew members, they dug into the limited storage and found some ornaments for the occasion. However, this appeared to be sufficient to make a significant impact on the moral of the passengers, now filled with new expectations. Children and adults went on caroling and conversations about traditions were exchanged with passion. The festive atmosphere growing on board helped to haste the passing of time and ease up everyone's impatience to see the American continent.

And this was a good thing, for the officers and officials spending most of their time on the upper deck at the command post, followed with increased intensity and concern the unfolding events gripping the entire planet. Returning to the American East Coast, virtually a homecoming to safety, lessening the tension as they were crossing the mid distance across the Atlantic, raised now reasons for new disquiet. The news arriving became more alarming by the minute.

Joseph Godson followed closely the development of the events, as he had been cleared by the Pentagon after the Intelligence Agency communications, and along with the Commander Matthew Johnson and his officers, waited for data and orders for the itinerary that might change.

The old Cuban military bases have been overlooked for decades, and for good reasons, the failing Cuban economy not posing a threat to the United States. Since they could not sustain any substantial upgrading or modernization of the troupes, the Cuban military did not represent a first priority to the American government for over 45-50 years, having nothing to be concerned about for a long time.

With the international tensions growing in other areas of the globe and with several military engagements in the Middle and the Far East, the American national surveillance of this small and close to home island became somewhat neglected. Surreptitiously, Russian submarines made rounds of presence, stopping to Cuba to bring nuclear warfare and even drop some military enforcements in order to train the rusted Cuban army. Lately, their presence became more permanent, reminding of the incidents during early 1960 era, when JFK was president. Most recently, the Russian submarines got bolder, making frequent incursions close to the American coast, although remaining within the 'international waters' distance.

The Russian government locked in the nostalgia of multi-continental domination, cleverly manipulated for years the obsessions of other nations, in particular the hatred some countries had against the United States. Practically always supporting the Chinese, whether overtly or behind the scenes, the Russian frontrunners made also strong alliances with the Arabic nations fiercely opposed to the western influence of Europe and Israel.

Thus, the Russian regime obtained to oversee all the oil production in Iran and Syria, countries consumed with their loathing of America to the point that they preferred to allow the Slavic presence manage their natural resources, saving money from running themselves a poorly planned economy as a result of constant social turmoil and massive governmental corruption. The Russians were gaining from controlling most of the foreign oil exploitations and favoring their own production, while avoiding the crush of their own domestic disastrous economy. During this time, the Arabic countries had the Russians as a constant allied presence in the middle East to oppose the Israeli and Americans, without having to spend much in the process.

Basically, other super powers and many countries, regardless the race, religion, and ethnicity, had mounted a global movement for the destruction of everything that represented the western culture, along with the Christian and Hebrew believes.

Commander Matthew Johnson, who initially complained about having been given a mission to 'babysit civilians', was covered over his head with encrypted messages and stayed in contact with the major air-bases, from Florida, Virginia, Maryland, and Long Island. He almost regretted that his antimissile and anti-torpedoes operators had been limited to only two for the return voyage. And getting close to home, it grew also the possibility of an unexpected provocation from an unfriendly encounter with a heavily equipped adversary. There was not much left of his previous thrill of being home for Christmas, as a compensation for this mission he had considered until now almost humiliating.

On the third full day of the trip, Commander Johnson entered the meeting room with a derisive grin thinking of his comrades' little jealousy that he would be with his family for the holidays. But quickly his smile was completely wiped from his face when the first officer announced:

"It happened at home too! The Chinese lunched a satellite for the Iranians who detonated a nuke in high altitude, which disabled all electronics over most of northeast side of the country. New York, Washington DC, Boston, Phily, all are paralyzed. Only the Pentagon, the White House, and the main governmental locations equipped with anti-EMP attacks still functioning."

"We have ourselves a solid shield system for the protection of our proper operation, as you know', the commander tried to appear undeterred. "We will need to stay in close contact with *Freedom*, though, she is half a day behind us. We need to signal her to keep close by and let us see what lies ahead."

USS Independence continued vigilantly for almost two more days the trip home, the officers and crew straining to keep a good face as the apprehension increased, while the travelers became more jovial thinking that the next early morning they should enter the New York harbor.

Based on the latest data received, the orders were that *Independence* presents to US Navy & Marine Corps Reserves, in Brooklyn, Long island. Commander Johnson was ready to assemble his staff and about to notify the passengers, who were standing by for the captain's announcement regarding the last preparations in the view of disembarkation.

Passengers forming small groups, crowded some of the common areas close to speakerphones, all excited in the expectation of their arriving on land. It seemed that they had to wait forever for the Commander's voice to be, finally but firmly, heard. However, the announcement they were expecting sounded very different from what they imagined.

"Ladies and gentlemen, this is your Commander Matthew Johnson. As you might have heard, we are looking forward to our arrival to New York Harbor in the morning. I know you are, we all are, very excited about coming home. However, in order to avoid confusion and disorder, I ask you to follow these directions. I insist that this is an order and you all have to strictly obey it for your maximum security. You will assemble your belongings, but you have to keep ready the minimum necessary, which means a few clothes, secured identification papers under the plastic pouch given in embarkation, and your medication. You will wear the safety jacket at all times from now on, and stay in close contact with your siblings if you are a family. The crew members will be standing by for further instructions. And one more thing, the lights will be turned down, keeping on only the emergency ones."

There was silence for a few minutes following this announcement, nobody knowing how to interpret it. However, the travelers, who have already been subjected to many unusual situations, tried not to oppose, nor to question the orders. Trebor inquired that Maggie and the children, including Sara, had gathered together and were preparing as the captain ordered, then he whispered to Maggie that he was going to find Jo and learn more about the need for such orders.

As he arrived to the command area, Trebor went straight to his father.

"Dad, all seem under control for our arrival, right?"

"Well, with some strong prayers, that should be the right assumption", Jo answered to his son's interrogating look, then he added:

"We have been followed by a submarine. Russian and armed with nuclear head missiles. We don't know what game Russians are playing, but they circle us tighter and tighter. We need to see if they will let off as we get closer to protected territorial waters and if this is only an intimidation maneuver. But we are transporting close to 200 civilians under a reduced military personnel, and no measure is too exaggerated. This is too much even for the coastguards to handle at once."

"Dad, if they decide to torpedo us, a couple of those nuke missiles would leave nothing left of our ship, even one would be enough to sink us. Really, is there anything that can be done to save all these people?"

"Right, and even if we return the fire, we still can do that, we all get hurt, we don't keep nuclear warfare on board of this ship and our missiles would not inflict a hard blow to a submarine. And we would have to be the first to attack if we consider any chance of escape, and the orders are against it."

Then, Jo put a hand on Trebor's shoulder and said with a gentle smile:

"You see son, we need your strongest prayers."

DANGER FROM THE DARK

It had passed several hours of silent waiting, children have been given food, and many were asleep, as it was past midnight. The crew and the command team hoped that in 3-4 hours all would be over, the lights of New York City would make their show with a sky illuminated like the best Christmas ever, and, with the coastguards surrounding them on arrival, they would all sigh with relief.

Commander Johnson, tense like a rope guiding the largest ship against a storm, searched through his binoculars the lights indicating the coastal profile. His radar picked a few, still faraway, sandbars south of Long Island, but still no lights. And the shadow of the monster, one of the Russian subs, continued to show its dark nose, appearing and disappearing, from different directions, playing with their nerves.

"You, bustard, bloody son of a ...", he swore through his teeth. "Stay away from my ship! Those are civilians, all I am trying to do is to bring some children home. I want to see mine too for Christmas, for that matter. Have you forgotten, there has been a Savior longtime ago?!" the captain pleaded silently.

And, as the hourglass sipped its sand, minutes were passing with a torturing slowness. Around four in the morning, hoping to awake from this bad dream, the command group watched the big radar screen, and followed a few small points coming toward them from the shore, the coastguard vessels coming to meet them! Ready to shout in victory, they had, however, to smother the sounds coming out of their throat, for another, larger shadow was approaching from the deep at high speed.

As hard as this was to believe, the Russian submarine had decided to strike; if this time they were no longer able to close in, before turning around and staying away from the territorial waters, the Russians decided to make a last sneaky move and launch a missile.

The blow was terrible, the ship was struck on the left wing. The 2 MTU Friedrichshafen diesel engines hit, were shut down short. Commander Johnson scanned in a glimpse the ship's diagram and ordered the fire doors to be activated, in the attempt to completely isolate the damaged area. Seconds after, he ordered everyone on the large deck, close to the helipad where the two helicopters were secured. He realized that the passengers would not be in danger, so far, if they were brought on the upper levels. And he could guess that it would not be another blow, since he noticed that the dark shade of the submarine turned around after firing, and cowardly and quickly disappeared from the radar screen, reaching deeper waters.

Commander Johnson addressing his crew, tried one more time, against all evidence, to express confidence:

"As you all know, we are still running on our GE LM 2500 gas turbines and we have our 4 diesel generators for the ship's electric supply. So, we will make it if we keep our cool, brothers in arms." Showing determination, the commander knew that he relied on his combatants, more than ever.

In the process of bringing everyone on the large deck, preparations were made for their safe arrival expected in the next couple of hours. The crew and some volunteers trained in evacuations, checked that no one was missing, the order and calm were maintained, and that all passengers were well covered against the cold wind and wore the safety jackets.

Joseph Godson, after his large group was gathered and everyone felt safe with the close supervision of his two children and of his closest friends, took upon himself to descend below. Relying on years of experience and strong instincts, Jo started by checking carefully and methodically every corner to see if somebody was left behind. He was reassured that no one remained below the deck, as he was aware that the functioning of the ship could be done entirely from the command deck.

Jo proceeded to his private inspection with feline eyes and muted movements, his long training becoming a reflex switching on automatically. He was so far satisfied and ready to come back reaching a narrow spiral staircase, when, turning the angle of a tight corridor, he saw on the far corner of his right eye something moving. Indeed, a form dressed in the *Independence* uniform was crouched, tinkering with some wires, not very happy, and obviously in a hurry, for Jo heard him swearing in frustration. This triggered his caution, and approached the sailor without making any noise. Getting close to the back of the man, Jo realized in a flash that he had unfolded a roll of wires connecting plastic patties stuck to the door room of the gas generators, the only engines capable to provide electrical supply to the ship. He was on the process of setting the timer of a detonator and seemed inpatient, as Jo could distinguish a few words...in Russian:

"Davai, davai! sabaka!" Come on, Come on, you dog!

In a fraction of a second Jo immobilized the man from behind, and, while taking advantage of the surprise effect, at the same time he yanked the wires off the plastic. Once this done, Jo concentrated on the traitor, for he was strong and put on a fight. However, if the sailor realized that he was caught, he also noticed that no other person was around besides Jo.

"So, now we speak Russian in the Navy?", Jo humored the traitor.

"I will make sure with my life that this ship won't make it home", was the answer.

"And I will make sure with mine, that it will."

In their struggle, Jo became pinned under the spy who pulled a military knife and raised it to gain momentum coming down on Jo's throat. Jo grasped quickly the marine's forearm and twisting it, succeeded to return the blade striking the attacker in his left jugular. Jo could see his enemy's face twisted in pain and surprise, but this, in a last effort, falling on Jo's chest managed to bring the knife blade on the left side of his abdomen.

Jo, pushed the young man off of him, and considered him for a few seconds as he expired, the convulsions emptying rapidly his body of blood.

"Another who could infiltrate in the most classified operations. We must be too naive, we trust too easily", Jo thought, then he made a summary inspection of his abdomen.

"Bah, just a little nick, no big deal, we will take care of it later. Now, let's bring the Commander here to have a look."

THE UNTHINKABLE

Against all the efforts everyone made, the activity on the main deck felt chaotic. *USS Freedom* sailing along her sister Independence, caught up in speed and events, the ships exchanging intelligence and organizing a common front for disembarkation.

Half an hour away from the first buoys indicating their approach to Long Island with the southmost Long and Atlantic Beaches, and ahead on the west the of it, the Lower Bay and Brooklyn, two of the coastguard boats signaled their presence. There were spontaneous cheers from civilians and a sense of relief from the sailors. Quickly two more ships showed up and finally a fifth appeared. The first two boats radioed to the military asking permission to come on board and speak with each one of the captains. Once this granted, at each end of the two corvettes a coastguard quickly reached an opening in the gangway, and a guardsman rushed up to meet the captain of the respective ship.

"Commander Johnson, you cannot enter Jamaica Bay and go to the US Navy & Marine Corps Reserve. They are all mobilized for the defense of New York and Long Island. As you know, all control of the entire coastal area, I mean the whole northeast of the country operating under digital transmission and not protected against EMPs, is shot down. All public electrically powered services are out, lighting, subway, all communications, transportation, gas, fuel supply..., you see the picture."

As Commander Johnson thought "God have pity on us", then said aloud:

"We have to find a way to bring my passengers to a safe place and guarantee them a protected way back home. I did not bring them all the way here to turn around. And we have two disabled engines and the Russians subs are circling close to here."

"I am aware of that. What you might not know is that some commandos infiltrated New York, New Jersey, and Long Island, and further attacked the country, detonating the gas lines, blowing through the subway tunnels many buildings, roads and bridges. Even the hospitals have not been spared. The population is trapped in a few parks and isolated places not destroyed yet. And it is winter and almost Christmas!"

"Above all, Richard Munk continued, it is hard to take apart the real citizens from the terrorists in the middle of this pandemonium. NYPD, FBI, and CIA try very hard to identify those groups, and so far, many were found to be extreme Islamists. They came legally, as refugees, and hooked up with Russian and Chinese elements, who provided them with ammunition and guns they needed. After all, we are a free country, we welcome everyone to a better life here!', concluded bitterly Richard.

During this time, Commander Matthew Johnson, taking in the disastrous news, was thinking fast. Originally himself from New York, born and raised in Brooklyn, he played and had learned to love the waterways since he was a child. That had led to his present career, and at this moment an idea was forming in his mind. If he could advance into the Lower Bay then engage into the East River, longing Manhattan port side and Brooklyn starboard, once going under the Brooklyn, then Manhattan bridges, he could access Brooklyn Navy Yard.

The Brooklyn Navy Yard did not function for decades as a shipyard, and many modern transformations had been added, including commercial buildings and even a movie studio, but it still maintained five good piers and some of the docking facilities could allow a safe mooring. That made Commander Johnson feel confident that he could easily bring *Independence* and *Freedom* along the First Pier. He only needed to pass East Way, facing Front Avenue between the 2d and 3d Streets. But that was possible only if the way was open, which was another unknown to all of them.

However, Commander Johnson explained to Richard Munk his plan, and since nothing better was offered facing the terrible events, as they were advancing close to New York/New Jersey bay entrance, communication with the official authorities of the military and the city were exchanged and permission for both navy ships, obtained. Thus, an impressive convoy was formed between the naval war ships and the escorting coastguard embarkations, and their sight, hopefully, capable of dissuading any further attack.

Shivering under the blankets offered by the *Independence*'s crew, the passengers assembled on the main deck were unaware yet of how precarious their arrival laid ahead, and commentaries could be heard as the ship sailed close to iconic sites.

"Here is the Staten Island and this must be the Statue of Liberty, but why is she not lit, it is still dark, we can barely guess her shape..." and, "I don't know, but she looks crooked to me!", then another: "I thought she was taller..."

Then later on, "This must be the famous Brooklyn Bridge!"

"And this, ahead of us, looks like Manhattan Bridge!"

Others, joined in with different remarks: "But why their left ends seem down, and why Manhattan Island is in the dark? This is 'the city that never sleeps', and there are some flames back there, and those skyscrapers look like they have been bombarded!!"

"Yeah, what is going on?", followed by: "There is destruction everywhere!"

Questions started raining from all directions, while *Independence* advanced as the lead ship, and, with its passengers regrettably all under the open sky, it created a higher uneasiness to the captain, maneuvering his ship through uncertain waters.

For Captain Johnson had good reasons to worry, as he continued to receive further details of the situation, news he was sharing with his crew and the new friends from Trebor's group. Jo, in contact for a while with the headquarters of his agency, had been briefed in some issues which he was asked to pass on to the commander as well.

The two men had been trained and faced so many perilous operations, that their calm and self-control allowed them to keep a blade sharp focus, as they did right now.

Thus, Commander Johnson tried to show no sign of emotion sailing by his dear Brooklyn, which appeared in ruin, and knowing that his own family lived there. Not long ago they all waited with excitement for his return hoping to spend Christmas time together, thing that did not happen in a very long time.

Joseph Godson fought to keep his mind concentrated in helping his family and Trebor, and bringing his group to a safe haven, not letting the disappointment of the new difficulties deter them. And, as much as everyone hoped that their troubles would be at an end once arrived on American territory, he rebuffed a thought that nagged him now constantly: finding a hospital or a small emergency facility where he could visit discreetly once on land. The 'nick', the 'scratch' that the knife of the Russian pierced in the left flank of his abdomen, was a little deeper than he would have wished. And now, Jo was wondering for how long would he be able to stuff it with towels before it would be filled with the blood that was slowly leaving his body, and how much longer would he keep his composure without anyone noticing his injury.

"All hands on deck, engines to wake", the captain's voice thundered, and a new wave of excitement spread around. Then, all went like in a dream, and, as everyone was absorbed in the operations of the arrival, all went quickly.

The ship made a wide turn east, then, facing south toward Front Avenue, slipped between the 2d and the 3d Street, along the First Pier. Only when *Independence* came to a complete stop and securely moored, Commander Johnson allowed himself to sigh with relief. But this took only a few seconds, before he continued to give his attention to the arrival of *Freedom* and to her proper attachment to the quay.

Now it was time to proceed to the disembarkation, and leaving the ship and assembling everyone on shore was not much of trouble, the problem was that the passengers, or most of them, had nowhere to go. The two command posts, along with Joseph Godson, received no further instructions, and there were no orders of what to do from the time the refugees made it to the United States. At the moment, there were other monumental torments the government had to surmount for now.

CHAPTER 12 - THE NEW JERUSALEM

THE BIG APPLE IN RUIN

The crowd of the two ships assembling over four hundred people started spreading slowly, families and couples becoming aware of the reality and reconsidering their future plans to find their homes, if there was still a home. Trying to make sense of the conditions of the city and the streets, they were shocked by the changes inflicted by the many explosions having blown most of the buildings, the fragmented walls blocking the roads.

Confused and under great strain, some directed their steps a block away to the Commodore Berry Park. Instinctively, others followed and gathered to contemplate their new surroundings, disoriented. They were finally, all together, seamen and civilians, back in the United Sates, but were they home, yet?

The crowd noticed a figure coming towards the assembled people, calm, gentle, magnificent. As the sun made its presence sending the first rays to the American continent, Trebor was glowing in a light that was not due only to our star. And slowly, he started talking, his voice adorned with intense harmonious intonations, reached everyone present:

"Do not fear, my friends. Do not look at these ruins as our damnation. We are here to rebuild, to restart again. We have been given this great opportunity, this gift, to make a new world, a better, much, much better world than the one about to destroy itself. We have this mission to restart again, for us, for our children, and for all the generations to follow."

People got closer, attracted by the perspective of seeing a solution, a future. And, as they were listening, they were entranced.

"We will all stay together, until some can regain their own dwellings, or remain with us to settle in a new place. Together we can do it."

"Who are you?", a voice asked.

"Yes, who are you?"

"And why should we listen to you?"

Then someone said aloud:

"He is the New Messiah! I know Him, I was there when the pope declared him!", Agostino's voice was heard. "And he saved me!"

Then, a little voice joined in:

"He saved me too!" Ishmael stated.

"Me too", was Raj adding. Then more voices were heard, Sara, Wubit, and others:

"Me too, Me too!!"

"Is that true, are you the New Messiah?"

"I am the New Messiah as anyone of you is the New Messiah. There is a new Messiah in every one of us, in every woman and every man. For we all are the children of the same father, and high and divine forces are watching over us all."

Then Trebor added:

"Yes, there are immense powers, infinite powers, and God is represented everywhere. There is a celestial, intelligent, universal, and loving energy reuniting us all to God and this is our divine consciousness we all are part of it. We are guided and we can become infused with knowledge, we can find peace, we can all live in peace, harmony, health, and infinite prosperity if we stay harmonized with the higher powers of this celestial consciousness."

Some people tried to understand, to envision the ideas Trebor offered. Others absorbed his words with a deep longing for a blissful world, but they all wanted to hear more, all expectations directed now on Trebor, on the new path he showed to them.

"We must open our hearts and take this new chance, this divine opportunity to reconsider ourselves, to rebuild our world within, and here on Earth. This beautiful place has been given to us and we are destroying it. It has been the Garden of Eden, and we transformed it in garbage."

"But we can still rebuild the world we all want to live in. And we are helped, we are pardoned, and we are loved."

Some people became filled with hope, there was joy spreading within the groups of people, some were wondering how could they accomplish all this new world Trebor was talking about, when he explained:

"We all have our talents and special aptitudes. We all can do something for the fulfillment of our dreams and of the others'. And it is simple, one needs only to look into his soul and find out what his divine purpose is."

THE NEW JERUSALEM

Trebor started looking for a place to bring the people, to find ways to organize their new life. He opened the path going ahead, first reaching Fort Green Park, a few blocks south. Then, he continued through a deserted and damaged town, until reaching Brooklyn Museum along with its Botanical Gardens.

As the day was clearing from this dark and strange night, the light of this day of December 19 lifted the fog enveloping the city. And with it, the city let all see its wounds. But once arrived at the large expansion of the Museum, the preserved greenery of the park opened up like a new vision, almost untouched and full of promises. And there were other people. After entering deeper into the large grounds between the Botanical Gardens and the Prospect Zoo Park, they could see tents and many RVs grouped together, where human forms moved around. Some of them stopped seeing the new flock advancing, and came to meet the newly arrived.

It took only a few minutes for the two sides to exchange their story, and learn that some locals found this park safe enough to bring their families and friends, and organized a resistance to protect them against a possible attack from unfriendly elements. And the others found about the long and daunting exodus of the new comers, and the disenchantment they faced once arriving home. Words travelled quickly through the grapevine, and the travelers were encouraged to come along, getting closer to the center of the camping.

Soon, people went back and forth, and a flow of activity stirred into the camp life: some brought back blankets, some chairs, tables, cots, even some small tents appeared by enchantment. After a short while, trays with coffee, biscuits, and all kind of foods were presented to children and adults of the group.

In a little while, life in the camp took more shape. The command groups of the two ships learned that they were, indeed, on their own, and decided to stay together. The same for Jo and his close family and friends who traveled together, as it was for the refugees from the navy ships. They also learned from the people of the camp that most of the inhabitants of Brooklyn still alive sought refuge in that place until new times, and all together felt inclined to form a new community to survive and help each other.

By the end of the day, everyone had a warm place to sleep and a gigantic dinner was to start. If the food was simple, tables were set up everywhere, for all to share a meal together. When everyone was seated, someone proposed to say a blessing, and another asked that the New Messiah be the one to talk. Now, they were all looking for this New Messiah, some curious, some spontaneously considering him as their leader. Finally, Trebor stood up almost with embarrassment, then, as he smiled and looked around him, everyone felt illuminated by his smile.

"Alright, my friends. I will say the blessings, but as you know, I am no priest, and I do not hold any dogma. I only listen to my heart and I talk from my heart." Then he continued:

"Blessings, yes blessings! They are so many to say and so much to be grateful for. I give thanks to our celestial Father, to our Virgin Mary and her Holy Son, thanks to our higher guides and powers for bringing us all home. I give thanks for sparing us and for finding new friends in these times of distress. I thank the ones who gave us their science and dedication to bring us here, and to the ones that accepted us with open hearts."

"There is nothing more inspiring than looking for a new beginning in this devastation, to see people of all ethnicities and religions coming together in good faith and with the best intentions raising from their hearts. Yes, we are here to build in this place a better world, a more peaceful and more loving one, and for that we give thanks and we ask God for His blessings." Then Trebor added:

"We ask God to give blessings to this place, to His New Jerusalem."

STARTING A NEW LIFE

Shortly after raising tent and adopting the Botanical Garden as the home for the refugees, Captain Ricardo Montovani, Scotti Hunt, Matt Johnson, and Phillipe Robertson, the captain of *Freedom*, held an improvised pow-wow in order to consider the immediate needs of the group of refugees, and if needed, their defense. Joseph Godson was automatically included to the meeting, as was Trebor.

It was only when they all took the time to face each other that they noticed how pale Jo was. At that point, Jo had to let the rabbit out of the hat, and he admitted he had been injured during the altercation and apprehension of the Russian spy on board the *Independence*. Immediately, Commander Johnson called upon his medic, and without hiding their concern, they all looked upon Jo's care without delay.

A small group was formed, Dr. David Anderson and Rebekah, his wife, were promptly called along with a general surgeon found among the camp members. They accompanied Jo, who was transported at once on a minivan back to *Independence*, for treatments at the vessel's operating room. A Brooklyn resident having his own taxicab was the one who offered to drive the small team, and insisted that he knew a path still open until recently. And the good angels were with them, because they could arrive discretely and unscathed back to the ship.

Once the wound properly explored, irrigated, disinfected, and closed, then a good dose of antibiotics given intravenously, Jo could lie down for a good night rest. On the following morning, Jo seemed out of the woods, and, under the close supervision of Dr. Anderson's and his wife, they decided that they all could come back to the new village they called now The New Jerusalem.

However, the two ship captains, Matthew Johnson and Phillipe Robertson, remained with their ships along with a limited crew to protect their vessels, now that their passengers had found a place where they could stay. Somewhere, deep in his heart, Commander Johnson held a strong hope that, through the protected communication devices he had on board, he would be able to get in touch with his family.

One day later, still taking oral antibiotics, Jo felt much improved, to the great relief of his children and all the friends now part of their extended family.

The new settlement had organized security patrols and watch-shifts around the village, although for a little over 24 hours there were no explosions heard. Besides the fumes of smoldering carbonized debris continuing to consume slowly the last fires, there was an earie quiet over a city that lived under blaring sounds of detonations short time before.

In The New Jerusalem, everyone was getting ready for Christmas; children practiced their songs and added more to their long lists to Santa, just in case. Many were baking and cooking, others wrapping some presents, and some felt so confident that they even started decorating putting up batterie-operating lights. All that could be found in the stores around, now exposed open through their shattered windows and doors, allowed the people from the newly formed community to bring in food, water containers, and other supplies, including Christmas trees and many toys and decorations.

Overall, in The New Jerusalem, even the air was filled with hope and joy, while a spirit of high expectations and fellowship animated everyone. It was as if the celebration of Christ's birth became a true beginning for all of them as well.

While Jo was recovering, Trebor continued to communicate with the Commander and followed the news turning direction. There were representatives from many countries all over the world, taking upon themselves to express their nations' intentions, and came to the United Nations' building in Manhattan for an unified treaty to cease all hostilities. Under these premises, knowing the not far from there, just on the other side of the East River, the United Nations were in full session, Trebor was elated to spread the good news. It was so wonderful to see the spirits reaching high after so long and so much desolation.

"Just on time for Christmas", he thought.

MORE GOOD NEWS

"Greetings, Trebor, and good tidings!", Captain Johnson called Trebor with a cheerful tone in his voice. "How is your father?"

Then, learning that Jo felt and acted like everything was back to normal, he added:

"I have great news too: I found my family, I am with them right now, in our home in East Brooklyn. There are some damages, the garage is destroyed, but everyone is well. Thank God, this is all that counts. This must be another Christmas miracle. And I am freed for my duties from now, a Navy mate took over the command and I can be with my family for Christmas after all! But I won't be far away from you and we will stay in touch."

The animated conversation lasted for a little longer, Trebor sincerely delighted to learn that Matthew Johnson was with his family and that all was looking good for them.

"Well, I let you go now", the commander concluded, "please give my best to everyone and Merry Christmas! And by the way, do you know how many New Jerusalems are in the US? While I was searching the web for my family I checked it out: 138 so far, and in 6 different states! So, I guess we can add another one here, in Brooklyn!"

DEFENDING THE NEW JERUSALEM

In this Christmas Eve day, Joseph Godson, bound to his long-term habits and feeling so much more energetic since he had his wound taken care of, decided to make his own inspection tour on the edge of their new village. He went on a good three-mile circle, invigorated by the crisp winter air with the promise of snow for Christmas. With a nonchalant pace, in reality Jo was scrutinizing attentively his surroundings. He stopped a few times to chat with people who invited him for a cup of tea and for the famous Ruben sandwich, as it was getting close to breakfast time. Finally, he stood up and retracing his steps, went on to close his tour.

Jo was fueled with the good energy present in the village, happy to see how well people adjusted to these modest living conditions and how well they were getting along. The only thing he missed was Everest by his side, his faithful companion during his inspections looking too busy that morning, playing and entertaining the children of the camp.

Some other children in New Jerusalem went across Flatbush Avenue to the Prospect Park Zoo, all part of this expanded green area, and interacting with the Zoo kippers who stayed with the animals, were allowed to play with some of them. At the Zoo, the stranded employees, through their dedication for their job, discovered that remaining close to the animals could have in reality saved their lives, keeping them away from the areas targeted by the attacks. It had been a forbidding task for them to calm the animals from the frightening sounds of the blasts and to continue to maintain their care without new arrival of supplies. However, the people camping on the park, soon found out about their presence and they were readily integrated to the new village, while many of them volunteered to help with the care of the zoo residents.

The zoo continued its designation as an attraction for the children, and helped more than ever distract them from boredom or discouragement. Aided by parents and some of the care givers of the zoo, children had followed Maggie in the previous morning, who proposed to install a Nativity Creche. Children of the New Jerusalem were so enthralled with this project that this occupied their entire day, and this morning almost all the children, including Ishmael and Wubit, along with Sara and Maggie, were fussing around the life-size creche. Because many insisted, some of the farm animals were brought in as part of the pageant setting, and it was a general excitement having a real cow close to a real manger, a few sheep and lambs, even a little pig. And no one thought that they were too many, as the younger ones kept on asking for more to be part of the scene.

It was quite a picture to admire, as Everest found himself a part in the role of an improvised nanny, rocking the manger where the baby Jesus was placed, while little children were sitting on the lawn with sheep and lambs, holding them and giving them kisses.

Deep in these thoughts, and almost back to their camping place, Jo had the impression of seeing something moving beyond the ruins of the Botanical Garden's pavilion. It was inside the wrecked walls of the Eastern Parkway Brooklyn Museum which sustained severe damages and it was in no condition for someone to adventure occupying the sites. Jo turned on the spot to see what was moving and talk the person out of risking to get buried under the gravel, when the intruder swiftly hid behind a wall.

Jo broke into a run before the person could escape and arrived at the open wall of the exploded building, when a gunshot detonated and Jo fell on a pile of debris. An atrocious pain stunned him and went through his body like a lightning, as a bullet impacted and shattered his right shoulder. With the main artery bleeding profusely and losing the control of his hand, Jo quickly realized that he could not shoot his revolver in defense. He summoned, however, all his energy to climb up, holding on the ruined wall. There, he could clearly see the shape of a young man, wearing dark clothes and a black cap covering his head all the way down his neck.

With the sheer force of his will, Jo tempted to run after the man and made a few uncertain steps through the smashed bricks, while the attacker managed to get out and gained a good distance from the building. Suddenly, the young man stopped and turned around looking at Jo straight into his eyes, ready to cast a grenade. There was a moment that seemed to last an eternity, when the two men faced each other, Jo holding against a wall and studying his attacker, each one suspended into the other one's gaze.

At that time, Joseph Godson understood what the terrorist was about to do. And, as his blood was emptying his body, the time seemed standing still, and he reviewed his life story unfolding in front of him. One by one images scrolled and Jo could see himself as a child, then a young man, his training and his hobbies, his friends and his family, and then his beloved Mai. And every detail was filled with the magic of love and acceptance, until this very instant. Joseph Godson was at peace, he had found his children, he was reunited with them, and he brought them home. Now, he could be reunited with Mai, and finally be together for eternity.

SAYING GOODBYE TO THE BEST

The entire village was startled by the explosion. When the gunshot was heard, many people started running toward the museum, but seeing Jo fallen, they stopped on their tracks, bewildered. Then, all went up in the air with a deafening blast.

When the dust settled, Maggie and Trebor, with all their friends close by, went to find Joseph and retrieve his lifeless, mangled body. With pain tearing their hearts open, they carried him to their tent, and deposited him with infinite gentleness on a sleeping bag. Although his body had been thrown in the air and many bones were broken, his face was spared. And it was the serenity that Trebor and Maggie read on their father's final expression that gave them the courage to overcome their despair, to understand that Jo was telling them he had left this life gratified.

After a while, during which a vigil was held in the tent, Commander Johnson came along, having been informed of Joseph Godson's tragic death. He paid his respects, then took Trebor and Maggie aside. With all the consideration for the tragedy that all felt, Matt Johnson suggested that Jo needed to be buried without delay, albeit temporarily, considering the risk of decay without a cold chamber and with the Christmas Eve celebration on going. He advised them to make a very private ceremony, not alerting but the closest friends and family, insisting that this is the way Joseph Godson would have wanted, for everyone to go on enjoying life.

Matt Johnson stayed on for the preparations and he even provided a body bag he had brought with him from the ship, since they did not have a real coffin. The body was then placed on the commander's Jeep and the closest friends and family followed down to a small garden pavilion remained intact close to Washington Avenue. Buckets of roses, gardenias, hibiscus, orchids were placed around an improvised grave made as a flower bed. In a spontaneous and unconventional ceremony, prayers and chants were made, Lu Xiang burned his own incents and rung the bells he always carried with him. A priest of the village came along and conducted prayers where many nations and religions were represented. Then, his friends joined in a succession of eulogies, everyone applying their efforts to remember rather the good times spent together.

It was as if Jo and Mai were there, with them. Trebor and Maggie, although crushed with sorrow, seemed to be closer than ever and the tragedy had only brought tighter the new family they now formed together. Comforting each other, they realized how much strength they drew from the other one's presence, feeling that they would overcome all difficulties, and being reunited gave them consolation, courage, and hopeful expectations.

As the eulogies ended, they all followed a line and, one by one, casted a handful of dirt over the bag containing Jo's terrestrial remains. It must have been one of the most touching scenes to watch them saying their farewells, Jo's children, then Ishmael, Wubit, Sara, Li, Lu Xiang, Jamuna, Raj, the ships captains, Agostino, along with Rebekah and Dr. Anderson, Amanda and Sonia, Farid and Aisha, Randal, Jovanni, Phillipe, Deborah, and Joshua. All the friends that shared recently unimaginable tragedies and adventures, were there to say a last goodbye and wish their friend to find eternal peace and happiness. When Jo's body was covered with dirt, then with flowers, and when all was done, a howling pierced the air outside the door. It was so intense that it expressed all the suffering one's heart can ever contain. The cry that Everest let out like a wounded wolf, could not have described more sincerely the deepest of a human despair.

NATIVITY

The night was falling over the New Jerusalem in that Christmas Eve. The day had been quite gorgeous and the anticipation of Christmas kept the children outdoors, in a euphoric expectation of Santa Claus. When the parents, after calling many times for them to come inside the tents or the RVs for dinner, they had to promise them to go to the Nativity reenacting once the improvised mass would start.

There was a mystic feeling in the air, sensed by people of all faiths, not only by the children. And not only because of the magic of the Savior's birth, but they were all under the spell of the Christmas promise, the hope of a new beginning.

Soon, most of the members of the new community were reunited by the Nativity Creche, and Christmas carols started. Songs were resonating in a crisp, starry night, as the children begun their pageant.

At first, Sara did not want to go join the others. With her heart tight and mourning for Jo's passing, whom she considered like her grandfather, she was not up to rejoice. However, Wubit and Ishmael came for her, and Trebor and Maggie insisted for them to celebrate this special evening, so dear to all children.

Once she joined the congregation, and being part of the pageantry coaching, she forgot about her sadness, while her tender age gave in to the general exultation. Then, the time for gift distribution finally came, as many insisted to have a common merriment, since the presents were expected to be scarce that year. At least, bringing them all together it would feel like there were many presents. And since Sara was the one to help Santa hand out the gifts to the children, she ignored the cramp-like pains traversing her tummy.

"It must be something I ate, too many cookies!', she thought, as the pain, although sharp, would not last but a second, just lancing a little her abdomen.

When every child had received their toys and dolls, Sara took a deep breath and sat down by the manger to catch her air, happy her job was finished. Suddenly, the pain was stronger and lasting a good minute, and, as Sara became quite uncomfortable, she attempted to sit up.

Maggie was at her site in no time, alerted. When Sara, with a halted voice attempted to answer, Maggie saw her forehead pearled with perspiration and asked Trebor to fetch Dr. Anderson right the way. "It is about time," she whispered to her brother, with an understanding sign of the head.

Dr. Anderson and his wife, still lingering around after the pageant, approached the future mother. Rebekah helped Sara to stand, as Dr. Anderson wanted his patient to be taken to a more protected, private place. There, the time for him to run and grab his travel surgical case, his wife would be examining Sara. However, when Sara got on her feet, her waters broke, and the baby seemed to be in a hurry.

"Good, he thought, at least she won't need anesthesia."

Very gently, they carried Sara to the cottage close by, housing a couple of sheep with their new lambs. Room was made for the delivering young mother, with the help provided by Deborah, Sonia, and Amanda, who scrambled to bring sheets, towels, and, at Sara's insistence, the suitcase she had ready for the baby. And since there was hot running water available for the washing of the animals, along with a good size bench for their tending, the caregivers furnished also some basins and strong disinfectant liquid for them to clean. Then, they were standing ready to help with whatever there might be needed.

The villagers also gathered, tense and waiting around a camp fire, determined to stay close to the cottage. Maggie asked Trebor to bring the children by the village gathering as well, promising that she will keep them abreast with the progression of the delivery. Along with the women allowed inside, only Rebekah was the one with experience on the 'baby business' and assisted Dr. Anderson, her husband. They commented that this was the first time when they worked together during a delivery, admitting that they preferred this happy event to all the others they shared before.

In between the contractions that became stronger and more frequent, attempting to distract Sara from pain, Maggie joked telling her that she was the woman who had the most fathers and mothers pacing outside, nervous like all true parents and relatives. Sara laughed and cried in the same time, her contractions barely tolerable.

Dr. Anderson announced to the mother that the baby is 'crowning', meaning that he could see the top of baby's head. He knew that Sara must be in terrifying pain, and he admired this juvenile future mother for her courage and strength, for she did not complain, and if she could not retain at times a few moans, no screams were heard out of her mouth.

It was just a little after midnight, when with a last effort, Sara gave birth to a baby girl. There was no need to announce it, with a powerful cry, the baby made her own introduction into this world. Outside there were cheers of joy, everyone claiming that this was a miracle, the Christmas miracle! When, minutes later, Maggie handed the cleaned baby to the mother, Sara had the most luminous smile in her face:

"She is a miracle, a beatitude, she is my Béatrice!", she declared.

They gave a little time of respite to the new mother to meet her baby. When Sara felt again some contractions, she looked at the medical couple with worry in her expression, but Dr. Anderson reassured her:

"It is normal, it must be the placenta coming out."

However, Sara felt real pain again, and Dr. Anderson, concerned, examined her.

"I see another head coming out quickly! Another baby?!"

Indeed, within the next few moments, another beautiful baby was born, this time a little boy!

More cheers were heard as soon as the assistance was informed about the 'second miracle'. And everyone feeling the exhilaration of this special night, as the first snowflakes of the year started falling, children and adults all together, were ready for a celebration they would always remember.

The young mother, beaming with joy, soon welcomed her other baby in her loving arms. As she took him in her embrace, she already called him, Alexandre.

Maggie, probably more emotional than the mother, had tears streaming from her eyes with a joy she had never felt before. Trebor came in, not tolerating any longer to stay outside the door, and shared the joy with them, crying with no shame.

"Jo left this Earth, and now tells us that he wants us to rejoice with this double miracle!"

THE END

EPILOGUE

Peace finally came on Earth. People all over the planet were tired of fighting, of tearing each other apart and destroying their natural world. The new alliance created between the well-intended nations and the United States of America, played an instrumental role in establishing the foundation of this New World Era. The economical bases of rebuilding from the ruins was guided by the advanced technologies accessible to lesser fortunate countries, but through guidance and information made available, and not through monetary aides that could become subject to corruption and enslavement.

There was now a strong recognition given to the spiritual growth and everyone's connection with the universal consciousness, containing all the energy and knowledge present for all to harvest. The increased awareness in regard to this powerful energetic and spiritual field implied the new paradigm that we are all connected. Thus, sentient of the contribution and influence that everyone has upon the global conscience, the world was guided toward higher vibrations, elevating and benefiting to all.

It became a common knowledge that this shift to a higher dimensional energy made the transition to a more peaceful world, more loving and tolerant, bringing prosperity and happiness to human coexistence, now possible even on this plane of physical manifestation.

The New Jerusalem grew and rapidly took form of a lovely community, built solidly on stone structures and beautifully designed gardens. In the beginning, this was achievable mostly thanks to Trebor financial contribution, whose expertise acquired during his young years, found the right channels to transfer all his immense fortune and use it to the creation of this part of the new world. New schools, libraries, and medical centers were integrated along with parks and animal sanctuaries, and The New Jerusalem became an example for many other communities, Phoenix rising from the ashes of destruction and replacing gravel and ruins with new, ecological places of habitation.

People were ready for changes, for renewal, and along with it, for a better world.

The group of friends traveling and sharing so many adventures together, stayed together. Rebekah and Dr. David Anderson were among the first to set up a medical clinic for First Aid and Emergencies. Deborah and Joshua McClain started a school, and when the new, beautiful building was ready, classes were opened from the 1st to senior levels.

The former secretaries becoming flight attendants, Sonia and Amanda, married respectively Raj and Phillipe Prior, the former flight engineer. Sonia and Amanda started a kindergarten, and loved it. Raj shared his time between giving yoga classes and gardening, while Phillipe and Andi, the copilot, opened an electric vehicle transportation company.

Aisha married the love of her life and chauffeur, Farid, who worked together with Phillipe and Andy. Ricardo Montovani, if he could not recover his yacht, *Syrena*, managed, however, to bring his family form Napoli and, along with Stéphane, opened a restaurant. It became one of the most animated places around, the two friends engaging in verbal jousting, one louder than the other, defending the best cuisine of their country of origin. On one side was the Italian wing called The Little Vesuvio, where Ricardo was the ultimate boss, while Stéphane opened in the opposite aisle The Little Paris, just to annoy his friend.

Beshadu, using his former skills as a police officer, became the main agent for the organization Randal and Jovanni opened for the reunification of families separated during the last world confrontations.

Kuan Li became very soon proficient on driving the new Tesla electric cars, and was mesmerized by the simple but advanced technology he discovered. Getting up in age, he was still fast and energetic, forged by a life-long hardship. Always smiling and appreciating his new life like no one, he found his contribution to the community by volunteering to drive a school bus.

Maggie continued to assume the mother role for Wubit, Ishmael, and Sara, and along with her brother, Trebor, who play the father figure, they formed a family as life commended along. With time, Jamuna, always present and ready to help Maggie with the settlement of their community and family, gained Maggie's trust and affection. They eventually married a couple of years after their arrival to the US, and one could say that they lived happily ever after.

As Ishmael and Wubit followed regular school classes, Jamuna insisted that Maggie resumed her journalistic occupation for which she had so much talent. Indeed, Maggie opened a publishing company, and ran 'The New Jerusalem Daily News' as the editor in chief, along with several magazines with scientific, sports, and art profiles. Her publishing company, 'The Godson Twins', grew with the contribution of selected writers, and soon Maggie published her own book, 'Chronicles of a lifetime voyage'.

Jamuna himself, continued to feel the best being outdoors and discovered an inclination to gardening. He seemed to have a real 'green thumb', amazing everyone with his extraordinary flower and parterre designs.

Sara's babies were the joy of the entire community, and **Béatrice** and Alexandre never lacked the constant attention and affection of all around. Agostino loved to sit close to the children and the mother, constantly drawing their angelic faces. He filled scores of drawing pads with beautiful sketches, for the exquisite subjects were a powerful inspiration for the artist. It was no surprise to anyone when Sara married Agostino, and they too, lived to enjoy a blissful life together.

Lu Xiang continued to be a great attraction, and against an advanced age, he remained vigorous and engaged in the community. He even initiated special classes for children and adults, teaching meditation and yoga with the help of Raj, Jamuna, and even Beshadu. It was as if Lu Xiang discovered a new youth when he chose to stay in this new place, loving the children and infusing them with the desire to explore beyond the seen, the materialistic forms of life, and look deep inside their own soul. When Lu Xiang had his classes open, all his friends tried to make time to share the peaceful moments of meditation.

The New Jerusalem had its own mascot, Everest. Everest could be seen in many places, but mostly he liked to accompany the children to school and help watching the lady directing the traffic around the school hours. Everest was present during the field practices and no soccer or football game, nor any other sports events would begin without him giving the start with a bark.

The following spring, in a beautiful day, during a touching ceremony, the remains of Joseph Godson were moved to Arlington National Cemetery. He had found his final resting place, a hero amongst the heroes of his nation. His memory and work were saluted by officials, military, and civilian friends coming from all over the world to honor and recognize his dedication and his ultimate sacrifice.

And Trebor, one would wonder? Well, he immersed himself in the construction of the New Jerusalem. And if he did not find, yet, the woman of his dreams, the citizens of the new town declared him, against all his protests, as their mayor. Trebor was their ultimate leader, his brilliant mind and extensive knowledge in the matters of running successful companies, contributed to the flourishing of their new community.

At night, when he laid down to sleep, Trebor had no longer bad dreams. He traveled however, to higher realms, where he found beauty beyond belief. And he always talked to his celestial Father with a heart filled with gratitude. He thanked Him for the bliss his parents found for eternity, and for the peace he found himself in this place.

"Thank you, Father, there is happiness on Earth. And there is Peace."

Then, as always, Trebor ended his prayer in Aramaic, "L'alam, Al-mein, Amen."

("I seal my prayer in Truth, and Faith, and Trust" - Translated from Aramaic form Nag Hammadi Library, text of the Gospel of St. Thomas - King James version of the Book of John, 16-23 - 'Instructions of how to address a prayer to God'.)

ABOUT THE AUTHOR

Dr. Marinella Monk lives in the Panhandle of Florida, USA, with her husband, Robert. A retired physician, Dr. Monk enjoys writing, traveling, playing music, and taking strolls on the beach.

Dr. Monk's early education started with music, when she studied the harp at the Conservatory in Paris, France, and played with the Monte Carlo symphony orchestra.

A few years later, Marinella decided to study medicine and returned to Paris where she completed her degrees in Mesotherapy and Sports Medicine. Well into her three years of private medical practice in Paris, Dr. Monk met her second husband, Robert. Shortly after their marriage, they left for the USA, where her husband was born, and the newly formed family of his two sons and her daughter, started a new page in their lives, filled with challenges and adventures.

After completing the requirements for practicing medicine in the United States and obtaining her specialization in Rehabilitation and Pain Medicine, Dr. Monk served as Medical Director of Houston Rehabilitation Institute for nine years before opening her private medical practice in Destin, Florida, from which she retired in 2015.

Dr. Monk penned her first book, 'You Are Not Alone', at the insistence of her patients, and quickly produced a motivational guide to give inspiration to many facing life's difficulties. 'Gentle Therapy' followed, suggesting transformation of trivial routine activities into rewarding and meaningful occupations. The originality of this book is the addition to each chapter of the description of an imaginary place to visit, and encouragement to meditate, along with a piece of classical music, setting the stage to better reflect on that particular therapy.

Dr. Monk's third book is also her first fictional novel entitled 'Heaven Rediscovered'. In this book, through many adventures and tragedies, the author debates love and happiness here on earth and beyond. The events described in this story bring into consideration our purpose in life and our destinies related to the people we encounter, along with the reasons for these experiences. She questions what will happen to our feelings and connections once we complete this lifetime.

Made in the
USA
Lexington, KY